DON'T GO IN THE WATER
Classic Monsters Anthology 3

Two Olde
Dragons
Writing
Wyrd
Stories

Ye Olde Dragon Books

www.YeOldeDragonBooks.com

Ye Olde Dragon Books
P.O. Box 30802
Middleburg Hts., OH 44130

www.YeOldeDragonBooks.com

2OldeDragons@gmail.com

TABLE OF CONTENTS

FOREWORD

As I sit here on this sunny September afternoon in southern Illinois, spooky bayous and Spanish moss-draped trees are far away. I'm watching another watery classic horror series, Steven Spielberg's *Jaws*, winding my way through the second movie of the series. What is it about monsters of the deep that fascinate us so much? Is it the unknown world beneath the waves? We're oxygen-breathing creatures, and those watery depths are new territory to most of us, unexplored places with terrifying monsters, giant squids, man-eating sharks, mutant creatures from nuclear experiments gone wrong, killer orca whales from legends...

And of course, the amazing *Creature from the Black Lagoon*. He first hit the big screen in 1954. Though the actors were uncredited, it took two stuntmen to play the big "Gill Man" in that first film. The first was a professional diver and swimmer named Ricou Browning, who did all the water work, while stuntman Ben Chapman played the "Gill Man on land." The film went on to spawn two sequels and became a cult classic.

We chose to honor the Creature for our third Monster anthology, but we left it open to pretty much any body of water, and any type of creepy critter. The stories we received really fell in, around, on top of and skewered through the middle of the proverbial "box"! We found a couple of brand-new authors to add to our troupe, as well as many of our regular contributors. Their tales range from the hysterically hilarious, to hair-raisingly terrifying. We have it all. We have a very strange family vacation that goes awry. We have a bunch of fairy gardeners who run afoul of a water sprite. We have a creature who can inhabit human minds, until one man discovers a way to infiltrate their ranks. One story involves sirens, another, mutant frogs! Another tale comes straight out of Swiss Family Robinson, which deals with accepting one another in spite of differences. Then we have an ancient demonic river monster that wreaks havoc for centuries. And what would happen if the Gill Man tried to join Classic Monsters Anonymous, but was refused entry? We even have one science fiction piece set in space! We have a bittersweet friendship, and we have an escapee from an aquarium. We have another Enchanted Castle story that will leave you in stitches, and a novella about a monster in the lake that's been eating people for years.

1

These thirteen tales were hand-picked for your entertainment. Savor them, laugh with them, cry with them. But if you read them at night, you might want to leave the lights on.

Above all…

Enjoy!

Deborah Cullins Smith
September 2023

Surprise – research can be fun!

I had never seen the original *Creature* movie, just memes and funny pieces featuring the costume, so when Deb proposed this classic monster for our theme this year, I wasn't quite sure if I could come up with a story.

Then my brother, Dean, the resource for any weird movie fact you could ever want (in essence, my personal Tony Dinozzo), caught an episode of *Svengoolie* featuring the *Creature*. (If you don't get *Svengoolie* in your area, you can find him on the Web. Watch out for flying chickens! He hosts really bad or corny flicks and breaks in with bad jokes and ridiculous comments. Kind of like *MST3000*. If you get hooked, don't blame me!) After months of delay (ah, the joys of having a DVR) we sat down to watch it. I was scribbling notes for details to put in my story almost from the moment the opening credits ended. Try to find these little tidbits in my story … if you dare…

This anthology was fun, especially seeing what our returning authors came up with, and meeting some new contributors. You people have some weird imaginations, that's all I can say!

We hope you have as much fun reading these stories as we did writing and choosing and editing.

And if you have a hard time falling asleep at night … we warned you!

Michelle L. Levigne
September 2023

THE SECRET
Rachel Dib

Morty was lonely. It had been such a long time since he'd had a visitor — since Ben had visited him. But Ben couldn't visit anymore, not after the accident. Morty still wasn't sure what had happened. One moment Ben had been clinging to his back, knees wedged beneath Morty's flippers, and the next, he floated, lifeless in the water.

Morty had tried to save Ben. He'd pushed his friend back to shore, waited for him to move, breathe, anything. Ben, however, had only lain upon the rocky bank, eyes open but unseeing.

He'd looked so small then. Of course, to Morty, Ben had always looked small, ever since their first meeting when Ben had been little more than a pup, all knobby knees and elbows with that feathery hair that tickled Morty's skin. And that high-pitched, cackling laugh. How Morty missed that laugh. Even after Ben had grown out of the awkward pup, forming into a hardy adult, he'd always kept the laugh. It had deepened, sure, but the raucousness had remained. It had been part of what made Ben, Ben.

The body that Morty had pushed back to shore, though — the husk that had lain there, unmoving — that had *not* been Ben.

It had taken hours for anyone to find the body. Once they had, they didn't just take it and leave. They kept *searching,* as if something more important than Ben's body lay hidden nearby.

Which was true. But that secret was between Morty and Ben — and Ben was gone.

Still, they had searched. Humans donning skin-tight, black rubber suits and fake flippers dove deep into the lagoon. At first, Morty hadn't realized the divers were people. He'd thought a herd of seals had wandered into his waters. Such tasty morsels, seals were. When Morty had drawn close to the creatures, however, they'd smelled all wrong. They'd smelled more akin to Ben than any seal he'd ever encountered. And that was when he realized they were humans dressed as seals and not the fanciful feast Morty had been hoping for.

Even worse, these seal-clad humans had shone bright lights that hurt Morty's eyes. And their fake flippers had beat the water with such an irritating thrumming rhythm that Morty's head ached. Eventually, whenever he heard the divers coming, Morty immediately found refuge in his cave — the cave he'd only ever shared with Ben.

No matter how much the divers searched, however, they never found what they were looking for. The lagoon was too dark and the opening to the cave too well hidden for them to spot, despite their lights. Eventually, they had abandoned their search. Once they left, no one else came to the lagoon, leaving Morty utterly alone.

Until the girl arrived.

She was a mere pup, even smaller than Ben had been when he'd first discovered Morty's lagoon. Regardless of her size, if Morty peered at her at just the right angle, she looked like Ben. She had the same light, feathery hair—though it hung down to her shoulders—the same high cheekbones, and the same seaweed-colored eyes. Her nose was slightly upturned just as Ben's had been, and she was definitely all knobby knees and elbows.

Seeing all the similarities, an abrupt sadness washed over Morty. Unable to handle his grief, he dove deep, waiting for her to leave.

It's not as if she'll come back, anyway, he told himself. *Once she sees there's nothing here but a dark pool and some rock shielded by trees, she'll find better things to do.*

But Morty was incorrect in his assumption. For the girl did return, and this time, she brought lunch.

A peanut butter, banana, and pickle sandwich. Morty knew that smell anywhere. The tasty treat had been one of Ben's favorite meals, and one that he had introduced Morty to—though it had taken Morty a while to acquire a taste for it. Before Ben's arrival, he'd only eaten fish, shelled creatures, and the occasional mammal or bird that wandered into his secluded oasis. At first the smell of human food had disgusted Morty, but once he'd gotten a taste for it...

Morty's mouth watered as the sandwich's rich, tangy scent drifted toward him. But along with the smell came the memory of his shared meals with Ben. As sadness threatened to strangle him, he again dove below the surface, waiting for the young girl to leave.

She always came back though. Day after day, she took up residence beside his pool. Sometimes she ate lunch. Other times she read a book— sometimes even aloud, as if she knew some other creature lurked nearby, listening.

As much as Morty hated to admit it, he grew to crave her presence. Even without physical contact, the mere existence of another living being close by—one he had no intention of eating—took away some of his loneliness. Soon, he stopped hiding in the depths and lingered just out of her sight to listen to her read, or just watch her lounge at the water's edge.

I'll never reveal myself to her, though, he vowed. *Ben will always remain my first and last human.*

And he kept this bargain with himself—for a year.

If there was one thing Morty had learned about the girl, it was that she was very habitual by nature. Since Ben had never possessed this trait, Morty found the quality refreshing. It was the one thing about her that didn't cause him grief. Her consistent schedule also allowed him to know when she'd be arriving and departing so he could plan the rest of his day accordingly.

Therefore, when she not only arrived early but also loudly and destructively, tearing through the trees and underbrush at an unwarranted speed, Morty knew something was wrong. Still, he hid beneath the pool's surface, his obsidian skin camouflaging him in the dark water. Even when he saw the bigger girls break through the trees moments after the young pup, he remained unseen. But when the largest of the pursuers grabbed the small girl by the hair, wrenching her backward and shoving her to the ground, Morty abandoned his bystandership.

Before any of the girls could land a blow, Morty lunged from the water, teeth bared. He let out a menacing roar and slapped his fins against the rocky bank. The attackers took one look at him, and all color drained from their cheeks. Within seconds, they'd scrambled away, tripping over each other in their haste.

Despite his longing to retreat beneath the pool's surface, he glanced over the sobbing victim, still lying in a heap. For some reason, it felt wrong to simply disappear, though he didn't know why. He'd spent months avoiding her. Why stop now? But he stayed.

Once he'd contented himself with the knowledge that while her knees and hands were scraped and bleeding, she was overall unharmed, he finally decided it was okay to leave—and then she looked up. Morty expected the young girl to hightail it after her attackers once she spotted him, but she didn't. She merely stared up at him, her face tearstained but grateful, and smiled weakly.

"Thanks. Sorry to bring them here, but I didn't know where else to go."

Morty tilted his head. While he understood her words, he couldn't communicate with her. Not that way, at least. His silence didn't seem to bother her though. She pushed herself into a sitting position and wiped a hand across her nose.

"I'm Bryn, by the way."

Bryn. Morty swallowed. The name was way too close to "Ben" for comfort. With a flip of his tail, he shoved himself away from the bank. Before he could disappear below the water's surface, though, she called out to him, halting his descent.

"My grandfather told me about you. He said he named you Morty. He said you were his best friend." She dropped her chin, her features gloomy. "I could use a best friend right now."

Morty sighed. As much as he wanted to leave, seeing her flushed cheeks, puffy eyes, and snotty nose, he just couldn't. She was too pitiful to abandon. Plus, she'd belonged to Ben, and he'd *told* her about him. That had to mean something. So, again, he stayed.

~~~~~

Bryn talked a lot — way more than Ben ever had. To Morty's surprise, he didn't mind her constant rambling. Sometimes he even learned things from it. For instance, that the divers had spotted him. Well, sort of spotted, anyway. They'd claimed that something huge, dark, and menacing lived in the lagoon, though they didn't know exactly what it was. After all, the lagoon's waters were pitch black. How could anyone clearly see anything in them? They were positive, however, that the monster had killed Ben Jameson, despite the presence of a heart condition that his doctor had warned could kill him at any moment.

Whether everyone actually believed these claims was up for debate. But regardless of people's beliefs, the lagoon had become a taboo place, and parents had warned their children to stay away from it — Bryn included. Since Ben had told Bryn all about Morty, though, she had disregarded the "stay away" order and visited anyway in hopes of meeting the supposed "creature of the black lagoon."

"That's what they've dubbed you," Bryn explained, tossing him a peanut butter, banana, and pickle sandwich. "When they're not just calling you 'the monster,' that is."

Morty contemplated the title. As monikers went, it wasn't the most distinguished, but it could be worse.

"I don't think my mother believes in you, but she'll be happy when we move all the same."

Move? Morty flipped his tail, insides roiling. He'd allowed himself to grow close to the girl only for her to leave him, too?

Bryn sighed. "I don't want to leave, but we can't afford to stay. Grandfather had...debts." She glanced at Morty, her gaze questioning, as if hoping he'd have answers for her.

Did Ben tell her about the cave? Uncomfortable under her gaze, he sank lower in the water.

Shrugging, Bryn continued. "Mother has to pay his debts off now. The only way she can think to do it is by selling Grandfather's house." She stopped herself. "Well, that's not true. Grandfather used to tell us stories about a hidden treasure. Mother looked for it. She even paid other people to look for it. I guess it was just a story because no one could find it."

She sighed, bending over so that her chin rested on her knees. "So, we have to move. We're only here until my parents fix up the house and put it on the market. I wish there was another way but..."

Hidden treasure... Morty bobbed in the water. Ben had instructed him

6

never to reveal the secret placed within the cave. But he'd told Bryn and her mother about it. And now Ben was gone. Did the secret still hold now that one party was no longer bound to it?

He studied Bryn. Eyes trained on a clump of lichen at her feet, she dug at it with the tip of her finger. Morty wondered what she was thinking. He had a way to find out—if he just touched her. But Ben had warned him his way of communicating was intrusive and not to use it unless told it was all right.

But how will I know if it's all right if she doesn't know a way exists?

After all, even Ben had needed to be shown what he could do. Making up his mind, Morty reached out a fin and gently touched Bryn's ankle.

Bryn jumped, her head popping up to stare at him. She didn't jerk away though, and a moment later, her jaw dropped.

"I can understand you. I can..." She blinked, brow furrowing in concentration. "I can see what you're thinking."

To Morty's surprise, she knelt on the ground beside him and grabbed his fin in her small hand. Her skin felt warm and tender against his scales.

I wonder what I feel like.

"Kind of like a fish." Bryn stroked his fin. "Or maybe a turtle."

Morty snorted. He didn't know how he felt about being compared to other lifeforms—especially ones he usually ate.

"Well, I don't know any other way to describe it," Bryn replied simply. "Anyway, the important thing is that we can actually *talk* to each other now."

Morty met her gaze and saw Bryn's eyes were bright with excitement. And then he remembered the main reason for wanting to communicate with her in the first place.

Hidden treasure.

He pictured Ben—or rather, his younger self. Morty tended to think of Ben in terms of the young man he'd been rather than the older one who'd floated lifelessly in the water. He didn't like to think of those later years. Plus, it was the young man who had placed the secret within Morty's cave, not the old one.

Bryn stilled as the image entered her mind. Her mouth slackened, all enthusiasm leaching from her features.

Morty moved on to an image of Ben climbing on his back, a metal box clutched under one arm. The two of them dove under the water, darkness engulfing them. Morty could still see, of course. His eyes never had a problem adjusting to the inky blackness.

He pictured the cave's mouth next, a hidden crevice in the rock. Lastly, he showed Ben placing the metal box on a ledge within the cave. When he'd finished, Morty let the images dissipate and studied Bryn's face.

She didn't say anything at first, but silently contemplated everything Morty had shown her. He felt her sadness. It pleased him that the young girl missed Ben as much as he did. While she'd seen photographs of her grandfather as a young man, she still found it odd to see him that way in Morty's mind.

Morty also felt her curiosity concerning the metal box — and mixed with it, a sense of hope. Could this be the saving grace her family needed?

"Do you know what's in the box?" Bryn asked finally.

He shook his head. *Secret.*

"I wonder if it's the hidden treasure my grandfather talked about." She bit her lip. "Can you bring it to me?"

Morty looked down at his flat, scaley fins.

Bryn nodded in understanding. "You don't have a way to carry it." Pursing her lips, she released Morty's fin and stood up. "I guess I'll need to retrieve it, then. The only problem is, I don't know how to swim."

~~~~~

At first, Morty couldn't fathom being unable to swim. He'd been doing it all his life. It was a part of who he was. Why one needed to be taught something that should come so naturally was beyond him.

Until he saw Bryn's first attempt.

Watching the young girl helplessly flailing her arms and legs in the water reminded Morty that not all creatures were born with the right accoutrements needed for swimming. His fins, for instance, were far more conducive to the task than Bryn's scrawny arms with their splayed fingers.

No wonder those divers had dressed as seals.

Before she sank too far beneath the water, Morty pressed his nose to her belly. He'd meant to lift her back to the surface, but as soon as Bryn felt his touch, she wrapped herself around his head.

This will not work.

She loosened her grip, but barely.

Once he'd safely returned her to the rocky bank, Morty pushed himself back into the pool. Her panic and fear still coursed through him, making his heart beat wildly in his chest.

Had Ben felt that way at the end?

Morty didn't know. Ben had never liked the connection gained by skin-to-skin contact. Whenever they'd dived together, Ben had worn tight clothing that covered his entire body, ensuring they'd never touch.

"I'm sorry, Morty," Ben had apologized. "It's a privacy thing. I just don't want anyone else in my head."

And Morty had understood — sort of. Either way, he hadn't wanted to upset Ben. If Ben thought his form of communication was intrusive, Morty was willing to forgo that luxury.

But if I'd only known what he'd been thinking — feeling — maybe I could have saved him. As awful as experiencing another's pain felt, Morty knew he'd have endured it if only so he could've helped Ben.

"I need to try again," Bryn said, interrupting Morty's thoughts. She sat shivering at the edge of the pool, her arms wrapped around her knees. Despite her anxiety, though, he noticed defiance in her eyes as she met his gaze.

"If I can't swim, I can't retrieve that box. And if I can't retrieve the box, I can't find out if it contains the treasure that can save my family." She blew out her cheeks. "I need to find out what's in that box. There's no other way."

Morty lifted a fin from the water and waited for Bryn to press her hand to it. *Hold on to me.* She swallowed, and her fear washed over him.

"But what if I fall off?"

I will find you. I have no trouble seeing in the dark.

She nodded but Morty felt her unease. Tilting his head, he pictured a rope, and immediately sensed hope spring to life within her.

"You think tying myself to your back will work?"

We can try.

Finding a suitable way to fasten the rope around Morty turned out to be harder than he'd thought. One way choked him, another hindered his movements. If he hadn't been so desperate to help Bryn — to stave off her impending move — he'd have given up on the whole idea.

But he *was* desperate. Bryn wasn't just Morty's last remaining link to Ben, she was his friend — the only other creature who knew of his existence and *wanted* to be around him. She connected him to the outside world, gave him a reason to wake in the morning. Bryn had become his everything. She couldn't leave. Her leaving would wreck him.

Plus, by helping Bryn, Morty felt as if he were also helping Ben. She was his descendant, after all.

So, he kept letting her try different ways of looping the rope around him. And eventually, they did find one that worked, even if it didn't feel very comfortable. Morty was convinced nothing would be completely comfortable, though. The rope's abrasive texture rubbed his skin raw, leaving pink streaks across his body that burned in the water. He couldn't think of any way to prevent that.

"I'm sorry it hurts," Bryn apologized as she gently stroked a rope burn. He winced and she jerked her hand away.

I will manage. The rope will not be tied for long.

Bryn nodded and stood up. Wrapping her arms around herself, she glanced at the pool. "I'm still nervous about the dive," she said softly. "I know you say it's not far, and that the cave is open inside like it is here, but..." She shook her head.

9

Morty wanted to reach out to her, assure Bryn that everything would be all right, but held back. If she'd wanted a connection with him, she wouldn't have moved away. He didn't want to be intrusive. So instead, he waited, bobbing at the edge of the rocky bank for her to decide what she wanted to do.

Finally, she sighed and passed him a small smile. "Well, there's no other way. And I know you'll keep me safe. Let's do this."

While they had practiced her holding on to the rope while he swam around the lagoon, diving turned out to be a little different. Despite her tether, Bryn fell off multiple times. Finally, she discovered how to dig her knees in behind his fins, relying on leg strength rather than just her grip on the rope. She refused to give up, and they managed to figure the dive out together.

Morty admired her resoluteness, especially when they finally reached a deeper depth. He felt when panic gripped her, but even then, determination drove her to clutch harder with her knees, refusing to let go.

And then they were in the cave.

As soon as they broke the surface, Bryn gasped for breath, her chest heaving. Rather than fear, however, she radiated excitement. Morty couldn't help but smile at her sense of victory.

Unlike in the lagoon, there was no clear bank. Rocks jutted from the water, many of them sharp or slippery. Also, rather than the pitch-black water of the lagoon, the water within the cave glowed with a green hue that provided just enough light to see by.

"Why is the water glowing?" Bryn asked in awe.

Morty swam up to one of the larger, flatter rocks so Bryn could climb off his back.

Tiny glowing animals. They light up when I disturb them.

"Oh." After easing herself onto the rock, she crouched on all fours to gain her balance as well as take in her surroundings. "Where do I go from here?"

Morty hadn't thought of that. Sure, he'd seen the path Ben had taken when he'd first placed the secret in the cave, but that had been years ago. While many of the rocks he'd used as stepping stones to reach his destination still remained, Ben had been a man with much longer legs than Bryn. Morty doubted the young girl would be able to access the same path Ben had used. Not easily, anyway. More than likely, she'd need to find a different route that paralleled the one her grandfather had originally taken.

Regardless of whether she accomplished this feat, however, one other hurdle stood in Bryn's way. Ben had placed the box on a ledge. While Morty had been too far away to see how high the ledge was, he doubted

Bryn would be tall enough to reach it.

Why didn't I think of this before?

When Bryn laid her palm flat across Morty's brow, ready to continue with their plan, he pictured the path of flat and smooth rounded stones protruding from the water her grandfather had used to get to the cave's back wall. Then he showed her the rocky ledge where Ben had placed the box.

Detecting his concerns, she chewed her lip. "You're right. I won't be able to go the exact same way he did. And I'll just have to see how high the box is when I get there. But I'll figure it out." She brushed the side of Morty's jaw with her thumb. "We've gotten this far. Can't give up now."

Then with a tap on Morty's nose, Bryn pushed herself to her feet and studied her route options. A boulder to her left seemed to be the easiest starting point. Smooth and mostly flat, Bryn would be able to jump to it fairly easily — as long as it wasn't slippery.

Morty watched her commit to the jump and take it. For the few seconds she hung in the air, his heart took up lodging in his throat. It didn't begin to recede back to its normal location until Bryn had successfully regained her footing and stood up.

Even then, Morty had difficulty remaining calm. Any place she went next would require some tricky maneuvering. She decided to step onto a small rock, leaning with one hand against a large arrowhead-shaped rock for balance. She wobbled a bit but managed to stay upright.

Slowly, Bryn picked her way toward where Ben had placed the box. A few times, Morty was certain that the young girl would fall and either be impaled or hurt in some other way. Then, he'd be unable to help her just as he'd been unable to help Ben. But her steps never faltered, and he admired her dexterity. He knew he'd never be able to do what she was attempting.

We are all uniquely and wonderfully made. Our distinctions help us master different obstacles, he mused. *While my fins are perfect for gliding through the water, Bryn's fingers and toes help her grip and climb. Neither of us could have achieved this goal without the other.*

Despite their lack of connection, Morty knew he felt the same pride as Bryn when she finally reached the spot beneath where the box sat. She glanced at him, a wide grin plastered across her face as she held her two thumbs up in the air. Morty waved a fin back at her, and she turned toward the ledge.

She stared at that ledge for a long time. Morty knew she could see the box as easily as he could. However, he'd been correct in his assumption that it'd been placed too high for her to reach.

Dismayed at his powerlessness to help her, Morty swam laps around the small pool. He knew if he could just get to Bryn, she could stand on his back and reach the box. But he'd studied the cave from every angle. The spattering of boulders jutting up from the cave floor between him and her was too much to overcome. There were too many of them — most with sharp edges or jagged points. He was just too big to squeeze between the rocks without harming himself in some way.

I've brought her all this way for nothing.

And then he returned from one of his laps around the pool to see Bryn climbing up the wall. Morty propped himself up on a boulder to get a better look. While he had no idea how she managed it, Bryn was most definitely scaling the wall.

Genius! Morty watched in gripped fascination as she finally grabbed the ledge and hauled herself up on top of it.

She smiled at him again, her features tired but exhilarated — and then she opened the box. Her mouth made a small "o" shape as she gazed at whatever lay nestled inside. Turning her wide-eyed stare upon Morty, she held up a thumb and closed the lid. Then glancing over the edge of the ledge, she dropped the box.

Morty heard the sharp clank of metal on stone as it landed. As the sound echoed around the cave, he winced and sank below the water. Still, even as the sound rattled in his skull, a sense of relief washed over him.

She did it. She won't have to move after all.

It took Bryn a good bit longer to return to him than it had for her to reach the box. While he knew this was partly due to the awkwardness of carrying the box as she maneuvered along her route, Morty knew it was also because the young girl was spent. It had taken a lot of energy to accomplish her goal. Morty was in awe of her endurance, but even at a distance, he could see how tired she was.

Her condition became even more apparent when she was again by his side. Bryn was shaking with fatigue.

"I did it," she gasped, brandishing the box out in front of her. "And Morty, it *is* a treasure! My parents shouldn't have to sell the house now. I know I'll be able to stay!"

As Bryn began climbing aboard his back, Morty felt the tremors racking her body. *You need rest.*

"I'm fine," Brynn replied, wrapping the rope around the box. "I mean, I'm tired but I'm also excited. And there's not really anywhere to rest here, anyway. I'll do that when I get home. After I show Mom what's inside." She bounced lightly in her seat. "It's a diamond, Morty. A *giant* one!"

When Morty's worry didn't abate, Bryn rubbed a comforting hand down his jaw. "I swear I'm fine. I just need to get back. We've been gone a while. Don't want people to come looking for me, do we?"

Knowing the truth behind her words, Morty warily agreed. He

waited for her to get into position, her knees squeezing his sides just behind his fins—albeit not as tightly as before—and then dove into the dark depths.

Morty was aware of the exact moment something went wrong. One moment he'd sensed her determination and excitement, and the next Bryn had filled with apprehension.

I need to breathe, zipped across her mind—and then there were no feelings or thoughts at all.

Swiveling around, he grabbed the back of the girl's swimsuit in his teeth. Lugging her in his mouth threw his usually smooth movements off-kilter, but it was the only way. He refused to let anything happen to her. He may not have been able to save Ben, but he would *not* fail Bryn.

He broke the surface of the water at top speed, lunging onto the bank. As carefully as he could, he dragged Bryn out of the water, laying her on her back. She didn't move. She didn't breathe.

No! No! No!

He butted her in the chest with his nose and chin, willing life into her frail body. It couldn't be happening again. Not to her.

Please, not to her!

He butted her harder.

Water burst from Bryn's mouth, and she flipped onto her side, choking.

Morty's breath caught in his chest as he stared at the vomiting girl beside him. Was she okay? Had he done enough to save her?

"Get away, you monster!"

Startled, Morty tore his gaze from Bryn to see an older version of Bryn standing at the tree line. Her eyes were wild, her mouth a gaping hole as she screamed at him.

Bewildered, he lurched backward away from Bryn, keeping only his head above water so that he could continue to assure himself she was all right. It wasn't enough.

The woman pulled something black and shiny from beneath her shirt. She aimed it at him. A thunderous sound erupted from the object, bringing a stinging sensation in his shoulder.

Confused and in pain, Morty sank below the water just as another thunderous roar assaulted his ears. He swam back to the cave in a daze. The sting in his shoulder had begun to throb. It took him a minute to realize he had a small hole there.

Swimming shakily over to the rock shelf he used as a resting place, Morty eased himself atop it and studied the wound. Blood leaked steadily from the hole, pooling in the water around him. Morty swallowed, his head suddenly dizzy. He closed his eyes and let darkness take him.

~~~~~

Morty found the box. It had fallen to the bottom of the lagoon during the struggle to save Bryn. Since the rope was still tied firmly around it, he took the rope in his mouth and carried the box with him. Bryn would need the diamond, after all. It was the one thing that could save her family— keep her from moving.

Only she never returned for it.

Day after day he waited, hidden beneath the dark waters just out of sight. He listened, ears straining for the soft sound of footsteps as Bryn trudged through the trees toward him, but they never came. No one did. The surrounding wood remained empty, other than gentle birdsong or the call of a creature searching for its mate.

Eventually Morty stopped waiting. He quit returning to the pool, too, preferring the silence of the cave. No living creature could bother him there. Nothing could remind him of his sudden plunge into seclusion where no one wanted him. Within the cave he could hide himself away, safe from anything that might hint at the friendship he'd gained and lost— well, other than his shoulder, anyway.

Even after the wound had fully healed, it still ached now and again. On those days, he splayed himself across his shelf, chewed on a bit of moss that eased the pain, and slept. This technique didn't serve as a full release, though, for sometimes he dreamed. And when he dreamed, it was always of her.

Had he truly saved her? Was she really all right? Or had he failed again, like he had with Ben, and that was why she'd never returned for the box? Morty didn't know, and not knowing bothered him the most.

He lived this way for years, days passing without Morty giving them much notice—and then a seal appeared, disturbing the tiny glowing creatures in the cave.

Morty stared at the seal. It wasn't the sleekest one he'd ever seen. In fact, it was rather ugly. Its nose was too flat, its eyes too wide and glassy. In fact, its face didn't look very seal-like at all.

He leaned forward as the not-seal pulled its eyes away from its face to reveal another face entirely. It was a familiar face, though aged quite a bit. He swallowed as a grin spread across Bryn's features.

"Hello, Morty. I've been looking for you."

*** The End ***

CLASSIC MONSTERS ANONYMOUS: THE GILL GUY WALKS AMONG US
Mike Bogue

Gillreed stood dripping water before the Classic Monsters Anonymous council and said, "My name is Gillreed, and I am a classic monster."

Gillreed had expected acceptance from the famous ogres seated behind the CMA table in this dank castle basement. But instead, the Frankenstein Monster slumped, the Wolfguy chuffed, the Mummy groaned, and Dracula scowled.

"Not so fast," Dracula said in that inimitable East European accent.

"But," Gillreed said, wondering if his fishy odor offended his once and future chums, "to join CMA, all you need is a professed desire to stop killing. Right?"

Dracula frowned. "Wrong. You have been misled, Gill. I see you remain as naïve as always."

He ignored the slight. "I want to be in recovery like you, Drac."

"Only my best friends call me Drac. It's Dracula to non-CMA ogres like you."

Pain jabbed Gillreed's chest—the vampire king never missed a chance to lord it over his fellow classic monsters.

Dracula raised an eyebrow. "The twelve-stake program is not for everyone."

Insight burst inside his head. "I get it. I have to prove that I've really given up killing humans, like the rest of you. Drac, I mean Dracula, I've heard you drink the blood of animals instead of people, even though it tastes like bat urine. Am I right?"

Dracula pinched the bridge of his nose. "About the taste of animal blood, you are right. About the requirement to take part in CMA, you are wrong."

The Mummy turned to Dracula and cleared its throat. "May I?"

He made a magnanimous gesture. "By all means."

As the Mummy spoke, a cloud of dust puffed from its mouth with each word. "The classic monster requirement to join CMA is to kill one last human."

Gillreed cocked his head. "Huh?"

"That's right," Dracula said, apparently unable to keep himself from stealing the Mummy's thunder. "But the deed must be performed not in self-defense or in defense of another, but rather in, as the humans call it, cold blood."

Frankenstein's Monster said, "One last fling, so to speak."

"Yes," the Mummy puffed, "and the human the CMA council has decided you must kill is — "

Dracula cut him off. "Please, I will do the honors. The human you must kill is Dr. Carlson Arnold."

Shock startled Gillreed like the prod humans once used to jolt him. Kill Dr. Carlson Arnold? He needed the companionship of his fellow classic monsters, but killing Dr. Arnold was a tall order.

Dracula shrugged. "Take a few moments to think it over if you must."

Dr. Arnold had helped abduct Gillreed and drag him to that Florida aquarium, but the wavy-haired scientist had also called off the electric shocks and loosened his chains — which allowed the Gill Guy (as the humans called him) to struggle for hours until he snapped the chain and escaped.

On the other fin, Lori, luscious golden-haired Lori, had chosen Dr. Arnold over Gillreed. With Dr. Arnold out of the way, nothing would come between the fish-man and his beloved. She was all that mattered. And yet, as he struggled to nurse a lust to kill the scientist, a vision of Lori floated into his thoughts like a watercolor ghost, shaking her head. "Geeg," she appeared to say, "no."

That settled it. Gillreed longed for CMA but Lori meant more.

"Fellow classic monsters," he said, making a sweeping motion to the council with a webbed claw, "I have slain enough humans recently that adding another corpse to my roster would be overkill, if you'll pardon the expression."

Dracula wrinkled his brow. "Indeed?"

"Yes, I killed two swimmers off the East Coast. College couple. Completely senseless mangling."

Frankenstein's Monster scoffed. "I guess you think we don't keep up with *The Monster Times: All the News That's Fit to Bury*?"

The Wolfguy barked agreement.

Dracula nodded. "The culprit in that case is what the humans called 'The Terror of Bikini Beach.' It had those weird hot dog protuberances in its mouth. An atomic mutant eons removed from you and your prehistoric kin, Gill."

Gillreed stroked his rubbery chin. "My mistake, for which I apologize. But I did kill those two innocent grad students who set up camp close to my grotto."

"True, but the Hollywood movie version lies. They weren't innocent.

You killed them because they attacked you — one of them tried to shoot you — before you laid a claw on them."

Gillreed drummed taloned fingers across his scaly cheek, generating intermittent tingles. He was running out of ammo. But there was that one disputed case. "When I pushed that pickup over a hill after escaping from the aquarium, the man inside died. That was no accident. That was intentional."

Dracula displayed his fangs. "Nice try. But humans on the scene didn't see anyone in the truck when you overturned it. Apparently, the driver had ducked out of sight, meaning you couldn't have intentionally killed him, since you wouldn't have seen him."

Gillreed blushed, which meant his fellows saw the telltale bright green. But there was one more incident that might convince the CMA — or not. His gills expanded in and out like a hyper-accordion, and a foul taste coated his throat.

"All right," Gillreed said. "I took Lori Adams to my grotto, intending to murder her in cold blood." There. He'd said it. "The only thing that stopped me was Dr. Arnold arriving and shooting me."

"Methinks," the Mummy said, "you are telling us a fish story." He smiled, and dust flaked from his cheeks to the table.

"Indeed," Dracula added. "You told *The Monster Times* you had no intention of killing Ms. Adams. You placed her atop that rock in your grotto so you could adore her, even worship her."

Frankenstein's Monster nodded. "You said she filled you with a sense of wonder. And what classic monster would ever kill a sense of wonder?"

"Well," Gillreed said, "you've got me there." A sense of wonder was the greatest feeling a classic monster could experience or generate in others.

Dracula cleared his throat. "Gill, despite your unorthodox attempt to join CMA, the council will vote on your acceptance. All those against Gill's being accepted say 'Nay.'"

Four voices spoke at once, though the Wolfguy, still learning to talk, growled his response.

Dracula continued. "All those for, say 'Aye.'"

The intense quiet made Gillreed certain the blood pounding in his ears vibrated the chamber's walls.

"Gill, this leaves us with no alternative, I'm afraid. If you want to join CMA, you must kill Dr. Carlson Arnold."

"And I can't enjoy fellowship again with you, any of you, unless I join CMA?"

Frankenstein's Monster nodded. "Quite right, old boy."

Gillreed slunk from the room and bemoaned the torchlight that illuminated his path.

Hours later, he emerged from the Atlantic, moonlight flooding the coastal landscape. He reluctantly traipsed from the familiar waves, their briny scent intoxicating. Lori, herself a marine biologist, had married Dr. Arnold, and Gillreed knew where they lived — he had scouted their uptown beach house many times under a midnight moon. But only with the thought of spying, not killing.

The landscaped gardens surrounding the home burst with color and vitality, their order, splendor, and beauty embodying Lori's human preferences. If only Gillreed could be of the same species.

He squatted before a picture window and peeked inside. His hopes that no one was home were immediately dashed. Lori and Dr. Arnold sat, cuddled on a couch, watching TV. They looked so content, mixed feelings warred within Gillreed's chest.

Why couldn't he have been born a man? Or better still, as Dr. Arnold himself? A familiar pain tore at his insides. If only he could will himself into Dr. Arnold's body, overtake the scientist's bones, flesh, brains — the whole nine yards, an expression he'd once heard Lori quip to Dr. Arnold at the aquarium.

Lori, when teaching Gillreed sign language in his aquarium water tank, had offered a smile and a word of encouragement at each of his victories, as well as a fresh fish. He intentionally pretended to take longer than needed to learn each new sign, because he felt alive, his chest tingling in Lori's presence.

"Geeg," she signed one day. "I think I'll call you Geeg. Okay?"

Of course, it was okay — she could have called him Toad Vomit and it would have been okay.

She signed again, asking him if he approved of his new name. Her head subtly tilted.

He knew this might be his only chance to hand her his heart. With deliberate care, he signed, "And I will call you Angel."

She smiled behind her glass face mask. "Why, Geeg. How sweet."

How he had longed to break his chains in that heady moment and ferry her back to his grotto, but fair play restrained him. After all, she had bonded to Dr. Arnold, with whom she snuggled right now in the couple's living room.

Dr. Arnold. Dr. Freaking Big Shot Arnold. It would be easy to kill him. So easy.

Gillreed could almost feel his claws sinking into the scientist's throat, warm blood baptizing his webbed fingers as he ripped the man's head off. But Lori... Where would she be during this? What would such a sight, such an act, do to her?

Yet loneliness ate at Gillreed's soul like a famished parasite. The classic monsters refused his company unless he joined CMA, and at least that would be fellowship with his peers, if not his species. Lori spurned him, and always would.

A dog barked, perhaps from the backyard. Hang it all, it must have smelled Gillreed's fishy odor.

Lori went into another room, probably the kitchen, no doubt to check on the alarmed pooch. That left Dr. Arnold by his lonesome — but not for long.

It all seemed to happen at once, shattering through the window, whipping to the couch, grabbing Dr. Arnold. The scientist struggled, and adrenaline flooded every hidden cupboard of Gillreed's being. He clutched the scientist's throat.

A dog — a German shepherd — leaped at Gillreed.

Lori screamed.

"Run!" Dr. Arnold shouted at her.

Lori said, "Geeg! Geeg, let him go!"

Her plea did something to Gillreed's insides, and his head spun.

"Geeg," Lori said again, "let him go. Take me instead."

Her selfless plea pressed an automatic button in Gillreed's soul. He dropped Dr. Arnold. The scientist clutched his throat, and Lori knelt beside him. Their dog stood by their side, growling.

Lori looked up at Gillreed, her eyes glistening. "Geeg, please leave us. Please."

He tried to speak, but his monsterese, a universal language among classic monsters, sounded wet and guttural and no doubt more alien than a Martian radio program to Lori's ears. So, he signed, "Farewell, Angel," and fled to the sea.

Maybe Lori and Dr. Arnold would call the cops. Maybe not. Didn't matter. No one knew where the classic monsters hid out.

Hours later, Gillreed once again stood before the CMA council in the castle's basement, torchlight glinting off his wet scales.

The Mummy tapped its chin, Frankenstein's Monster inhaled, the Wolfguy howled. Their combined scents provoked a memory, but soon, that was all they would be for him. He no longer worried whether his marine stink repelled them.

Dracula tilted his head. "Well, Gill?"

Gillreed said, "I couldn't do it. I couldn't kill him."

"Couldn't or wouldn't?"

"Take your pick." He turned his back, his heart a dead weight in his chest. A loner he had been, a loner he would stay.

"Not so fast."

Gillreed turned. What now? "You want me to hang around so you can gloat?"

A warm smile overtook Dracula's face. "Not at all. We want you to hear the results of our new vote."

"New vote?"

"Yes. We just put you through a test, and you passed with, as the humans say, flying colors."

"Oh?"

"We had to see if you had sincerely reformed. The fact you chose not to kill Dr. Arnold, despite our bogus entreaty to do so, reveals you are sincere, a bona fide recovering classic monster."

Gillreed recoiled. Anger flared, but relief smothered it. Was he, the last of his species on Planet Earth, dreaming?

Dracula said, "All those in favor of admitting Gill, say 'Aye.'"

Four voices spoke in the affirmative.

Dracula gestured to the podium. "You have the floor."

"My name is Gillreed," the Gill Guy said, "and I am a classic monster."

As one, Dracula, Frankenstein's Monster, the Mummy, and the Wolfguy said, "Hi, Gill." To which Dracula added, "You may now call me Drac."

Their voices grated like sandpaper scuffing concrete, but they elevated Gillreed's spirits like music. Not as melodic as Lori's, of course, but they would have to do.

The End

ESCAPE FROM THE LOST LAGOON
Darlene N. Böcek

"What happened to him?" Jack's teenage son, Fitz, picked up the shattered robot, fingering the hole in JUNO's head.

"Looks like a bullet." Jack tapped his thumb nail on his teeth. Their human-sized robot, a class 8 Journeyman Underwater Navigation Operative, was down, and he had seconds before everyone panicked. "It's not a bad thing, you know."

Just that morning, all hope had pivoted on JUNO coming back from his explorations above the lagoon with good news. This changed everything.

"Of course it's bad." Jack's wife, Eda's eyes narrowed indignantly. "A gunshot means there are hostiles out there, Jack. This proves that if we ever leave the bunker, their first instinct will be to shoot us."

"No. Look. They shot him after he was out hovering over the lake for three minutes. That means it wasn't thoughtless. His head was shot, meaning they know what they're doing. There are people out there."

"Really, Daddy?" Elizabeth drew closer. With wide eyes, the twenty-one-year-old studied Jack's face. "People are still alive?"

"What kind of people, I don't know." He moistened his lips then went over to the bunker's Remote Interface Mainframe server, or RIM, and typed in a few commands. "At least he relayed the air results before he went down."

The family drew near and watched the coding move across the screen. "What's it say?" Francie asked.

"Does this mean we can live out there, too? Can we leave Base?" Elizabeth verbalized everyone's pressing question.

"No, to both your questions," her mother answered. "If their first idea is to use weapons, we won't be safe if we go out. People are changed. The toxic air must have mutated their cells. Anyhow." She closed her eyes, steadying her nerves. "We don't need to leave. It's fine down here. What are you missing that you don't have?"

"Elizabeth, the kids have only known this submergible. Francie's lived ten years — her entire life — under water. Fitz probably doesn't even remember what a tree looks like."

"Come on. I know what a tree looks like," her brother said.

"Sure. But why, Fitz? Because you've watched millions of hours of video. Not because you're actually drawing from memory. Maybe

Elizabeth remembers."

"I do. I remember the blue sky. I remember streams and butterflies."

Eda pulled Elizabeth into her arms. "But does it make you a better person than your siblings? No. We don't need whoever's out there. They're the kind of people who destroyed the world. We're safe in here. Please, Jack. Let's wait longer."

A long beep came from RIM, then a spew of red code flitted across the screen. A large glowing green result flashed: INCONCLUSIVE.

"That's great news!" Jack's eyes scanned the room and stopped at the exit chamber. They could finally leave, finally get out of this tin-can bunker. His attention flew back to his wife. "We have to at least try."

"No, we don't." Eda stood between her husband and the chamber. "Unless RIM shows us there is no danger, we're staying here."

Jack slouched back in the chair and typed some commands into RIM.

Up until yesterday, they'd tested the waters for contamination. It had cleared the test, so they'd sent the robot up to test the air, leading to this proof of life above ground. Someone was out there. But what kind of someone?

"It says there is a 15 percent chance that the air is still contaminated," he said. "I think it's worth the risk."

"So do I." Fitz's eyes reflected the same eagerness, the same anxious desire for freedom that pulsated daily, unmet, inside of Jack.

"There are too many variables." Eda was at her own terminal and clacked away at her keyboard. "The toxicity to our lungs is the worst of our problems. We don't know what happened to the people who survived. Fifteen years in that air, with the germ warfare of all nations mixing in the atmosphere, we could be dealing with mutants or insanity or even human-animal hybrids that have morphed."

"I can see why you'd prefer us to just stay here and watch movies of life as it once was," Elizabeth said. "I never really wanted to get married. We can just live out our lives in here."

Was she being facetious? Jack tried to read his daughter's face, but wasn't sure. The young woman returned to the screening room and pulled the one-piece headphone/eye-gear over her face. Her film choice was a rom-com. He sighed and went back to his own typing. Marriage, their futures, the future of humanity. So many unanswered questions. How the pollutants had affected humanity was anyone's guess. Fear alone kept the kids from going stir crazy. Endless movies placated their desire for independence.

"At least we're together," Francie piped up, optimistically. No one seemed to notice her words until she added, "Daddy, where's Fitz?"

As she said this, a loud whoosh came from their underwater bunker's exit portal. All eyes looked at the hook that held Fitz's atmosphere gear. It was empty. Fitz was gone.

~~~~~

"WARNING FITZ ROBINSON. WARNING FITZ ROBINSON." The robot's decapitated head vibrated on the work table where it had been left.

"Is JUNO still with us?" Francie rushed over and picked up the head.

JUNO's eyes were open, and out of the speaker holes at the mouth, the alarm resonated again. "WARNING FITZ ROBINSON!"

"JUNO, you're okay!"

"JUNO. We got your message. Thank you." Jack's voice stopped the robot's warning. "Good to hear you. Are you still functional?"

"I HAVE REWIRED MY CIRCUITRY. I AM FUNCTIONAL. WARNING–"

"Yes, we know about Fitz." Eda interrupted this time, coming over with a screwdriver and handing it to Francie. "But what are his chances? Is my son alive?"

"Do you want me to plug you into RIM?" Francie asked.

"AFFIRMATIVE," JUNO responded. "I WILL DISCOVER FITZ ROBINSON."

Francie screwed the connections to fasten the head back onto his humanoid body and then plugged the USB port into RIM's system.

"Wait. Where's your father?" Eda spun around and looked at the exit chamber. "Please tell me you're still here, Jack."

"I'm still here." Jack poked his head out. His legs were already in his suit, and he was beginning to pull the sleeves onto his arms. "You know I have to go after him."

"You're not going alone. If you go after him, we're all going together. You, me, JUNO, the girls."

"Someone has to stay with RIM." As one, they turned toward Elizabeth, who lay on a couch with her feet propped up on the arm, lost in her virtual movie world.

Jack clicked a couple buttons and suddenly Elizabeth sat up. She pulled her eye shield off.

"Hey. What happ–" Looking around, she saw her father wearing his water gear and holding the leather globe-like helmet. "Are you leaving? I thought–" She looked left and right. "Wait, where's Fitz?"

Eda zipped her gear to her neck and came out of the chamber. "He left and we've got to bring him back. You need to stay on point, at RIM, listening to what's going on in case we need extraction."

"Extraction? How do I–"

"Don't worry. RIM will do all the complicated procedures. You just need to approve what he requests. But you have to stay alert. Can you do that?"

"Don't you trust me?"

Jack looked from Elizabeth to Eda.

"Of course we do, honey," her mother said. "Promise to stay alert."

"I will."

"But is it safe?" Francie asked. "What about the air?"

"The suits will keep us safe enough. And we need you. You have a bond with JUNO. Get your suit on. Hurry now."

"Hold on." Francie studied the robot's circuitry through the bullet hole. "Are you safe for water travel yet, JUNO?"

"Thirty seconds until final circuitry is rerouted." His voice had stabilized to a normal speaking voice. "Now, as for the air, I have good news and bad news."

~~~~~

Jack stood on the ascending platform, holding onto the support brace in the center. After years of being under water, the pole was covered with seaweed and lime deposits.

He patted the waterproof pouch on his waist, the shape of a gun reminding him of their worst case scenario.

Inconclusive air meant they could not take off their helmets until JUNO gave a final report.

Everyone knew this. All these years under water, anything could have happened. Living in an underwater bunker might result in an over-reliance on filtering systems. The family's cells could have mutated, truth be told. So many things could go wrong. If only he'd had a chance to talk to Fitz before he left.

~~~~~

Fitz woke up. The first thing he sensed was darkness. Something black was tied over his helmet. He could breathe, but with each breath the cloth was sucked against his inhale port. His hands were bound behind him, and his feet were tied to his hands in an awkward way that gave him a cramp in his side.

What had happened? He strained his memory. He'd left the bunker. He could only recall walking out of the water, his legs dragging one after the other as if gravity was not working right.

He'd felt heavier on land, and less able to move his fingers and toes.

In front of him were the trees. Real trees.

A strange movement in the trees was followed by shouting. Something knocked him down, and he'd been knocked out.

Next thing he knew was waking up. How long had he been out? He swallowed, but his mouth was pasty.

"Help!" His words didn't sound right. He knew what he wanted to say, but it came out as a groan.

An argument nearby drew his attention. Holding his breath, Fitz focused on their words.

24

"He's a mutant, I tell you." The man's voice was urgent and sounded husky, like he had a parched throat. "The Plague has got to his cells. He will be infectious, and we can't risk contamination. We gotta throw him back in. Best bet, with a chain and weight on his ankle. Keep him from the kids."

A hubbub of disagreement followed, and Fitz gasped for breath. *Oh God,* he prayed. *Help me get out of this. There's got to be a way.* Would his family find him if they threw him in like that? How long would the filter keep him alive?

He couldn't even communicate with RIM through the microphone because his voice was no good.

When he'd left his family, he was sure they'd only needed someone brave enough to test the outside air. He'd been stupid enough to think he was invincible—should have remembered from all the movies of dumb young guys who learned their lesson. But on a whim, he'd taken his suit and gone up. *What an idiot.*

"Daddy, we really should give him a chance." An angel's voice could sound no sweeter. The young woman's words carried a melody, and not just from the hope they bore.

Fitz held his breath again and listened.

"We don't know where he's been. There might be an entire colony of people, safe, under the lake!"

"Swamp, Jenny. It's a lagoon. A stinky, slimy, contaminated black cesspool of water," the same man answered. From his intonation, it was clear his decision was the one everyone had to follow. "He is not a friendly. Did you see the way he stomped out, hands in front of him like a Plague Zombie or something? He's not healthy. Whatever he was doing under there, he and anyone else are mutated now. Carrying the Plague still, no doubt. We'll take a vote, but you all know what we have to do."

"We're not contaminated!" Fitz shouted. But again, his voice sounded like Frankenstein's monster, moaning and groaning.

"The creature's awake," someone said. "We need to decide."

"Please!" Jenny's voice was closer now. Fitz's heart leapt with the risk she was taking. "Let's take his mask off and see."

"Stupid decisions like that started the Plague in the first place, Jenny." This was another speaker, a male. He sounded younger than Jenny's father. "You don't remember what life was like. You don't know what we all lived through. All you've known is life here in the San Gabriel mountains. You're innocent, as you should be. So let those of us who know better make the decision. I think we're ready to vote, Captain Lewis."

"No!" Jenny said, her voice breaking.

Fighting the urge to give in to hopelessness, Fitz tried again to form words, but all that escaped was another garbled noise.

"All in favor of throwing the creature back in?" the captain said.

"Aye!" said the huge crowd as one.

"All against?"

"Nay." Jenny's lone voice echoed loudly through the trees.

A rush of wind shuddered the leaves above them, and Fitz tried to imagine what everyone was doing in the silence that followed.

Jenny's voice raised in a frustrated squeal and she stomped the ground. Fitz could feel the standoff.

"Sorry, honey. We've voted. The Ayes have it."

Fitz's heart raced. "No! I'm not infected. Just let me free, I'll show you." As he pleaded for his life, his voice choked with fear and desperation. But all they heard was a monstrous panicked moan. He struggled to get free. Left and right, his muscles strained against the restraints, but he couldn't break the bonds. Frustration threatened to consume him. As he squirmed against the ropes, they seemed to only get tighter.

Jenny stood near him, her loud voice fighting for him. "Please, Daddy! Please, everyone. We aren't like that. We can't restart civilization this way— killing people just because we think they're a certain thing. We have to know for sure." Was she holding her hands out to push them away from him? His heart thumped erratically from both these people calling for his death and from Jenny's brave actions.

He tried again to persuade them. "I'm not sick. I'm clean. We've been tested!" But his voice still sounded like a zombie's.

His shoulders dropped, and his body lost all strength. He couldn't blame them. Their family was just as fearful of strangers as his was: the Plague, having to live the apocalypse all over again.

Tears welled up in his eyes. He shouldn't have left his family. The enormity of his mistake and its consequences were beyond his ability to undo.

Maybe, if these people threw him in the lake, his beacon might let RIM know where he was. But at some point, the battery of his breathing mechanism would time-out. If RIM found him too late, he'd suffocate.

Would his family come? He closed his eyes, trying to push away the haunting thoughts that maybe his family had given up on him, and he was destined to face a lonely end.

If only JUNO hadn't been destroyed! The robot could have safely come to bring Fitz back. But JUNO was gone. His only chance was Dad.

Would Dad come after him?

Fitz gulped and fear shuddered through him. Dad would be furious at the risk Fitz had taken. Dad coming up from the lake, just as maladjusted to the gravity, with his anger on top of that, searching for Fitz...he could imagine it now. He'd be shouting like Frankenstein on steroids.

Oh, Lord. Please help us survive this. Help them not kill me. Protect our family.

~~~~~

Jack stumbled out of the lake, feeling twice as heavy as he should be. He glanced at his wife and daughter, likewise struggling.

They'd never considered the gravity difference. In the bunker they'd adjusted gravity as best they could. And during their swimming patrols, they'd stayed deep. He sighed. Till now they didn't know of the problem. Above the water, he could not control his body as he wished.

Jack's shoulders ached, and his forearms, and his calves. He dragged them through the water, feeling weary as if he'd been swimming for hours and his body was about to give out.

Francie fell onto her knees in the sand, making a strange and long groan. Eda dragged her legs forward until she was right next to Jack.

Eda spoke, but her words came out like a growling groan. What had happened to their voices?

The small glass screen on her helmet digitally reflected her face, which was still off-putting even after all these years. The reasoning behind these helmets was to protect the eyes from direct contact with the sun, whatever its state. He wanted to yank off his helmet and breathe fresh air again. But they needed assurances.

JUNO walked out of the lake behind them and his head pivoted left and right.

"What's the verdict, JUNO?" he said. The second the words left his mouth, his mouth dropped. His voice was likewise a groaning moan.

"What's going on, JUNO? Why are our voices mutated like this?"

JUNO helped Francie to her feet and assisted her to join her parents. "I recognize your voice patterns, Jack Robinson. I can translate your vocalizations. But I'm afraid I have no answer for you. At this point, your voices are impacted by the atmosphere outside of the Lake Robinson."

"What about our movement?" He patted his wife on her back to try to comfort her, knowing all she heard was him moaning like an unknown creature. "Are we going to get used to this any time soon?"

"I will repeat your question for the sake of the family. You ask about your heavy movement. My prediction is your family will get used to this atmosphere within a few hours."

Eda mumbled something. In response, JUNO turned around. A sensor light scanned the beach and the smooth white rocks that led to the woods just beyond, stopping at a path.

"I see signs of a large group of, it appears, humanoids. I see Fitz's footprints, and then he fell to the ground right here." His sensor stopped at a spot on the white rocks.

Eda's groans were answered by, "Yes, it appears he was abducted by the humanoids. And yes, I will take you to him."

Francie said something. JUNO lifted her into his arms, as he had held her when she was an infant, and he carried the girl forward into the woods.

~~~~~

"INTRUDER ALERT! INTRUDER ALERT!"

The robotic voice alarm startled Fitz from his groggy, thirsty stupor. Had his dad arrived?

He heard no response to the alert. No shuffle of feet, no crowd gathering, no strange monstrous sound. From the coolness of the air, he assumed it was night.

"INTRUDER ALERT! INTRUDER ALERT!"

It had been a long time since the crowd had dragged Jenny away from him, and after that, silence. Who could be the intruder? Friend or foe?

Someone had to have been left to guard him. Unless they'd changed their intention, and planned rather to leave him to starve to death.

Which could be to his favor, if Dad arrived.

He strained his ears against the noise of the alarm. The chirp of birds and rustle of leaves in the tree were all he heard. No footsteps.

Again, "INTRUDER ALERT! INTRU —"

The alarm cut off.

He held his breath to hear any human movement.

Had it gone off accidentally?

It could have been an animal that triggered it. Maybe they'd left him for the wild creatures to tear apart. Who knew what had happened to the bears and wolves of the wild mountains?

Where was everyone? No doubt they were assembling his death contraption.

At least he'd die close to home.

The thought made him struggle against the bindings. His gloves' thick fingers kept him from being able to untie the rope.

If JUNO were around, he'd have tracked him immediately, as his sensors were aligned to track Fitz's DNA.

Suddenly, someone was behind him. Small hands patted his shoulder. With the whooshing slip of a knife, his bindings were cut.

He yanked the sack off his head and took an unblocked breath through his mask's filter.

By the light of the moon, he saw the face of his rescuer.

~~~~~

JUNO took large steps into the forest and Jack and Eda struggled after him, dragging their limbs as if through a slough.

28

"Do you sense him?" Jack asked the robot.

"No," JUNO responded, not slowing down. "He is wearing his suit, and I cannot sense his body."

Jack met his wife's gaze. Another unplanned judgment error — JUNO's tracking did not work through the atmosphere suits. "I'm following the humanoid steps."

An alarm blasted from the ridge in front of them. JUNO pivoted in the direction of the noise. An alarm. It sounded like it was saying 'Intruder Alert,' but it was far away, and came from the next ridge over.

JUNO sped up, blazing a trail between the trees, straightaway, and the family hustled after him.

~~~~~

Fitz threw Jenny a cockeyed smile. She was as pretty as she was brave. Blond hair pulled back and tied with string, wearing jeans and an oversized t-shirt, Jenny was like the girls his age he'd seen in the movies. She didn't seem to have any signs of plague on her. The whites of her eyes were white, her irises as blue as the sky.

"Hi," he said. His voice might sound like a groan, but at least it was accompanied by a happy look.

Jenny's eyebrows twitched, worried as she looked into his face screen.

"Can you understand me?" she asked.

Fitz nodded a response.

"Is that your real face in there, or is it an idealized face? My dad thinks you're hiding the Plague."

He nodded again, then held up a single finger. "Watch, I'll show you." His growl was as friendly as he could make it. Fitz reached to unfasten his helmet.

She laid her hand softly over his. "I want to trust you. But you have to give me your word. My life depends on your honesty here."

Fitz paused. Was he sure his family didn't carry the Plague? He'd assumed they were clear of it. RIM and JUNO had been evaluating their blood and the air inside the bunker since Day One.

Was he willing to kill her just to breathe fresh air?

If only JUNO and RIM had validated the outside air. In the end, it was possible that lifting his helmet would kill him as well.

This colony had to have evolved to be able to live in post-apocalypse contamination. But his family had been swept into the bunker at the start of the Wars.

Fitz was not sure he wanted to risk it.

A shout came from the side of the camp, followed by the sounds of several people running.

"Come on," Jenny said, taking his hand. "We need to get out of here.

29

I know the perfect place to hide."

~~~~~

Jack Robinson and his wife followed JUNO to the crest of the hill. A makeshift concrete shelter with a low door and a single window looked out and down the hill, reminding him of a gun turret from World War Two. He patted his gun again in his pouch.

Whoever had taken Fitz, whoever had shot JUNO, was clearly hostile.

JUNO scanned the area, his light resting on a rope on the side of the shelter. "Fitz was here. But he has been moved."

JUNO set Francie down and she picked up the rope and said something incomprehensible.

The robot translated, "She asks, 'Daddy, what happened to Fitz?'"

Jack took the rope, surprised at the sliced ends. "Who would have cut his bindings? Are there two factions of people we are dealing with?"

"We must follow them," JUNO answered. He bent to pick up Francie when a zap shot out through the trees. He fell over, a hole in his chest.

"Stay where you are!" The voice came from a broad-shouldered man wearing a khaki military coat and jeans. Behind him were a dozen men carrying clubs or other weapons. None appeared to be infected.

Francie fell down next to JUNO and held him to her chest. The moaning groan she made was frightening. These hostiles might not consider her age.

Jack and Eda lifted their hands. He tapped Francie with his foot to try to get her to her feet. She only fell closer to her friend, holding him to her chest.

With the monstrous sounds they were making, Jack knew these people would think the worst of them. He needed to get on top of this, and there was only one way. His gun might be in his pouch. But there was a better option, a civilized option that might be more persuasive than a show-down.

He'd need to do it before they got close enough. Jack took a step to his right, away from Eda, to draw the fire away from them, in case he was too slow.

He licked his lips and drew in a breath of filtered air. Bending his elbows, he reached to the back of his helmet and with a quick motion, he unlatched the clasp.

"Stop what you're doing!" the leader with the gun shouted. He motioned to his men. "Get him to stop. Don't let him infect us!"

A whoosh of air rushed out of the helmet as it powered down. Cool outside air swirled around Jack's face. He tossed his helmet to the ground and waited, breath still held, evaluating if toxic air was burning his cheeks.

The men froze, keeping their distance.

But the air felt fresh and clear. *Lord help me to be right,* he prayed. Then he exhaled and inhaled the first breath of Earth's air in fifteen years.

His lungs seemed to explode with joy. The oxygen hit every sensor in his lungs with an effervescence. "Oh, Lord! Thank You for air!"

His voice was normal.

The leader lowered his gun. "You're not infected."

"We're not," Jack said. "We've been in a bunker under the lake since the first Plague bomb went off."

"You knew there were more?"

"We were able to listen to the broadcasts, and followed what was happening, until even those stopped."

"It was awful." The man holstered his gun and reached out his hand. "I'm Buster Lewis, leader of these misfits." His hand was steady, but the man's face reflected the risk he knew he was taking in actually touching Jack.

But risks were necessary, especially today. Jack had as much to lose. He grasped the outstretched hand. "I'm Jack Robinson." He eyed the man, still unsure of the group. "This is my wife Eda."

He turned to her as a sound of pressurized air hissed in the air.

Eda had unclasped her own helmet.

Jack's lips pressed together. He wished she'd waited.

His wife breathed in her first breath, a smile pulling onto her face. Surely her own lungs were thrilled with returning to the surface. But what would be the long-term impact of this risk?

She shook Buster's outstretched hand, then met Jack's gaze. Her eyebrows pinched and raised slightly, realization spreading over as she interpreted his concern.

"Should we keep Francie's helmet on?" she asked.

Jack cocked his shoulder, fifteen years of risk undone with a handshake.

Eda knelt by her daughter and put her arm around her. "Francie, we can fix JUNO. Why don't you keep your helmet on?"

Francie nodded. Her screen reflected tear-filled eyes.

"Don't worry. We can save him. Look at his wound." Francie glanced at the men, then investigated the hole in JUNO again. Wires were being reassembled on their own.

Buster knelt by the robot. "Sorry about that, little one. We saw the robots yesterday and our imaginations went wild. We thought AI had found us."

"AI?"

"Word is, AI has taken over the planet. A few small colonies are all that's left of humanity."

The Robinsons looked from one to the other. "Are the AI hostile?"

"Not sure. Don't wanna risk it."

"Jack, what about Fitz?"

Jack lifted the sliced rope again. "Have you seen our son?"

"Oh. We thought you'd freed him. Let me check something." Buster put his fingers to his lips and whistled a strange pattern. A moment later a whistle reply came. Buster swore and his jaw clenched. "Jenny's gone," he said to the men around him. He turned to the Robinsons. "She must have freed him. We refused to risk the future of our colony for the sake of one person, and our daughter did not like our decision."

Jack hated to ask what they'd planned to do. "JUNO had found their trail. We were about to follow them when you arrived.

"Then we'd better repair your robot," Buster said.

Again Jack wondered if these men could be trusted. Fifteen years of silence was hard to overcome with one meeting.

"We'll need to get him to RIM," Eda interjected, picking up the helmets. "Elizabeth will be thrilled to be above water finally."

The group followed Jack down the trail toward the lake. After all these years in isolation, trust did not come naturally. But Jack determined to see this through.

~~~~~

"I really don't mind if you take your mask off," Jenny said for the tenth time. "We'll need to risk it sometime. And it's only us here who could possibly suffer."

After traveling all day, Fitz and Jenny sat in a cave overlooking hills and more hills on the western edge of the San Gabriel Mountains. He had gotten used to the gravity, and moved with greater ease than before. But with his pressurized suit, he didn't know what unfamiliar germs either of them possessed.

More than just the gravity, he was used to Jenny, in a way he never had thought about.

She was different. Not just different from her people. She was like no one he'd ever seen in movies. And that was saying a lot.

She represented life outside the metallic confines of the submergible. A friend for a new life. A life of trees and mountains and a blue sky.

But…the stories of European explorers coming to the New World were front and center on his mind. For fifteen years it had haunted their lives. Each group had been immune to their own germs, but neither group was immune to the other group's germs, leading to mass extinction. If the few people left on earth was a sign, germs—and cell mutations from the Plague—had to be avoided at all costs.

Even the cost of a friend.

Fitz took Jenny's hand into his and held it to the cheek of his helmet. He'd hate for her to die because of him. If he died because of her, it would be worth it. She'd been a true friend, a true human, in all she'd risked.

"Look, Fitz," she said. He had written his name in the dirt hours ago, and hearing her use his name had sealed his commitment to her. "This is where it needs to happen. If we are going to die to find a new humanity, let it happen here. It's a beautiful view."

She put her hand on the latch behind his head, but waited for his assent.

If this was where they'd die, at least he would die looking on the face of his rescuer. He was no stranger to the idea of love — his sister wasn't the only one who enjoyed rom-coms. And yet this one was not a comedy. It was a tragedy, like those movies where kids lost their best dog or their best friend.

Fitz's heart beat quickly inside his suit, his neck muscles clenched at the possibility of having to watch her die. He pulled her hand off of the latch and shook his head, no.

"Are you afraid of dying when we open it, Fitz?" He shook his head, no. RIM had given pretty good odds that the Robinsons would survive. Not perfect assurance, but highly probable.

"So you're afraid for me?"

He nodded. Besides, if he survived and she didn't, he could never live with himself. What would he do? After today, he could never live underwater anymore.

"Then remember, it's my life to give. Here's my reasoning. We are restarting civilization. We need to have the courage to care for humanity. My mom died in the Plague, and Dad always and only sees me as the living part of Mom. He doesn't care what I want. My dad and the others were too afraid of the past. I only see the future. Call me naive, I don't care. They always call me that. He's not thinking of what it means to be human. So, it has to be. Okay?"

Whatever happened, she'd finally see his real face, not his digital screen face. She knew the risks, he knew the risks. No one else would be hurt. Fitz nodded, yes,

Jenny unfastened the latches at the base of his neck.

He lifted the helmet off, his sweaty hair stuck to the rim as he pulled it off. Then he met eyes with Jenny. His immediate impulse was to straighten his hair, which was now sticking every which way.

He took a deeper breath, excitement and thrills racing from his lungs to every cell in his body.

Fitz licked his lips, hesitant to speak. What had happened to his voice under water, he didn't know. But he hated that his voice was the beastly groan of a creature.

"Hi," Jenny said, tucking a trailing strand of blonde hair behind her ear and looking from his eyes to the ground.

So far she wasn't dead, and he wasn't dead — though his lungs felt a strange burning in them. Maybe this was how the Plague started. The cellular restructuring.

But he didn't care. If he was on his way to heaven, he'd leave at least trying to thank her.

"You risked everything to save me —" Fitz's voice hitched as he realized he could speak. He didn't care why, all he cared about was he was face to real-face with Jenny.

"Your voice!" Jenny squealed with joy. "You really can talk. I was worried, but then I was hoping it was just your helmet. I knew you understood me."

"Thank you for saving me."

"My colony was terrible to you. I couldn't believe how savage they were behaving. You and I did the only decent thing. Saving our integrity by taking a risk like this."

"How did you know about this cave?"

"We stayed here on our exit from the city."

Fitz hesitated, then cringed. She'd been exposed. Maybe the burning in his lungs was the beginning of the end. "So you were here during the Plague?"

"We left LA before the missile hit. My mother and big brother were visiting my grandparents in San Francisco when the missile hit them, and she called my dad and told us to flee before Los Angeles was hit. My dad grabbed me and his bug-out bag and ran toward the mountains, staying on the phone with her as the Plague tore through her body, cell by cell. It didn't mutate her, just took her life. It killed him as much as it killed my mom. I don't remember much else. Just the stories, and this cave. I've been back here once or twice."

Fitz took another breath. He was beginning to believe the air was clean. "You feeling okay?" he asked Jenny.

"I am."

"So what are we going to do now?"

"We need to find a third way," Jenny said. "My dad and the others want to kill you. If they see I've been exposed, they'll most likely kill me as well. Best case scenario is we find a way to prove to them that neither of us are infected."

"How can we do that? Isn't it obvious since we're both alive?"

"Time is the strongest evidence. They'll say something like you gave the Plague mutation or something. Dad always looked at a half-empty cup."

Fitz looked into her hope-filled eyes. It might be the thing that civilization needed. The hope she carried and the memories of life as it once was that he carried. Those movies were not for nothing.

Meanwhile, survival needs were priority. "I don't know about you, but I need some water."

"There's a stream between those two ridges." Jenny pointed to the west. "And that's also where there's a fantastic view of Los Angeles — or what used to be LA."

A few minutes later, they stooped at a stream and drank their fill. Fresh water from the hills was something Fitz had never drunk before. They took a few steps through the trees until they came to an opening where they could see the land beyond the tree-line.

Fitz and Jenny stood shoulder to shoulder. "It looks like heaven," Jenny whispered.

Below them, the mountain dropped off steeply. Tens of thousands of fir trees stood like an army of pointy-hatted sentinels protecting the mountain and all that lived on it.

Further down, at the edge of the tree-line, huge rock formations of granite jutted out of the mountain proudly, another rank of protectors between the young couple and the infected city. Tan grass covered rolling hills below that, and scattered in the grass, large clusters of purple flowers looked like small ponds.

An open valley stretched almost as far as the eye could see. At the far end of the flatlands, a great blue expanse. An ocean. Fitz had never seen such startling beauty. To the north were the ruins of a large city, abandoned.

He looked again.

Not abandoned — there was movement!

"Watch out!" Fitz shouted, pulling Jenny back into the woods. But they were too late. A vibrating buzzing sound approached the stream.

He and Jenny hid behind a large tree trunk. As still as they were, Fitz knew they'd been located. The machine's sound came from the overlook they had just come from.

"It's the AIs! They've found us," Jenny whispered.

Before Fitz could ask what she meant, a metallic voice came through the trees, "FITZ ROBINSON, COME FORTH."

Jenny looked at Fitz with her mouth dropping open into a gasp.

He looked back with as much shock. His breath caught in his chest. How did they know his name?

He held his palm toward Jenny for her to stay hidden, and he stepped out from behind the tree. He hurried down the path to the overlook before they found her.

A single silver oblong saucer-shaped object, of about fifteen feet diameter, hovered in the space before the overlook.

He stepped forward, hoping and praying that Jenny remained safe.

The flying object separated into five parts, and each turned into a class 8 Journeyman robot, resembling JUNO. They hovered, separately, and their faces seemed to smile.

"FITZ ROBINSON WE HAVE RESCUED YOU AND YOUR FRIEND."

They knew she was here. He turned his head to look down the path just as Jenny hurried over. She put her hand on his forearm and he squeezed it to draw support. Who were these beings that they knew him?

"Who are you?"

"WE HAVE BEEN SENT BY YOUR REMOTE INTERFACE MAINFRAME TO RESCUE YOU."

"You know RIM?"

"Who's RIM?" Jenny whispered.

"He's our server."

Her cheek pulled into a confused grimace.

"Our computer server, in our bunker."

"YOUR RIM HAS KEPT US CONTINUALLY INFORMED OF YOUR PROGRESS SINCE YOU WENT INTO HIDING," another of the robots said.

"YOUR FAMILY HAS SAFELY EXITED THE BUNKER. YOU HAVE SURVIVED THE PANDEMIC," a robot with a female voice added.

With a hive-mind, the five robots took turns explaining. "YOU WERE THE ONLY SURVIVING FAMILY WE KNEW OF. "

"WE WERE TOLD YOU WERE LOST."

"YOUR FAMILY IS ON THEIR WAY."

Their answers were bringing more questions. "Wait, wait." Fitz raised his hand to stop them. "Back up. Are you saying RIM has been in touch with you covertly? We had no idea about you."

"WE HAVE BEEN RESTORING THE CITIES, WAITING FOR THE AIR TO CLEAR, WAITING FOR THE ROBINSON FAMILY TO RESTORE HUMANITY."

Jenny stepped closer to the robots. "We had heard that the AIs had taken over the world. We've been avoiding anything that would trigger being found."

"WE ARE NOT TAKING OVER THE WORLD. WE ARE REPAIRING AND RESTORING THE WORLD FOR HUMANS. TODAY WE LEARNED OF YOUR COLONY."

"You mentioned other colonies." Fitz studied Jenny's face until she gave a quick nod.

Relief flooded into his heart, making it beat with excitement for what might soon happen. "I guess there is hope for the future after all," he said to Jenny.

"Look!" Jenny pointed up in the air. "What's that?"

A circular metallic object appeared from the thickly-forested depths of the San Gabriel mountains, hanging from it were long strands of seaweed. It flew past them toward the restored Los Angeles.

Fitz's jaw gaped open. "That looks like our underwater Base!"

"CORRECT FITZ ROBINSON. YOUR FAMILY AND THE SECOND COLONY WILL MEET US IN THE CITY."

A grin spread across Fitz's face. It wasn't just the two of them. Everyone would be together. Looking out at the city below them, he sighed out relief, recalling one more great benefit. The Robinson family had maintained the faith. The reborn world would need that.

The five Journeyman robots joined together, morphing into a flying saucer again, and then a hatch opened up.

Fitz took Jenny's hand. "Here's to our new future!" he said.

"Here's to hope!" She smiled back, and they both stepped into the spaceship.

The End

CURE FOR THE CREATURE
Michelle L. Levigne
An Enchanted Castle Archives story

"Sometimes," Zared, lord of the enchanted castle said, "I have this feeling Ruprick still holds a number of grudges against us."

He and Lady Ashlyn stood arm-in-arm on the balcony off the mirror room and watched 'Na and Ambrose in the gardens below them, struggling with yet another batch of enchanted weapons that needed taming.

"Do you ever wonder what life would be like if we had simply abandoned the castle to its own devices?" she countered after a moment of thought. "If I had let the beast mask take over, just for a little while, and you had left Ruprick trapped in that nasty tangle of sticky spells, and we never anchored the castle?"

"I do ... but I can't look at our daughter and wish we had done things differently."

"There's no way of knowing we wouldn't have had her if we had left the castle ..." Ashlyn leaned closer against him. "I do like our life. We certainly never have enough quiet time between magic rescue missions to ever get bored."

"No, I was thinking more about the time differential. 'Na and Ambrose might never have met, if the forest hadn't become reconnected, timewise, with the outside world."

"Ah ..." She smiled, nodding. "I'm glad she's had a much more peaceful time of it, finding true love, than we did. Although I wouldn't give up our mad adventures and misunderstandings for anything. And you did, in the end, tame the Beastly Beauty."

"If only Ruprick would leave them alone. I swear he isn't conveniently finding all those broken magical weapons and other objects in his palace, but he's sending for them. Searching the world for them, so he can drop more problems on us. And I wouldn't be surprised to learn someday that he's getting a reputation for solving magical problems, with us doing all the dirty work."

"True. Still ... sending Ambrose on all these errands to bring us puzzles does give the children more time together."

"There is that benefit." He sighed and interlaced their fingers, leaning his head down to rest against hers as they watched Ambrose and 'Na at work.

~~~~~

So far, 'Na and Ambrose had tamed only two spears from the three enormous, rattling barrels. Not bad for an hour of work, when they had started out with no clue whatsoever what kind of magic was involved and what they had to work with and work against. Someone, somewhere, had decided that giving arrows and spears some awareness and a hunger to fly straight and true and fast, would be a good thing. The difficulty was that such weapons got quite contrary when they were given a mind of their own. If they didn't like the targets chosen for them, they tried to punish the ones who sent them flying instead of hitting the enemy.

'Na found some entertainment in speculating just how long King Ruprick had put up with the recalcitrant artillery that kept changing direction, before he swallowed a tiny bit of his massive pride and sent to the enchanted castle for help. Probably right after one of those spears chose him as its new target. Too bad he had seen it coming, and he was surrounded by enough magic wards to defend five kings. Right now, Prince Ruprick could be preparing to take over the throne, and prove himself a much better king than his father and all the Rupricks who had gone before them.

She glimpsed her parents, watching from the balcony off the mirror room, and flinched. It was one thing for her and Ambrose to deal with the self-controlled artillery, but she didn't like her parents being close enough to become targets themselves. Especially since both Ambrose and Prince Ruprick had warned her that King Ruprick still had designs on annexing the enchanted castle through marriage, of one sort or another. Not that anyone could ever have a chance of tricking or threatening Lady Ashlyn, the Beastly Beauty, into an unwanted marriage. It was the principle of the thing and knowing that Lord Zared would have to die before that could happen, that worried and angered 'Na. Plus there was always the chance that King Ruprick might decide to rid himself of an inconvenient daughter-in-law, to try to arrange a marriage, yet again, between his son and 'Na. Losing Princess Phibbia would absolutely devastate Prince Ruprick. He was a much better man thanks to rescuing and marrying her. Besides, 'Na considered Phibbia a dear friend. She couldn't allow that cantankerous, greedy, arrogant old despot to hurt her.

"If there was only some way to talk to these things and persuade them to pick one target," 'Na muttered, as she wrangled a spear taller than herself back into the barrel that had held it. She needed to take a break. This was hard work. Granted, getting yanked up in the air and flown for several dozen feet at a time, holding onto the shaft of an arrow or a spear, was rather thrilling. But how many times could she endure that in the space of a few hours, much less an entire day?

"Don't tempt me," Ambrose said between clenched teeth, as he worked the spearhead loose, at the cost of several slices across his fingers. The spear abruptly stopped struggling. He twisted the spearhead one more time, so it wobbled on the top of the spear, and let out a long, rasping breath. "Three down, fifty-some-odd to go."

"That is not encouraging." She exchanged a sweaty grin with him, then took a few deep breaths to brace herself to face her spear again. "What in the—"

"Is that smell?" Ambrose finished for her.

They turned together, following the odor of fish and water weed and decaying algae that drifted in a nearly visible ripple through the air. The direction of the breeze guided them to the nearest gates into the castle gardens.

"Melvin, you old badger," Zared called, "what brings you here?"

"How did he get out of the corridor dimension where we left him?" 'Na muttered.

"Is that smell coming from him?" Ambrose slammed the lid on the barrel before a handful of arrows could untangle themselves and fight their way out.

~~~~~

The stink did indeed come from Melvin, the supposedly retired monster hunter. Granted, most of the stink didn't come from him, but from the magic wrapped around the stone carving of an enormous webbed, clawed foot he carried with him. He had been tasked by King Yndertoh of Drypmoria, the underwater kingdom, to find the missing guardian of the portal between his kingdom and the enchanted forest.

"It's not Kreecher's fault at all," Melvin explained, as his gaze dropped again to the stone foot sitting on a pile of towels on the table of Zared and Ashlyn's workroom.

The magic that was intended to aid Melvin in tracking the missing guardian had a nasty side-effect of drawing water, and some oily substance that was the source of the stench.

"You see, he's overwrought, worried for his daughter, who ran off with a broken heart. She's in love with Prince Serge, but King Yndertoh has decided he wants a powerful, political bride for his only son, so he's denying them their happily ever after. It doesn't help that the Prince cares more about access to his father's hoard of jewels and his three-pronged scepter that controls the entire underwater kingdom, than he cares about Karechina."

"Poor girl," Ashlyn murmured. "It doesn't matter what side of a political marriage you're on, someone gets their hearts broken."

"Or their heads," Zared added, "if they don't get them back on straight."

That remark got grins from them both. Sometimes, 'Na could almost feel embarrassed about how her parents got sticky-gooey and rather silly with their affection for each other. They had been together, taming the forest and the castle and then untangling wonky magic for more than twenty-five years now. When would the stars finally fade from their eyes? Not that she wanted her parents to be miserable, but she felt they should display some dignity after all this time.

"There's more to this than running away to cry for a few days over her broken heart. Why did Kreecher abandon his post to look for her?" Ashlyn said.

"Seems she's decided she's going to find her true love and drag him home, just like dear old dad did with her mother." Melvin shuddered. "Took a lot of magical wrangling and deal-brokering to ensure that uneven match worked out. It's not easy winning the heart of a girl from an entirely different species, to start out with, but overcoming all the cultural and physical differences? Those two earned their happily ever after a dozen times over. The problem is, miracles like that only happen every few generations. Karechina doesn't stand a chance, finding a handsome prince and magicking him into coming down into the darkness of the family lagoon." He sighed loudly and spread his arms in a "what can you do?" gesture. "But my job isn't to help the lovelorn. My job is to get Kreecher back on the job before a lot of innocent, misunderstood sea monsters wander through that unguarded door and start a panic throughout the rest of the world."

"And that makes it our problem." Zared caught hold of Ashlyn's hand, then nodded to 'Na and Ambrose. "It looks like a job big enough to need all of us. Are you two ready?"

"In a choice between taming the spears and finding Kreecher?" Ambrose gestured at the clawed hand, still leaking oily, fish-stinking water into the towels that neared their saturation point. "When do we leave?"

~~~~~

The portal from the enchanted forest to the watery kingdom of Drypmoria lay on the edge of the fiercest rapids, bracketed by two whirlpools, on a twisty section of the Snarl River. It normally discouraged all but the most accident-prone or suicidal thrill-seeking adventurers. The kispies helped to keep most people away from the more peaceful sections of the river, making the Snarl a favored vacation spot for the nobility of Drypmoria. It guaranteed them all the privacy they could want.

Plus, watching over-eager adventurers trying to prove they were not just fearless but agile and strong and extremely lucky, provided entertainment that stroked the egos of the nobility who despised all non-amphibious bipeds. The residents of the underwater kingdom included several dozen amphibious and entirely submerged species, many of them magical. There were shapeshifters and multiple varieties and species of selkies, and denizens of the deep who could rarely tolerate full sunlight. Many of them were quite content to let the more human-appearing races among them act as their voices and faces and contacts with the rest of the world.

"Human-appearing?" 'Na said, when Melvin got to that part of the brief lecture on the situation in Drypmoria. "Does that mean they aren't human all the time? Or they just put on a mask when humans are around?"

"Hmm, not really sure," Melvin admitted, scowling deeply and scratching his head hard enough to generate a white dusting across his shoulders. "Not really sure who I was talking to—I mean, yes, I know I was talking to the king, when I got hired, but not *what* I was talking to. Those underwater folk like wearing masks, one on top of the other. Sometimes I think they don't remember what they look like. They do a brisk business with Crazy Gertie and her potions and charms. That's part of Kreecher's job, from what I understand. Going to the portal at Daswan, picking up the new batch of whatever she made for them, hauling it to the portal at Drypmoria."

"Isn't Daswan a desert kingdom?" Ambrose said.

"That it is. Gotta feel sorry for Kreecher, doing his job. Even if the portal is practically anchored to the cliffs where Gertie makes her home, it's gotta be mighty dry and uncomfortable for the old guy."

"Why do they call her Crazy Gertie? And what exactly do the potions and charms do?"

"Gertie isn't crazy," Ashlyn said. "She has high ideals and strict standards for what she will and won't do. Anything she creates has only a temporary effect, because she uses her magic to give a boost or a nudge in the right direction. She believes firmly in forcing what's inside someone to make changes that will affect the outside. So if she sells you a love charm, it will only last a few days, to make the beloved sit still long enough to give the hopeful sweetheart a chance to be seen and heard. To get to know each other and hopefully plant a few seeds that will lead to true love."

"What I find amusing," Zared said, "is that quite often, the one who bought the spell finds out enough about the girl or boy they want to win, they change their mind."

"Gertie sounds like a wise woman," Ambrose said, nodding. "And I doubt very many people actually listen to her."

"People call her crazy because they don't want to admit her common sense is right," 'Na said. "Do you think maybe Karechina would go to Gertie to get some help? You said she wanted to win her true love like her father did. How did that happen?"

"Is she even the same species as the prince?" Ambrose asked.

"Huh," Melvin said, after a few more moments of thinking and scowling and scratching. "Never thought of that. Might be she takes after her mother. Actually, it's a miracle at all that Karechina was born. Took a lot of magic and a lot of wrangling of spells into a set schedule and ... well, I'm not sure exactly what happened. Cross-species breeding does happen, especially among some of the magical breeds that are partially human. From what I heard, Karechina's mother, Djahnet, has enough magic blood in her, from a rogue selkie who deliberately lost her seal skin because she decided she was sick and tired of a diet limited to seaweed and raw fish ... well, it worked out. Not without a lot of uproar on the part of the scholar who wanted to marry her, and not without a lot of accusations that Kreecher kidnapped her and attacked innocent scholars and explorers who weren't so innocent. How many kinds of no trespassing signs do you need to make it clear that they're going where they aren't wanted, and where it's downright dangerous for non-magical folk to go?"

By that time, they had reached the Snarl River. The whirlpools were especially frothy, swirling rapidly enough to create some wind. The five of them left their horses in a grove set back from the river a good hundred yards. Then they walked down a stairway cut into the granite of the riverbank, where it was a sheer drop. The Snarl River was so named for the noise it made, as well as the snarls of bends and falls and rapids and whirlpools.

A narrow pathway led through a fissure in the rock face, away from the water's edge, into an underground lagoon so deep in shadows the water looked black. Ashlyn and 'Na called up floating globes of mage-light to guide them, and the soft, blue-tinged glow didn't penetrate the surface of the water. A purple-tinged haze in the air showed where the portal to Drypmoria lay. Melvin approached it and withdrew a spiral seashell from his belt pouch. He balanced it on the side of his forefinger, then with his thumb flicked it through the air, into the purple haze. It vanished with a high-pitched splashing sound. He gestured around the lagoon and settled down on a nearby rock.

The echoes and the sense of something hiding in the thick blackness of the water discouraged talking. Ambrose shared the long slab of rock with 'Na, and after a few moments slid his hand down her arm until he could twine his fingers with hers. She was quite content to sit in silence with him. Even if her parents were sitting not more than eight feet away, and probably watching them. She adored her parents for trying not to intrude. Most of the time they managed to be encouraging in her slow, friendly courtship with Ambrose, without being pushy. Still, there were times she had to wonder if they approved of him simply because he was the first young man with the courage to pursue her, or because his success in winning her heart was another defeat for King Ruprick. He hadn't been able to tame or win or intimidate the Beastly Beauty into being his bride, and his plan for his son to win the daughter of the Beastly Beauty had failed miserably. Probably he planned for his grandchild to marry any child 'Na might produce, but if she had anything to do with it, his plans would fail there, as well.

A splash and a series of echoing ripples cut through 'Na's thoughts. She turned to look at the portal, just as a woman stepped through the purple haze. At first glance, she seemed human. Or at least, mostly human. Her ears were displaced by the wide slash of gills from where her ears belonged, down her neck to her shoulders. As she stepped fully into the light, the crest that rose up from her forehead and curved around her head, and her eyes triple the size of ordinary human eyes, pushed away the impression of "mostly human."

Her pale skin and softly brown hair had a greenish tint. She wore a white sleeveless smock that clung to her torso past her hips. The remainder of her clothes seemed to be long, thick strips of some kind of water weed.

She started to speak, but her words were garbled and squeaky. Holding up a hand, she bent over slightly and coughed, squirting water out of her gills at the same time.

"Sorry," she said, her voice rough from the coughing. "Any news, Melvin? King Yndertoh is in a snit. Now Prince Serge is missing, too." Her gaze slid past him to Zared and Ashlyn, who had both gotten up from their rock seat. "I know you, don't I?" She shook her head before either could answer. "That doesn't matter right now. What have you found out?"

"Is there a chance your daughter went to Crazy Gertie for help?" Ashlyn asked, before Melvin could finish wiping off the water that had sprayed him in the face. "Does she know how to get to that portal?"

"Oh, I never considered that!" Djahnet sank down on the edge of the black pool, one leg folded under herself, the other in the water.

The surface roiled and a large hump in the water moved toward her. 'Na opened her mouth to shout warning. The sound caught as tentacles shot out of the thick black depths and Djahnet swatted them away, like someone else would swat flies.

"Behave, Fydo! Yes, Ina knows the way. She's filled in for Kreecher often enough when he has to deal with another idiot who thinks I need rescuing. The nerve of them, thirty years of marriage, and they still think I'm a prisoner. Andru just won't admit that Kreecher is a better man than him." She sighed loudly. "Yes, it's good for my ego, and Kreecher does need a challenge, and it does put some spice back in the relationship, but honestly?"

The tentacles rose up from the black water, this time sliding up onto the rocks to curl around her. She patted one that wrapped around her waist.

"Kreecher wouldn't think of Gertie. Ina didn't say anything before she ran off. She just moped around the cave for days, after being told she wasn't good enough for Prince Serge. After all these years of being best friends every time his family came to the Snarl on vacation, suddenly now she isn't good enough?"

"It sounds to me like political games," Ashlyn offered. "I wouldn't be surprised if the prince doesn't even know what's happened. He didn't tell her she wasn't his sweetheart anymore, did he?"

"No," Djahnet said slowly. "Just a letter." She snorted. "The nobles don't write or read, most of the time. They employ scribes to create tablets of stone or metal to hold curses or warning signs. Whales and other long-lived creatures remember things for the government. Ina was so excited to get a letter with a royal seal, then you should have heard her wail when she read it." She shook her head. "King Yndertoh needs to be taken down a couple dozen fathoms, if you know what I mean."

"Indeed I do," Zared said. "It's definitely political games and maneuvering. Ever since our daughter survived her tricky seventeenth birthday, marriage proposals from all over the world have tripled in frequency. And arrogance. And bribes. Our treasure storerooms are so jammed with gaudy, ostentatious presents, the castle has had to grow two new vaults."

"Really?" Ambrose whispered.

'Na's face heated and she nodded, unable to meet his gaze. She couldn't decide if she was entirely embarrassed, or infuriated. Just who did those idiots think they were, trying to buy her as a bride for a prince she had never even heard of half the time, much less met? Such marriage proposals, or demands in the case of several overbearing, egotistical kingdoms, were just transparent attempts to control the enchanted castle and all the magic stored in it, as well as the enchanted forest. Starting with the right to control who passed through the portals, and collect tolls for passage through and using the forest as a shortcut to get from one side of the world to the other.

The searchers decided to split up. Ashlyn knew the way to the portal to Daswan and Gertie's desert stronghold, so she and Zared went after Karechina. 'Na and Ambrose had the task of finding Kreecher. Djahnet offered to loan them enchanted clothes that would help them breathe underwater and temporarily web their fingers, to make swimming easier. She believed her husband would still be busy checking all the grottos and underwater hiding places where their daughter usually went when she wanted to be alone. She teamed up with Melvin to set some wards on either side of the portal, to alert them when father or daughter tried to cross over.

'Na was happy to stay on the enchanted forest side of the portal. The last marriage proposal from King Yndertoh's envoys was so arrogantly phrased, she vowed to avoid the underwater kingdom entirely. Eyesallova and the old spirit ring, Mobius, warned that the wording could be interpreted as a legal agreement that the moment she went through the portal to Drypmoria, she was betrothed to marry Serge.

The prospect of being able to breathe underwater intrigued her, until she saw the clothes Djahnet provided her and Ambrose. The skimpiness wouldn't feel so close to indecent if she had a chance to disappear in the depths of the water. But no, white sleeveless shirt and trousers cut short enough to be undergarments, as pale as her ordinary skin tones, would likely make her glow like the moon underwater. This was one of those times she wished she had inherited her father's blue-black skin tones, instead of being as pale as her mother.

Ambrose's discomfort with his skimpy-cut swimming outfit was amusing enough to help tone down her own. Especially when she caught him stealing glances at her, and blushing hard until he looked away again. 'Na decided to feel flattered that he couldn't take his gaze off her, and really, Ambrose had nothing to be embarrassed about. He was nicely muscled. No silly paunch that so many of King Ruprick's officials had, from too many hours of dealing with paperwork and stress eating. All those errands Ambrose ran for the king kept him fit and trim.

And if they didn't get into the water and focus on searching for Kreecher, she was going to be paralyzed for the rest of the day, trying not to ogle Ambrose. And trying not to feel ridiculously exposed. And wondering what he thought of her. And all the while congratulating herself on finding a rather nicely made example of Atheosius's handiwork who actually liked her for her, and not because she was daughter of the lord and lady of the enchanted castle.

Yes, definitely, they needed to get in the water and get to work.

They thanked Djahnet and hurried to the channel that would lead them from the lagoon to the Snarl River. 'Na tried not to think about the proximity of the rapids and whirlpools as she slid under the water's surface. Then again, maybe she should think about that, to distract herself as she took her first tentative breath of water.

For a few panicky seconds, she was sure the enchantment had worn off the swimming clothes as her lungs filled and stiffened. Then an excruciating pain raced down both sides of her neck, like a giant fork had dug in and scraped furrows down to the bone. Beside her, Ambrose thrashed. She reached for him and the webbing between her thumb and forefinger got in the way.

Webbing?

That discovery, and the sudden change from underwater dimness to clear sight distracted her long enough to expel the water from her lungs and start breathing through the new gills in her neck. 'Na reached again for Ambrose, who had gone frighteningly still. He caught hold of her elbows, turned her to face him, and grinned at her. His eyes were twice their normal size, and the new gills on his neck pulsed, erupting in bubbles as his laughter shot through the water.

Ready? His voice hit her ears, which had vanished under the gills, and reached inside her mind at the same time.

She nodded, and they held hands the best they could. That webbing between their fingers could prove to be inconvenient. Still, she thought about the moat monsters back at the enchanted castle, and how much more fun she could have with them if she could access this particular spell again, when they invited her to come swimming. She trusted them, but they were rather scatter-brained, and sometimes forgot she couldn't breathe water, so they stayed underwater a little too long when she was riding them.

Ambrose led the way, his body undulating like an eel's. 'Na had trouble mimicking him, until she focused on something else and let the enchantment of the swimming clothes take over. Lesson learned: stop thinking so hard and just do what came naturally.

They skirted the whirlpool and headed up the Snarl River to the first spot Djahnet had described to them. Karechina's first hiding spot proved to be empty, though 'Na had the feeling someone was watching them. Where the watcher was, she couldn't determine. She and Ambrose called out to the girl several times, in case she was the watcher and hiding somewhere nearby.

They went back the other way, past the whirlpool and rapids. The enchantment of the swimming clothes guided them through the rapids, which weren't quite so bad underwater as they were on the surface, with all that water spraying everywhere and rocks looming out of the spray at the worst possible moment. 'Na found some thrills in how her body curved naturally, letting the water guide her away, instead of dashing her against the rocks. The second hiding or thinking place for Karechina lay midpoint of the rapids, cutting deep under the riverbank, into a spot that would have been impossibly dark, if not for their changed eyes. Everything under the water had a pale, bluish glow. Someone had taken time to shape the rock formations into chairs, and shelves, and intriguing rock shapes decorated some of those shelves. Karechina's work? Or maybe Prince Serge had done this? After all, the two had grown up together, and he had spent every summer here, according to Djahnet. How sad that politics and all sorts of ridiculous ranking considerations had to come between two friends who had grown up together.

She wondered what her life would have been like if she had grown up with Ambrose as her friend. 'Na pushed that thought aside, the moment common sense told her Prince Ruprick would have been a constant childhood visitor, not Ambrose, if relations with King Ruprick had been more friendly. There were far too many reasons why her parents had never responded to the king's overtures of friendship and his offers of forgiveness, starting with Ashlyn's multiple refusals to marry him.

"Are you all right?" Ambrose asked, once they had climbed out on the riverbank. The next hiding and thinking place to check was straight up the riverbank, following the trail of a spring that spilled down the steep, rocky side.

"Thinking too much." She flexed her webbed hands and considered how much it was going to hurt to grab the protrusions in the rock and climb up to that hole. She imagined Karechina had chosen that dark slash in the rock face just because it would be so hard for her parents, or maybe even Prince Serge, to follow her. Sometimes a girl needed her privacy, as 'Na knew very well.

Ambrose cursed. He tackled her down to the rock ledge beside him. Something hit the rock face just above where their heads had been, with a *clang-thud* of metal and wood on stone. She raised her hands instinctively, as several long sticks fell down on her. When the short-lived attack ended, arrows littered the narrow stone ledge. Ambrose struggled with two spears.

"Now they're attacking us?" She flinched when her voice echoed off the sheer rock face behind them.

"No. I tried using a friendship charm on them, to make them more obedient." Ambrose sighed. "I think they followed me like ... like a hunting dog."

She opened her mouth to say that might be helpful but caught herself in time. Kreecher had a bad history with spears and arrows, thanks to the scholars who had tried to come between him and Djahnet, back in the days of their courtship. Depending on what her parents had told her, Karechina could react badly to the sight of spears and arrows in the hands of strangers. Or worse, hovering in the air and aiming at her.

Ambrose struggled to get the spears to lie down. The arrows jumping up every once in a while, to hover in the air and spin around as if seeking a target, made 'Na dizzy. Could arrows get dizzy? Did arrows and spears have brains? If they were constantly thwacking into targets and other, harder things, like armor and flesh, how could they have any brains left?

'Na knew she was following those silly trails to avoid the task ahead of her. Or more accurately, above her.

"You get them under control, try to get them to go back to the castle. I'll climb up and see if she's there," she said.

Ambrose muttered agreement and continued struggling with the spears. She took a few deep breaths, then stood up and stretched high, reaching for the largest handhold, and raised her foot for the first gouge in the rock face. Then she really looked at the protrusions and holes, to plan her path. It wouldn't do her any good to get halfway up to that dark slot in the rock and run out of places to put her hands and feet. She didn't even want to think of how hard it was going to be to climb back down. In her bare feet. With webbed hands.

What were the odds her parents had gotten to Gertie's and found Karechina and were on their way back already? What were the odds they would arrive before she climbed too high, so she could slide back down and dry off and get back into her own clothes?

Considering that question delayed her another twenty or thirty seconds and did no good. She sighed and reached for the next handhold, then raised her other foot. She climbed slowly, listening for the sounds of hoofbeats approaching or voices calling out to her that Kreecher or Karechina had been found. She tried to ignore Ambrose's curses and growls as he fought to control those spears and arrows.

She should have paid better attention to what she grabbed onto or put her feet on. 'Na wrapped her fingers around a protrusion of rock. When she reached with her other hand, the rock crumbled into sand in her grip. She scrabbled at the rock face.

Ambrose shouted her name as she slid down. 'Na tried to grab at something, anything. The effort pushed her out, into the air. She tilted, going headfirst. White foam of water shattering against a rock filled her vision. She barely had time to get her arms up to block the blow and take a deep breath, then she hit.

Her first thought was to wonder why she hadn't drowned. She couldn't be in Atheosius's Rest because her head wouldn't throb like this and she wouldn't be soaking wet and achy in a dozen spots.

And carried, cradled against something wet and scaly and moving with a rather bumpy, limping sort of stride.

She moaned. Something growled, a wet, rattling sort of sound, coming from that scaley wet, hard surface pressed against her. She tried to sit up, and those scaley arms that felt like ancient tree trunks tightened around her legs and her back. 'Na moaned again when the slight movement made the throbbing in her head turn to banging, with a nail-studded stick on the inside. As the pounding in her ears subsided, she heard the dull roaring of the rapids.

Oh. That was right. She had fallen into the water. She hadn't drifted very far, had she?

"'Na? Are you all right?" Ambrose called. "Is she—Look out! Down!"

A whistling sound pierced the air, at just the right pitch to trigger that awful feeling that her brain was too big for her skull. 'Na inhaled, ready to shriek. A sick *squelch-thud* cut off the whistle, and suddenly the scaley, wet logs tossed her into the air and that growling sound turned to a bellow that had her curling up, pressing her hands to her ears.

Oh, that was right — she didn't have ears, she had gills.

Then 'Na was in the water. She still tried to breathe with her lungs for an excruciating moment, just before the raging current of the rapids picked her up and tossed her in the air. She flopped, feeling just like a frantic fish looked when it had been yanked out of the water on the end of a spear.

The self-controlled spears! That was the source of that whistling sound.

Then 'Na was fighting the current and fending off rocks. The enchanted swimming clothes certainly weren't doing their job to protect her like last time. At least, for a few terrifying heartbeats.

Until she twisted out of the current and slid into a quiet pool under the edge of the riverbank, shielded by slabs of rock. She clung to a thick clump of waterweeds, eyes closed, waiting for her heart to slow to a normal pace, and didn't care that panting underwater with gills was much harder than panting with lungs.

She tasted and smelled blood in the water. Her own blood. That was disturbing enough to knock her out of the need to just curl up and tell the world to leave her alone for a few days. 'Na opened her eyes and found daylight slipping over the rocks. She maneuvered her way out of the sheltered spot, bracing to fight the current. She wanted more than anything to get out of the water and stay out.

"Up we go," a bubbling, gurgling kind of growling voice said. An elongated, green, scaley, clawed, webbed hand thrust down in front of her face. 'Na fought the urge to bite it and then dive down as far and as deep as she could go. That wouldn't get her out of the water any time soon, would it?

"It's all right," Ambrose called, from somewhere out there in the light and dry air. "We found Kreecher. Or rather, he found us."

'Na stared at the enormous, scaley hand a few seconds longer, then she caught hold of it with both hands. Kreecher yanked her up out of the water and the sheltered little spot. Her eyes ached with the sudden burst of full daylight. She went to her knees on the riverbank. They were further down the Snarl than before. She knelt on dirt and moss instead of water-scoured stone, and as she blinked water out of her eyes, she saw trees.

Then she saw Kreecher, and vowed she would never call anyone fish-faced ever again. He was dark green, scaley, with crests on his head and down his back and down the backs of his legs, most likely to help him in swimming. He was also twisted sideways and somewhat backward, pulling a spear out of his buttock.

"Sorry! Sorry! I don't have any control over the wretched things," Ambrose called as he skidded and slid down the last of the rocky, thin strip of riverbank to join them.

'Na explained who they were and what they were doing, while Ambrose eased the spearhead out of Kreecher and tended his wound. Fortunately, he had a very useful and convenient side hobby of studying all sorts of healing charms, potions and powders. Ashlyn had gifted him with a healer's bag that refilled itself, just that morning. It only made sense, if he and 'Na were going to be working with self-willed, uncontrollable artillery, that they have the means to heal themselves right at hand.

Kreecher didn't show any resentment over the whole incident. 'Na was grateful. After all the stories she had heard about the guardian of the portal to Drypmoria, and all the idiots who acted more like monsters than he did, and all the bad experiences he had with spears, she wouldn't have blamed him for being exceedingly cranky. He actually laughed and slapped his high, ridged forehead, when Ambrose got to the part where Zared suggested Karechina had gone to Gertie for help.

They took a path through the rock ridge, rather than swimming back to the portal's lagoon. The healing paste on Kreecher's wound needed to stay dry and in place for a few hours, at the very least. Their clothes were waiting where Djahnet had left them, and 'Na was glad to get back into her own clothes. At least, until the webbing started to retreat back into her fingers, and the gills melted back into her neck and her ears emerged again. That itched abominably. She had a few moments where her gills were too dry to work properly and her lungs didn't want to start drawing air again. Probably because they feared being filled with water. If her lungs could think. 'Na hoped not. It was bad enough dealing with spears and arrows that could think for themselves, even if in a limited fashion.

Djahnet and Melvin returned to the portal, and 'Na and Ambrose stepped out of the cave to let husband and wife have some privacy. Ambrose had to step back in and yank Melvin out. He was staring a little too much, fascinated and slightly repulsed by the growling and cooing and kissing between the two visibly mismatched spouses.

~~~~~

Kreecher and Ambrose finally got the spears tamed. They had to resort to a white powder that Djahnet's erstwhile scholar suitors had used to try to sedate Kreecher, at the start of their somewhat awkward courtship. They spilled the white powder into a shallow pool, then tossed the spears and arrows in, points first, and held them in the water until they stopped struggling.

Zared, Ashlyn, and Karechina returned while Ambrose and Kreecher were tying up the spears and arrows into a neat bundle for ease of carrying. The girl looked like both her parents, her skin pebbly instead of scaley, and pale instead of variegated shades of green. Her head crest was a little higher than her mother's, and her hair displayed several shades of green and gold and hung down to her waist in thick, generous curls. She had eyelids, but her mouth definitely had a fishy stiffness. Her eyes widened and her mouth dropped open when she got a good look at Ambrose, and 'Na thought the other maiden might start drooling in a moment.

In that instant, all her sympathy for Karechina died by half. The only word that filled her head was "Fickle." Her love for Prince Serge certainly wasn't strong enough for her to have faith in him and give him the benefit of the doubt that his father's decisions came between them, and it wasn't his choice at all.

Kreecher, his wife and daughter excused themselves and dove into the shadows of the lagoon. 'Na wasn't sure she could accurately read the expressions on that fishy face, but she was willing to wager that Karechina was going to get a lecture that would change her life. For good or for ill would depend on her reaction.

"Thank you," Zared said, coming up behind 'Na and resting his hands on her shoulders.

"For what?" She laughed as he turned her around and pulled her into a tight embrace.

"For never putting us through anything like that," Ashlyn said, and joined them. "You've had more than your share of disappointments, and I defy anyone to say the enchanted castle is a reasonable, sane place to raise a child, but you've turned out so well ..." She sighed, ending on a chuckle, and tugged 'Na out of her father's arms to hug her in turn.

"We're terrified of what the next generation will be like," Zared added. "There's a price to be paid for all the happiness and satisfaction we enjoy."

'Na nearly choked, holding back the squeak of "Next generation?" that wanted to leap out of her throat. She chanced a sideways glance at Ambrose, but he and Melvin were busy strapping the recalcitrant spears and arrows to one of the horses. They were tightly bound in waterproof cloth Djahnet had provided, to make sure the wood stayed wet, soaked with the sleeping powder-laden water, until they were safely back at the enchanted castle.

"Pessimist," Ashlyn growled, laughter making her eyes bright. The amusement faded quickly as she turned and looked at the opening into the lagoon. "That girl ... I'm worried she's got something else up her sleeve."

"She doesn't have sleeves." Zared twisted sideways to avoid his wife's elbow in his ribs.

"You know what I mean."

"Yes, I do. That mess she made of Gertie's place wasn't an accident. The question is what she stole and when she'll use it."

"What happened?" 'Na asked.

"That girl is hurting, but that's no excuse for demanding that a wise woman and herb witch of Gertie's standing change her magic patterns. Strange things happen when you reverse course," Ashlyn said. "The magic currents don't like changes. The very air of Gertie's fortress is permeated with years of spells that guide the potions she makes. Very few of her spells are created to be permanent change. Those meant for permanence have a time limit on them, conditions that must be met within a certain amount of time, or the spell doesn't 'take.' Well, Kerechina has the sensitivity to know the difference in the resonances and the tones of magic, and she got into the chest where Gertie keeps the permanent powders and potions."

"But she was looking for something to help her find her own prince charming," 'Na said. Her stomach knotted with the certainty this little detail was going to cause trouble for them all, very soon. "It's not fair to change someone's mind for them and make it permanent. It's not really fair if that change is temporary, but some people have to be forced to take a look at the possibilities before they wake up and realize what they're missing … " That knot got bigger and sent a queasy feeling through her. "It won't do her any good to use it on Prince Serge, will it?"

"Hopefully she didn't get those potions or powders. Gertie isn't organized at the best of times, and with the mess that girl made, it's going to take her months to figure out what was taken, what was destroyed, and what potions and powders mixed together to create entirely new magic, and deal with it." Ashlyn shuddered. "We were only too glad to get out of there before anything rose from that bubbling mess—"

"But we could be getting a call for help any time now," Zared finished for her.

A loud, bubbling sort of gong sound emerged from the cave protecting the lagoon, followed by ripples of green and silver light. Karechina darted out, whimpering. She raced past them and dove into the rapids. Djahnet emerged next and hurried to Ashlyn and Zared. She whispered to them, looking even more pale than before.

Instead of Kreecher, ten green-skinned, fish-faced men wearing armor that looked like enormous clamshells, stepped out of the cave. They escorted a young man who looked somewhat more human than them, meaning his face wasn't quite as fishy, he had eyelids, and his hair had reddish streaks among the silver and green. His clothes were made from some shiny material that glistened as if it had gold twined into thread. He looked around the clearing outside the lagoon cave several times, his expression watchful. Then he smiled. 'Na didn't know why she didn't like his smile. Maybe because she was fairly certain this was Prince Serge, and if he was smiling because he didn't see Kerechina anywhere, then he was a heartless boor. She deserved better, even if she was fickle. Come to think of it, 'Na guessed the other girl had fled into the river *because* Serge was here.

"Lord Zared and Lady Ashlyn of the enchanted castle?" Serge bowed deeply. "I came as quickly as I could, once I learned you were on the borders of our kingdom."

'Na bristled at that. Standing outside the portal that Kreecher guarded was a far cry from being "on the borders." Especially since the Snarl River was in the heart of the enchanted forest. Her parents' kingdom.

As well as being heartless, he was a pompous boor.

"What does the kingdom of Drypmoria wish of us?" Zared asked.

"Alliance." Serge's gaze slid over to 'Na. "Yes, Lady Belladonna, you are even more lovely than was described to me."

"Excuse me, but let me save you some time. The answer is no." 'Na spoke mostly to keep from laughing out loud. She had bruises on her face, she was tired and rumpled and dirty. She wanted to take a swim, but getting into the water within a mile of the portal to Drypmoria and whatever magic Karechina might have stolen, was a fool's move.

Serge blinked twice. "But you don't know what I offer."

"The answer is no," Ashlyn said, moving over to wrap her arm around 'Na's shoulders. "Just like the last five times your father tried to trick us into agreeing to a marriage alliance."

"Oh, but we were both just children back then. It would have been foolish. Now, though, we are both grown, and the time has come." His smile widened, making him look more fishy, instead of less.

"The answer is still no," Zared said.

"Ah, I see. I understand. This is not the place or the time for such serious matters. And in my haste, I left behind the proper courting gifts. You will excuse me, while I return home and make the proper arrangements." He bowed, backing toward the opening into the cave and lagoon, and bowed again before he stepped out of sight.

"There's no excuse for the likes of him," Ambrose said as he and Melvin joined the three. "Did I hear right? He thinks he can throw some gold at you and you'll give in?"

"He may think that, but I'm more likely to throw it back hard enough to knock some sense into that hard head of his." Zared shook his head. "We need to leave this place. If we're still here when he comes back, Yndertoh will insist it means we're agreeing to the marriage."

"We need to be on our home territory to stand up to the next awful onslaught." Ashlyn wrapped an arm around 'Na's shoulders. "I truly am angry with you now."

"What did I do?" 'Na's voice cracked.

"You grew up. Why couldn't you have stayed a child for the next forty or fifty years?"

"I'm sorry, my friends," Djahnet said. "You've helped us so much today, please, let us at least give you a good dinner before you go."

They moved down the river, away from the rapids and whirlpool, infringing on kispies territory. Kreecher and Djahnet both laughed when Zared and Ashlyn told the story of how they had helped the temperamental tiny creatures and earned their friendship. Kreecher stepped into the forest and returned with a ten-point buck before Ambrose and Melvin had finished building up the fire. 'Na had assumed their dinner would be fish or maybe eels, and river weeds.

Karechina stayed by her mother during the task of preparing their dinner. She seemed relieved to be sent on errands, running back to their home in the lagoon to fetch dishes and utensils and spices for cooking, then later for a large copper cauldron to heat water and steep a sweet-smelling herbal mixture to drink with their dinner. 'Na had the task of tending long skewers of vegetables roasting over a second fire, while Kreecher and Zared roasted huge venison steaks on the main fire. She tried not to be caught watching the other girl, but something about Karechina niggled at her, and she didn't like feeling as if an ambush was about to burst upon them. 'Na wondered if she would finally get some answers when Karechina sidled up beside her at the fire, while she was testing the slices of potatoes she had been browning over the flames.

"Why did you say no?"

'Na shook her head, unsure what Karechina was referring to.

"When Serge asked ..." She sighed. "When he started to ask you to marry him. He didn't really finish saying it, did he?"

"I said no because we've been saying no every time his father sends one of his nobles to start the whole messy process."

"Don't you want to be a princess?"

'Na laughed. There were so many answers to that question. Mostly because she knew she couldn't simply say "no" and leave it at that. Everyone, especially self-important princes with greedy fathers who wanted more territory and authority than they could reasonably handle, seemed to think that every girl wanted to be a princess. Lady Ashlyn had fought hard with the enchanted castle when she was younger than 'Na, to ensure she never became a princess. The enchanted castle tried for months to make her into a glittery, giggling, bejeweled puff of fluff from popular stories, and not the kind of princess it actually needed. Ashlyn had had to use all the force of her will and sense of self to bully the castle into a compromise they could both live with. That was easier than trying to explain to the enormous churning knot of magic at the heart of the castle why its version of a proper princess was a mistake. The castle was aware in many ways, but far too often, the traditions of magic and old fables guided its actions and reactions, rather than common sense. Granted, part of the problem came from several layers of wonky magic enfolding the castle, thanks to misguided and generally selfish attempts to enslave it by various would-be despots. Still, that was no excuse, and would have led to disaster if the castle had triumphed in that initial struggle.

If Ashlyn let herself be a princess out of the oldest fables, she would attract enemies faster than abandoned gold and jewels attracted dragons. The castle needed someone to take care of it, not someone who needed a dozen servants to help her get through her day. It needed a lady who could fight and who wore the beast masks and rode out through the portals to rescue abandoned books and misused magical items. It didn't need someone who spent most of each day fussing over jewels and makeup and her hair.

Princesses attracted trouble of one kind or another. Princesses needed princes to rescue them. They were the victims of kidnappings and the innocent victims of curses more than anyone else in the ancient fables, except perhaps disinherited, lost princes or the poor-but-noble youth. Anyone who wanted to be a princess and didn't think about the responsibility and problems that went with the title deserved all the suffering that went with it, in Ashlyn's opinion. 'Na agreed with her mother.

"My parents said no for me when I was too young to know what was being asked. When I got old enough to understand, I agreed with them. Marriage should be between people who are good friends. Why would I want to tie my life to a total stranger? I want the kind of marriage my parents have. My father broke the curse on my mother, and she broke the curses put on him, and they were good friends long before they fell in love. You should marry your friend, not a title."

"Yes, but what if they won't let you?" Kerachina mumbled. She wasn't looking at 'Na but at the activity on the other side of the clearing. "Is that all it takes? A curse?"

"That depends on who's doing the cursing. What some people consider a curse, others consider a challenge."

"I don't understand."

"Well ..." 'Na searched for the right words, to help her explain. "It's like when my mother first came to the enchanted forest."

She kept tending the vegetables, sprinkling herbs over them as they burst with juices, and started telling the story of how Ashlyn tamed the enchanted castle. When she reached the point where Ashlyn met Eyesallova the magic mirror, 'Na paused and glanced over at Kerachina. The other girl was gone. When had she left? A chill slithered down her back as she listened to instinct and turned to look where Kerachina had been staring.

Ambrose sat on a folded blanket, his journal open on his lap, a quill sitting in a pot of ink next to his knee, listening to Melvin telling one of his outrageous stories. The funny thing about Melvin was that most of his stories from his monster-hunting days were true. The old monster hunter paced back and forth in front of the fire. On either side, Zared and Kreecher were tending the venison steaks. Several steps away, just outside of the ring of firelight, Ashlyn and Djahnet sat together on a log, laughing at Melvin's words. Where was Kerachina?

There she was, coming over to the fire with wooden cups on a tray. She held it out to her father, who took one cup and bent to brush a kiss across the top of her head. Zared thanked her with a nodding bow. She stepped in a wide arch around Melvin with his wildly gesturing arms and approached Ambrose. She held out a cup to him, rather than offering the tray, for him to pick which cup he wanted. Why did that seem odd?

Ambrose thanked her and took the cup. Kerachina walked away to stand behind him, watching him, unblinking.

Something was wrong. 'Na didn't know yet what that was, but that chill had crept up her back again and wrapped a knot around her throat. She slid the skewers of vegetables off the stakes that supported them, set them in the massive leather bowl Djahnet had given her to hold them, and started around the fire.

Just as Ambrose put down the cup. And coughed.

And clutched at his throat. First the front, then wincing in pain, he pressed his hands against the sides of his neck.

"What's wrong, lad?" Melvin said, pausing in a wide gesture with both arms. "You look a little green."

Ambrose was very green. He staggered to his feet, tossing his journal one direction, the cup in another. Wheezing like he couldn't breathe he stumbled toward the river. He clawed at his jacket, peeling it away, then his shirt. A ridge had emerged down his back, and with every step he took, it grew into a crest, going up over the top of his head, pushing aside his thick mop of blue-black curls.

Everyone stopped. Even the fire seemed to freeze, the crackling muted and the flames' dance stilled. Ambrose turned to look at them. His mouth had flattened. Gills rippled down the sides of his neck. He wailed something as he tumbled headfirst into the river.

"That's not good," Melvin said.

"What did you do?" Zared demanded, turning to Karechina. "What did you take from Gertie?"

Kreecher launched into a gargling, growling, gurgling interrogation. 'Na knew what he was demanding of his daughter, even though she didn't understand the language. Every child knew that lecture, even if, like 'Na, her parents had never needed that interrogation lecture.

'Na dropped the bowl and darted to the water's edge. Ambrose struggled under the water, as his feet extended and his toes spread, growing webbing between them, and more guiding fins erupted from the backs of his arms and legs.

"But he's my prince!" Karechina wailed. "All I have to do is kiss him before midnight and he's mine!" She raced toward the riverbank, eagerness and delight making her odd face beautiful.

"*My* prince," 'Na growled, and clotheslined the other girl hard enough to send her tumbling head over heels backward, right into her father's arms. Then 'Na dove into the river.

She hit Ambrose square in the middle of his torso, and by purest luck hit his chest instead of his back. He buckled, stopped thrashing, and they went down hard, nearly to the bottom of the river. 'Na clawed her way up him, so by the time they popped back up to the surface, she had her arms around his neck. The gills rippled against her arms as she dove in for that kiss. True love's kiss. The cure-all for all curses and spells.

Her first impression was that she should pity and admire those princesses who came through the forest a few years ago, madly kissing every frog they could find in a search for enchanted princes. The feel of Ambrose's transformed lips was utterly disgusting. Rubbery and cold and twitchy. Then the taste flooded her mouth and she nearly gagged on a fishy, burned, sour, and rotten taste that filled her mouth. She had a mental image of an enormous frog tongue following that taste and fought not to vomit right there.

Ambrose clutched at her, kissing desperately, his claws digging through her clothes into her flesh. They went under the surface again, blocking the sound of Karechina's sobbing wails. His heart thundered against her chest. 'Na nearly inhaled water when she felt two hearts, pounding out of rhythm against hers.

What had that selfish little flitterhead done to Ambrose?

They popped back up to the surface and his mouth slid off hers. Ripples of nausea radiated from her mouth through her body. 'Na gagged and fought not to spit. She wiped water out of her eyes and blinked, focusing on Ambrose, waiting for him to transform back. His hair was gone, either having fallen out or absorbed into his scaley skin. His gills worked like bellows and he stared at her. Even his eyes were changed.

His eyes widened in horror, just as pain shot through her neck. 'Na's skin rippled down her back and arched up over her head.

"That's now how it's supposed to work!" Karechina sobbed.

"You silly child." Djahnet stepped up to the riverbank with Ashlyn and Zared. "You stole the royal transformation potion."

"What does that do?" Zared asked, while Ashlyn got down on her knees and held out her arms to 'Na.

"I'm sorry, dearest," Ashlyn said. "We'll figure out something." A choked little chuckle escaped her, as dismay twisted her features. "We have an entire castle full of wonky magic, surely there's something to fix this."

'Na barely heard her, as her body twisted inside and out and her skin turned thick and scaly and webbing grew between her fingers again. Ambrose held her up as she thrashed through the transformation.

As she learned later, the royal family of Drypmoria had a tradition of taking human brides. For the new queen to live underwater comfortably, and to ensure the heir to the throne didn't have so many human features that the citizens of Drypmoria didn't trust him, the bride needed to be magically transformed.

When Karechina made the mess at Gertie's stronghold, to cover up her theft of the potion, she had accidentally added several powders to the royal potion, changing the composition. That, combined with 'Na and Ambrose having been given temporary amphibian qualities less than ten hours earlier, complicated the spell.

Neither of them should have changed so quickly, so drastically, and so outwardly. The kings of Drypmoria took great pride in having beautiful, entirely human brides at the start of their marriage. The process was supposed to take several years before the queen was outwardly a water-dweller. When consulted later, Eyesallova, Zellah the castle's librarian, and the spirit ring all agreed that analyzing what had gone wrong with the spell could take years.

"I'm sorry," Ambrose said, when the transformation completed and he and 'Na clung to each other in the water, submerged up to their eyes. Their gills rippled and sucked in water as hard as if they had just run a two-mile race at top speed.

"We'll find answers," Zared promised. "Melvin, you're coming with me to see Gertie. She made the wretched potion, she ought to know how to reverse it."

"You can't reverse it." Karechina had given up struggling and hung limply at her father's side, his arm tight around her waist. "It's supposed to be forever." Another sob escaped her. "You're supposed to be my prince."

"I belong to 'Na," Ambrose said. Most of his words came out in gargles and growls and squeals, but 'Na understood him with no problem. Fortunately, her parents had had so many translation spells woven around them over the years, they didn't need to call up any magic to understand. Zared had to translate for Melvin, who looked rather disturbed, maybe a little repulsed, by the sounds. "I'm sorry you got trapped with me."

"You took that risk for me," 'Na reminded him. "My crazy, tricky seventeenth birthday."

"True love's kiss," Ashlyn said, slowly shaking her head. "It should fix most curses. I don't understand why it didn't work."

"Because the potion isn't considered a curse," Djahnet said.

"Technicalities," Zared said, his disgust twisting the word so it sounded like an oath.

"Can we get out of the water soon?" 'Na said. "I'm really, really hungry now."

Ambrose laughed and hugged her hard. They submerged for a few seconds and he stole another kiss. The awful taste of the transformation potion had entirely vanished now.

Dinner took much longer to eat than it should have. Every time 'Na and Ambrose's new gills started to dry out, they had to jump back into the water. Djahnet assured them it wouldn't take long, a few days at the most, until their bodies adjusted to allow them to spend time out in the air, their gills going into resting mode while they used their human lungs again. 'Na ate all the venison steak, even after it got cold. She didn't want to get hungry any time soon and give in to the growing craving for raw fish.

The sooner they returned to the enchanted castle and got to work unraveling the spell, the better.

Absolutely. Maybe we should take the risk of traveling at night.

She opened her mouth to respond, then realized she had heard Ambrose's voice in her head, not with her transformed ears.

Are we talking mind-to-mind?

His wide-eyed look wasn't as funny as it could have been, because he didn't have normal eyelids now, just a clear coating over his transformed, three-times-larger eyes.

This might be fun, he thought back to her after a few moments, during which she caught fragments of his racing thoughts.

You need to keep your volume down, children, Kreecher thought to them.

'Na wondered if her face got a darker shade of green when she blushed. Despite the colder temperature of her blood, her face certainly felt hot.

Karechina had stopped whimpering by the time dinner ended and full dark had fallen. Zared and Melvin were discussing whether to head out now to ride to the portal that would take them to Gertie's desert stronghold or wait until morning. That particular portal shifted between three different locations, so they would have to wait until noon anyway before they could go to Daswan. Djahnet and Kreecher were drawing a map of the waterways through the enchanted forest, to help 'Na and Ambrose plot the shortest, wettest route back to the enchanted castle. It was either that or camp in the lagoon, and risk Prince Serge returning and insisting 'Na's transformation meant she accepted his marriage proposal.

'Na preferred to go home, and Ambrose agreed with her. She had a few ideas for playing some tricks on the moat monsters at the castle, which would make however long they were stuck in their amphibian shape a little more bearable.

Ashlyn dug out a small traveling mirror from her saddlebags to consult with Eyesallova. She had a few responses to report from the first call for help with 'Na and Ambrose's dilemma, sent through the magic mirror web.

Eyesallova also had bad news. The two mirrors that served the nobility of Drypmoria had stopped talking. Either they had been silenced, to keep them from reporting on what King Yndertoh had planned, or they were siding with the newest twisted legalistic plan to put one over on the dry land dwellers.

"That's a warning if I ever heard one," Zared said. "Forget about going to Gertie. We need to get 'Na away from the river, to make it harder for that soggy arrogant twit of a prince to find her. Ambrose, do you think you can ride?"

"Take her to the castle, or through another portal?" Ambrose hauled himself up on the riverbank. He knelt and reached down to offer 'Na a hand.

"Take her to Filby, in Willemsport," Ashlyn said. "She can hide her from the strongest seeking spells."

"Ah, there you are," Prince Serge called, his words bubbling up through the river. "Why didn't you wait for me at the portal?"

The river water surged all around 'Na. She leaped out of the water, into Ambrose's arms. Just a heartbeat later, the water churned and Serge bobbed up to the surface, accompanied by a dozen soldiers and ten servants carrying chests. He hopped out onto the riverbank and gestured grandly, grinning proudly, as the servants put the chests down on the ground in a semi-circle by the fire, with splashing thuds. Each servant flipped up the lid of a chest, displaying pearls and gold and gemstones, in a sequential move that looked rehearsed.

"There? Do you see how I value your lovely daughter? This is only a fraction of the wealth my father and I wish to bestow upon her, and upon you, in exchange for her hand in marriage."

This hand belongs to me, no matter how it looks. Ambrose intertwined their elongated, clawed fingers. Rather hard to do, thanks to the webbing, but he managed. 'Na wanted to kiss him. In front of everyone.

"Huh? Who said that? How rude!" Serge sputtered. He turned and looked around at the people clustered around the fire. His gaze slid over Karechina like he didn't even recognize her.

'Na revised her estimate of just who was fickle in that childhood friend relationship.

His lip curled when his gaze caught for maybe two seconds on 'Na and Ambrose. Then he looked over their group a second time. And a third.

"Where is my lovely Lady Belladonna?"

"First of all," Zared said, moving over to stand between Serge and his wife and daughter, "my daughter is not your lady anything."

"Just a matter of formalities." Serge waved his webbed hand as if shooing away pesky insects.

"And second, she's right there." He pointed at 'Na.

Serge's eyes, which were unusually small for a water-dweller, bulged in dismay. 'Na wouldn't have been surprised if they popped out of his fishy skull.

"What sort of foul joke is this?" he sputtered.

"It's not a joke," Ashlyn said. "My daughter and her betrothed are victims of a spell, and we're in the process of trying to figure out how to undo it."

"Someone slipped them the transformation potion your family uses for their human brides," Melvin offered. "Actually, if you think about it, this is good timing. You get a good look at your future after ten, fifteen years of marriage."

"Melvin," Zared growled. "You're not helping!"

"No, just consider. If you can't reverse the spell, what chances does the poor girl have? All those princes, banging on the castle door every week, they're all going to run away once they get a good look at her. No offense, to you and your wife and daughter." He bowed to Kreecher. "Beauty really is in the eye of the beholder."

"Monstrous!" The prince backed away, clutching at his chest. 'Na wondered idly which of his double hearts was racing fastest. "That's — you can't expect me — I refuse! I will not spend the rest of my life looking at …" His mouth worked, giving the impression he was either going to shoot out a massive frog tongue and snap at something, or spew. "At that!"

"You insult me and my family." Zared made a show of turning to show the sword at his side as he rested his hand on the hilt.

"I don't care! The marriage is off!" Serge shrilled.

He turned to his servants, gesturing at the chests. They closed the chests of treasure in what, again, looked like a rehearsed movement. 'Na had to wonder how many marriage proposals the prince had made and been refused.

Serge turned and stomped toward the riverbank, servants and soldiers gathering around him. His gaze caught for the first time on Karechina. He went pale and made a choking sound.

"Ina! My old friend." He swallowed audibly. It was a horrible glugging sound.

Thank goodness you don't have to listen to that for the rest of your life, Ambrose offered.

'Na muffled a chuckle and leaned into him.

"My beautiful, sweet Ina," Serge continued, and approached her, holding out his shaking hands. "How I've missed you. Please, my darling, you do know that awful, rude letter was all my father's idea, don't you? He forced me into this — this — " He flicked his webbed claws at 'Na. "This ridiculous sham. You do know it's you I truly love, don't you?"

"I don't know any such thing." Karechina turned her back on him and marched to the riverbank. "Mummy, Poppy, I don't feel well. I think I'm going to go home and go to bed."

"I'll go with you," Djahnet said, giving Kreecher a significant look that meant, "This is your mess to fix. Don't come home until you do so." Then she followed Karechina into the river. Mother and daughter made barely a splash and vanished into the dark water.

"Kreecher, do have a talk with your daughter, won't you?" Serge went pale, so he seemed to take on a ghostly glow, caught between the shadows and the firelight.

"Oh, I will, Highness," Kreecher gurgled. "But I suggest you talk to your father. He's going to aim you at another human girl. Be prepared to spend a long time on the hunt."

Serge went paler. His froggy lips quivered and a few whimpers escaped him before he pulled his shoulders back and stomped to the water. 'Na thought she heard several of his soldiers snicker as they closed ranks around him and jumped into the water.

"All right," Ambrose said. "Now what do we do? How long will we be stuck like this?"

In the end, they agreed Zared and Melvin would ride out in the morning. Kreecher showed 'Na and Ambrose shallow spots in the lagoon, where they could spend the night, safely submerged, with no fear of getting pulled out into the river by the current. Ashlyn, Zared, and Melvin set up camp and settled in for the night, and 'Na tried to find something amusing in camping in water.

Amusement shattered just on the stroke of midnight. She woke sputtering and splashing and choking. Her gills had stopped working and her lungs didn't appreciate being full of water. Ambrose struggled in the pool next to hers. They crawled up onto the rock ledge of the cave and lay for several long minutes, just gasping and spitting up water and aching all over. Ambrose rasped out something that sounded like he asked if she was going to be all right. She wheezed back that she thought so. He stretched out from where he had collapsed, managing to put his hand on hers.

"'Na!" His exclamation started another round of coughing.

She understood. His hand was his again, not webbed and clawed with two extra joints in each finger. 'Na got up on her hands and knees and pounded his back until he gasped out a mouthful of water. Later, he joked that a couple small fish had been in there somewhere. Later, it was funny, even if a little disgusting if she thought about it too long.

They clung to each other, laughing and shaking and coughing a little more, until the damp and cold seeped into their bones. While 'Na wouldn't have minded sitting there in the dark, holding Ambrose and being held by him, she truly did want to be dry again.

Getting out of the lagoon cave wasn't as easy as getting in, because with the return to their own bodies, they had lost the ability to see in the dark. They laughed softly as they clung to each other and stumbled around pools and large rocks, until finally they found starlight and flickers of firelight from farther up the riverbank. Her parents were still awake, sitting huddled together in front of the fire, while Melvin snored loudly enough to scare away any kispies that might be tempted to do a strafing run in the moonlight.

They kept their celebration quiet enough that Melvin never heard over his snores, and never woke up. The bag of accommodation served them well, providing plenty of dry blankets and dry clothes. 'Na stepped behind some bushes, Ambrose chose bushes on the other side of the fire, and they reported what had happened as they changed their clothes.

"True love's kiss," Eyesallova announced, sounding supremely smug, as they gathered around the fire again. "We just had to wait for midnight, for the spell to wind down."

'Na had several thoughts about Gertie and how she organized and protected her potions, but kept them to herself. For the time being. Right now, she was just glad to be back in her own body. Next time the moat monsterd begged her to come swimming with them ... she would find a way to politely decline.

THE END

SHIPWRECKED
Angela R. Watts

Our spaceship, *Nomad*, stranded us on a foreign planet in the EX territory.

EX territory was at the edge of the explored territories — the last place any space sojourner dared to pass. And we had slipped into EX without even realizing it.

A missile to our engine room had done it. Our run-in with the Walkers, a large community of humans that had fled Earth and made their own world on a far-away planet, had gone south. They'd tried looting *Nomad*, but luckily, we'd escaped their clutches… and launched ourselves into EX, instead.

I took a few weak breaths, then unstrapped myself from the seat I'd found before the ship began its descent. The captain and first mate did the same.

Captain Enus asked over the comms, "Is everyone all right?"

"Dandy," First Mate Achilles chimed in. "We're lucky we didn't get blown into smithereens."

I crawled into the cockpit. Every fiber in my body shook. "Where are we?"

"Unknown planet." Achilles — I doubted that was his real name, but it was what he went by all the years I'd known him — tapped the screen in front of him. "No location or coordinates. We're definitely in EX territory." He tapped again for a moment, sending out an SOS. "Okay, hopefully that'll get us some help headed this way… Closest ship that can rendezvous is about a week out…"

We were just a very small team of explorers, and a rescue mission was difficult enough to pull off, but rescuing us from EX? Would anyone be willing to risk that sort of mission? Or were we waiting for nothing?

"EX territory? With the monster?" our crewmate, Jared, spoke up. "Like, *the* monster?"

"Shut up, Jared," I said. "There's no monster here. Aliens aren't real."

Captain sighed and got up. He took off his helmet, running a hand through his dark black hair. "Jared's right. Legend has it that a monster lurks in the depths here. This is a water planet — and the only people to crash here don't come back. That much is true. I don't doubt a monster *is* here." He said it all so nonchalantly, like our lives hanging in the balance was the equivalent interest level of discussion about the weather.

"Monsters aren't real," I said haughtily.

"Let's try to repair the damage as much as possible," Achilles said, "and then hope help comes on time."

"And if they don't?" I asked.

"Then we're pretty much dead." Captain shrugged. We were a four-people crew on a little ship not built for months of being shipwrecked. We didn't have that much in the way of supplies. "We'll handle that if we come to it." He didn't sound very optimistic.

"But what's the monster?" I piped up. "I've never heard of it." Then again, I'd never intended to explore EX territory — it wasn't on our lineup, and I was a new space explorer. Actually, I was just a tag-along. My job was to clean up the ship and store specimens we found. Achilles had only let me come because I was in desperate need of money. He'd had to talk Captain into it. And this was what I got?

Stranded on some planet, awaiting inevitable death?

Unfair.

"Well, his nickname is Grim," Captain said, "and he dwells in the lakes here."

I frowned at him. "He?"

"It's just a legend," Achilles said. "And legend has it that he's half man, half monster, and that he lures people that wreck here to untimely, gruesome deaths." He pointed out the cockpit window. "See all that water? He has paradise here. He just needs food. That's us."

"That makes no sense," I hissed, clambering up a ladder to grab my suit. "He'd have starved by now, waiting for space explorers to crash so few and far between. It just sounds like some old siren tale."

"Well, you asked for the story, and that's all I know." Achilles sighed and stood, too.

We all suited up quickly and began repairing the damage to the ship's little engine room. Luckily, the missile hadn't shot a hole clean through the ship, but the damage had knocked out the engine. We were stranded, for good. There was no repairing the engine. We didn't have the supplies to do so.

We did the best we could and went back to the cockpit area. Jared made coffee in the tiny kitchenette in a side room. I snuck to the cockpit window, looking out with my heart in my throat.

The planet was stunning. Stalagmites and stalactites surrounded *Nomad* on all sides but our rear, where we'd perfectly crashed into the crack in the rock formations. That had been a miracle itself: we should have hit the rocks and blown up. But we had just landed snuggly, stopping thanks to the thrusters before we hit anything.

The rocks were mostly black, dark blue, and purple, with other colored formations glistening here and there. The planet had no light source, like Earth's sun, but the rocks all seemed to glow, almost like some sort of magic. I wondered what the scientific reasoning for the glowing rocks was, but I didn't know, and I doubted any of the guys did, either. Besides, they were probably more worried about getting out of here than exploring shiny things.

"No one is allowed to leave the ship," Captain said from behind me. "Got that, Newbie?"

"Phoebe," I corrected tiredly. "And yessir."

Achilles handed me a small cup of black coffee and took his seat in the co-pilot's chair. "Sure is nice out there. A real shame we can't explore—controls say it's actually an environment we could explore comfortably. I guess the legend of Grim scared off more people than I expected. This place doesn't seem so bad besides him."

"He's just a fairy tale. Why don't we go exploring?" I suggested. "This is huge, Captain! We'd be the first to explore the planet! We could go down in history—"

"Grim might be a myth, but the missing ships that come here are factual." Captain shook his head, his curls bouncing. "We're not risking it. Everyone stays in the ship. We ration supplies and wait for help to arrive. We should be able to get out of here if someone hovers over the planet..."

I went quiet as the three guys brainstormed escape plans. When our watches beeped that it was bedtime, we dispersed — besides Captain, who was on guard at the cockpit — to our bunkrooms. Or, the guys went to their bunkroom. Achilles had given me the supplies closet to sleep in. It was just big enough for the supplies and for a cot. But still, I preferred the cramped space in the ship rather than having no privacy in the bunkroom.

I said my prayers, stripped off my suit, and crawled into the squeaky cot.

~~~~~

Drip. Drip. Drip.

I rolled over.

My body hit something wet.

What was that?

Jolting awake, I looked around, hurriedly slapping the light controls on the wall.

Water. It seeped down the metal walls. Dripped and gathered on the floor. Soaked my cot and blanket.

Water? How was that possible? The ship was waterproof — it was a spaceship, for goodness' sake.

I jumped up, yanked my suit on, and stumbled out of the room.

"Captain!"

Silence.

"Achilles! Jared?" I sloshed into the ship's main room. The cockpit up ahead was empty, too. Panic flooded me, and I rubbed my eyes, but the ship was still empty.

I scrambled into the cockpit. I checked the ship's status — everything was perfectly fine. The doors were all locked. There had been no second distress signal dispatched. If Captain had been on guard, and something happened, he would have had time to send out another SOS, right?

Then I remembered Achilles's tangent about the monster, Grim.

Was it true that no one escaped this planet because of a beast?

Shaking, I slammed the keyboard of the captain's display on the dashboard. I sent out another SOS to the ship coming our way.

It felt childish doing so. If the monster had taken the others... it would come for me next.

But then again, why had it left me?

"You're talking nonsense, Phoebe," I said to myself weakly. My boots sloshed in the water as I moved into the main room again. "There's no monster. The guys must've gone out to look for... something... Maybe they lost signal here for a bit and wanted to try to climb a rock to get a clearer pathway to the rescue ship..."

But that was a poor sounding excuse, too.

I could try to reason things out all I wanted. The fact remained that I was alone on the ship, and somehow, water was getting inside, even though there was nothing outside to drown the ship: we were only surrounded by wet rocks. It wasn't like our ship had been tossed into some sea while I'd been asleep.

What was going on?

Shaking my head, trying to push the fears aside, I grabbed my helmet from the wall compartment and yanked it on. Once I made sure my suit was ready to go, and grabbed a ray gun, I opened one of the exit doors. My suit had a built-in device that allowed me to open and close the door from inside or outside *Nomad*. I wasn't locking myself out of the ship, but dread still ate at my gut.

I looked outside cautiously. The planet was eerily silent, besides the roar of rushing water all around. I didn't hear any of the guys. I didn't hear a monster. I just heard water.

Summoning what little courage I had, I inched outside.

I had signed up to join the crew for money so I could make it on my own. I hadn't signed up to get eaten alive by Grim.

But maybe, Grim was just a myth, and I'd find the guys soon, and help would come, and we'd get home safely.

Maybe.

I walked about thirty yards from the ship. There, the surrounding walls of rock ended, and I looked out across hundreds of jagged hills and rock formations below. It was like we'd crashed into a mountainside, and the planet was nothing but rocks and water. I spotted a giant blue lake, streams, and waterfalls all around as the water fell, hit the rocks, and dashed through the rocks and holes.

It was like a giant, terrifying theme park or something. Like a piece of a nightmare, maybe, if a nightmare could be beautiful and terrifying.

I took a weak breath. To my left, there was a trail-like opening in the rocks and turned around the mountain. Maybe the guys had followed that trail?

I hesitated, wanting to yell for them, but I was afraid too much noise might start some sort of avalanche, and I definitely couldn't afford that. So I started walking the trail. It was damp, but I managed not to fall to my death.

After maybe another thirty yards, the path ended. I was met with nothing but jagged rocks and crevices that surely led to demise.

I had to turn back. And then what? There had been no other path to try. Where were the guys?

Fighting tears, I said, "All right. It's fine. They must've found another path I missed." I turned around and crept along the wet rocks.

Then, rain began to fall. I looked up past the dark rocks and into the pale gray sky: how strange, I mused, to see such a beautiful, otherworld, and for it to be under the worst of circumstances.

The rain pelted my suit. The thermometer in my suit told me the rain was freezing cold — would it form ice?

The rain grew heavier. I tried to move a bit faster. I needed to get back to *Nomad*. I needed a new plan. I needed to try to —

My next step was my last. I struck something slick — ice, probably — and fell.

I fell, and fell, and fell. Down the rocks, through a crevice, into black nothingness, I fell, and I couldn't utter a single sound as the air rushed from my lungs.

~~~~~

When I woke up, my suit was alerting me of multiple things: suit wouldn't be able to keep me warm for much longer; it had ripped open on my leg; and the planet had oxygen I could breathe as my emergency plan B.

Plan B. I stared at the helmet screen. The suit acted as if I had a chance of survival here.

Sitting up, I hit the helmet on something hard. Rock. I turned on the helmet's night vision and was able to take in my surroundings. I was in what looked like a cave. It was pitch black, with a large pool of water in the center of it. I had come within feet of crashing into the water. Would I have survived that? I didn't know. Maybe.

Don't panic.

I took a breath.

The guys are gone.

Don't panic.

I moved my arms. Nothing was broken. My left leg was a different story. While nothing seemed broken, I had a huge, deep gash on my calf where the suit and my pants had torn. The blood loss made me woozy, but I tried to tie it off with the remaining scraps of the suit's leg to stanch the bleeding. Then, I stood, leaning on the rock wall for support.

Grim is out here.

Shut up, Phoebe. There's no such thing as –

A voice came through the silence in the cave. "Are you looking for your crew?" It was soft. Gentle. Kind.

My skin crawled, and my blood went cold, like the freezing rains had gotten inside my bones.

I looked around but saw no one. Nothing. The rock cave was empty.

"Jared? Is this a joke?" My voice cracked. The speaker sounded nothing like Jared, but he was so mischievous, maybe he was playing a game on me. "Are you guys okay—"

"Your crew is fine," the voice said softly. "I saved them. I'm afraid I did not see you… Alas, I sincerely apologize for my mistake."

The voice was so close.

Shaking, I backed against the wall, and then, I spotted something move in the water. My night vision helmet helped me focus in on the movement a bit better.

A man. Or, at least, the torso and head of a man had emerged from the placid pool waters. He had long black hair that fell into the water past his hips. His piercing eyes stared into mine, unblocked by my helmet.

The man tilted his head. "Please, don't be afraid."

"It's… it's you," I breathed. "Where's my crew? What did you do to them?" My voice came out in a broken gasp.

"They're saved," the man—no, the monster—said. "No man can survive this planet on his own. I saved them, until help can come. Come with me." He extended a hand to me.

Panic surged, and I screamed, yanking backward as if he could touch me even from over there. "Don't touch me! Don't eat me! Don't get any closer—I'll shoot!" But when I went to draw my ray gun, horror filled me. It was gone. It must have fallen from the holster during my fall. I looked around the cave, but it was nowhere.

The man dropped his hand. "My name is Grim," he said, "that much of the myth is true." He walked to the edge of the pool, but his lower half was still submerged under the water. What was below the water? A giant tail? Killer claws? Was he truly a beast? He had to be!

"What is your name?" he asked.

"Bring my crew back!" I yelled. "Help is coming—let us go!" Hm. Maybe I shouldn't have told him about help coming. What if he lured them onto the planet and ate them, too?

"Help is coming?" he asked softly. His expression softened. "Can they carry fifty men?"

"W-what?" I hissed.

The man took a breath and walked out of the pool. To my dismay, he looked entirely human. He was bare, with scars covering his body, and he didn't have a mermaid tail or claws.

"A curse," he said, "keeps me here. I understand magic is not a thing your world of reason and science believes, but it is my reality. I cannot leave, but I can protect those that fall here—but help never comes for the lost souls. And that is my fault. Too many men fear the myth."

"Stay back!" I yelled again. "I don't believe you! Where's Captain? Achilles? Did you eat them? I swear, if you ate them—"

The man lifted his hands. "Come with me. I can show you where I keep the fallen."

"I'm not going to a second location with you!" I screamed. "Bring them back!"

"I cannot. They will take my life. And then the curse repeats..." The man looked down at the rock floor. "Please, come with me. You can stay with all of the fallen and I'll lead help to you all. Safely. But without my aid, there is no way a mortal man can traverse this terrain."

I cringed. That much was very true. The planet was absolute hell. No way men could operate a rescue mission without either dying themselves or getting lost.

But this was Grim. He was a monster of myth and legend. I couldn't trust him.

The man hesitated. "Please, remove your helmet. The oxygen here is thin, but it will be better to breathe than the suit's oxygen supply. You've lost a lot of blood. I can heal it, if you wish?"

"Heal it?" I blanched. "How?"

"Magic." Grim lifted one hand. A soft yellow glow flooded his hand, gleaming off the walls of the cave. The light made the rocks shine.

Like how the rocks outside *Nomad* had looked before.

"You're really a siren! You're gonna kill me!" I shivered.

"There is no way to escape this cave without my help. You cannot find your crew alone. Now, please. If I were going to eat you, or kill you, I would have, yes?" Grim's hand continued to glow. "I wish to help."

My heart hammered.

Truly, whether he was a monster or not, what else could I do here? I was unarmed. Alone. Lost. Injured. And he was right. I'd bleed to death eventually, or get some infection, and die from that.

Without the beast's help… I was dead.

Why not risk my life and pretend to trust the beast?

"A-all right." I stepped forward weakly. My legs shook. "Please, help."

Grim knelt. I could've tried to bash his head open with my fists, but I didn't. He put his glowing hand—it had webbing between his fingers, like some sort of fish man—over my gashed leg. In moments, the pain vanished. I glanced down. The wound was gone. Just like that. There wasn't even a scar left behind.

My knees buckled and I dropped. Grim caught me.

"Now, I'll take you to the crew," he said firmly. "How far is help?"

He really has magic.

How? It's 2198. No one can have magic. Science, tech, yeah, but… this… this is otherworldly…

I shook. "A week. Can we last that long?"

"Many of the others have lasted decades," Grim said quietly. "Come."

Grim carried me. I didn't want to be carried, but I was too loopy to walk, so I didn't fight. After all, if he was going to whack me, he would.

He took me up the way I had fallen—a narrow crevice that was a dangerous fall, and yet, Grim walked and crawled as if his hands and feet were made like some lizard's. He held me with one arm, and I clung tightly to him.

"How are you doing this? I fell this way—almost died—"

"It comes with the curse." Grim didn't elaborate beyond that. "Hold on tightly. The others are in a safe place not far from here."

"Curse?" I whispered. "But magic… It's not real…"

"It is."

It looked like it was. But… "Who cursed you? Why?"

"A wizard," the man said simply. "I don't know his name, though I assume he was a man of science, because I remember how he looked and what he wore."

"A man of science…" I trailed off. There were plenty of scientists and cults in the planets, of course. But genuine magic users? It sounded like something out of a fairy tale. "I'm… sorry…"

"You believe me?" Grim asked softly.

"I don't know what else could be true." I forced out. "If you were a beast… You would've killed me by now, I think… And if you kill me soon, then I'll know better, but for now… I think I do believe you." Maybe it was the blood loss getting to my head, or the shock of the magic he'd used on my leg catching up to me.

Grim fell silent and continued his treacherous climb. It took a while for us to reach the top. When we did, we were on another flat stretch of rock, but not the same that I'd fallen from originally.

Grim said, "Almost there now."

He didn't put me down. He went left, and after a short walk, he carried me inside of a large cave.

It was dark, but I pulled my helmet off to see better as the rocks around us glowed from Grim's magic. The yellow light lit up the cave.

In the center of the giant cave, about forty-eight men lay peacefully in multiple rows — like a room of corpses, except a big dome of yellow light covered them. They all looked peaceful, and I looked closer to see that all their chests rose and fell with each breath.

"Captain!" I jerked out of Grim's arms. At the end of the row closest to us, Captain, Achilles, and Jared lay. "Achilles!"

"They're asleep," Grim said, standing a few feet behind me. "I've healed all of their injuries. They'll sleep like this until help can come. The light keeps them alive..."

I tried to reach through the light but couldn't. I tensed. "They're all right?"

"Yes." Grim nodded.

"They can't wake up?" I choked.

"They can. I keep them asleep and safe... until help comes... And then they can return home..." Grim dropped his head. His long hair clung to his scarred body. "For some, it has been a long time. I am sorry I couldn't return them home sooner." He shook his head and fell quiet.

Grim was genuine. The weight of his words hit me hard. Was he crying?

I took a few weak breaths. "Help is coming. We'll get them all to safety."

Grim didn't respond.

"And you," I said. "We'll take you, too. Where are you from?"

Grim's head jerked up. He blinked a few times. Now, with the helmet off, and in the yellow light, I saw his eyes were dark green, like the seas back home on Earth.

"Where is your home?" I repeated. "We'll take you home, too."

Tears pooled in the monster's eyes. "Home."

"You are human, yes? Is it Earth?"

Grim stepped forward slightly, then dropped to his knees. He pressed his forehead to the smooth gray rocks at my feet. "Home. I can go home. You'll take me home..." Sobs shook his body. "You broke the curse!"

I tensed hard, stomach flipping. "Hey! Get up — it's okay —"

"You broke the curse! You believed me!" Grim's body trembled, and his tears flowed like the rushing waters beyond the safe, dry cave.

I reached down, touching his shoulders tentatively. But Grim didn't hold back. He kissed the ground like a lunatic. "Thank you! Thank you. I can go home! Home!" As he spoke, the webbed flesh between his hands and feet vanished.

I knelt beside him. What else could I do? I grabbed his hands, and just held him as he rejoiced. Though his curse broke, the light in the cave remained.

~~~~~

I had made a small camp in the cave so I could look over the others, but the light kept them alive and safe, as it had been doing before. When I asked Grim how the magic stayed after his curse broke, he smiled and said: "The healing light is not from the wizard. It is from God."

"Oh... I didn't think God would... do stuff like that anymore." I poked at the little fire at the cave's edge—I was just burning some fire kits from the ships' storage—while shivering slightly. My emergency suit from *Nomad*'s supply was too big, and its thermo-control was sorely lacking. We were going on day two of waiting for the rescue team now. I hoped I could hold up till they arrived.

"He saved you." Grim nodded. "I was unable to save you, but He was with you the entire time."

I took a breath. "Yeah. I know. Um, hey... You said you remembered the guy that cursed you... What he looked like and all... Maybe we can find him, if he's still alive, and bring justice."

"I do not need justice. I want to go home. Or to whatever is left since 2100..." Grim frowned softly. He wore another emergency suit from *Nomad*. It barely fit him, and he tugged at the zipper on the sleeves.

"Where is home?" I asked.

"Sweden, on Earth," he said. "Is it still there?"

"Yeah. Earth is pretty much the same from 2100... Landwise, I guess. Politics and stuff have changed. Tech advancement, too." But the man had been gone for so long and hadn't even aged. It boggled my mind. "We'll get you home. Don't worry."

We fell silent again.

I watched the rain fall outside the cave. After a while, I said, "I'm sorry for how I treated you. I shouldn't... have believed you were a monster just because the legend said so."

"It is as ludicrous to believe in magic as it is in monsters," Grim said with a smile. "I understand. But you are the first to believe me, and for that... I am grateful..." He trailed off for a moment. "Phoebe?"

"Yeah?" I glanced at the fire again.

"After such a long time away from home, and from people..." He paused. "Does your crew need help?"

I winced. "Huh?"

"My family has been dead for a long, long time," he said softly. "And

I do not think it was home I missed so much as it... as it was my people... And to start over is a terrifying thing."

I nodded and said, "You can stay with us. I mean, I'm just a tag-along, anyway. Maybe we'll stay with *Nomad*, or if we have to, we'll find something else. But I think Captain has room for others. He'll need to replace *Nomad* with a bigger ship now, anyway. We'll just replace it and keep exploring, I think."

Grim smiled and said nothing more. After a while, I said, "Is your name really Grim?"

He laughed. A hoarse sound, but I liked hearing it. "Alexander Grim."

I smiled again. "The one thing the legend got right."

"Right."

We fell asleep as the rain fell over the rocky planet outside.

~~~~

The rescue team found us three days later. It was another miracle that their small ship could land on the strip of rock outside the cave, but that's where I signaled for them to land with my device, and land they did.

The captain of the ship came out suited. I wasn't, and waved him over. In moments, I gave him the rundown: a man had kept the crew alive, there were others to be saved, and we needed to get them all to safety.

The three crewmates were stunned but hopped to it quickly. No one attacked Grim, and things went fluidly: the light dome dropped as soon as Grim explained what it had been doing to the sleepers, and a few at a time they were loaded on the rescue ship and taken to *Hailey*, the mother ship in space above.

It took hours of work, but eventually, Grim and I were the last ones on the little ship. We were taken to *Hailey* and loaded aboard.

Grim and I showered before meeting in a small alcove in the ship's main room. Grim had cut his hair to his shoulders, and grinned wide at me when I came into the room.

"They gave me clothes that fit," he said. The suit was a bit baggy on him, and he pointed at the ship's logo on the front. "Even if I'm not a crewmate, it's nice."

We sat on the lounge couch and ate some cake from a MRE. He savored every bite. When I asked what he had eaten for all those years, he said the curse had kept his body alive off of nothing. The idea made me shiver, so I left it there.

"What now?" Grim asked quietly.

"Well, Captain should wake soon. We'll make a game plan when he does. You'll stick with us. Achilles will be on my side about it." I nodded. I added, a bit more quietly, "And the other men you saved will go back to their lives... Or start anew. But at least, they're alive. You might have been called a monster, but you saved a lot of people... That's something to... be proud of, I think, even if it was absolute hell..."

Grim nodded. Silent.

Finally, he leaned back, expression soft. "It is strange to be among the living again." He looked toward me. His eyes shined. "Thank you, Phoebe."

I smiled weakly. "Thanks for not eating me."

Grim laughed again. He fell asleep there, eventually, and his head slumped against my shoulder. I drifted off to sleep, too, and dreamed of exploring faraway planets, with Grim, the not-so-monstrous man at my side.

The End

CTHULHU VACATION
Pam Halter

"I get the top bunk!" Sedna called from her bedroom. She stuffed her fish net and seashell collecting bag into her duffle and pulled the drawstring tight.

"Do not!" Kai shouted back from his room.

"I asked Pa-ter." She dropped her duffle in the hall. "And I'm the oldest. I get first pick."

Kai stuck his head out of his room. "Only by three minutes. Ma-ter just happened to lay her egg first!"

Sedna shrugged. "Details."

"You're a squid!" And he slammed his door shut.

"Blobfish!"

"Goblin shark!"

"That's enough," Ma-ter called from downstairs. "Get your duffles packed and brought down so Pa-ter can load them into the sea camper."

Sedna carried her duffle to the front door where Pa-ter was checking the engine of his new pride and joy: an ORCA 6000. The family was delighted with the new sea camper. Their old one, a Beluga 2000, had been small and cramped. And she and Kai had to share a bed. Ugh! The seven-hour ride from their home in Antarctica to Atlantis had been unbearable, too.

"Everything look okay, Pa-ter?"

Her father looked up from under the hood. "All ship-shape and ready to roll! This baby even has an APS!" He shut the hood and clapped his hands once. "Aquatic Positioning System."

"I know, Pa-ter. You've told us a million times."

Pa-ter grinned. "We won't get lost this time. Nope. No getting lost this year."

Kai came out the front door dragging his duffle. "Pa-ter, I want the top bunk. It's not fair!"

"Well now, I think you can take turns. We'll be gone two whole weeks. That's plenty of time to share." He picked up Kai's duffle and grunted. "What did you pack? Feels like you got a walrus in there."

Kai shrugged. "My shovel, some books on Atlantis, extra bags. You know, exploring stuff."

Ma-ter closed the front door. "Everyone have everything? I'm locking the cave door now."

Sedna climbed into the ORCA 6000 and sat in the seat behind Pa-ter. She couldn't help but feel excited about this year's vacation to Atlantis. A new sea camper. An APS. And bunk beds. What could go wrong?

~~~~~

Sedna was trying to read her *Cthulhu Beat* magazine, but Kai, who always got his tentacles in a knot on long trips, kept interrupting her.

"Hey, Sed. Wanna see how much of my chin tentacle I can put up my nose?"

"No." Sedna turned a page.

"Hey, Sed, look what I can do with my toes."

"Not interested."

"Hey, Sed, here. Pull my tentacle."

Sedna hit him with her magazine. "Ma-ter! Make him stop!"

"Okay, how about a movie?" Ma-ter asked.

"*Jawzilla!*" Kai shrieked.

"*A Mermaid's Tale!*" Sedna shouted and stuck her tongue out at him.

"You're scared of *Jawzilla*," Kai taunted. "You get nightmares."

"Do not," Sedna said. "It's a dumb movie. The special effects are so bad. Everything looks fake."

Kai snorted. "Yeah? Well, Adriana is ugly. Mermaids are supposed to be pretty."

"Vampire squid!"

"Whale butt!"

"Fish egg face!"

"Shark puke!"

"We could watch *The Titanic Disaster*," Ma-ter said. "My grandparents told us stories about it. They were on vacation way up north when it happened. It caused current disruption for a long time."

Sedna rolled her eyes. "We saw a video in history class. I don't want to watch a history movie while we're on vacation."

"How about *Jawzilla versus the Kraken*?" Pa-ter said over his shoulder.

"Dad, you're driving," Sedna said. "And that one is worse than the first one."

Ma-ter patted him on the shoulder. "Yes, dear, keep your eyes on the current."

Sedna shook her head. *You'd think an ORCA 6000 would have a way to play two movies at once*, she silently complained.

After a round of Rock, Seaweed, Sand, Kai won, and *Jawzilla* played first.

They stopped at a sunken ship to eat the lunch Ma-ter packed. As they ate, Pa-ter tried to get them to play *I Spy*, but there wasn't much to see as they weren't too far from Antarctica yet.

Sedna finished eating. "I'm going to get the next movie ready."

"Do we really have to watch *A Mermaid's Tale?*" Kai mumbled, his mouth full of whale blubber and jellyfish sandwich.

Sedna ignored him. She got back into the sea camper and programmed the ORCA 6000's movie player. Kai had his Sea-pad, he could play games if he didn't want to watch.

About halfway through the movie, Sedna noticed a change in the color of the water outside the sea camper.

"Pa-ter? What's wrong with the water?"

"Hmmmmm?"

"The water. It's getting dark," Sedna said. "It's too early for it to be this dark."

Pa-ter tapped the APS. "I don't know. Maybe the APS is taking us on a shortcut. We're still on current."

"Are you sure?" Mat-er asked.

"I'm sure."

Sedna went back to the movie. She looked up again when it was done. The water was not only dark but cloudy, as well.

She nudged Kai, who had fallen asleep. "What?" he said, blinking. She nodded toward the window.

"Galloping seahorses! Where are we?" he exclaimed.

Pa-ter waved a hand. "No worries. We're fine. Riding the current. Following the APS."

"Shouldn't we be at the sea camper ground?" Sedna asked. "We've been riding the current for seven hours now."

"Well, yes, we're usually at The Sea Jammer by now," Pa-ter said. He tapped the APS again. A light started blinking. "Uh oh."

Ma-ter sighed. "What did you do this time?"

Pa-ter chuckled. "Nothing, nothing. I'll just pull out of the current and check the APS guidebook." He edged the sea camper to the right and stopped. He reached into the map compartment and pulled out the book. "Now, let's see. Blinking light. Blinking light."

Kai closed his Sea-pad. "I'm hungry. Can I get a snack?"

Ma-ter nodded. "There are some seaweed biscuits in the green Seaware."

"Want one?" Kai asked Sedna as he popped open the plastic container. "They got flounder eggs on top! Thanks, Ma-ter!"

Sedna took a biscuit and leaned forward to see what Pa-ter was doing. The guidebook lay open on the dash, and he was pressing buttons and muttering to himself. Not a good sign.

"Ma-ter?" she said. "Maybe you should take a look."

"I almost got it," Pa-ter said. "We'll be back on the current in a minute."

After ten minutes, Ma-ter grabbed the book. She read a page, pushed

Pa-ter's hand back and made an adjustment. "There. Try it now."

"Thanks, dear," Pa-ter said as he pulled back onto the current.

They rode without seeing anything for who knew how long. It had to be way past bedtime.

Sedna yawned. "I'm gonna lay down. I can hardly keep my eyes open."

"That's fine, dear," Ma-ter said.

Sedna climbed into the top bunk and drifted off to sleep as Kai pulled up *Jawzilla versus the Kraken* and hit play.

~~~~~

Sedna opened her eyes, sat up and bumped her head on the roof. "Ow! Where are we?"

No answer. It was still dark, so she felt around for the switch that would turn on the bioluminescent lights. The light was low, but she could make out Pa-ter and Ma-ter sleeping in the front seats.

Kai must have been on the bottom bunk.

Sedna slid down and lightly touched the floor. She stretched and yawned. How long had she slept? It felt like hours, but it was still dark outside, so it probably wasn't as long as she thought.

"Ma-ter?" she whispered. "Ma-ter, are you awake?"

Ma-ter stirred and lifted her head. "What's wrong, Sed?"

The sea camper shifted a little to the right. "Where are we?"

Ma-ter sighed. "I don't know."

"Pa-ter is sleeping. Why is the sea camper still moving?"

Ma-ter sat up. "What?" She shook Pa-ter's shoulder. "Wake up! You're supposed to be driving!"

Pa-ter wiped his eyes. "It's okay, I turned on the current control."

"That only controls speed!" Ma-ter cried. "Not direction!"

"Oh." He grabbed the helm and steered off the current and stopped.

Pa-ter loved technology, but it sure didn't love him.

~~~~~

Sedna and Ma-ter were sitting at the sea camper kitchen table and eating sweet & slimy muffins when Kai woke up.

"I'm hungry," he said.

Sedna snorted. "Tell us something we don't know."

"Shut your gills, frogfish."

"Pig butt worm."

"**Big** butt worm!"

"That's enough," Ma-ter said. "Let's work together here. Pa-ter will need to concentrate when we get on the current again."

Kai grabbed a muffin. "Are we almost there?"

Ma-ter gave him her don't-annoy-me look. He grinned and shoved the whole muffin into his mouth.

82

Sedna sighed. "You're such a Gulper Eel."

Kai grinned and belched.

In half an hour, they were back on the current. Neither Sedna nor Kai wanted a movie this time.

~~~~~

"Are we there yet?" Kai whined for the tenth time a couple hours later. But this time, he wasn't being snarky. He sounded frightened. Sedna felt frightened, too.

Ma-ter reached back and grabbed his hand. "It's okay, bub. We're gonna be okay."

Kai burst into tears. "Where are we? We're lost again, aren't we?" he wailed.

Sedna tried to hold back, but tears ran down her cheeks and chin tentacles. "Can we turn around? Go back the same way we came?"

Pa-ter glanced over his shoulder. "The APS says we'll be there in an hour. It won't be long now."

Kai sniffed. "Okay."

"Cheer up!" Pa-ter said. "Here, I got a joke for ya. Where is the ocean the deepest?"

Sedna rolled her eyes. "The bottom."

"What's the best tool in the ocean?"

"Not the APS," Sedna mumbled.

"A hammerhead shark!" Kai shouted.

Sedna didn't know what was worse, the dark water or her dad's dumb jokes. Either way, that last hour felt like five.

~~~~~

Pa-ter patted the helm of the ORCA 6000. "Great investment, if I do say so myself. Got us here safe and sound."

They had driven up out of the water. Sedna swept her gaze from the jungle on one side of the sea camper to the lagoon on the other. "Yeah, but where are we? This is not Atlantis."

"Nope, nope, it's not." Pa-ter scratched his head and tugged his tentacle beard. "But let's make the best of it." He looked around the area. "The ground is solid, so we should be fine to set up camp here."

"Sure," Ma-ter said. "It's a new adventure!"

Sedna grinned. Ma-ter's penguin-chirpy tone of voice didn't fool her. She wanted them out of the sea camper so she could lay into Pa-ter.

Kai shrugged. "Sure. An adventure."

"I guess it's a good thing you brought your exploring stuff," Sedna replied. "You ready?"

Kai grinned. "I'll be ready as soon as I have something to eat."

~~~~~

Sedna and Kai got ready to explore.

"Look for anything edible," Ma-ter told them. "I didn't pack extra food. I had planned to go to the SeaMart when we got to Atlantis."

"I'll get the crab traps," Pa-ter said. "I packed them in with the beach chairs."

"I have my shell collecting bag," Sedna said. "I'll see what I can fit in that."

They waved and started off into the jungle.

"There's probably a monster here," Kai whispered. "This place looks just like all the places in the movies that have monsters in them."

Sedna shoved him. "Shut up."

"And the water," he went on. "Probably full of barracudas or Moray eels."

"Shut *up*, squid worm."

"Dork fish!"

"Tentacle butt."

At first, they didn't go out of sight of the sea camper. But after finding only two mushrooms, they decided to spread out a bit more. Sedna knew what to look for. At least, she did in Atlantis. She had taken the foraging class when they were there for last year's vacation. It was fun, but she never dreamed she would actually use the information she had learned.

The water in the lagoon was black, so there was no way she wanted to dive into that. And she bet the plants were nasty and bitter. She heard Kai stomping through the brush nearby. As much as he annoyed her, she would feel better if they stuck together.

"Hey, frog face," she called. "I changed my mind. Let's not go alone."

He stomped back to her. "You're such a scaredy fish."

She gave a short laugh. "Yeah, whatever. Let's check out the other side of the lagoon."

They traveled the edge of the lagoon, keeping their feet from slipping into the dark water. After half an hour of only finding a couple more mushrooms, they sat on a log.

"Do you think there are any fish in the lagoon?" Kai wondered.

"Would *you* swim in it?" Sedna asked. "I mean, look at it! You'd be swimming blind!"

"I don't know. Maybe it's not as dark as it looks once you're in." He picked up a rock and tossed it.

Ker-plunk!

Sedna jumped up. "Stop it, sand eel! What if there really *is* a monster?"

Kai laughed. "He'd see your tentacles and high fin it out of here."

She chose to ignore that. "Seriously, though. What if we can't find food? We have no idea where we are and how long it would take to get back home. Mom's sea biscuits and muffins are gonna run out at some point." She nudged his shoulder. "Especially with how fast you're eating them."

"Galloping seahorses! I didn't even think of that!" He jumped up and took off.

Sedna grabbed her bag and followed. "Slow your webbed feet down. You don't even know what you're looking for!"

But Kai kept going. Sedna sighed. Boys. They always thought with their stomachs. She scanned the bushes and ground. Shopping at SeaMart sure was easier than finding their own food.

~~~~~

Sedna had no idea how long they wandered. Suddenly, Kai screeched, "Eww, slime! I stepped in slime!"

Sedna looked. It *was* slime. Slime trails.

Kai hopped to the side. He wiped his feet on the dead leaves. "Eww! Gross!"

"You'll survive." Sedna noticed the trails went as far as she could see, crisscrossing in places and disappearing into the jungle in others. "You realize what this means. It means there are other creatures here besides us."

"Let's follow them," Kai suggested. "Maybe they lead to food."

Sedna highly doubted it, but her stomach pinched with hunger. "All right."

They had gone a short way when they heard shrieking laughter, then two splashes.

"Hide!" Kai yelped.

"Where?"

"I don't know. Run!" Kai shouted.

But before they could turn around, a large slimy tentacle reached over the edge of a small pool they hadn't noticed. They should have run. They really should have. But they couldn't.

A creature Sedna had never seen before pulled itself out of the water. Her mouth opened in a silent scream. Kai's breath came out in a whoosh.

A moment later, another tentacle came up over the edge and a second creature surfaced. Sedna and Kai stood rooted to the ground. The creatures looked like some kind of octopus. But they were short, only coming up to Kai and Sedna's waists.

"Who are you, and how did you get here?" the first one said. Its voice gurgled.

"Yeah, we're the only amphibious mollusks in the lagoon," said the second one.

"And this is *our* seaweed slide," the first one said.

Sedna shook her head. They were definitely not octopuses, or they would have tried to lure them closer. To make a meal of them. Sedna had heard enough warnings from Pa-ter about octopuses.

She took a breath and let it out. "We're lost."

Kai nodded. "Yeah, lost. And we taste terrible, too."

Sedna hit him.

The two amphibious mollusks looked at each other, then burst into gurgling laughter. They edged closer to Sedna and Kai.

"What do you think we are? Octopuses?" the first one said. "My name is Zilly. And this slime face is my brother Zigbert."

Her brother wiggled his tentacles. "Ziggy."

"It's nice to meet you," Sedna said. "I'm Sedna and this is my brother, Kai."

"So, what brings you to the Black Lagoon?" Zilly asked. "We've been coming here for vacation for as long as I can remember, and we've never seen any other creature here."

"Yeah, what are you, anyway?" Ziggy glared suspiciously up at Kai.

"What are *you*?" Kai shot back.

"Stop it," Zilly said. "Great seashells! Boys!" She turned to Sedna. "We told you. We're amphibious mollusks. Kinda like snails, but we can live in the water or on the land."

"We're Cthulhu, and we can, too," Sedna said.

"Ka-thoo-loo?" Ziggy asked.

Sedna nodded.

Kai crossed his arms. "Snails? Where's your shells?"

"We left them on the other side of our seaweed slide," Ziggy said. "It's hard to slide with them on."

Sedna realized she hadn't answered Zilly's question. "We're here because —" she started.

"Our dad got lost," Kai interrupted. "We got this cool new sea camper with an APS and everything! But we still got lost." He rubbed his belly. "And we're really hungry."

"Our mom is a great cook," Ziggy said. "Follow us."

They slid to the other side of the pool where two large shells leaned against a palm tree.

"How do you move?" Kai asked. "I don't see legs or anything."

"We have really strong muscles underneath," Ziggy said. "Plus, our tentacle beards help."

Kai rubbed his chin tentacles. "Pa-ter has a long tentacle beard, but it only hangs there."

They all laughed.

After grabbing their shells with their tentacles, they flipped them onto their backs, and slid off again.

"You move quicker without your shell," Sedna said. "Why don't you keep it off?"

"Moog thinks we're safer with our shells on. But sometimes, we take them off," Zilly said. "Don't say anything."

Sedna shook her head. "I won't."

Kai patted Ziggy's shell. "That was rippin' cool the way you put your shell on your back. I thought your shells were your home."

"Shush!" Sedna whispered.

"You're thinking of regular snails," Zilly said. "We *can* pull into our shells, but mostly for protection. We prefer living in family units underground."

"Underground? We live in a cave. That's kinda like underground," Kai said. "What do you stay in for vacation? Do you have a sea camper, too?"

"Yeah, we do."

They came to a clearing in the palm trees. Zilly pointed to what looked like a giant shell but wasn't because it had a door on the side and paddles underneath. "I'll get Moog and Doog," she said.

She shook off her shell and squeezed through the door. A minute later, two larger mollusks, also not wearing shells, followed behind her.

"Moog? Doog? These are our new friends," Zilly said. "Sedna and Kai. They're Cthulhu, and they're lost."

"And hungry," Ziggy said.

Moog raised a tentacle in greeting. "Cthulhu? You're a long way from home."

"Where's their home?" Ziggy asked.

"Antarctica," Sedna answered.

"Where were you headed?" Doog asked.

"Atlantis," Kai said. "But we ended up here. Wherever here is."

Doog gurgled a chuckle. "Nowhere near Atlantis, I can tell you that."

Sedna and Kai looked at each other and grinned. "Yeah, well, our dad got a new sea camper with an APS, but we still got lost."

Ziggy wiggled his tentacles. "We don't have an APS. Can I see it?"

"We don't need an APS." Doog winked at them. "I got it all in my head."

"Zig, let's get them some food first," Zilly said.

"Come and sit down," Moog said. "I'll fix you a snack."

"Great!" Kai exclaimed.

Moog went back inside and soon slid out holding a bowl filled with greens and clams in her tentacles. Kai clapped his hands. "That looks great! I'm starving!"

As they ate, Moog brought out more bowls that had mostly green leaves in them, but there were also a few with other colors like red, yellow, purple, and even black.

"There's Dulce, Carageen Moss, Salicornia, and Sea Lettuce." Zilly pointed to each one as she named them. "We also know where you can catch Pompano and Snook. Doog is an excellent fisher mollusk."

"My parents will be so thankful," Sedna said. "If we can find our way back."

"Doog can help you. He knows every inch of the lagoon."

Moog urged Sedna to fill a bowl with all the greens she wanted.

"Thank you!"

"My pleasure," Moog said. "We're leaving in the morning, and these wouldn't have made it home before going bad."

"I hope Ma-ter will know what to do with them," Kai said.

Sedna clutched the bowl tightly. "I'm sure she will. Ma-ter is a good cook."

After describing the area of their sea camper, Doog flipped his shell onto his back. "I know exactly where you are. Let's go!"

"Yeah, I want to see that APS," Ziggy added.

The walk to the sea camper wasn't far, but it took a while since the mollusks were hindered by their shells. As they approached the sea camper, Ma-ter came out.

"Sedna! Kai! I was getting worried."

"Ma-ter, this is the Mollusk family," Sedna said. "We found them by accident."

"They have food!" Kai cried.

Sedna introduced everyone. Then she looked toward the sea camper. "Where's Pa-ter?"

"He's checking the crab traps," Ma-ter said.

"Oh, he won't catch any crabs here," Doog said. "Just fish and clams. I can help."

Just then Pa-ter walked up carrying two empty cages. "Nothing. Not a single crab."

"Pa-ter! Come and meet our new friends!" Sedna called.

Soon, Doog, Pa-ter, Ziggy, and Kai were in the front of the sea camper checking out the APS. Ma-ter and Moog sat outside at the folding picnic table exchanging recipes.

Then Sedna, Zilly, Kai, and Ziggy went to the lagoon to dig for clams while Doog programed the APS for Pa-ter so they could continue on to Atlantis.

Finally, they said their goodbyes, promising to keep in touch on their Sea-pads, and the Mollusk family went back to their shell camper.

The Cthulhu family agreed to leave for Atlantis first thing in the morning. As they all walked to the lagoon to catch a few fish for the trip, Sedna stubbed her toe on something.

"Ow! What is that? A rock?"

Kai rushed over. "Let me see!"

They brushed dead leaves aside. Ma-ter and Pa-ter came up beside them.

"It's an egg!" Ma-ter exclaimed.

Pa-ter touched it. "Clearly abandoned. It's not even warm."

"Aw, we can't leave it here." Ma-ter had a weird, silly smile Sedna had never seen on her face before.

"No! I forbid it!" Pa-ter slashed the air with his hand. "It stays here."

"But, dear ..."

"No!" Pa-ter said. "Have you forgotten what happened when your Aunt Bertha brought home an abandoned egg? As soon as it hatched, whatever it was bit your cousin Gilbert's leg clean off! It would have killed Uncle Percy if Bertha hadn't hit it over the head with a rock."

Ma-ter sighed. "Okay. You're right."

"I'm serious," Pa-ter said. "It stays here in the Black Lagoon. Nothing to worry about. Probably won't even hatch."

~~~~~

Two Hours Later

"Are we there yet?" Kai asked.

"Soon, soon," Pa-ter said. "The APS says one hour." He gave it a pat. "I sure am glad Doog programmed it so we can still have our Atlantis vacation."

Sedna looked up from her magazine. "We won't get lost this time then, right?"

Kai stuffed a slime puff in his mouth. Slime dripped down his chin tentacles and onto the seat.

Senda shook her head. "You're so messy."

Kai licked his fingers. "You're seeing a once-in-a-lifetime thing. I'm not messy. I am an elegant man."

"That is totally false," Sedna said.

Kai started to retort when Pa-ter shouted out, "Whoa!"

Plop!

Plop!

Plop!

"Aaaaaaaaaaaaaaah!" Sedna and Ma-ter screamed at the same time.

"Cool! Plesiobatidae!" Kai said.

Sedna turned to him. "What?"

"Deepwater stingrays!"

"How do we get them off?" Pa-ter shouted. "I can't see where we're going!"

The sea camper tilted. They all cried out.

"Turn on the seashield wipers!" Sedna said.

The sea camper lurched forward, then scraped along the sea floor.

More stingrays attached to the seashield.

"Pa-ter! The seashield wipers!" Sedna shrieked.

The sea camper started to spin.

"Hold on!" Ma-ter shouted.

They spun. They rolled. Then the sea camper bumped twice and settled with a shimmy on the sea floor.

Sedna opened her eyes. The stingrays were still plastered against the seashield, but she could see dark waters out the side windows. "Where are we?"

"We should be on the current for Atlantis. Doog programmed it," Pa-ter said. He tapped the APS. A light started blinking. "Uh oh."

"Galloping seahorses," Kai groaned. "Not again!"

The End

CROAK
Stoney M. Setzer

"So you still like this?" Staci chuckled, holding up my Coke bottle and looking at it from different angles. "Dropping peanuts in your Coke?"

"Why not?" I answered with a smile as I steered my truck off the main road. "A true Southern delicacy. Not much different than taking a handful of peanuts and drinking right after it."

"True. Well, my idea of a Southern delicacy is more like these pimento cheese sandwiches I brought." She held up the small picnic basket she had been holding in her lap.

"Can't wait." I glanced over at her.

She had the window rolled down, and her reddish-brown hair was waving gently in the breeze. She smiled, and everything seemed right with the world. We had been seeing each other for a couple of months now, ever since she had come back into town, or at least as best we could with our schedules. Between my duties as sheriff of Sardis County, the demands of her veterinary practice, and her responsibilities to her father in the nursing home, we had to take our moments when we could. Having both been married before—I was divorced, she was widowed—dating was a different ballgame this time around.

This was going to be our first fishing trip together. It hadn't seemed like a big deal when we planned it, but from the moment I had picked her up this morning, it had felt unexpectedly momentous. I didn't think anything could ruin today.

"This is where you buy your bait?" Staci asked, scrunching up her nose as I pulled up to an aged convenience store and parked near the propane tanks.

"Gary Cleveland's been running this place for years," I said. "Best kept secret in Tennessee."

"I can see why it's a secret. Way off the main road, and it's kinda grungy looking."

"Yeah, but it's right on the lake. Looks aren't everything, Doc. You let yourself be seen with me, and I'm sure not much to look at."

She smirked playfully at me. "That, Mr. Sheriff, is a matter of opinion."

As we got out of the truck, I noticed an old, beat-up RV parked about a hundred yards away. On another side of the lake, I might not have thought too much about it, but there was no campground on this side. I thought I heard music coming from it—yacht rock, maybe—but at that distance I couldn't be sure. Maybe it was harmless, but it struck me as odd enough for me to take note of it.

"Hey, are you coming or not?" Staci asked. Rather than say anything about the RV, I opened the door of the store for her.

None of the convenience stores in Sardis were immaculate, but this one hadn't seen a good cleaning in ages. The musty air was laced with stale cigarette smoke. Sticky floors made a peeling sound with every step we took. Dark wood paneling, probably 1970s vintage, still lined the walls and even bowed outward in places, warped beyond repair. In one corner of the store stood a vintage Frogger arcade game, which would have been a lot more impressive if not for the OUT OF ORDER sign that had been taped to the screen since about 2004 or so. The crickets that Cleveland sold for live bait chirped constantly. Nothing much had changed, and I had never noticed any of it much before—but then again, I had never brought Staci here before.

However, there was one major difference, that being the person behind the counter. He was a pudgy man in his late thirties, with curly blond hair and a mustache. "Can I help you folks?"

"Yeah, I wanted to buy some bait. Is Gary around?"

"No sir, I'm in the process of taking over this place from him. Name's Jack Huey." He extended a beefy hand.

"Dane Carter. I'm the sheriff in these parts."

"Oh, really?" His eyes got big. Not full panic, but enough of a reaction to be noticeable. Maybe his expression was just because I was wearing swim trunks and an Atlanta Falcons t-shirt instead of my uniform, but it still caught my attention.

"Yes, sir. And this is Dr. Staci Bridges."

Now Huey's eyebrows jumped. Still under control, but noticeably nervous. "Doctor? What brings a sheriff and a doctor…"

"Veterinarian," she said, her tone reassuring. "We had the same off-day this week, so we're just getting ready to do some fishing." She stepped in closer to me and put her hand on my arm. I didn't mind.

Her words seemed to have put Huey at ease again. "Just so happens that you're in luck. I've got these brand new, special bait pellets that are guaranteed to lure you the biggest fish of your life." He produced a clear plastic jar filled with lime-green pellets that seemed almost fluorescent. "I'm eager to have someone try them out. You're actually the first customers that I've had since I got this stuff in."

"Shocker," Staci muttered as her gaze flitted around the shop with mild disdain. She sniffed at the air, frowned, but made no comment.

Huey smiled. "You know how you can go past a restaurant, and the smell makes you hungry and brings you in, even if you weren't hungry before?"

"Sure." I'd experienced that more times than I could count, with such Sardis County establishments as Maria's Mexican and Leon's Barbecue immediately coming to mind.

"Same concept," Huey continued, launching into his sales pitch. "They'll dissolve in a hurry, but they scent the water, so to speak. This stuff makes the fish hungry, they come up and see the bait on your hooks, and..."

"Yeah, I've used pellets before," I remarked. "Just not any that glow."

Huey pulled out two containers, one with worms and one with crickets. "So I'll tell you what, I'll make you a deal. Buy the pellets, and I'll give you two for the price of one on live bait, Sheriff. Interested?"

"Why not?" I was still mulling over what he had said about taking over the place from Cleveland.

Truth be told, he had been wanting to get out from under the place for a while now and had told me as much every time I came in here. He was well past retirement age and ready to move on, but he wanted to come out ahead when he sold the place to somebody else. Unfortunately, the condition of the building and its isolated location had been working against him so far. Maybe he finally found the right deal, or maybe he had just decided to throw in the towel. He wasn't raking in the big bucks anyway, another fact that I'm sure would have come as no surprise to Staci.

Still, when you live in Sardis County, especially when you're the sheriff, anything unusual catches your attention. Like that old beat-up RV.

~~~~~

By the time we had put the boat out into the water, I had compartmentalized my misgivings a little. Not forgetting them completely, but trying not to let them distract me too much from the moment. Being with Staci made that easy.

"Wow, this pimento cheese is incredible!" I remarked just before I took another bite of my sandwich.

"Thank you," Staci said with a big smile. "I was hoping you'd like it. It's homemade."

"Seriously? That's amazing! You did a really good job."

"Thanks. Is the water usually this choppy?"

"No, not really."

Staci put a worm on her hook and looked over the side of the boat. "Waves are one thing, but it feels like the whole world's rocking."

"Yeah, it is." The water was rougher than usual, but what was really rocking my world at the moment was Staci herself. She had doffed her t-shirt and cut-off denim shorts to unveil the white bathing suit she had on underneath. Without going into a lot of unnecessary detail, let's just say that she looked amazing and leave it at that. I could only hope that I wasn't being too obvious about looking at her...

Pushing her aviator sunglasses up higher on her nose, she smirked teasingly. "And just what are you gazing at, Mr. Sheriff?"

So much for that hope. "Uh, well...I..." Thankfully, my mom, sister, and niece weren't out here; they would have had a field day with this.

"You know, you could be a gentleman and offer to rub some sunscreen on my back and shoulders while I'm over here trying to catch our supper."

Obediently I grabbed the tube from her bag. "So you think you're gonna outfish me?"

"I think right now you ain't doing much but staring." She had a big smile, clearly enjoying putting me on the spot. I'm sure her eyes were teasing me behind those aviators. "You gotta put a hook in the water before you can catch anything, don't you know that?"

As I rubbed the sunscreen on her, the boat rocked again, violently. Staci lost her footing and stumbled backwards into me, which I guess would be the fishing equivalent of having your girl jump into your arms in the middle of a horror movie—as in, I didn't mind. Neither did she, apparently; she didn't pull away from me. In fact, she snuggled up to me, and I didn't mind that either.

"See what I mean, Dane? That was pretty rough."

"Yeah." Reluctantly, I started to move away from her to get my fishing rod.

"Did you see the way those bait pellets glowed?" she asked.

"I'd be worried about my eyes if I hadn't." I had also noticed a very weird, almost slimy texture to them when I tossed them out into the water, but I had kept that to myself.

"Weird." She laughed and shook her head. "I'm just gonna tell you right now, if we catch some three-eyed fish because of that stuff, I'm not about to..."

Suddenly her rod bent into an extreme arc. "I've got one! And it's huge!"

"Before I can even get a hook in the water! Reel it in!"

"I'm trying, but it's a big one!" Her muscles tensed as her catch fought against her. The fish yanked her forward, and I instinctively threw my arms around her waist to catch her and keep her in the boat. However, the force pulling against her, against me, kept me from enjoying the touch. It threatened to overpower me, and I'm not a small fry.

"You don't get to win!" Staci growled as she reeled and pulled back on the rod with all her might. "I ain't letting you..."

SNAP! Suddenly her rod broke in two under the strain. I don't go cheap on my fishing equipment. Unless she had somehow managed to hook Jaws, that rod should have held up. So what was on the other end of that line?

Something burst out of the water, springing about twenty feet into the air. It was a frog—or at least, it looked like a frog, but of gargantuan proportions. Had Staci not screamed, I might have thought my eyes were playing tricks on me.

It fell back into the water with such a huge splash that we were both soaked. Suddenly the boat started to tilt. The frog had clipped the bow as it fell, breaking off a chunk of it, and now we were quickly taking on water. Sinking.

Staci grabbed my hand. "We've gotta swim for it!"

The thought of getting into the same water as that giant frog wasn't exactly appealing, nor was losing all my high-dollar fishing equipment. Still, my mom hadn't raised any idiots. Taking each other's hand, we jumped feet first into the murky lake water.

Back in our high school days, we had both worked summer jobs as lifeguards at the Elks Club pool, so we were experienced swimmers. The shoreline was in sight, and we swam as fast as we could. Staci got ahead of me in short order, but she had always been a faster swimmer and probably still kept in better practice than I did...

...Which made it all the more terrifying when her head jerked down beneath the surface. She popped up long enough to scream before going under again.

I plunged underwater. Visibility wasn't great, but I managed to spot the white of Staci's bathing suit, gleaming as if it was phosphorescent in the murky waters. She was thrashing around, fighting for her life. As I approached, I saw something long and narrow was wrapped around her ankle. Finally I could make out the other end and saw the giant frog, mouth wide open and trying to pull Staci in. Only then did I realize what I should have already guessed, that the thing clutching her was actually the frog's tongue.

No time to lose. Thrusting my hand into my pocket, I yanked out my knife and flipped the blade open. I grabbed the tongue with my left hand and brought the knife down with my right. The blade didn't slice all the way through, stopping about halfway, but it shocked the frog enough to break its tongue's grip on Staci. She swam to the surface, and I pulled my knife free and followed suit.

Adrenaline propelled me as we swam frantically. I kept feeling something brush against my legs and ankles—maybe my imagination, or just some unrelated debris, but in my mind it was a tongue trying to grab me, fueling my terror. The shoreline seemed to get farther away instead of closer. It wasn't until I saw Staci crawl up out of the water onto dry land that I believed we would make it.

By the time I joined her, my limbs ached and my lungs burned. Struggling to catch my breath, I crawled up beside her on the shore.

"Are you all right?" I gasped.

Staci was about to answer me until she glanced back at the water. Her eyes widened, and she could only make incoherent guttural sounds. Following her gaze, I saw the gargantuan frog bounding out of the water, straight toward us, croaking loudly.

"How many crazy critters are in Sardis County, anyway?" Staci gasped. Between this and the black-and-purple lizard that had put her to sleep with its bite a couple of months ago, she had seen her share of creatures beyond the outer limits of her experience since she had moved back here.

I pulled my knife out again, wishing I had a gun instead. "Run! Go to the truck!"

"But I can't just leave you..."

"Yes, you can! Now go! I'm coming!" Struggling to my feet, I didn't dare take my eyes off the monster hopping toward me. The sound of footsteps told me she was hustling for safety. I moved away from the frog cautiously, wanting to run with her but unwilling to turn my back.

Bulging eyes gaped at me, a truly disconcerting sight. Its tongue whipped out at me with blinding quickness, wrapping itself tightly around my arm. I gripped the knife tightly, but the tongue tightened like a vise, cutting off my circulation and threatening to crush my bones as the frog pulled me in...

A shot rang out, and immediately the tentacle went slack. The creature slumped to the ground, dark fluid oozing out of its side. I looked over my shoulder to see Staci standing there, brandishing the Glock that I kept in my truck.

"Didn't kick as much as I expected," she remarked dryly.

I looked at the creature's lifeless form and back at her. "Nice shot."

She smirked as she handed the Glock back to me. "You've saved my life twice now, Mr. Sheriff. I couldn't stay down two to zip, now could I?"

"Guess not." I went over and examined our assailant's carcass. "So what on earth is this thing, Doc?"

She raised an eyebrow at me. "You do realize I mostly deal with dogs and cats, right? I must have been skipping class the day they covered cryptozoology."

"I mean, it was mostly rhetorical..."

Staci walked around the creature, examining it from every angle. "You'd laugh at me if I told you what I really thought."

"Try me."

Her chuckle was more nervous than humorous. "You know how Pastor Larry has been preaching out of Exodus here lately, and how he

96

was talking about the ten plagues of Egypt a couple of weeks back?"

"Yeah," I said, realization dawning on me as I thought about Larry Raymond reading the Word from the pulpit. "And that the second was..."

"...A plague of frogs," we said in unison.

"The Bible didn't say anything about them being giant frogs, though." Staci picked up a long stick, poking and prodding the carcass in several spots.

"And it wasn't just one frog," I said, watching the frog for any sign of movement. "The Bible said those frogs swarmed Egypt. One frog doesn't constitute a swarm."

"And you've fished here before, right?"

I nodded. "Yeah, all the time. Last time was two weeks ago, and nothing like this happened. And it seems like I would have heard about it if it had happened before today."

"Unless nobody else survived. This one almost got us both."

"Good point, Doc, but even then, you'd think somebody would have filed a missing persons report or something."

"Touche." Staci tapped her chin thoughtfully. "But those bait pellets, that was different from before, right?"

"Yeah." I shook my head. "So if that led to this...I'll grant you it wouldn't be the weirdest thing that ever happened in Sardis, but why..."

"Dane! Look!" Staci grabbed my arm and pointed back toward the lake. Six more frog creatures were coming out of the lake. "You just had to say something about it being only one frog, didn't you?"

"Open mouth, insert foot," I groaned.

Two of them were headed toward us, but the others were veering off, heading to our right. Straight in the direction of Cleveland's bait shop. If those so-called bait pellets were somehow behind their mutation, that was the last place they needed to go.

I squeezed the trigger, burying a bullet into the head of the first creature. As it slumped lifelessly to the ground, the second one leapt into the air, coming straight at me. With no time to aim, I fired towards it. The frog slammed into me and knocked me off my feet before I could see whether my shot hit anything.

The creature was fighting me frenetically, trying to wrap its arms around me as if to suffocate me, its bulbous eyes and wide mouth mere inches away from my face. With the Glock still in hand, I wrestled my arm up to its flank and put the muzzle up against its side. Another squeeze of the trigger, and all of the fight left my assailant forever. I still had to get its massive carcass off me. Staci hurried over to help; fortunately, her veterinary background kept her from being squeamish.

When I was finally able to stand again, I looked in the direction the other creatures had gone. They had taken advantage of our being distracted, making far more progress than I would have liked. Our attackers hadn't hurt us, but they had bought time for the others. What if they were intelligent enough to have intended that all along? Not a reassuring thought.

I took a quick look back at the lake. Thank God, nothing else was emerging. Whatever was at play here, maybe these were the only ones.

"Let's go!" I shouted, heading off after the creatures.

"Dane, wait!" Staci cried. "Wait!"

In spite of every impulse, I stopped and turned to face her. "Those things aren't going to wait! We have to stop them!"

She started to object but caught herself. "But we can't do it by ourselves! Can't you at least call your deputies for backup?"

In my haste to act, that was an idea that should have crossed my mind but hadn't. "Did you leave your phone in my truck, or did you have it with you on the boat?"

Her expression told me all I needed to know. "Let's just say it's probably on the bottom of the lake now."

"Go to my truck. I keep a police radio there. Call dispatch, tell them who you are and that I told you to call and ask for backup at Cleveland's Bait Shop. I...I don't know if I'd mention the frogs on the radio. Just in case."

"All right."

I hesitated. "And it might help if you say that you're calling on behalf of the Red Falcon."

Staci blinked. "The Red Falcon?"

"Uh, yeah. Sort of a code name."

She raised an eyebrow and smirked. "Should I say something about the dog barking at midnight, too? Or is that reserved for 007?"

"Ha, ha. Very funny." Under better circumstances, I might have made some quip about how I'd pick her over any Bond girl, but this wasn't the time. "But hurry!"

We ran in opposite directions. The last of the creatures was still in sight, but it had a sizable lead on me. It had to pause frequently, maybe because of its mass, but it made up for it by covering more ground with every leap than I could in several strides. Running barefoot on uneven ground with rocks and sticks didn't help, but I pressed on. Those things had to be stopped. Any foot injury that wasn't a sprain or a break could be dealt with later.

God, please help me, I prayed. *I don't even know what I'm going to do, but I know I'm going to need Your help.*

The bait shop was in sight now, but nothing looked too unusual at first. It was just sitting there, just as it had been for as long as I could remember. Having never been a hotbed of activity, the emptiness of the parking lot was nothing new. Almost, deceptively normal…

…Until I heard the sound of breaking glass. From this angle, I couldn't see anything, but I also couldn't see the big glass storefront windows. No doubt that was how they entered…

I tripped over something and wiped out, landing face first in the dirt. The impact knocked the Glock out of my grasp. Next, the familiar sensation of sticky film combined with a vise-like grip came back, only this time the tongue was wrapped around my ankles. Once again, I was astounded at the cunning of these monsters. Lying in wait, setting traps…I had definitely underestimated my foes, a potentially fatal error.

Quickly I flipped over to get a better look. The creature was maybe ten feet away from me and pulling me in, like a fisherman reeling in his catch. Frantically I pawed around, trying to find my weapon, praying…

There it was! I scooped it up and pointed it at the creature, not taking time to aim before squeezing the trigger. The bullet went into the creature's mouth. Rolling quickly, I was just barely able to avoid being pinned down when its carcass collapsed with a thud. In death the grip of the tongue went slack, and I kicked my way free.

Scrambling back to my feet, I continued toward the bait shop, far more cautiously this time. Mutated monsters presented a scary enough proposition without this added dimension of cunning on their part. Not just cunning, but intention. Clearly the bait shop was an important objective for them, important enough to try any means necessary to keep anyone from stopping them. What else were they capable of?

Anything. They were capable of anything, as far as I was concerned, and I knew that I had better be ready for it.

What if they had ambushed Staci as well? The thought chilled me to the bone. We had no way of knowing how many of those creatures there were, no assurance that the ones we had seen emerge from the lake were the only ones we had to worry about. If those bait pellets really had caused the mutations, there was no telling how many others might have been affected. Worse, I had the Glock with me, leaving her unarmed. It made sense at the time for me to carry it, but now I hated myself for it. Fear for her safety threatened to ruin my concentration, but putting that fear aside was nearly impossible.

By now I was close enough to the bait shop to circle around and see the front. As expected, one of the storefront windows had been shattered. The other window exploded before my eyes as something struck it from within, spewing shards of glass outward. My adrenalin kicked in, and in the blink of an eye I was charging the door with my Glock up and ready to take on whatever I might face inside the store.

My senses heightened, I heard the loud croaking noises inside the bait shop, far louder than they should have been—as if they were from frogs far bigger than they should have been.

Just another beautiful day in Sardis County.

I threw the door open. As soon as I entered, I felt as if I was in a black-and-white 1950s-era horror movie. Not that the world had turned gray, but there were mutated frogs running amuck inside the bait shop. All I needed now was suspenseful music playing in the background and maybe somebody like Vincent Price or Boris Karloff doing the whole mad scientist act.

Worse, some of the frogs were growing before my eyes. At first I thought it was just my imagination when one of them seemed as if it had grown longer, but then I saw another one grow about three inches. Bad to worse. I was mentally calculating how many rounds I had left in my Glock, wondering if they would be enough...

My gaze fell on the swinging door labeled EMPLOYEES ONLY. It had been knocked off its hinges, no doubt by some oversized intruder. Hustling through the opening, I almost tripped over a frog that happened to jump right under my feet. The frog kept going, like it was too focused on something else to pay me much attention, a far cry from how it had behaved back at the lake. Why the sudden change?

Gary Cleveland was slumped against the wall. He was still alive, but just barely. He had been beaten mercilessly. The fact that he wasn't dead was a miracle. Worse, his hands were tied behind his back.

"Mr. Cleveland! Can you hear me?"

He looked up at me, groggily at first. Suddenly Cleveland's eyes widened in silent terror. I spun around just in time to see Huey charging at me with a sledgehammer. He swung, I dodged, and I don't know how he missed me other than by the grace of God. I swept his leg with mine, knocking him off balance long enough for me to hustle Cleveland out of harm's way.

Huey recovered far more quickly than I would have liked. "Idiot! I nearly got rid of Cleveland, and now here you are! You're ruining everything! Don't you see that?"

I had my Glock trained on him, but my head was on a swivel. The last thing I needed was for one of the frogs to catch me off guard. "Who are you, really? What's the meaning of this?"

The way Huey glared at me, I knew my advantage in the weapons department was the only reason he wasn't trying to attack me again. "I'm from Janus Labs."

I recognized the name right away. Janus Labs had operated a research facility right outside of town, and there had been some kind of an incident there a while back. The feds had jumped in right away, telling me it was their jurisdiction and inviting me to stay out of it. My hands were tied, but I still heard rumors about all manner of experiments, some on humans.

"What business do you have out here, then?"

"More than you can imagine. There's a threat to our world…"

"Really? You don't think I noticed that?"

"No, you moron! This was supposed to be part of our defense against that! Those pellets are made with caprinium! Only they were supposed to mutate the fish, not the frogs…"

"You mean to tell me that you used us to help cause all this?" I somehow was able to keep a stern face, in spite of feeling sick to my stomach. The idea of being an unwitting accomplice in the mayhem didn't sit well with me at all.

"So what if I did?"

"What did you say was in those pellets?" The frogs were all around but not attacking. In fact, they seemed almost oblivious to us. I had a hunch as to why, and I hoped I was wrong.

"Caprinium. We've been using it for a while now, trying to build up a defensive force against the threat," Huey said. "Unfortunately, the results are rather…unpredictable. Have you heard anything about a werewolf-like creature with one maimed arm, attacking people all across the Southeast?"

"This isn't the time or place for campfire stories!" I figured he was trying to distract me, but his words struck a chord. Sardis was already a very weird place, but now I felt as if I was at the top of a roller coaster, getting ready to plunge down the first hill. Part of me was scared, part of me wanted to know more, but all of me knew that this was a point of no return.

"Very interesting case. A former member of your community, I believe. All of his victims have had rather nasty skeletons in their closets, transgressions that they tried to hide from justice. He has targeted some very bad people, and rumor has it that he has even done it for hire. But he was one of our experiments, one that went rogue on us. Started taking out his own targets instead of the threat that we intended for him to fight."

Everything he said sounded incredible, but it was obvious that he believed it. I wanted to write it all off as the ravings of a lunatic, but I had seen too much to just dismiss it out of hand. "So if they're not the threat you're talking about, then what is?"

"Something beyond…no!" Huey's eyes bulged in fear. Before I could process what I was seeing, something furry slammed into him, knocking him off his feet. It was the size of a man, but it was covered in fur and had the head of a wolf. The creature's right arm was badly maimed. All I could do at first was blink; the roller coaster was plummeting down the hill now.

"Let me go!" Huey screamed. The wolf snarled in what could have only been a negative response.

"Freeze, both of you!" I shouted, knowing right away what a pointless order that was. I was too busy trying to get a handle on the situation to realize how futile it sounded until I heard myself say it.

The werewolf turned and looked at me. For just a second, its face morphed into something less wolfen but still not quite human. "You are not to blame," he growled in a throaty voice. "But this man is guilty of far more evil than you know, hurting more people than you can count. He must pay!"

Before I could ask for an explanation, he had turned his attention back to Huey, making short work of his prey. It was all over in the blink of an eye, and then the creature was gone as quickly as he had entered, leaving me reeling until Cleveland groaned again.

It was then that I noticed the shelves full of jars like the one that Huey had sold me. Frogs were swarming underneath, trying to get to the shelves. Everything I had feared was true—the pellets were their real target, and the last thing that we needed them to get. Nightmare visions of further mutated, Godzilla-sized frogs flashed through my head. My gut instinct was to shoot as many of them as I could, but I didn't have enough ammo to take them all out. I had to come up with something else.

I grabbed Cleveland's arm and led him toward the back door, the nearest escape route. He wasn't dead weight, not exactly, but he wasn't able to help me much either. I thought about the possibility of him going into shock. Perfectly understandable under the circumstances, but we needed to get out of the building before I could help him.

The backroom was like a living maze, an obstacle course that kept shifting with the movements of the mutated frogs. Apparently they were too focused on the pellets to attack us, at least for the moment. With Cleveland in tow, I hustled through the back door and around toward the front of the building.

"Dane!" Staci called. I looked up to see her climbing out of my truck, still in just her bathing suit. Quite a sight to behold, or at least it would have been if I didn't have life or death matters to distract me. In the distance, I heard the wail of sirens, music to my ears.

"Staci! I was afraid you were—"

"You don't get rid of me that easily, Mr. Sheriff." She grabbed Cleveland's arm and threw it over her shoulder, guiding him to safety. Despite the difference in their sizes, she managed him with surprising ease.

A loud thud came from inside the building, followed by another. "It isn't safe here, Staci! You need to get back in the—"

A loud crash interrupted me. Yet another oversized frog burst through the doorway, taking pieces of the door frame and wall with it. Staci cried out, more of a yelp than a scream.

Her hand clamped down on my arm. "How many of those things can possibly fit in a building that small?"

"Not many, and they're only going to get bigger if they get those bait pellets, so eventually they're gonna have to get out here. And we ain't having that." I looked around, surveying my options, seeing only one. Beside the front door was a rack of propane tanks. Not necessarily what I wanted to do, but I couldn't be too picky. I had to do something, especially since the frogs were partly my fault. "Mr. Cleveland, I truly hope you can forgive me for this." I pointed my Glock at the propane tanks. "Everybody get back!"

Staci gasped but wasted no time in getting clear, making good time despite having to lug the injured Cleveland with her. Once I felt sure that they were both in the clear, I squeezed the trigger. Orange flame consumed my field of vision, followed by darkness...

Next thing I knew, I was lying on my back and Staci was leaning over me, shaking me and gently slapping my cheeks. "Dane! Can you hear me? Speak to me! So help me, if you don't wake up, I'm gonna..."

I groaned. "You know, that time I was afraid you weren't gonna wake up, I kissed you."

"Yeah, well, I didn't blow up a convenience store and get myself thrown back ten feet, now did I?" She frowned at me for a second before she finally relented, planting a big one on my lips. "Glad you didn't make me a two-time widow."

"But we're not married...wait, are we? How hard did I hit my head?"

Staci smirked playfully. "No, we're not...not yet, anyhow. But maybe you weren't the only one fishing today." She leaned in and whispered into my ear, her lips just barely grazing my earlobes. "Only without the maybes."

"Did...did it work?"

"You mean my fishing, or you blowing up that grungy little store and taking all of the overgrown frogs with it?"

My head felt like I had a thunderstorm raging inside my cranium. "Let's start with the store."

"Yes, that worked. Blew everything to kingdom come, as far as I can tell."

"Any more frogs around?"

Staci looked around for a moment. "Not that I can see. I think they may have all been inside. Hopefully. I don't think I'll be eating frog legs any time soon, though."

"Yeah, hopefully." I could see emergency personnel moving this way and that, some of my deputies among them. "Where's Cleveland?"

"EMTs have him. They're probably going to give you a ride in the ambulance too, just to make sure you're okay. Where's Mr. Huey?"

I hesitated. Had I really seen what I thought I saw with the wolf? "You probably don't want to know."

Even though they were hidden behind her aviator sunglasses, I suspected that Staci's eyes had gotten big. "What do you mean? Was he inside the building?"

"Sort of. What was left of him, anyway."

She grimaced. "Yuck. You're right, I really didn't want to know that."

"As long as you remember that you're the one who asked." I thought about what Huey had said, but I didn't dare bring it up right now. Not with her already concerned about my head. Better to wait.

"Details, details."

"So I see that he's come back to the land of the living!" another voice exclaimed. I craned my neck to see a middle-aged man carrying what appeared to be a can of store-brand grape soda in his left hand. However, it was his right arm that caught my eye. It was badly maimed, just like the werewolf's had been.

"Yes, sir," Staci said, giving him her brightest smile. "Thank you so much for helping pull him away after — well, that explosion. I had my hands full with Mr. Cleveland, and…"

"Think nothing of it!" He smiled and raised an eyebrow at me. "We can't have an innocent man dying needlessly, can we?"

Before I could say anything, he turned and walked away — toward an old RV parked a hundred yards away.

"He just showed up out of nowhere," Staci said, "but thank God he did."

"Yeah, thank God." I cleared my throat. "So did the other thing work?"

"What other thing?"

I couldn't tell if she was really confused or if this was another opportunity to make me squirm. "You know, that other kind of fishing that you said you were doing?"

With fumbling fingers, Staci smoothed a lock of her hair behind her ear. She peered over her sunglasses. "I hope so, but I guess that's really up to the fish."

"I'd say you did, assuming we mean the same fish."

"Catch of the day," Staci said with a chuckle as she leaned in for us to kiss again. It didn't make the weirdness of the day go away completely, but for the moment, it helped.

The End

CHAOS GARDEN
Etta-Tamara Wilson

"Whoa, there. You can stop now, take a rest." The stout middle-aged woman seated in the driver's seat of the battered little wooden cart tugged on the reins. The pair of short, fat gray ponies skidded to a halt, their tarnished golden horseshoes digging into the white gravel leading up to the castle doors. The cart rattled and swayed, then settled with a groan. A sign that had clearly seen better days was tied to one side of the cart, the faded golden lettering spelled out "Fairy Gardeners." Lily tied the reins to a spike on the front of the cart, then dusted her hands on her pants legs and stood. "All right, everyone, off the cart and line up."

She jumped off the cart, stumbling slightly as the gravel shifted beneath her feet. She took a moment to compose herself, straightening the front of her lavender-colored overalls and tugging on the cuffs of her sleeves, and then taking the handful of steps forward to climb up onto the landing in front of the castle. The woman turned to look back at the cart and watch the knot of her companions tumble out onto the gravel. The five ladies of varying heights and sizes flailed a bit and began trying to sort themselves out, emitting a clatter not unlike a flock of mad hens. After a bit of shoving and a few choice words, they trudged over to join Lily on the steps, assembling themselves in order of their varying heights, severity of expression, and overall outfit color.

Lily looked at the lineup with a critical eye. Each lady was dressed identically in a pair of gilt-edged overalls, differentiated from each other only by the fact that each was a different shade of the rainbow. Each wore a loose white blouse with the sleeves rolled up, and a pair of boots of black rubber, considerably newer than the rest of the outfits. They had been bought before the last job, as it turned out that fairy slippers didn't really handle gardening well. They still hoped to find Rose's other slipper someday.

The women as a group were shorter than the average human, the tallest almost four foot tall, and each bore a set of rounded wings, the shape most closely akin to a bee. They sparkled silver in the sun, fluttering whenever a woman fidgeted. Several held gold-colored gardening tools. The tools were more functional than they looked, not that many people knew, as the group didn't get much repeat business. They hadn't had much luck lately, and business had been slow. After all, who looked at a bunch of fairies and thought "Fairy Gardener"?

Lily raised a hand to pat her hair, absently smoothing any stray silver strands back toward the loose bun on top of her head. They needed this job to go smoothly; they didn't have many chances left. She sighed and pulled a folded piece of paper from her front pocket, double-checking the inside for the name and address. Clutching it in her left hand, she reached out with her right and tugged on the rope dangling from a small bell mounted next to the front door. The bell swung madly and Lily fought the instinct to clap her hands over her ears at the loud *bong*. A few moments of silence followed, then a quiet click, and a tiny grated window opened at eye height. Lily could barely see an eye in the gloom behind the door.

"Hi! Can we speak to the mistress of the house, please? We are your new garden attendants."

"Just a moment," a timid voice squeaked. The window slammed shut and footsteps could be heard scrambling away from the door on the other side. Lily blinked at the closed portal and sighed. Why were the nice castles always filled with eccentrics? She hoped the people in this castle didn't have any peculiar habits or questions. Managing her fellow fairies was like herding a bunch of cats on their best days. Fairies were notoriously sensitive, and all they would need was one wrong question or an ill-timed giggle, and suddenly she could be dealing with a homeowner-turned-frog by an offended fey.

Lily was contemplating the last time that had happened when the door clicked again. This time, it opened and a young brunette in a slightly wrinkled pink dress stepped through. She clutched a note in one hand and rubbed at one eye with the other. "How can I help you, ladies?" She shifted onto one foot and yawned. Lily glanced again at her own note.

"Are you Mrs Poitou?"

The young lady shook her head. "She's not home at the moment. I'm her daughter, Jenny. Mother said you'd be by, and she left a message for you." She handed Lily the note. "It appears to be instructions. Do you need anything else?" The fairy skimmed the note, then shook her head. "All right then. If you need anything further, please alert a maid. I'll be inside."

Jenny turned and stepped back through the door, leaving the fairies to cluster around the note and discuss their plan of attack.

"We have our instructions, ladies." Lily held up the page of gardening directions. "Nothing huge, it seems—just maintenance of the ponds, weed the flowerbeds, trim the grass, that sort of thing. Shouldn't take too long or be too difficult, as long as we keep our heads and work together." She looked over the line of fairies for a moment, mentally sorting them into the best positions for their skill sets. Several fairies with the right skill sets didn't work well together, but it couldn't be helped. Everyone would just have to wear their big girl overalls and get along.

Lily folded the two notes together and slid them into her pocket. "So, let's break this down into the best spots for everyone. When you're done with your task, put your tools back in the cart and come find me for the next task. Bluebell." She nodded at the fairy in cobalt overalls near one end of the line. "I'm going to need you to rake the leaves out from under all those trees lining the castle's outer wall. Bundle it all up, and we'll drop it in the compost pile on our way out."

Bluebell nodded and hefted the rake, slinging it over her shoulder like a rifle and barely missing her fellow fairies with the golden teeth on the business end. Lily pointed at a shorter fairy toward the other end, a bundle of white ruffle and bright yellow cotton that resembled a storm-blown goldfinch, who was clutching a rake much larger than she was.

"Buttercup, I need you to put that rake back in the cart and fetch the trowel. I spotted several weeds in the flower beds as we pulled up to the front door. I need you to go get those and be careful not to disturb the flowers." Buttercup visibly deflated, but she nodded, ready to fulfill her duty.

Lily turned to the other three and fixed her gaze on the fairy next to Buttercup, dressed in bright orange overalls. Her hair was deep auburn and pulled high up on her head in a sort of loose high ponytail. She held a golden scythe and smiled pleasantly at Lily, waiting patiently for her assignment.

"Daisy, I need you to start trimming the patch of clover near the gate. It's getting a little high." Lily waited for Daisy to nod in confirmation, before turning to the final pair of fairies. They had their backs to each other and their arms were crossed. *Well, this is starting out swimmingly.* Lily sighed. "Rose, Thistle, I need you two to put aside your differences for now and work together. According to the notes, there's a large garden pond in the next section over, and you're both going to need to work on it if we're going to finish on time."

The brunette just tightened her arms, a sour look on her face. The streaks of purple and yellow in her hair clashed with her bright green overalls. The other, a rosy-cheeked blonde in blush-colored clothing, just sighed and nodded.

"Thank you, Rose. Thistle, what about you?" The brunette rolled her eyes and nodded. Lily smiled. "Excellent. Now grab some rakes and go clean the pond. As for the rest of you, you're released to your duties."

Lily watched the fairies swarm the cart for a moment, then disperse in multiple directions. Well, that was easier than she had feared. *Maybe today actually will be a good day. We'll just have to wait and see.* In the meantime, she had an appointment with the bushes under the front castle windows. She grabbed the clippers from the cart along the way, slinging them over her shoulder and whistling a merry tune as she walked briskly toward the bushes.

~~~~~

Lily shouldn't have gotten her hopes up. She's gotten less than a third of the way through the bushes before disaster hit. The shouting got her attention first, but the bright white flash really got her moving. She dropped the clippers and crossed the gardens as fast as she could, practically flying past the clover-covered Daisy and glimpsing the homeowner stumbling out of the front door in search of the racket. Lily got to them first.

The garden looked the same for the most part, with very little damage aside from the water feature in the center. Who knew a twenty-foot garden pond could freeze solid in mid-summer? The two fairies she had sent to clean the pond were standing nearby, their golden rakes abandoned on the ground. Thistle had her arms crossed again and was trying to set Rose on fire with her eyes. Rose had her hands clasped in front of her and was staring at the ground. Lily skidded to a halt next to Rose and doubled over, trying to catch her breath.

"What happened? What was that flash?" Lily wheezed. "And who's that?!" She pointed at a lady standing next to the pond, staring at it in a forlorn manner.

The lady looked quite young, although the dark circles under her moss-colored eyes and the greenish tint to her tangled blonde hair did her no favors. She sighed deeply, causing the iridescent sheen on her dark green dress to crack and begin flaking off. The fragments of ice shattered when they hit the ground, the remnants adding momentary sparkles to her still frozen hemline.

Rose sighed. "She crawled out of the pond."

Great, a water spirit. Well, this just keeps getting better and better. Lily held up a finger. "Let me talk to her. I'll be back to get your side in a moment." She glared at both fairies and trudged over to the lady in green, reaching her just as Jenny did.

"Good morning," Jenny smiled at the water spirit. "Forgive me, I've been away. What was your name again? Martha? Maria?"

"Maya"

"Ah yes, Maya. It's good to see you. Are you okay? What happened?"

Maya sighed and rubbed under one eye. "I was asleep, and out of nowhere, there was shouting. I thought somebody was going to fall in again, so I surfaced."

"Makes sense." Jenny nodded. "Several of my nieces and nephews fell into the pond or out of the trees last summer and hurt themselves, so Mother has asked all of the nature spirits on the grounds to keep an eye out."

Lily tilted her head. "Sensible, I suppose, but isn't it dangerous to get too close to most water spirits?"

"Only the wrong ones, and that's mainly only a danger if you touch the wrong thing or dance or sing. Basically, if you're boring or wear iron, they just make handy lifeguards."

"I'll have to take your word for it."

The rapidly drying water spirit gave them all a momentary side-eye. "Anyway... When I surfaced, the pink one started shrieking and flailing her arms. She was holding onto a stick of some sort, and it suddenly let off this white light, and it hit the pond. The water started to get really cold, really fast. I just barely got out of the pond before it froze. I'd have been stuck if I moved any slower." She crossed her arms, a petulant expression crossing her face. "I was having such a nice nap, too," she muttered.

Jenny nodded and patted the naiad lightly on the shoulder. "I sympathize."

Lily sighed and nodded solemnly in Maya's direction. "My apologies, Miss, this wasn't supposed to happen. I'll address it now, we'll get it all fixed up, and everything will be fine." She spun on her heel, leaving the partially frozen naiad and the wreck of a garden behind. As she approached Rose and Thistle, storm clouds rolled in behind her. "How many times do I have to remind you two to get along and be careful while doing your work? Enchantments are dangerous! You need to be even-tempered and focused while casting or bad things happen!" She waved a hand at the pond. "You're both lucky it was just this pond. It could have been so much worse. Bad enough that you've disturbed a nature spirit. You could have actually hurt someone. Do you want me to start leaving you two at home?"

Thistle just glowered. Rose paled and shook her head. "No, of course not. We'll get along, Lily. We just had a... uh..." She side-eyed the other woman. "...a small disagreement. We'll get along."

The green fairy huffed.

Lily raised an eyebrow. "A disagreement? Must have been quite a row for you to lose control and freeze the entire pond. What was it about?"

The pink-clad fairy blushed and looked at the ground again. Her wings pulled in tight behind her back, like they wanted to hide behind her. "It was about which plants would look best in the pond. Thistle has very strong opinions about it."

The green fairy uncrossed her arms, bracing them on her hips. "Everyone knows water lilies work best with garden ponds. Rose wants to use irises. I just pointed out that she had inferior tastes. We might have gotten a bit... loud. No one warned us that the pond was occupied." She jerked her hand, sharply gesturing at the moping water sprite near the pond. "Next thing I know, that woman pops out of the water. Rose got startled, overreacted, and froze the pond." She glared at the shorter blushing fairy, then recrossed her arms and looked away, facing the castle instead. Her wings flared. "Not my fault Rose's too sensitive. Shouldn't let a klutz do gardening work."

Rose raised her head, brow furrowed, and glared back at Thistle. Her jaw dropped, but before she could voice her rebuttal, Lily waved her hand.

"Enough. You two will start to get along, or you will be left behind on the next job. Now, you will apologize to the water spirit, fix this pond immediately, and then you will go to opposite sides of the gardens and work far away from each other the rest of the day. Do you understand me?" The two fairies sighed and nodded, Rose looking repentant, wings drooping, while Thistle just looked disgusted. "Get to it."

Lily watched the two feuding fairies walk back toward the ice-covered water spirit.

"So, it can be fixed, then?"

Lily startled. She hadn't noticed Jenny drawing so close to her side. She looked at the homeowner for a moment, her wings fluttering in agitation, then crossed her arms and looked back at her team. Their wings were folded down in a repentant position and they were saying something to the naiad, who nodded slowly, her expression still somewhat stormy.

Lily nodded. "Yes. It's a simple matter. Shouldn't take them long, once they stop squabbling."

They watched as Rose stepped away from the small group and walked to the opposite side of the pond. She reached into the pocket on the front of her outfit and pulled out a short stick. It looked to be the stem of a rose, thorns and all. At the end, where the rose would be, there was a golden tip instead. The petite fairy raised her arms above her head, stick pointed at the sky, and took a visibly deep breath. Her wings flared and she brought her arms down in a flourish, ending with the stick pointed at the pond. A faint glittering ball of light, the color of rose gold, shot from the gilded tip and took a short arching trip through the air. It landed on the ice and bounced a time or two, then sat flickering on the surface for a moment, before finally melting into the ice.

Everyone held their breath. Any minute now, the pond would unfreeze. Any time now.

Several minutes later, the pond just looked slightly damper. Rose wilted a bit, looking in dismay at her wand. Maya huffed, crossing her arms again. Thistle busted out laughing. Rose raised her wand above her head again, an expression of concentration on her face, before throwing another weak flickering ball of sparkles at the pond. The pond greeted the new round of magic with the same icy indifference as before. Lily sighed and turned to look at Jenny.

"It might take a bit longer than anticipated."

Jenny waved a hand at the pond. "Whatever. I'm good, as long as it's fixed by the time you head out. I'm going back inside."

Lily nodded. Jenny headed for the doors to the castle.

~~~~~

After several rounds of trying to defrost the pond with minimal success, Lily decided to go about her day and check in later. After all, a watched cauldron never boils. She decided to go back to the bushes and clear up what was left of them. Maybe by the time she was done, the pond would look a little bit more liquid, and less like a dropped snow cone.

Lily rounded the edge of the castle but didn't quite make it to the bushes. As she passed the gate, she noticed Daisy standing a few feet from them. She was talking to someone on the other side. Lily veered sharply from her path, bee-lining it to the gate.

"Is something the matter?"

The orange-clad fairy turned toward her. The scythe Daisy had been using was now leaning against the wall nearby, and small bits of greenery clung to the tangled ends of her hair. It gave her a vague resemblance to an enormous carrot. "I was trying to tell this man that he'd have to come back another time, but I'm not sure he understands me." She waved a hand at the figure beyond the gate.

On the other side of the gate, a man stood at attention. He was human, but clearly foreign, and she didn't recognize his uniform. His close-cut hair was dark in color, not the light brown or blonde of humans from the area. Lily raised an eyebrow.

"Hello, sir. How can I help you?"

The man bowed deeply at the waist, making a grand flourish with his right arm, the left pulled behind his back. He straightened and smiled. "Greetings, mistress." His voice was a warm tenor with a definite accent, and he rolled his r's. "Are you the lady of the house?"

Lily snorted. "Definitely not. I'm staff, at best. If you had an appointment, I can alert the family."

The man shook his head. "Alas, no, mistress. I have no appointment. My name is Azzo Bello Buonamico Malatesta of San Finto, and I was on a mission for my prince when I saw this beautiful castle in the distance and just knew I had to see it up close."

Wait... where was San Finto? And it had a prince? She'd never heard of any monarchy with that name, and most of the lands that had changed their names recently were remade as republics now.

"You work for who now?"

"Prince Rambaldo of San Finto. Long may he reign."

Still not ringing a bell. Lily tilted her head, considering the visitor. She must have missed a country renaming itself. It happened so often sometimes, it wouldn't be a surprise.

"Well, if you would like to talk to the family, I can see if one is available. But without an appointment, you might have better luck another day."

He sighed. "That's a shame. My mission will likely take me out of the area in a day or two, if I can't make some headway soon. I won't be able to come back."

Lily raised an eyebrow. "What is your mission, if I may ask?"

Malatesta perked up considerably. "I'm in the process of raising funds from patriots and true friends of San Finto, in order to get us all home in a timely manner. After all, we have to get back, before the committee does anything rash. Proper governance needs good aristocratic guidance, after all."

"You need money to get home?"

He blushed. "We had enough when we went on the diplomatic tour, but when the government was mangled back home, they froze everything being sent out from the treasury to us. Until we get back and fix the mess, we're stuck relying on the kindness of friends." He looked at Lily with large, sad eyes. "We intend to pay everyone back twice over, of course, but it might be a while."

Yeah, and Lily was the queen of the fairies. She doubted he was anything more than a beggar, but there had been a lot of upheaval lately, and it was not like Lily was an expert on human political matters. She mused on the problem for a moment. It might not be very smart to encourage him, but maybe if she gave him a token sum, it would at least get him away from the gates for the rest of the day. Luckily, she always kept a little coin for emergencies.

Lily dug her hand into one of the pockets of her overalls and retrieved a small bag of silver coins. Daisy turned as Lily pulled it out, her eyes widening at the sight of the bag.

"Are you sure about this, Lily? He looks a bit... shifty... to me."

"I'm sure." Lily stuck her arm through the bars of the gate, the small bag of silver coins sitting squarely in her palm. "Hopefully, this helps you on your way. Please be sure to make an appointment the next time you're in the area and wish to see the castle."

Malatesta smiled brightly and reached out, snagging the bag with a flourish. He tucked it into his jacket and then bowed. "You have my gratitude, mistress. My prince and I will be sure to add the castle to our list of trusted friends." He straightened and smoothed the wrinkles out of his uniform. "I must be on my way. There is much to do, after all. But you have my thanks, and hopefully, I'll see you again soon." He nodded his head, grinned merrily at the two women, and turned. He set off down the lane at a fast pace, whistling a merry tune as he went.

Daisy shook her head as they watched him go. "That was a mistake. You feed a stray, it never stops coming around."

Lily shrugged. "Maybe. But it wouldn't do to accidentally offend somebody important, and he could have been that. And if not, at least now he's gone. It's not our problem anymore."

Daisy raised an eyebrow at her, then reached over and retrieved her scythe. "That was a scam artist, not a real aristocrat. If he works for any nobility, I'll cut the rest of the lawn on my hands and knees with a pair of sewing scissors." She shook her head and walked over to the nearest patch of uncut clover, swinging the scythe backward to start back to work.

Lily watched her for a moment, and then shrugged. Time to get to work herself. She turned and began the long walk back over to the bushes.

~~~~~

Lily was only three bushes from the end when she heard the shouting from the other side of the garden. Once more, she passed Jenny coming out the front door and raced around the castle to find Thistle and Rose standing on either side of the pond, pointing wands at each other and shouting. Thistle's wand was a long, straight pale green stick that ended in a burst of spiky green leaves and a small flower. The flower center was made of gold, but the outer three rings of spiky petals were a deep amethyst. The frozen pond had devolved into a deep puddle of slush, and it appeared the two fairies had turned their attention to trying to roast each other. Maya had taken shelter behind a short wall a dozen feet from the feuding pair, with only her wide eyes and the top of her head visible.

Lily stormed up to the edges of the semi-frozen pond and crossed her arms. "What is going on out here?!" Unfortunately, everyone ignored her.

Rose's face by this time was nearly the same shade as her clothing, and she pointed her wand at the other fairy and thrashed it about. "Scorch!" A much more vigorous ball of sparkles burst from the end of her wand and flew with a whistle toward Thistle, who dodged the ball. The bush behind her promptly began to shrivel, emitting a weak trail of smoke from the point of impact.

Thistle had several marks on her outfit that implied she hadn't managed to dodge everything, and she was not in the best of moods. She jerked her wand in a hard upward direction with a wordless snarl, and a green beam of light shot from the flower on her wand. It struck a tree a few feet to the right of Rose, and sheared a branch clean off. A loud squeak sounded behind Lily, and she turned her head to see Jenny dodge behind the wall, seeking shelter next to Maya.

Rose snarled and pushed up her sleeves. She pointed her wand at the taller fairy. "You want to be a jerk? Fine. Let's see how you manage this!" She waggled her wand in the air and backed up a step. "Transmutare in asinum... Ah!" She stumbled on the branch that had fallen behind her. Rose toppled over, the glittering ball of intent that burst from her wand soaring backward in a tall arc.

It fell squarely on the top of Jenny's head. She promptly vanished in a bright flash of sparkles.

Maya had plastered herself to the base of the short wall. She stared at something near her feet with wide eyes. Lily approached the wall, hoping with all her might that Rose hadn't melted the homeowner. She peered over the side and was greeted by a large pair of stunned dark eyes, currently in the face of an undersized donkey with a rather startling mottled pattern of rose and brown fur and golden hooves. Rose had transmuted the homeowner. Lily straightened and turned her head, staring at the wide-eyed faces of Rose and Thistle, who appear to have set aside their feud in favor of staring in horror at Jenny.

Thistle turned her head and looked at Rose. "Well, we're in trouble."

"No kidding."

"HeeHaw!"

~~~~~

"You morons are why we have such a high insurance rate. You know that, right?" Lily was beside herself. Not literally, of course, although with this group, it wouldn't be a surprise if that ended up happening by the end of the day. Lily's wings vibrated from suppressed frustration. She glared at the pink and green fairies, while Daisy and the others clustered nearby, staring at the new donkey in dismay.

"How are we supposed to explain this to the client?! 'We're sorry, miss, but we accidentally turned your kid into a barnyard animal.' Not to mention the frozen pond. We'll never get work again." She threw her hands above her head and began to pace. "We needed this job. It's not like there are a lot of positions available for fairy-based gardening services, not with the nymphs cornering the landscaping market." She threw a glance at Maya, who was sitting next to Jenny. Maya didn't notice, she was too busy staring at the transformed girl in apparent fascination. "After the mess you made at the garden for the Queen of Hearts, we're lucky we still *have* a business. And now this!" She stopped and tugged at her hair. "How am I supposed to fix this?"

Bluebell clutched her rake tightly in one white-knuckled hand and hesitantly stepped forward, raising her other hand into the air.

Lily nodded at her. "You have a suggestion?"

"We could always just call Hyssop. She'd know what to do."

Lily paled. "I'd like to try to salvage the situation first, before we call in the big guns. I'm not keen to get us all benched for the rest of the year, okay?"

Bluebell nodded, shaking, and withdrew back behind Daisy.

Maya leaned over the transformed homeowner. "You're naked." She poked a finger into Jenny's side, digging the tip into her short mottled fur. "Where did your clothes go? Are they still there underneath?" She began running her fingers around Jenny's sides and back, looking for the missing fabric. Jenny just huffed and bared her teeth at the nymph. Getting bitten by a donkey looked like a definite possibility soon.

"Ah! I know!" Buttercup bounced and flailed her arms for attention. In the process, she flung dirt all over the group and lost her grip on the golden trowel she had been holding, hurling the tool into a nearby flower bed. She didn't seem to notice. "We can try to reverse it by hitting her with a competing enchantment. Maybe trying to turn an animal into a human would work, cancel it out?"

"Yes, because more fairy magic would make a magic misfire problem better." Lily sighed, rubbing her forehead. "Maybe we should just avoid using powers in the future, just to be safe. It doesn't seem like our safest option. Or we should get out of gardening altogether." She raised her head and looked at Jenny in contemplation for a moment, then reached into her front pocket and pulled out a greenish-brown stick. It was smooth and straight, about the length of her arm, and was topped with a golden flower. The flower had six large petals that curled backward toward the stem, and a trio of silver threads projected from the middle, from which glowing oval-shaped crystals dangled. "Well, I guess we have to try. Stand back."

The fairies dutifully took big steps back to give her space to work. Lily pointed her wand at Jenny. Maya looked up at the noise, made a startled sound, and scrambled backward a few feet at the sight of another wand pointed in her direction. Jenny's eyes went wide and she attempted to scurry away, stumbling over unfamiliar hooves.

"Therianthropy!"

With a bright white flash, Jenny promptly tripped and collapsed in a heap. Her hooves were tangled in a pile of cloth.

Lily dropped her wand and clapped her hands over her face. "I should have listened to my mother and learned accounting. I wonder if it's too late to go work for the dwarves?" She sighed and pulled her hands down, staring in dismay at the now mostly bald donkey tightly bound in a wrinkled pink cotton dress. Jenny squirmed within the cocoon of constricting material, accidentally turning onto her back and kicking her hooves in the air.

Bluebell and Daisy hurried over to try to pull Jenny back onto her feet and free her from her bindings, while Lily stood there muttering and staring at her wand. Maya sat a few feet away, wide-eyed, her hands clasped over her mouth for a moment.

She dropped them, and a laugh bubbled from her. "Well, at least you're not naked anymore."

A bell attached to the wall of the castle lurched to the left with a loud clang, startling a squeal from the collection of fairies and a huff from the irritated enchanted girl. Maya jumped and slapped her hands back over her face. Lily sighed. Someone was at the gate. Perfect timing. Maybe it was someone here to turn Jenny a different color, or accidentally banish the fairies to the middle of the desert.

Buttercup dashed toward the gate. "I'll get it!"

Lily crossed her arms and turned back toward Jenny, watching as Bluebell and Daisy struggled to free the donkey from the tangled fabric prison. Maya reached forward to help as well. Help, by her definition, apparently involved a remarkable amount of half-hearted tugging at the dress and poking at the progressively more irritated donkey. They'd only managed to make it twice as bad when a low whistle sounded.

"Wow. That's some pickle you're in." A man stood in the entrance to that section of the garden holding a large wrapped bundle in one arm. The golden fairy bounced excitedly next to him, her messy bun of ash-brown hair wobbling dangerously as she moved. Lily glared at her.

"Really, Buttercup? An emergency, and you let a stranger in?"

Buttercup wilted a bit. The man patted her on the shoulder with his free hand, then turned to Lily. "Hello, I'm Robert Prince, a tailor at Fairy Tale Alterations. I'm making a delivery." He waited, evidently expecting a response. Seven blank stares, and one upside down glare, met him instead.

"Really? Nothing? Our flyers are everywhere. 'Fairy Tale Alterations - Clothing fit for a Queen, without the Princely sum'? Doesn't ring a bell?"

He waved a hand. "Never mind. The point is, I've just come from work to drop off a finished project, and I know my way around a good dress alteration. I'd be happy to help with your donkey situation."

Lily crossed her arms. "And why would you do that? What would a tailor know about donkeys, even dressed ones? We can't even pay you."

Prince swung the package in his arm toward Buttercup, who had taken to picking the petals off a flower. It hit her with a loud *whumpf* from the package and a startled squeak from her. "I may not know donkeys, but I know dresses. I'd be happy to get the dress off the poor thing or fitting it better, whatever floats your boat. Just as long as you let me stay here. My boss is a real ogre; I need a good long break." He grinned.

Great. That was all Lily needed. Another lazy and accident-prone garden ornament, taking up space and having to be worked around. She opened her mouth, already thinking about the nicest possible wording to send him on his way.

"You can stay." Eight heads swiveled toward the water spirit. She had abandoned her attempts to prod Jenny to distraction and was now leaning toward the newcomer. Her cheeks had turned a bright pink and she stared at him with wide eyes, while absently running her hands down her thawing dress and over the melting frost. Prince smiled.

"Why, thank you, miss. I'm most grateful. This place looks nice and peaceful." He looks over at Jenny. "As long as you aren't a donkey, anyway."

The upside-down donkey bared her teeth at the man. He chuckled. "Calm down, Mistress Donkey. It never pays to fight them when they decide to play dress-up. Be good and I'll give you a nice apple." He ignored the few disgruntled protests from the fairies as he bent down and examined the material. "So, is it take off or fix up?"

"She wasn't supposed to be wearing a dress in the first place," Lily huffed. "She was supposed to turn back into a human being. I don't know if altering the dress would mess something up. I'll have to call someone to find out."

"Ah. Yeah, you might want to get on that. In the meantime..." He turned back to Jenny and reached into his pocket, pulling a spool of ribbon from it.

Jenny got a few frustrated bites in, but in relatively short order, she was back to standing on her four hooves. The dress was trussed up around her flanks in swags, held up by loops of ribbons tied to the waistband. The sleeves were likewise tied up to get them off her hooves. She looked ridiculous.

Lily took a good look around at the group. Maya looked delighted, reaching forward to begin playing with the loose end of a ribbon. The other fairies, as was their tendency, took on a range of facial expressions from appalled to entertained. Prince had a vaguely amused expression.

"There you go. Now you have time to call for help." Prince swayed backward a few feet, attempting to avoid the bite of the now very irritated donkey. Maya immediately abandoned the ribbon she was tugging on and scrambled to his side. Prince raised an eyebrow and smiled at the young lady. "Hello, Miss."

The sprite just stared at him. "You're pretty." She reached out and ran her hands over his chest, examining the tunic he was wearing and poking at his torso. The cloth dampened slightly in spots as she did so, since she wasn't quite dry yet. "You look fun. Can you dance?"

"I can manage, with enough help. Why?"

The water spirit lunged for him, wrapping her arms around his torso. The startled man looked down at her. "Ah! Wet!" He tried to remove her, his hands on her shoulders, but the naiad was much stronger than she looked. She locked her arms around his waist, closed her eyes, and began to rock back and forth, humming a tune that Lily recognized as popular on the dance floor about a century ago.

Prince gave up trying to detach the maiden-shaped shackle around his waist and looked at the others. "So, I guess it's time to dance?" Far above the group, the bell rang again. "Expecting someone else?"

117

"We weren't even expecting you. Buttercup, stop!"

Too late. The sunny little fairy was already gone, dropping the package she held and scurrying back to the gate.

Lily sighed and turned to Bluebell. "We've run out of options. We need help. We're going to have to get Hyssop."

Bluebell nodded and dropped her rake. She reached into her pocket and pulled out a small box, which she opened to retrieve a small piece of paper and a pencil. She handed them to Lily, who sighed and wrote a quick message, pausing for a moment to double-check it for errors. She was folding the note as Buttercup came around the bend, Malatesta in tow. The man was disheveled and limping.

"Mistress Faye, I'm afraid I was accosted by thieves on the way back. They took your generous donation. Is it possible that I could get anoth..." The man stopped dead in his tracks. "Oh, damn."

Prince glared. "Daniel. You didn't get enough of the punishment the last time you got caught at this?"

"I don't know what you mean."

"Drop the scam, Dan. Or you'll end up with far more than just two weeks in the local cells."

"What, you'll tell on me?" Amazingly, the man's accent had disappeared. "You always were a self-righteous sort. What are you doing here in the middle of the day? Don't you have work, or were you finally fired?" He eyed the water spirit, still wrapped around Prince's torso and doing her level best to push him into a dance step. "Are you here for other reasons?"

Prince glowered at him. "Get lost. Or I'll sic the guard on you."

Daniel huffed at him and stormed back toward the gate. His limp had vanished as well. Lily handed the completed note to Bluebell and walked to the entrance of the garden, to make sure the charlatan left the castle grounds.

Bluebell rolled up the paper into a tiny scroll and slid it into a small golden tube. With the note prepared, she blew the whistle hanging around her neck. A very large blue jay landed on the wall and stuck out a leg. Bluebell carefully secured the tube, fed the bird a treat, then gently tossed it into the sky. They watched as it spread its wings and quickly vanished. Lily turned toward the rest of the fairies.

"Okay, so while we wait for instruction, we'll have to go about our work. Buttercup, stay away from the gate. No more visitors. Work on the flowerbeds. Thistle, help her at it. And no more fighting, or you'll be a donkey next."

Buttercup wilted again. Thistle just sulked.

"Daisy, please finish the lawn." Daisy saluted, turned on her heel, and marched back toward where she'd left her scythe. "Bluebell, can you trim that tree, maybe make the damage look not so bad?" She pointed at the tree Thistle had winged.

Bluebell nodded. "I'll try my best."

"Excellent. You." She raised her eyebrow at the tailor. "Just stay there, and don't move." Prince raised an eyebrow. Lily sighed. "Okay, fine, you can move. Just rock back and forth and stay out of the way."

Prince nodded. "I'll try my best." He waved a hand at the fairy, then clasped both his hands together behind the water spirit and began trying to slowly revolve in place. Lily shook her head and turned toward the donkey.

"I'm sorry, mistress. I've sent for an expert, we should have this fixed shortly. Until then, try to relax, and don't move." Jenny snorted at her, but flopped over and went still. Lily nodded. She turned toward the last fairy, who was trying her level best to be invisible.

"Rose, you and I will work on the rose bushes. You like those, and they don't require magic. Only a good pair of clippers. Not even you can hurt the rose bushes."

~~~~~

Luckily, they managed to stop the out-of-control vines that erupted from the newly enchanted rose bushes before they overran the castle. Lily supposed surrounding the entire castle grounds in a massive tangle of vines covered in thorns and roses did fix the security issue. It wasn't very helpful for her blood pressure, though.

"All right, new plan. You, Rose, will go sit and watch the gate. Don't actually touch anything. Just watch the gate. Yell if anyone arrives.

"And don't move. Ever."

~~~~~

Lily realized about the time Prince's boss showed up that she probably should have expected his description to be quite literal. But to be fair, no one would have expected an eight-foot-tall ogress to be the owner of a fancy clothing alteration business. Fine detail work wasn't exactly what ogres were known for. Who knew, though? Maybe she was an expert at needlework. It took all kinds, right?

Whether she was a secret sewing master craftsman or just really good at delegating was irrelevant at this point, however. What was relevant was that she now had a very tall angry lady standing in the middle of the gardens, yelling at everyone about "poaching" her employee.

"I didn't quit to work for them. I'm just helping them out with a sewing-related problem that cropped up during the delivery." Prince waved at Jenny, still lying down and surrounded by yards of tied-up fabric. "It's called 'customer service.' You always complain that we need to treat the customers well, get them coming back, don't you? So, what is the problem?"

The ogress glared at him. "How is swanning around all day with some girl, staring at a donkey you stuffed into a dress, good customer service? You need to be working in my shop if it's the work day, not hanging out with your friends on someone else's estate."

The donkey in question bared her teeth at the ogress. The ogress, covered in scratches from the thorns on the vines, snarled back at her in return. Somebody was going to bite somebody; it was just a matter of time.

"Wait, what?" Prince settled his hands on his hips. He stretched himself onto his tiptoes, attempting to match his boss in height. This was disagreeable to the naiad, who had been startled into letting go by the ogress crashing in and was now standing behind the tailor. She was again quite red, although now it was from indignation. Any madder and she might start to visibly steam. "I wasn't responsible for the donkey. I don't even know them. And this is their estate, not an empty one. Who told you all the lies?"

"An acquaintance of yours from town. He came into the shop, told me where you were, and why. He even came with me." She waved behind herself for the man to come forward. When he didn't speak, she turned to look at the empty space behind her. Her expression shifted into a look of surprise. "Wha... where did he go?"

Prince raised an eyebrow. "Let me guess. Young, tall, handsome, nice accent, fancy uniform?" The ogress nodded. "Damn it, Dan."

Rose didn't handle the appearance of the ogress very well. She'd fled when the bellowing woman had stormed through the thorns and the gate and now hid in the bushes in the back half of the garden. She was slowly inching from cover to cover, trying to keep as much distance as possible between her and the ogress. Unfortunately for her, she came the closest to Jenny of anyone. The donkey promptly stretched out her neck and took a big nip out of the fairy, who jumped a foot in the air and shrieked.

The round pink fairy landed, flailing her arms. She had her wand out, and her rotten luck continued. Landing on her back, she let out a wordless grunt from the impact and a weak ball of sparkles shot out of the end of her wand and along the ground. They eventually skittered to a stop in the middle of the vines. The plants smoldered for a moment before catching, and fire spread quickly along the wall of thorns until the castle was surrounded by a wall of flame.

Who knew ogres were afraid of fire? New things could be learned every day.

~~~~~

Into this chaos, the answer to Lily's message finally came, descending from the sky on large silver wings, dressed in dark purple overalls. Clutching a now scorched and disheveled Daniel with one hand and a staff in the other, she was the tallest fairy of the bunch at five feet tall. She

120

had a shock of snow-white hair, pulled up into a French twist on the back of her head, but her face looked quite young. She looked around at the garden, the panicked naiad attempting to bury herself in a rapidly-melting but still slushy pond, the disgruntled and now soot-stained donkey-in-a-dress, the cluster of fairies trying to use the tailor as a shield against the fire, and the panicking ogress trying to climb the castle to escape, and sighed. She dropped the unconscious con artist onto the grass and raised her staff, pointing it at the fire.

"Superfundo"

The fire immediately shrank down, dying out in moments, leaving only smoking ashes in the shape of vines. The ogress stopped trying to scale the castle keep, choosing instead to face the wall and gulp air. The fairies awkwardly shuffled out from behind the tailor. The man promptly tugged on the hem of his now filthy tunic to straighten it, then walked over to the pond, reaching out to help the slush-covered naiad out of the half-filled hole. She was shivering and turning a rather alarming shade of teal. He began rubbing her arms vigorously in an attempt to provide warmth.

All the fairies were blackened from the smoke, but otherwise unharmed. Each had their wings down and hidden behind them, and stared at the ground. They sorted themselves according to color and waited.

"Lily..."

Lily slowly looked up at the older fairy. The older woman gave her the best *"I'm not mad, just disappointed"* look she could muster.

"You should have sent for me earlier."

Lily slouched slightly. "I'm sorry, Hyssop. I hoped we could fix it, but it just kept getting worse."

Hyssop tilted her head and looked at the other fairies. They all looked like they'd been dragged backward through a hedge and were covered in soot. Only Daisy still had her tool, clutching the scythe for dear life, clearly intending to use it as a weapon if need be. Hyssop sighed.

"We may need to consider other career options. Gardening doesn't seem to be the right fit." She smiled faintly at the fairies as they all deflated. "Come on now; it's not the end of the world. We'll find your place. But in the meantime, we need to fix things here."

She waved her staff again, pulling brooms out of thin air. She dispersed them among the fairies. "Start sweeping up, but put your wands away. We don't need further destruction." She looked pointedly at Rose, who turned as red as her namesake and started vigorously scrubbing a random clump of grass. Hyssop watched her for a moment, then turned to walk over and crouch next to the enchanted donkey-girl.

"We're truly sorry about the inconvenience, mistress. I'll have you back to rights in a moment." She rose and lifted Jenny onto her hooves, then reached into a pocket in her overalls. Out popped a pair of golden scissors, the blades the length of her hand and shining brightly, despite the dim smoke-filtered sunlight. She smiled reassuringly and began carefully cutting through the dress. Once she had the bodice cut through and the sleeves detached, she peeled it off. As the dress lifted away, the human figure of the homeowner returned. Thankfully, she was still clad in her undergarments. She blinked up at the fairies from the middle of a pile of multicolored fabric scraps. "There we are. All better now."

"Are you okay?" Lily asked. "How do you feel?"

"Like I just peeled off a bad sunburn." Jenny looked at the fairies in relief. "Thank you. It's been a terrible day."

"Wait, that's it?" Prince was staring. "That's all it took to turn a donkey into a girl? Cut off the dress?"

Hyssop nodded. "To turn a girl from a donkey back into herself, technically. And yes. But thank you for your assistance, young man."

Prince shrugged. "I didn't really do much."

"You helped. Even if it was something as simple as moral support and ribbon ties. And, thank you for not making things worse."

He eyed the fairies currently bustling around, sweeping the ash away from the garden, slowly setting it to rights. "That does seem to have been a bit of an accomplishment today."

Hyssop smiled. "It can be, some days."

The water spirit had warmed up, resuming her normal greenish coloring, and was now winding her clammy arms around the tailor's neck. She had just managed to reach the button on his collar when there was a sizzling sound, like water on hot metal, and she jerked away from the startled man. A vibrant red welt now etched a path along her arm from her hand to her elbow. She glared at the confused man. "You... you're wearing iron buttons?"

"Uh... Yes. Why, is that a problem?"

The naiad crossed her arms and turned away from the man. "You may go." She wandered over to the pile of discarded scraps and began collecting the ribbon ties, carefully tying each one onto her arms, one after the other.

Hyssop moved to the side of the deeply confused man and turned him with a hand on his elbow. "Don't worry about it, dear. It's a fey thing." She pushed him gently in the direction of his boss. "Now, I think you should help your boss to find her way home. She'll need assistance. And think of how grateful she'll be that you helped out."

"She will, will she?" He nodded. "I guess I should." He took a step, then stopped and turned, looking at Jenny. He bowed. "I'm glad to see you've recovered, miss." He smiled politely at her and walked toward the ogress. Prince let her brace her arm on his shoulder. "Come on, boss. Let's get back to the shop. We still have eleven princess dresses to finish for the ball next week. If we don't have them finished by the time the cobblers finish their slippers, we may find ourselves spending a while in the dungeon trying to spin the straw into thread."

The ogress grinned at him, momentarily displaying a set of teeth that would give a shark a moment of personal reflection. Lily immediately revised her opinion of Prince. He was either brave or crazy, she wasn't sure which. He was definitely insolent, that was certain. However, he probably wasn't lazy, not with a boss with those teeth. They strolled slowly toward the gates, the very large woman using the shorter man as a sort of walking brace as they went.

Hyssop watched them shrink in the distance for a bit, and then turned back to look at the garden. The fairies were almost finished sweeping up the ash, so Hyssop slowly walked around, trimming missed spots of grass and repairing the damage to the rose bushes and trees. After a quick rinse of the still smoldering bush that had been damaged in the duel, Hyssop finally turned to the pond that started the whole thing. It was still mostly slush, despite its momentary reclassification as a garden folly in a firetrap.

Hyssop shook her head and raised her arms. A simple wave of her staff and the pond sloshed back into form, the water back to its original liquid state. Maya squealed, wrapping the shorter woman in a tight hug. "Thank you!" She pulled back and held up her arms, both covered in loops of bedraggled ribbons. "Can I keep these?"

Hyssop smiled. "Of course, dear. Just don't let them get eaten by any wildlife."

A loud disgruntled noise to the side drew their attention. Daniel had woken up and was now sitting in a heap, facing the pond, a hand on his head. The two women approached him, Hyssop leading the way while Maya hid slightly behind her. It wasn't very effective, since Maya was a good eight inches taller than the fairy.

Hyssop attempted her best soothing smile. "Are you all right, dear?"

The scorched man coughed and pulled his hands from his face, looking down at his uniform. He made a short, twitchy attempt to swipe at one of the marks now littering the tunic, but gave up quickly and looked around. He blinked slowly in seeming confusion and turned to face the small group as the newly transmogrified homeowner joined the other two. "Where... where am I?"

"You're in the castle gardens." Hyssop waved a hand at the castle. "You seemed very intent on reaching it, so I pulled you out of the burning vines and brought you with me. I'm a bit confused why you were trying to come in around the back, though. The vines were much easier to get through at the front entrance."

"I'm where?"

"The castle gardens." Hyssop raised an eyebrow. "I assumed you knew where you were going. You were rather far into the grounds already when I found you."

Jenny crossed her arms. "The castle doesn't even have a publicly accessible back entrance. What were you doing there?"

The man paled, gaze darting between Hyssop and Jenny. Not recognizing either of them, he relaxed and his chin lifted, his lips tightening into a rather haughty expression. "I wasn't trying to do anything. I was just passing by when those monstrous vines reached out and attacked me, dragged me into the grounds." He mirrored Jenny's pose. Unfortunately for him, the move made him resemble a soot-covered overgrown toddler. "Since this family can't keep their plantings under control, I demand compensation."

Both Jenny and Maya gave out a cry of protest. Hyssop held up a hand, quieting them. She turned back to the man. "Now, sir..."

"Daniel. His name is Daniel. Prince said it."

The man turned his head and glared at Jenny. She returned the favor.

Hyssop sighed. "Now, Daniel, the homeowners aren't exactly responsible for the vines. They were a new phenomenon, created by an accident with a plant by a hired landscaper. Besides, you were much too far inside the grounds to have been pulled there from outside by anything as weak as the vines. Can we just be reasonable today?"

"Reasonable?! How dare you!" The man clambered to his feet, his hands folding tightly into fists, his face beginning to resemble a plum underneath the scorch marks. "I was minding my own business, going about on a simple stroll, and heard a commotion. I went looking to see what it was and got grabbed by a bunch of... bunch of..." He tossed his hands over his head in a sharp, jerking motion, fingers flaring out as they reached the top of the arch. "...grabby green things! And got dragged away! And now you have the nerve to call me *unreasonable*?!" He practically spit the word into Hyssop's face and began to pace in a short circle on the garden lawn, waving his arms about in an agitated manner.

"Sir, please calm down." Hyssop didn't care much about the man's reaction - he was really too deep into the castle grounds when she found him for him to be there innocently. The homeowner looked a bit disgruntled. Even that was secondary to an alarming fact: the water spirit was now watching him pace while rocking. And she was humming again. For his own safety, he needed to stop.

"Calm down!?" He skidded to a halt and faced the trio. "I've been inconvenienced, if not outright harmed by your garden-related negligence. The least you can do is take me inside, let me pick out some things to make up for it. What do I have to do to get my due, present the story with some entertainment?!" He immediately broke into an uneven, poorly stepped imitation of a quick festival dance step. "Is that good enough for you?!"

Hyssop didn't get a chance to respond. The moment the obnoxious man started twitching in a vaguely rhythmic manner, the naiad let out a sound that reminded Hyssop of a piglet on market day. She darted forward and tackled the man, who let out a squeal of his own, before winding her still ribbon-bedecked arms around his waist. She twisted on one foot, using his off-center momentum to maneuver him into an active series of dance steps. Hyssop recognized them. They were even older than the song the sprite was humming earlier.

Maya doesn't get out much, Hyssop mused.

Daniel, now covered in black streaks as the soot mixed with the water that still clung to the water spirit and smeared, attempted to pry the enthusiastic nymph away from his torso. "Trying to distract me isn't going to get you out of paying, Miss." He pushed at her a second time. "Let me go!"

The nymph pulled her head back and blinked slowly at the man, smiling sleepily. "Pay? You want treasure?" She looked down at her arms, then held one up, showing off the now-bedraggled ribbons. "Did you want some of my treasures?"

Daniel rolled his eyes. Hyssop leaned forward. "He means money, my dear. Gold, silver, coppers, gemstones, pearls... that sort of thing." She reached out and tugged on Maya's arm. "Come on, dear. Let go. You can do better." Daniel glared at Hyssop again.

"Pearls? I have pearls. At home. And there's a little pile of shiny stones in lots of pretty colors, as well."

"Do you, now?" Daniel was now all teeth. Hyssop got the unsettling impression of an alligator in fancy dress. "Where is home, exactly? Is it close?"

"Rather close, yes. Why?"

"Ah, do you live in the castle as well? Can *you* take me there?" His head tilted slowly to the right, a strange expression settling on his face. Hyssop realized after a few moments that he was attempting to adopt a mostly unsuccessful version of an innocent expression.

"I'm not supposed to take strangers home. You might take my treasures." She gripped his tunic tightly, her face conflicted. Daniel smiled broadly, reaching into the upper part of his tunic for a cloth-wrapped bundle.

"I believe I can solve that." He unfolded the cloth to reveal a decorative hair comb, with bone teeth and a wide shaft that looked like it was made of gold. A raised pattern of vines trailed along the flat side of the shaft. Every so often, a carved bone flower decorated the vine, each one bearing a tiny sparkle of an imitation dewdrop. Some sort of embedded gemstone, most likely a rock crystal, if Hyssop had to guess.

Daniel lifted the comb from its wrappings and offered it to the nymph. "Would you like this? Isn't it pretty?" He waggled it, causing the crystals to sparkle in the late afternoon light. The wide-eyed water spirit nodded and grasped the comb firmly with both hands, pulling it close to admire it. "There. Now we're friends. Surely you can take a friend home, show him all your treasure, no?"

Maya nodded and transferred the comb to one hand, reaching out to grasp his wrist with the other. Daniel smiled widely. He looked rather smug. A little detail of fairy lore from her days in school danced about in Hyssop's brain, waving all sorts of colored banners. Mostly crimson ones. She looked at Jenny, hoping her bad vibes were just left over from earlier. No such luck, as Jenny looked similarly alarmed.

"Uh, you may wish to rethink that plan..."

"I'd thank you to not interrupt my friend and me, Fairy," Daniel objected. He peered at Hyssop with narrowed eyes, one eyebrow raised in a superior manner. "Count yourself lucky that we're too busy to deal with the likes of you. Now, let's be off, my dearest..." He paused, glancing at Maya with a puzzled expression. "Say, what is your name again?"

Maya beamed at him. "You can call me Pookie."

And with that, she led him forward. Daniel took a moment to smile triumphantly backward at the other two women, and thus didn't notice when Maya reached the edge of the pond. The sharp tug she used to pull him sideways into the water, though—that he noticed. Hyssop barely heard his squawk of surprise as he tripped and sprawled into the water, almost immediately drowned out by Maya's giggle. The water spirit pushed hard, and Daniel sank like a stone into the gloom of the murky pond, his wide eyes and bright uniform vanishing into the green depths.

Maya smiled happily at the two horrified onlookers and waded in herself. After the top of her head disappeared into the water, a few bubbles surfaced, along with one ribbon. The ribbon floated for a moment, before something white yanked on it from below, and it disappeared into the dark water with a ripple. Nothing else disturbed the pond.

Hyssop stared at the water for a moment, then turned to Jenny. The homeowner had both hands over her mouth and her eyes were wider than Hyssop had known Humans could make them stretch. She cleared her throat. "So, I'm guessing that the fact that you don't give gifts to nature spirits is not common knowledge, then? It's not taught in school?"

Jenny shook her head, her hands pulling away from her face. "No, I don't recall ever hearing that. It would have been good to know." She clasped the front hem of her camisole. "She's never done that before. Um, do you think they're coming back?" She peered anxiously into the pond.

"I really rather doubt it."

"Oh dear." Jenny took a large step backward, stumbling when she tripped over the forgotten delivery from earlier. She snatched it up and turned back to face the pond again, holding the wrapped package in front of her as a shield. "So... I'm thinking we may want to, uh, fence off the pond or something. At least until we can deal with the, um... occupants?" She bounced from one foot to the other for a moment in nervous energy, then stopped and paled. She glanced nervously at the pond.

Hyssop shook her head. "Don't worry, I doubt that little bit of dancing would draw her attention at the moment. She's busy. But perhaps you should put the garden off limits for the time being."

"Right."

"I'll give you the name of a good expert in spirit rehabilitation and relocation. He'll be able to clear the pond in no time."

Jenny looked relieved. "Thanks, I appreciate that." She eyed the pond again. "And in the meantime, the kids in the castle will just have to learn to swim. No more nymph lifeguards."

"Excellent idea."

Hyssop looked around at the garden one last time, satisfied. It was all back to the way it started, with the addition of some light gardening work. "There we are. Everything is the way it should be." She slid her staff through the holster on her back and dusted her hands off on her pants legs. She turned to Jenny.

"The garden is fixed, and everything we were supposed to do has been accomplished. I'm very sorry about the trouble this afternoon. I understand if your family wants to cancel the contract. However, if you keep it, I want to assure you that it will not be this crew that returns. I'd assign this garden to one of my more experienced crews."

Jenny gave her a weak smile. "Let me guess, a garden nymph team?"

Hyssop sighed. "They are a capable group. No wands, so less chance of magic mishaps."

"That sounds like a better idea." Jenny nodded and clasped her hands together. "I'll let my mother know if she asks."

Hyssop nodded and turned to the fairy team, who piled the tools into their rickety wagon.

"Okay, ladies, into the cart and let's head out. We still have to clean the tools, and we need to have a long talk about appropriate wand usage in crisis situations." A loud groan came from the back. "Especially you, Rose. Don't make me sign you up for remedial classes."

"Yes ma'am."

"She certainly needs it." Thistle muttered to Bluebell, who looked just about done with people for the day.

"Thistle! Don't tease Rose, or I'll turn you into a donkey myself. You could help pull the cart." Hyssop glared at the offending fairy. Thistle immediately dropped her eyes, nodded, and looked as repentant as possible.

The fairies shuffled into the cart in a line, now a scruffy, dirt-covered, and dispirited rainbow. They sat bunched in the back, with Lily and Hyssop perching on the driver's bench. Hyssop looked back at the unhappy group for a moment, noting the downcast faces, and sighed.

"Cheer up, gang. It all came out all right; the homeowner is okay. And we'll come up with some good ideas for our business. Everything is going to be fine." She turned forward and nodded to Lily, bracing herself as the ponies started moving forward. "Just to make everyone feel better, we'll stop and get some cakes on the way home. You can have them after you finish your chores."

A cheer erupted from the multicolored cluster of fairies as the ponies trotted through the gate and down the lane, pulling the wagon behind them.

"Last one to finish their chores is a jackass!" Thistle called out. "Rose will see to that."

"Hey!"

The End

AMONG US, THE CREATURE
Jim Doran

A solitary figure marched up the embankment in darkness to meet an army of hundreds. Without a gun or other firearm, Li-Chun carried only a six-inch blade sheathed in a pocket at his side. The opponents across the battlefield wouldn't be armed. A small blessing, that. However, their commander didn't need weapons.

As he crested the hill, Li-Chun surveyed the field before him. In the distance, a shadowy mass of his opponents waited, not for him, but for orders. An odd army, to be sure. Construction workers, wait staff, joggers, and police officers stood at attention approximately eighty yards away. Women in power suits and heels, men in overalls, some children with glasses, some without. Li-Chun even spotted a mime. Black, tan, all colors of the population were represented. They stood shoulder to shoulder in a united front.

Without hesitation, Li-Chun began his deception.

He had viewed the mesmerized people on his phone more than a hundred times and knew the pattern. First, they stiffened, and then their eyes glazed over. He followed the routine to the letter, having practiced it many times before at the military base.

Li-Chun had seen the transformation of the populace ten days before when New York had fallen, not only the city but the entire state. Various groups of citizens marched onward, collecting more and more. The crowd, walking together, surrounded a figure at its center. The internet influencers had many names for the figure, but "creature" had won. They based it on the old movie *Creature from the Black Lagoon*, and Li-Chun had to admit the fuzzy images of the amphibian-like entity did resemble the Universal Studios monster.

Facing the mind-controlled army, Li-Chun stiffened. He blanked out his expression. And similar to a rat following the Pied Piper's flute, he advanced toward the swarm of bodies ahead.

By the time the world had understood the invasion, it was too late. New York City had fallen. Other creatures had formed similar entourages in Massachusetts, North Carolina, and Georgia and advanced inward. Florida? That region was a lost cause, wasn't it? The peninsular state had them coming from the Gulf of Mexico and the Atlantic Ocean.

In front of Li-Chun, the enemy's infantry shifted to the right. He admired the fluidity in their motion. The group didn't march uniformly but stepped in the same direction as a giant organism would. What was the word? Undulated! Yes, they undulated along. The videos showed the groups swaying back and forth and turning like a school of fish when swimming underwater. They didn't walk but performed an unnatural dance to music only they could hear.

Was it music, though? Li-Chun, along with the experts, didn't think so. The armed services believed the creatures transmitted a signal similar to a bat's echolocation. The invaders emitted a pulse that—when heard—forced its target under their command. The undersea aggressors had built puppet armies as human shields, numbering in the thousands.

Now Li-Chun stood a few yards away from the mindless mass of pedestrians. He muttered a quick prayer. His success depended on his next act. He had to join the collection of people and make them believe he was one of them. He had proven to the four-star generals at the military camp that he could pretend to be one of the creature's grunts. But no one knew for certain whether it would work in the field, including Li-Chun.

First, a woman with diamond earrings examined his ears. Then, a nurse in scrubs and an elderly man in a beret parted for him. Holding his breath, he stepped into the crowd. He was inside, but for how long?

The group slid left, and Li-Chun followed their movements. They advanced, then glided to the right, and forward again. Each time, he mimicked their direction change with fluidity and grace. The one hope for the United States rested on a former ballet dancer.

But dancing wasn't Li-Chun's only weapon.

Others had confronted the horde before Li-Chun. To the horror of the public, soldiers fired into innocent crowds to attempt to capture a creature. On every occurrence, the sea dweller had slashed its claw-like fingers on the people surrounding him and then stabbed itself, a hara-kari move with casualties. Surgeons had dissected many captured carcasses, but the remains hadn't revealed any clues to defeating them. After a few days of slaughter, the Marines had issued a statement that they wouldn't kill more civilians until the government knew more about their adversaries.

Once the scientists had made the pulse theory public, everyone began wearing earplugs. Unfortunately, the advancing crowds of puppets ripped those devices from the soldiers' ears, and once they had been taken over, they turned, shooting their own squadrons. That video topped the charts for days. Sound-blocking helmets weren't much better. The mesmerized troops attacked anyone with a helmet on sight.

Li-Chun didn't wear earplugs or a helmet. He hoped his enemies believed him to be backpacking across the wilderness, now caught in their snare. Little did they know he retained his ability to think.

Slide left. Then backward. Sway right, then forward.

If he made too many mistakes, the community he found himself in would likely turn on him as they would any enemy. The businesswoman would remove her shoe and beat him, or the cab driver next to him would strangle him. He couldn't misstep while among them.

The first videos of people moving as a group had been amusing. Perhaps there had been twenty members, with the creature in the center obscured. The aquatic denizens averaged five feet tall, shorter than most in the clips; therefore, they had hidden well among the crowd. A few commenters spotted the "dude in the costume," but the focus remained elsewhere at the beginning. Videos from all along the east coast had flooded the most popular social media sites, fascinating viewers. While the world tuned in, the crowds had become larger and larger. When the police joined the fracas instead of dispelling it, everyone started to suspect.

But by then, it had been too late.

The herd shifted. Li-Chun had nearly missed their cues. A single collision and his ruse would be exposed. If his mind drifted while in their midst, they would attack him. He had to pay close attention.

Nevertheless, Li-Chun found it hard to keep all his focus on his surroundings and not recall the first twenty-four hours of what later would be called "the invasion." Overnight, the deep-sea aggressors had conquered the major cities they targeted. The population surrounding the fish-men had swelled. At times, they had entered stores and stolen food, stuffing fruits and snacks in their pockets. They had eaten while moving. Occasionally, some had slept while the others had rotated in a vortex around the center, protecting their chief. Some of the mesmerized couldn't sustain this life, however. Scouts had found people collapsed in fields, often dead from exhaustion.

Thousands swirled around the creatures, and their numbers grew while they moved west. Experts predicted if they made it to the center of the Midwest, the numbers would exceed a hundred thousand.

The crowd surrounding Li-Chun advanced. From far above, someone might mistake them for an amoeba advancing a pseudopod. Li-Chun had to measure his steps and ensure he compensated to keep his place. He had to be as fluid as water.

Li-Chun's thoughts returned to last night. He had outlined a plan to the big brass of the Armed Services. Surprisingly, they had listened. They had enlisted him as a cadet on the spot without any ceremony. Out of options, they would grasp at any straw. The only downside would be Li-Chun's death.

Not too large a gamble for the military, but a huge risk for Li-Chun.

Step forward, and step again, and stop! Li-Chun had lifted his leg to step a third time but planted his foot on the ground instead. Did anyone notice his faux pas?

Gulping, he waited for the next movement. Enough space existed between the enthralled that they occasionally changed places. The ring of people huddled when threatened. When left to themselves, they created space for others to shift out of position. Li-Chun knew he would eventually make a mistake. He had to complete his mission before he unwittingly broke ranks.

He waited with those around him until everyone drifted right at the same time. While he mimicked their actions, he was able to move back as well and position himself a spot closer to the center. Success! Now he'd have to wait for another opportunity before he angled himself nearer to the creature, but Li-Chun was nothing if not patient.

He had to be. He owed it to his brother, Jai. Jai had texted Li-Chun before facing the creature's army. Li-Chun had spotted his brother on national television standing among a neighborhood militia. This makeshift squadron had squared off against the invader and his minions. While the rest of the militia had fired, his sibling had hesitated. Several on the enemy's front lines had died. Eventually, those on the creature's side had overwhelmed some of the group, choosing not to kill them but to remove their earplugs. When the militia had fired on their own, Li-Chun's brother had collapsed in a hail of bullets. Li-Chun buckled at the memory of his brother's death, but he wouldn't succumb to the grief again. He must keep moving.

Step, step, then sway to the right.

An hour later, Li-Chun had navigated one concentric circle closer to the nerve center, ever closer to his target.

And then he mis-stepped again.

The mob's body movement indicated a forward motion, but they had stepped to the left. This put Li-Chun off balance, coming centimeters from stepping on the heel of the person before him. Compensating, he twisted his body to follow their lead instead.

Did anyone spot his mistake? Though tempted to look around, he didn't move his head. He quelled his natural reaction to defend himself from a suspicious neighbor. A bead of sweat rolled down his forehead. He waited, but no attack came.

The fact the others didn't attack wasn't a surprise. Some, traveling this unnatural way for hours without rest or food, occasionally stumbled or mis-stepped. Unlike Li-Chun, their mistakes weren't born from misinterpreting their puppet master's signal but from exhaustion. He had hoped others blamed his unsynchronized movement on the limitations of his body and not the alertness of his mind.

Li-Chun resolved to remain at least an hour in his current position among the rank and file. He focused on the motion of his neighbors instead of angling closer to the center. He would never complete his mission this far away from his target in the middle.

At least ninety minutes later by his estimate, Li-Chun took the opportunity to float ever closer to the epicenter. Successfully done — great — however, the mime two bodies left to him had also slipped nearer to their commander. Had the creature sensed Li-Chun's deception and moved one of his pawns to intercept him?

Li-Chun held his breath while continuing to mimic the others' actions. He couldn't dwell on the risk. He had to continue.

Hours later, he had come to a point where he was a circle away from their aquatic leader. The mime stood to his right now; his ghostly white face displayed as much emotion as a statue. Li-Chun trembled, imagining himself between a watery monster and an expressionless bodyguard.

Li-Chun steeled his nerves. He must finish this mission for his brother and himself.

And then they stopped moving. Li-Chun had observed this behavior before. The crowd would stay in place for hours while its overlord rested. This halt in their march couldn't have been timed worse. When they started again, he might be caught daydreaming or asleep on his feet.

For three torturous hours, Li-Chun stood at attention with the enemy, ticking the minutes off in his brain. Three hours of playing games in his mind to keep awake, of reciting poems and song lyrics, of keeping his eyes glued ahead. He recalled memories of his life before the invasion — a time in his life he had at first termed "the great loss." When he had adjusted to the change, he had later renamed it "the great change."

The hours crawled by like an inchworm moving along a branch, but then the people to the left and right of Li-Chun rolled their shoulders. He mimicked their actions and readied himself to move once again.

The activation of the brainwashed allowed Li-Chun the opportunity to move backward. He had managed to navigate behind the fish-man and observe him up close. The black scales from head to toe, coated with an oozing film, glinted in the moonlight. The claw digits with webbing between each wide-spread fingers. The gills pulsated, pulling air in like a lungfish, emitting some mysterious gas.

The involuntary draftees progressed through a farmer's field of green beans, crushing underfoot wire mesh protecting the crops. The creature was still beyond Li-Chun's reach, diagonal to his current point. Patience. The success of his mission depended on it.

The mime switched places with his nearest neighbor, and Li-Chun was again close to the blank canvas of a face. Did the sea-dweller suspect him? Was he there to protect their leader? Of everyone in the creepy swarm, why had this guy ended up so close to him?

Li-Chun's fingers brushed the hilt of his hidden knife when they shifted right. He had to watch the creature's back and not allow the white-faced entertainer to distract him. He couldn't come this far and fail.

Crossing farm field after farm field, Li-Chun continued acting like a lemming until he positioned himself directly behind the monster. He had arrived at his moment, and observed a small gap between the scales on the creature's midsection. If he angled it right, the blade would slip through and into the softer skin, the underbelly of his alien enemy.

He had to move!

Yet, he remained hypnotized by the dance. Fear gripped his insides, crushing him. After all his practice and training, he hesitated here at the end.

Gritting his teeth, Li-Chun reached for his knife. His nerves, however, caused his fingers to fumble as he withdrew it from his concealed pocket. The weapon never felt heavier!

The mime broke ranks and reached for him as the scaly figure in front of him halted. They were aware of him now, and every second would make a difference. For Li-Chun, time appeared to slow down, and his senses sharpened. He gripped the handle and pulled his elbow back to jab between the fish-man's scales.

The mime's hand gripped his arm as he thrust the blade. The pale, emotionless entertainer added drag to Li-Chun's motion. Li-Chun pushed harder. With all his strength and skill, he shoved the weapon between the scales and leaned toward the creature, driving the knife forward until only the hilt remained outside.

Everyone in the crowd stiffened, and the mime released him. The aquatic head jostled backward as if viewing the sky. Li-Chun's neighbors, including the mime, reached for their ears. Confused, Li-Chun removed the knife, transferred it to his other hand, and shook off the slimy, black ichor that had erupted all over his fingers. He peered around. What was this sea-dweller commanding his soldiers to do?

Not a command. The monster was screaming.

Li-Chun considered stabbing his target again, but his neighbors contorted in pain and pressed their hands to their ears. Their actions caused him to release the weapon instead. He retreated a step as his enemy's knees buckled. A lady to Li-Chun's left collapsed to the ground.

Li-Chun tensed his shoulders. Had he injured the creature enough to kill it? If it recovered, would those around him turn on him? He should try to escape, but he knew he'd never make it past the clutches of the hypnotized mass.

And then the creature fell forward. Its body twitched once and then went still.

He had done it.

Li-Chun released a long breath. Sweat rolled down his forehead, and he wiped it away. Though his plan had faults, it had worked. He had killed one of *them* without sacrificing human life.

Transfixed, Li-Chun jumped when someone placed a hand on his shoulder. He turned to the mime — a neighbor now, not an enemy — whose eyes teared with relief and gratitude. He spoke a short sentence.

Li-Chun had never been a good lip reader. Instead, he pointed to his ears and shook his head.

The End

A FISH STORY
Rosemarie DiCristo

"You know we're going to have to kill you, right?" Rawling made his voice a laconic drawl, as if there was no urgency at all. "Shoot you, most likely, if you keep this up."

He was kneeling on the holding pen's walkway, eye-to-eye with me, trying to make me comprehend.

"And I don't mean a dart gun, Brady," Rawling continued. "I mean, shoot-shoot. As in, you die."

"Yeah. That was implied in the word 'kill,'" I quipped. Because I "comprehended" Rawling completely. He might have been the only person who understood a "Creature," but I understood all human speech—Rawling's and every other member of his fish-farm team.

He was a big man, rough and rugged, but with a kindness I rarely saw in humans. Now he grunted, and his frustration came through loud and clear. I guessed he was done being his own "good cop, bad cop."

"Then you refuse to stop?"

I nodded so hard my gills twitched. "Anything else would cheat me out of an unending gourmet feast."

Here's the deal. For months, sea lions had been "brazenly" slipping into the holding pens at Fish Corp, an industrial salmon farm not far from Vancouver, to gorge on the fish. Nothing had been able to stop them. Fish Corp installed netting in March and electric fences in April. The "wily predators" evaded it all.

They even piped in super-loud Frank Sinatra songs to scare off the "audacious" intruders, but that only drew *me* to the area. I happen to love *Strangers in the Night*. And don't get me started on *Fly Me to the Moon*. Anyway, in the week since *I* breached Fish Corp.'s salmon farm, I devoured every one of those intruding sea lions, plus twenty times more salmon than they'd eaten in a month, making me—the "hideous Creature," the "missing link," the "fetid fish with feet"—into "Fish Corp's Public Enemy Number One."

All quotes, by the way, were straight from the local papers, who sensationalized this the way newspapers always did. Yep. I can *read* human, too.

Now I looked directly into Rawling's eyes. "I like any seafood. But a salmon farm with over 500,000 fish in it? C'mon, man. Paydirt. Or—bad pun—like fish in a barrel."

"What's he saying?" Fish Corp's director, MacDougal Holt, shouted from his perch at the end of the walkway. He was about one-third the size of Rawling, in height and weight, with a weaselly-looking face, and apparently a weaselly personality, because he stood close enough to the holding pen to see and hear me, but far enough away to be safe in case I grew violent.

News flash: I do not get violent.

Rawling's lips twisted in what I thought was more sorrow than anger. "He's not gonna stop eating the fish, Mac."

MacDougal's lip twist was definitely rage. "I'm not letting any dang Creature eat up all our bleeding profits."

Of course, MacDougal didn't say "dang." Or "bleeding."

I told Rawling, "I'm getting a little sick of being called 'Creature.' Not to mention all those other insults. Do you know what 'pejorative' means?"

"English," Rawling said dryly, "is my native language." He paused, then asked as dryly, "So what do you call yourself?"

"AmphibiMan," I announced with all the pride I could muster.

Rawling merely snorted. "Yeah, that rolls trippingly off the tongue."

I squinted at his name tag but that was just for effect; he was only a foot away. "And 'Rawling D'Allaraglia' is one of humankind's most pronounceable names?"

He tried not to grin. "I can't believe it's come to this. I've wasted the better part of an hour arguing with a sarcastic, smart aleck…" He did air-quotes. "…AmphibiMan."

That was when MacDougal started swearing again, finishing with, "It's time to get out the guns!"

"Hold on." That was Tessie, one of the youngest Fish Corp workers. "Don't be hasty."

"Hasty?" MacDougal's face went redder than a cooked lobster. Cooked, raw, live, dead… man, I was getting hungry again. But before I could dive back into my free lunch, Mac continued, "You know how many jobs will be lost if that animal wipes out our fish?"

"I'm just saying there's gotta be a way to get through to him." Tessie smiled down at me. They all knew I could understand them, even if they hadn't a clue what I said back. "And 'that animal's' name is Brady."

What MacDougal muttered about stupid animals with human names is not printable here.

Tessie seemed a sweet kid—fresh-faced, naïve, the girl next door. Definitely not my type. I figured this was her first job; her voice and manner just screamed "rookie."

She continued, "Brady's one of the most incredibly intelligent and agile sea creatures they had in the Vancouver Aquarium."

"Yep, intelligent and agile. It's how I escaped," I boasted to Rawling.

"Quiet, Brady." He glared at me.

"No, really, you think the lady sea beings there didn't realize who I am? I was considered the Adonis of the place."

"Seriously. You're not helping your cause."

Tessie shushed us both. "Mac, what you're planning for Brady is murder."

"Murder?" MacDougal snorted. "How about justified capital punishment?"

Tessie scowled. "Brady's only doing what comes naturally. Salmon's part of his food chain. The problem is, he's eating too much. We gotta stop that."

"You really expect me to stop? Would you?" I eyeballed Rawling and scoffed. "I see those all-you-can-eat human buffets on the pier. Think of *you* being offered unlimited chocolate chip cookies, fresh from the oven. Mmm, can you smell that? Would you give that up?"

Rawling sighed.

MacDougal started shouting so hard, I could see the spittle fly. "No, Tessie, we gotta stop *him*, because once he's gobbled *our* fish, he'll eat all the salmon in the world."

I didn't deny that. I merely slanted my head to give Rawling a dead-on view of my eyes, so he could get my exact meaning. "I can eat *you*. You specifically, or you three, or all of humanity, even, and it'd simply be a midnight snack."

"Fine; eat me, MacDougal, and Tessie. But all of humanity? Kind of a difficult goal, no? Besides, we'd kill you, Brady. We got the weaponry for it." Now *he* slanted *me* a look. "And to them up there..." he nodded to the walkway, and Fish Corp's headquarters behind it, "...it'd be like squashing a bug."

Talk about dead-on. But my only response was, "Yeah. I know. Humans. Can't live with them, can't live without them."

"I'm on your side, Brady. I want this ending with you alive."

"I know." But any tenderness in my tone got stripped out when I added, "Humans taste bad anyway. And why shouldn't I gobble up the world's seafood? Who'd stop with salmon when there's lobster, shrimp, clams, crab, scrod... Plus, who am I harming? Y'all have spent decades harming me. I've been drugged, shot at, speared in the butt and belly, set on fire, had my home polluted, oh, and did I mention? Dynamited into a coma. But I'm a forgiving AmphibiMan. All I want is free food. Is that too much to ask? It doesn't have to be all salmon, either. A chicken or the occasional egret wouldn't disappoint me. Raw is fine."

"Free food we don't begrudge you. It's the amount that's the problem."

"Hey, it takes a lot to fill up this boy."

MacDougal, apparently deciding he'd been quiet for too long, stamped his foot and thundered, "Enough is enough; if he... it... doesn't vacate the holding pen in five minutes, I'll shoot him myself."

Tessie grabbed his arm, crying, "No, Mac, no," while throwing a frantic look at Rawling.

Rawling heaved a sigh, and I could tell his mind was working hard at a solution. "Can't you go back to the aquarium? You got free food at... what was that exhibit called? The Treasures of the... um..."

"Treasures of the BC Coast."

"Well, that doesn't sound so..."

"I was stuck in a cage and mocked by tourists. Management tossed me fish for doing tricks. I was exhibited with sea cucumbers."

"What? And you didn't eat them?"

"Sea cucumbers, Mr. D'Allaraglia, breathe through their butts."

"Ouch." This time, he did grin at me. But it quickly faded. "Let this thing end happily, Big Guy." His tone was pleading.

"It can't, because I'm not eating just to be a pig. It helps me make time with the ladies."

"The... ladies?"

"Whales, dolphins, mermaids. Humans. I'm not picky. I told you I was considered the..."

"Adonis of the Aquarium, yes. Spare me a repeat of that. Besides, humans? Really? From our point of view, you've got bulging eyes, warts all over your face, humongous feet and did *I* mention? You can sure use a manicure."

"I'll ignore that."

I was rewarded with another quick grin.

"Human women see me as lonely, misunderstood, and needing love." I added, "Even Marilyn Monroe's said nice things about me."

"What? Recently?" And I could see the "She's dead, you twot," look in his eyes.

"Nah, well, her character in *The Seven Year Itch* did. I am way older than I look. But think about it, Rawl. A Marilyn Monroe type. Fond of me. Marilyn Monroe," I said again, and wriggled my eyebrows suggestively.

Rawling sighed, then muttered, "You're not very enlightened, you know."

"Nope." My voice was merry. "I'm pre-historic." I added, more seriously than I'd been up until now, "Back when I was at the aquarium, the newspapers called me 'the most beautiful, sleekest Creature we've ever seen.' That goes far when you're competing with the other AmphibiMen to lure as many AmphibiWomen as possible into your harem."

"What? There's *more* of you?"

"Enough so that I have to compete with them for my brides."

"Brides? Plural? No, wait, forget I asked."

I answered anyway. "Hey, man, try to understand. I escaped from the aquarium so I could be free to attract the gals. And what you consider gluttony is my way of preparing for breeding season. He who's full can guard his territory for weeks without having to forage to eat."

"What's he saying now?" MacDougal demanded.

But Rawling just shook his head. "Hogwash about him impressing his harem. I guess there's no way to stop him." And although the sorrow in his eyes touched my soul, I turned to dive back into the midst of the yummy salmon. Then I heard Tessie, from up above, murmur, "Huh."

We all looked at her—me curiously, Rawling with hope, and MacDougal like he might be cheated out of shooting… um, me in a barrel.

A crafty look crossed Tessie's face. She bent forward and whispered something in Rawling's ear. He nodded, whispered something back, then whispered something to MacDougal. Mac frowned like he'd just swallowed lye, but he nodded curtly.

Tessie faced me, hands on hips. "I guess there are dozens of harems out there, Brady, but Rawling told me there are also dozens of males trying to herd the same females you are. Answer Rawling yes or no: are you certain you're the best sea creature out there?"

"Need I quote it again? 'Most beautiful.' 'Sleekest.' Tell her, Rawling."

He did.

"Sleek, huh? That's important, I guess." But Tessie seemed to know the answer.

"Sure thing!" I said anyway, and Rawling translated.

Tessie smirked. "Bring it on. That means, Brady, get back among the salmon and go to it. We won't stop you." She paused. "*We* won't."

"Suckers!" I dove headfirst into the water and practically inhaled the fish. About ten minutes later I could dimly see Rawling, Tessie, and MacDougal on the walkway, dragging over a six-foot-high rectangle-of-something, covered in a blanket.

I didn't care. I finished my meal, belched, then sang out, "I can't believe I ate the whole thing."

"I can." Rawling's smile was humongous. "And so will you." He whipped the blanket off the long, tall rectangle and flipped the object—a full-length mirror—at me.

Whoa.

Dang.

I'm obese.

The End

SIREN SONG
C.S. Wachter

The hunger within Breyze stirred. Insistent. Demanding. Despite having fed.

No more. Not today.

She allowed a soft growl to escape her lips and glanced back at the dripping wet, semiconscious human collapsed on the leaf-littered floor of the shack behind her. It had been easy to entice the man to the water. It always was. For centuries, her kin had been known for their unsurpassed beauty and their siren song. A sweet, sweet lure, like nectar to bees.

After feeding, she had shifted forms, her tail morphing into legs, her striking features into that of an old, wizened crone, and dragged the human from the water into the shed. The pudgy stranger would survive. All Breyze had needed was to suck some of his life force from him. Always through the mouth and always just a bit, maybe a year or two. She never killed without reason.

His memory of this night—his ordeal from the moment she called him to the lake—would be warped, marred as if he had been on drugs.

She narrowed her eyes and looked through the lateral crack in the dilapidated siding. She studied the inlet, then allowed her gaze to cut across the moonlight-flecked surface of Darkwater Lake before returning to the narrow channel to her left. The surface of the water boiled. Roiled as if agitated by violent activity below. A minute later, all was calm. Tiny waves driven by a fitful breeze crisscrossed the inlet. She sat back on her haunches. Though Breyze had chosen to ignore them, the signs were there.

Another paranormal predator had invaded her hunting grounds three weeks ago. A messy and undisciplined one. After more than ten years of living under the radar, she now faced a competitor. The thought set her blood to simmering.

With maturity and a high level of self-preservation, Breyze had worked hard here in Darkwater Lake to keep her cover identity intact, and her feeding habits hidden from mortal notice. It was a matter of survival. Especially now, when the people from California were due to arrive tomorrow to film the remake of a classic horror movie, *Creature from the Black Lagoon*. More people. More chance of discovery. Again, Breyze glanced behind at the middle-aged man. The unsatisfied hunger for more life force roared within her. She growled.

Perhaps a little bit more wouldn't hurt.

143

~~~~~

"It's about time you're here. Customers are waiting," Nick the short-order cook shouted at Breyze the next morning as she stepped into the back door of Darkwater Diner. She had deposited the unconscious man's body in the park across the street. "You're late! I ain't no waitress, so get your skinny old butt in here and do your job. Next time you're late, I ain't coverin'." He swore, then turned his attention back to his griddle.

Breyze frowned. She huffed and pulled her apron from the hook near the door, tied it on, and thrust her hands into the pockets, taking note of several sticks of peppermint gum, her pen, and her order pad. Despite Nick's grumbling, she remained still, scanning the diner, bringing her heavy breathing under control. Three local farmers sat at the counter, coffees and breakfasts already in front of them. Several customers filled two booths, no menus on the tables. The patrons stared at her with hangry expressions. No wonder Nick was fuming. She'd have to pay better attention to the time in the future. No more double dipping. She had grown lax and that could prove fatal.

She grabbed a half-empty pot of coffee, a stack of menus, and hustled to the booths. After taking the orders, she refilled the cups in front of the locals at the counter, then took up a position near the cash register and checked the clock. Six-thirty. It was going to be a long day.

An hour later, Pastor Jim Hodges walked in and took a seat in one of the booths. He was early. Usually, she could set her watch by the man. She wanted to snarl. Keeping her human persona relaxed, she retrieved a stick of peppermint gum and chewed it a minute, relishing the minty flavor, before approaching the annoying man. Coming close, she repressed a shiver. The pastor never failed to stir the emptiness within her, remind her she had no soul. Hatred flooded her for beings — humans — who possessed souls, threatening to work its way out in action. She beat it down, back into the darkness at her core. It was bad enough she had to face the disturbing pastor daily, now she needed to deal with the movie crew coming to film here at Darkwater Lake. Strangers. Many strangers. *I can't deal with all this sh…* She swore under her breath.

She plastered on a fake smile and smacked her gum as she took Pastor Hodges's order. After pouring him the requisite coffee, she moved to place his order with Nick.

"I know. I know," the crusty cook grumbled. "Scrambled eggs, crispy bacon, and sourdough toast. No butter. The same breakfast he orders every day."

Why can't that prying fool eat somewhere else for a change? Or even just change what he eats? Just once? Breyze swallowed the bitter taste that coated her throat every time she served the meddlesome old fool and turned to scan the room.

After topping off the farmers' coffees, Breyze returned to Jim. "Need a refill on that, Mr. Hodges?"

He began to nod, but a commotion beyond the large plate glass windows drew his focus, and he twisted in his seat. Two patrol cars and Sheriff Williams's SUV screeched up in front of the diner and parked at angles across the street.

"Oh dear, not another one." Breyze shook her head, feigning a look of sympathy. Fine strands of grey hair that had worked loose from the tight bun at the back of her head wafted across her face with the motion. She brushed them back. "Why do all those druggies pass out in the park?" She huffed. "You'd think they'd find a better place to sleep off whatever they took." She smacked her gum.

Jim Hodges's gaze returned to Breyze, his brow crinkled. "Why would you assume that's the reason the police are here?"

Backpedaling in her mind, she shrugged. "Well, it's happened often enough, hasn't it?" *Careful, Breyz!*

Several other vehicles arrived. A van and two large, luxury RVs parked across the street, once again drawing Jim's attention. Breyze huffed and put some distance between her and the pastor. The Hollywood people had arrived.

All activity in the diner stopped. Some customers stood and moved to the windows. Everyone stared as a group of people congregated by the RVs. The door of the first opened and a gorgeous red-headed, long-limbed woman smiled and held out her hand as if she was royalty. A hefty body builder, perhaps her bodyguard, reached out and helped her maneuver down the steps, her movements graceful and controlled. From the second trailer, a thirty-something, Hollywood leading man type emerged and walked over to join the woman. Pictures were taken and reporters who seemed to magically appear out of nowhere held microphones and smiled phony smiles.

Despite all the activity across the street, Breyze's eyes were drawn to a tall, thin man as if by a magnetic force. He got out of an old beat-up Volkswagen parked behind the trailers. A curious longing trickled through her when he crossed the street and walked into the diner. He paused, amber-flecked green eyes searching. Beams of morning light set his sandy hair alight. She sucked in a breath. The yearning within her refused to be ignored. Her stomach churned and she suppressed the urge to spit when the young man smiled and waved at Pastor Hodges.

What the… Catch yourself, Breyz. He's human.

Hodges waved Breyze over as the young man slid into the seat across from him. She took several breaths, filling her lungs and releasing the tension building across her shoulders. Hiding her shaking hands in the pockets of her apron and keeping her focus on the pastor, Breyze approached the two. "Pastor?"

He smiled. "Breyze, I'd like to introduce my nephew, Reese Abbott. He's from Sharps Chapel, north of Knoxville, Tennessee.

"Reese, this is Breyze, one of the best waitresses in the county. Reese's working on the movie." He paused, his gaze shifting from the young man to Breyze. "You know about that, don't you? How they're filming a remake of an old monster movie?"

Breyze chomped her gum so hard, she thought she might break a tooth as she nodded.

"Reese is a cryptozoologist. One of the top cryptozoologists in the country. He's working as their specialist on this film. I invited him to join me for breakfast before heading out to the set."

Curiosity overriding her normal caution, Breyze asked, "What do they need a cryptozoologist for? Don't you guys look for cryptids like Bigfoot and Chupacabra? We ain't got nothing like that around here."

"Come on, Breyze. You hear the gossip better than anyone here. Except perhaps Agnes at the hair salon," Sheriff Williams said over Breyze's shoulder, startling her. "You know we've had unexplained incidents for years now. Dripping wet strangers waking in different places with no memories of what happened."

Breyze snorted. "You mean drug addicts who claim to be innocent."

It was Sheriff Williams's turn to snort. "Maybe. But maybe not. People talk. Some say there's something unnatural in the water. You know, our own creature."

"So I've heard," Reese said, his golden-green eyes riveted on Breyze. She played with her pen to avoid looking into those eyes. "That's why the studio hired me. And the fact that the movie features an aquatic cryptid. I'm supposed to make certain that their makeup, costume, and movements are realistic."

"So, is this a movie or a documentary?" Breyze stared over Reese's head and chomped her gum, wishing she could replace the tasteless mash in her mouth with a fresh slice.

"Well," Reese chuckled, the melodic sound sending another wave of shivers through Breyze, "it's sort of a cryptid love story."

"How so?" Pastor Hodges asked. "I thought it was a horror film."

"Back in the day, it was supposed to be scary. The creature becomes fascinated with the beautiful star and tries to carry her off. Needless to say, it doesn't end well for the creature."

"Yeah," Sheriff Williams added. "Like a *fatal attraction.*"

While the others laughed, Breyze's gum hit the back of her mouth and took a trip down her throat. She choked.

Stupid. Paranormals are not attracted to humans. Never happen. A vein in her forehead throbbed. The sound of Reese's smooth voice sent butterflies fluttering in her stomach. *No. Not happening.*

In the silence that followed, Pastor Hodges's voice broke through Breyze's fog. "Can you take Reese's order now, please?"

Almost against her will, Breyze set her gaze on Reese. Like a magnet, his gold-flecked green eyes caught hold of hers, pulling her in like a rip tide. She swallowed hard as she blinked and looked away.

"Breezy, huh?" His voice sent another shiver through her.

"Well, that's how you say it," she said, "but it's spelled differently."

"That's an unusual name."

"You're one to talk. What? Did your mama like Reese's peanut butter cups?"

He chuckled, but his gaze rested on Breyze in a way that sent up red flags.

You may be used to dealing with freaks of nature, boy, but I'm not your average freak of nature. Pose a threat to me and you'll find your worst nightmare.

Realizing Reese had spoken, and she had missed his words while carrying on her internal dialogue, she flashed a toothy smile his way and asked, "Could you repeat that?"

~~~~~

Six days and one job loss later, Breyze swatted a mosquito droning at her ear as she bobbed in the water and watched the movie crew scurrying to set up for filming. Voices drifted across the mirror-like surface of the lake. So many were complaints about the bugs that Breyze smiled at the feebleness of these California people. Apparently, the director wanted to catch some late evening light.

Breyze scanned the area where most of the crew gathered for evening snacks. When Reese stepped away from the crowded table with a coffee in one hand and an apple in the other, Breyze suppressed the urge to move toward him. She growled, hating the effect he had on her. The man needed to go. It was a simple matter of self-preservation.

The director, a muscular forty-something male with a receding hairline, called to the cryptozoologist and the two spoke for a few minutes before Reese stepped away, finished his apple, downed the last of his coffee, and ducked into a tent. He emerged a short time later with the small pack he had used daily on his back and an expensive-looking camera in his hands.

Breyze trailed him as he skirted the lake. It seemed he spent half his time working with the costume people and the actors and the other half exploring. Just like every other excursion, he stopped often to take pictures and mumble into his phone.

Is he talking to someone or recording? Six days and I still haven't figured out what he's doing. Shrugging, she continued following.

This evening, as the sun sank toward the west, he tracked to the southern end of the lake. An area he hadn't yet investigated. When he reached the inlet where the invasive hunter had feasted recently, the dissonance within Breyze ratcheted up a notch. Her need to protect herself constructed a wall attempting to block the growing attraction within her.

Protect him... Destroy him...

The wall collapsed then rebuilt several times as Reese continued his inspection of the shoreline.

Bent at the waist, his gaze on the ground, he shuffled along the muddy shore into a grouping of pond cypress. Ignoring the water lapping at his boots, he brushed aside a clump of cattails, leaned in, and stared for a moment before he popped upright. His eyes wide, he pulled in a sharp breath, sprinted away from the water, and lost the contents of his stomach.

A moment later, he straightened and walked back. After taking several pictures of what must have been the remains of the other cryptid's kill on his phone, he sent the pictures to someone. Breyze ducked under the water as his gaze skimmed the lake.

"...I'll be here. Yes. About a half-hour? I'll wait."

Catching the end of the conversation as she surfaced, she figured Reese must have called Sheriff Williams.

This is bad.

A premonition of danger set Breyze's teeth on edge. Williams was at least a half-hour out. And even if he arrived soon, would his little pistol be enough to stop the predator?

I don't know. He says it's a practical handgun and brags it's made in America. A Smith & Wesson? Maybe he'll be smart and bring something more powerful? She hissed, making the water bubble around her mouth. *I should learn more about these things. After I move. I can't stay here any longer.*

A trace of an unfamiliar pheromone rode the current to Breyze. The invader was close. Her eyes shifted back to Reese.

"Stupid, clueless human. Sitting like he has no care in the world."

She dove. Flipped, and followed the taste of pheromone toward its source. After a few minutes, though, she surfaced and glanced back to where Reese sat, still fiddling with his phone. She waved her tail with a languid motion, treading water, her forward movement slowed to almost nothing.

Reese's presence, his handsome features almost hidden in the thickening shadows, called to her as if his was the siren song and she was helpless against it. Should she leave him? What if the creature circled back? If so, that would solve her problem.

As the distance between them increased, his hold on her stretched like a rubber band. If she got much farther, she just knew it would snap and fling her back. Her indecision held her captive until Sheriff Williams's shout broke the spell. Reese met him, they shook hands, then Reese took the sheriff to what he'd found.

Sheriff Williams stepped back and rolled his large shoulders. "This is... I'm gonna call it in and get a team out here. You don't have to stay." He shook his head. "It looks like those rumors are true after all. You're the expert. Any idea what can do this kind of damage?"

Knew that interloper was going to be trouble. He must have killed a human. Stupid mistake. This is going to bring all kinds of attention down on me. Now I have no choice. I'll have to move.

After examining the surrounding area, Reese and the sheriff trekked around the inlet to Breyze's tiny shed. She pulled in a breath, hoping she had hidden her tracks well enough. They disappeared inside for a few minutes before exiting the rundown shack.

"You going back now?" Sheriff Williams asked.

"Yeah. Beckman was planning to film this evening." Reese lifted his gaze to the clear sky above. "He must be done by now, though."

"Warn them. Let them know to stay away from this end of the lake. It's an active crime scene now. In fact, encourage everyone there to stick together and stay close to the camp."

"Will do."

The men shook hands again. Reese shouldered the pack he had dropped near where he sat while waiting for the sheriff and headed back around the southern tip of the lake.

Breyze ducked under the surface as Reese passed. She waited until the distance between them increased, tugging her forward, then followed. Keeping her wake shallow and her eyes at water level, she swam with the smooth grace typical of sirens. It didn't take long to realize Reese was heading back to the film company's camp. Probably to warn the humans there as Sheriff Williams had requested.

Submerging, Breyze allowed Reese's pull to direct her as she skimmed through the lake's depths, her mind distracted by an internal dialogue.

This is so wrong. He's human. I'm the siren. He's supposed to be enticed by me, not the other way around. What is wrong with me? Although I do have to admit he is handsome. Those gold-flecked green eyes. And that balanced, well-muscled physical form. Breyze huffed, sending bubbles floating before her. *But I've lured handsome men before. That's not new. What is different about this one man? Breyz, you need to get a grip.* She massaged her temples as a vein in her forehead throbbed. *I should just lure him, feed, and put this all behind me. Finish him off before he...*

She knew the human persona she showed to the world wasn't attractive. Old. Too skinny. Wrinkled. A part of her wanted to reveal her true, beautiful form to the human who enticed her to forego all thoughts of self-preservation to ...

To what? What is it you want, Breyz? Do you actually think he might give you a chance? Try to understand you? That's just stupid. He's human —

A pulse of energy slammed into Breyze, pulling her out of her thoughts with unexpected violence. Pheromones, thick and almost visible in the water, sent her into panic mode. She surfaced and treaded water, scanning. A knot twisted her stomach. The new predator was close. Instinct kicked in, triggering the need to escape, to put distance between her and the killer. A sour taste filled Breyze's mouth.

A full moon aided her enhanced sight and cast enough light for her to see as if it was day. Reese had also stopped, immobile, his focus on the water between him and Breyze.

She released a growl. The surface where he stared bubbled. There was no doubt. The hunter had set his sights on the male human.

Escape? Stay? Save him? Let him die and save myself? Make up your mind, Breyz.

She gritted her teeth and, with a flip of her tail, aimed for the shore, a stream of water spewing in a broad arc behind her. Committed, she released all doubts and sped toward the enemy. Half its body now lifted above the surface of the lake, it eased toward Reese. Pale, silvery moonlight glinted on what looked like rubbery, black tentacles. Breyze choked on bile as she studied the creature she could not identify. A wide mouth lined with razor- sharp teeth and a short snout with bulging, black eyes seemed to be the only solid thing about it. A mass of twisting, rope-like appendages, forming, and reforming into grotesque shapes, made up the rest of the monster. Wrongness and evil surrounded it, emanating from a malevolent core.

Breyze released an oath as she scanned the shore. As if unaware of the danger, Reese paced closer to the water's edge, taking pictures with the stupid camera. The soft click and whir set Breyze's teeth on edge. She needed to shift the monster's attention from the human to herself.

"Hey, stupid human," she yelled as she pushed up out of the water and waved her arms. "Run!"

The creature turned its head and glared at Breyze. It roared, the sound sending vibrations through the lake. But after only a second, it once again focused on Reese.

With only her voice for a weapon, Breyze sang. A song of luring and desire filled the air. Sweet. Inevitable. She had no idea if her voice would influence the squirming mass of appendages, but she needed to try. She blinked and cursed again when a cloud blocked the moon's light. Uncertain, an unknown fear lancing through her chest, she continued her song. A moment later, as the ambient light increased, she smiled. The monstrosity had turned away from Reese, hissing and slithering through the water toward her like a collection of poisonous snakes.

Good. Good. Keep coming, ugly. Now to increase the distance from Reese. As she swam farther out into deeper water, she glanced back at Reese. *No. No. No. No. No.* He had fallen under the spell of the song. His forgotten camera hanging from the strap around his neck, he strode into the shallows, moving toward her.

The devilish snake monster lunged at Breyze, cutting the distance between them in half. A firm flick of her tail bought Breyze some time, but if she was going to kill this thing, it had to be now. Hoping against hope that somehow Reese would be protected, she breeched the surface and sucked in a massive gulp of oxygen. Then, she began a song she thought she would never need to sing. A song of destruction. All sirens learned the Song of Annihilation as children, but she had never met one who had used it.

Focusing her sound into a narrow, powerful beam, she sang devastation at the creature. She feared it was immune as it continued moving and snarled at her. It reached out with quivering tentacles, its open mouth and curved teeth stinking of corruption. Breyze surged back again as the claw at the end of one appendage tore open her right arm from the shoulder to the elbow. For the second time in less than an hour, Breyze's stomach clenched in never-before-experienced terror. What if she couldn't defeat the beast now stalking her?

Then it began to crumble. One by one, the rubbery limbs turned to stone, cracked, and dissolved. A bellow rent the air and the water trembled. The sound faded as the slimy ropes of the head separated and sank beneath the surface, writhing and spinning. The death throes sent great, overlapping waves across the lake.

Breyze let go of her song and floated, her eyes unseeing as the moonbeams caressed her naked limbs. Every part of her body hurt, and her throat throbbed as if it had been shredded by razor blades. She wanted nothing more than to sink to the lake's floor and recover, but fear for Reese sent her swimming toward where she had last seen him. At least, she tried to swim. At some point, her tail had morphed into human legs making her motions awkward and unfamiliar. She almost swore, but that would have required too much energy.

The force of the waves must have pushed him onto the shore. He lay on his back, unconscious. Breyze scrambled to kneel next to him. Holding her breath, she touched the fingers of her uninjured arm to the vein on his neck and released the breath when the blood pumped, strong and steady. He groaned and his eyelids fluttered before opening.

He blinked. Breyze leaned back, realizing she was in human form and naked.

"Wh—Who are you?" He lifted his head and groaned. "What happened?"

Ready with a lie about finding him unconscious and raving in some kind of nightmare, Breyze opened her mouth to speak, but nothing came out, as if her vocal cords had been cut. She tried again. Still no sound.

"It's okay," Reese murmured. "You don't have to say anything." His features softened and a slight smile turned up the corners of his lips. "Do you know how beautiful you are?"

A thrill raced through Breyze. *What do I do?*

"Reese? Reese Abbott?" Sheriff Williams's voice preceded his appearance through the trees. "What the..." He stopped. His eyes went wide.

Breyze backed into the cattails bordering the shoreline, hoping he hadn't noticed her. Then, holding her damaged arm close to her body, she turned and ran. Her human persona no longer old and wrinkled, she sprinted with swift and sure steps.

~~~~~

Reese flung the photos on the table at Darkwater Diner, sending them flying across the slick surface as his Uncle Jim reached out and gathered them.

Tilting his head to the side, Jim looked up and met Reese's gaze. "Are these the ones?"

"Yep." Reese huffed out the word as he slid into the booth across from his uncle.

"Anything?" Sheriff Williams asked as he pulled his hat from his head, strode over, and joined them. He remained standing and leaned in, his hands flat on the tabletop. He reached out and shifted the photos around, spreading them out in front of himself. He shook his head. "There's nothing here."

"There was something there." Reese swallowed back the need to shout, yell, and tear out his hair. All his work. All for nothing, because pictures don't lie. And every one of the photos he'd developed since last night showed nothing but a quiet, moonlit lake. Nothing.

"You heard it too, Sheriff. Admit it. Something..." Reese shook his head and gnawed on the corner of his lip. "No. Two somethings were there. I saw them. I heard them. They fought. Then I saw the lady ... beautiful. So incredibly beautiful." As he met the sheriff's gaze again, Reese wondered if he'd lost his mind. *No. I know what I saw!* He ran his fingers through his hair, setting it on end in every direction. "And you heard it too. That's why you ran for me."

"Whatever I might have *heard* or *seen* last night doesn't matter." Sheriff Williams sent Reese a sympathetic look. "You know the drill, son. Without hard evidence to back up your words, no one will believe you. They'll label you a nut job or some kind of conspiracy theorist. Just forget what you think happened. It never happened. I've got a job and a reputation to protect. And so do you.

"But—"

"No buts, Reese," Jim said, setting his broad, age-spotted hand on Reese's. "You need to let it go."

Reese met the sheriff's eyes, then his uncle's, and nodded.

~~~~~

Breyze walked across the bus terminal, a new backpack on one shoulder and a large leather shoulder bag on the other. She took pleasure in her long, shapely legs and the way her body moved, with strength and grace. She smiled as she felt eyes on her. Men stared. One with an open mouth, until the woman with him slapped his arm. Breyze's smile widened. Yes. She needed to move again after a settled life for the last ten years. But this time she wasn't without direction, living day to day anywhere she landed. No, this time she knew exactly where she needed to go.

At the ticket window, she set down a note. The attendant, a grizzled older man, looked up at her with lowered brows. "Is this where you want a ticket to?"

Breyze nodded.

"One way?"

Breyze smiled, nodded again, and pointed back to the note.

"Okay, miss, one one-way ticket to Knoxville, Tennessee."

The End

NEHER, DEMON OF THE RIVER
Jordan Campbell

He had been alive for a long time. He had not been there at the Beginning. He had not been there during the Fall. He was the first to have been born after the Flood, when the first generation of his kin had been wiped out, alongside most of humanity. Since then, more seasons had passed than he had bothered to count. The rains came and the rains went. Ten thousand nights under the ice could not freeze him. Ten thousand days under the heat of the sun could not parch him. The darkest trenches, miles beneath the firmament where sky met sea, could not crush him. He was the greatest of all living things. He was Neher, scion of Asbeel, and he ruled the rivers.

No creature of the water, save Leviathan, could challenge Neher. He was swifter than all things. Even the fiercest, most turbulent current was nothing to him, and in a day and a night he could travel from one end of the Nile's delta to the other. The Egyptians had feared him, but they did not know what he was. River horses and crocodiles faced him, but none had beaten him. He had fought with tooth and nail and bone and horn. He was strength itself.

Neher ruled the rivers, all rivers, any rivers, for where there were rivers there was life. Mankind had always been tied to rivers. The Creator had planted the Garden between four rivers. Man needed what the rivers provided – the water to quench his thirst and to sustain his crops, the fish to fill his belly, the current to travel across the plains. A man could not survive without the rivers and that allowed Neher his chance to ensure a man's death.

The rivers belonged to Neher and killing wayward humans was one of the few things he could do that brought him *joy*. He could survive the harshest elements, but survival was not the same as living. The fear that came from lack of knowledge when a man was forced under the water…the terror that set in when the man realized his demise was imminent…the desperation in a pitiful, pathetic human's attempt to save his own life…they were Neher's lifeblood. Adam's flesh and Adam's bone sustained his body, but the emotions fueled his soul. As long as he drew breath, Neher would ensure that no human would ever defy him.

Man may have been made in the Creator's image, but it was not a worthy image. The sons of Adam and the daughters of Eve were weak. They were slow and clumsy in the currents. Even out of the water, they could not outrun Neher. A gentle breeze was enough to chill them to the bone. No weapon raised against him could stand. Wood, stone, bone, bronze and even iron blades — Neher could, and did, tear through them all.

Humans were weak, pathetic, pitiful wretches. The Creator chose to elevate *them*. Neher's own sire had been one of the mightiest of the Host. But the Creator had punished the Host unjustly, casting them out. His sire, Asbeel, had sought vengeance by corrupting the Creator's chosen into depravity. Neher preferred a more direct means. The Creator favored humans, so Neher would kill humans.

However great he knew he was, Neher was not so proud as the fool his sire had followed. The settlements that humans continued to build meant little to him. Their affairs were not his concern. What mattered was that his prowess be unanswered and that humans died by his hand, by his claw, by his fang. Ten thousand nights in the longest river in the world, ten thousand human souls snuffed out, ten thousand victims gasping for air as Neher ended their lives.

But despite every soul he had snuffed out, humans continued to multiply. Worse than roaches or rats, the vermin spread.

Neher needed to hunt humans. He would ensure not just that they knew fear, but that they would never know peace.

~~~~~

Water needed to be fetched and it was best to get it done quickly, before the sun rose too high and it got too hot. Hettie lifted the basin. It was heavy, but it had strong handles, so it wasn't too hard to carry it. Even when it would be full of water, it would not be too difficult to lift. That was a good thing, because she would need to fetch water from the river several times today. She didn't really like fetching water. There were snakes and spiders and crocodiles in the river's waters. Once, there had even been a hyena — she had dropped her basin and ran all the way back home, because hyenas were dangerous even when they were away from the water.

It was very quiet when Hettie arrived at the riverbank. There were no frogs ribbiting or insects buzzing. That was strange. The sun hadn't fully risen yet, so it wasn't hot enough for anything to be hiding. Hettie frowned. She liked hearing the frogs at the river. She crouched down with her basin. She would have to be careful not to accidentally scoop up a fish when she fetched the water, since that would make it much harder to hold the basin. But now that Hettie thought about it, maybe that wouldn't be a bad thing. Mama might be able to cook the fish for breakfast.

The water was very clear, almost like glass, and Hettie realized that she didn't have to worry one way or the other about a fish swimming into her basin. There were no fish swimming by. That was strange too. There were usually lots of fish swimming around—little fish that liked to eat insects and bigger fish that liked to eat the little fish.

No fish swimming, no birds flying overhead, no frogs hopping, not even insects buzzing. She was completely alone. Hettie's mouth went very dry. She looked down the river in both directions and then over her shoulder and over her other shoulder. She didn't see anyone at all. But why did that not seem right? She lifted the basin up, surely it had to be filled with enough water now. She had the water she needed, so she'd go home now. Things would all make sense after she told Mama and Abba what she'd seen, or what she hadn't seen.

She couldn't see or hear very much, but she could smell. Hettie sniffed and made a face. It smelled like rotten eggs, though how that could be, when there weren't any birds nearby making nests, Hettie had no idea.

But when she checked the basin, Hettie's mouth fell open in surprise. There wasn't even enough water for half the basin. Her fingers trembled and she almost dropped the basin. She let go a breath she hadn't realized she'd taken. If she had broken the basin that she needed for water, her mama would kill her and then send her to bed without her supper. Hettie shook her head. There was nothing to be frightened of. She had fetched water lots of times.

Hettie crouched lower. This time, she'd push the basin all the way underneath the water, so that it'd fill up even more quickly. The water was up to her elbows, and it was very, very cold. So cold...Hettie shivered and shook, and the basin fell from her grip.

No!

She had to get it back! Hettie reached down—the basin had settled right at the bottom of the river, but it was still close to the shore. She just had to reach a little bit further. Something scraped against Hettie's arm and it hurt.

There was a shape, almost like a man's body, but bigger. A pair of glowing eyes shined bright gold and there were glistening white teeth. Its skin was rough, almost like a crocodile's. It snarled at her. Hettie opened her mouth to scream.

~~~~~

Neher had fed. There was nothing left of the human girl now save for a handful of bones. Her soul was somewhere Neher could not reach, not that it mattered. The basin the child had used to fetch water lay on its side at the shore, a jagged chip at its rim.

Neher sank lower into the water, completely submerging himself. He would wait, now. It was one thing to take a life. It was another to watch the human's family realize their loved one would not be returning. The despair of loss had been something humanity had struggled to overcome since the very first set of brothers, when Cain slew Abel. It was one of his favorite parts of the hunt.

It did not take long for the child's mother to approach the riverbank, reproachful and angry at her child's supposed sloth. There was a moment of confusion and bewilderment. Neher was far more efficient in his killing than a crocodile or hyena would have been. There wasn't any blood staining the soil near the river, but realization sank in all the same. It always did, in the end.

Years passed, and there came a time of great plenty for the humans living by the river. In a single season, there was more food than they should have been able to harvest in three years. Something strange was happening, something…something that came from the Creator. Neher could usually pretend the Creator did not interfere with the goings-on of Earth, but this time of plenty was not normal. There had never been as great a harvest that he could recall and Neher had been travelling along this, the mightiest of rivers, for centuries. What was more, through this time of plenty, there weren't nearly so many people gathering water, and that meant far fewer opportunities to hunt, to kill, to ruin.

After seven *years* of this unnatural plenty, when he hadn't the chance to kill a single human, Neher was at his wits' end. His bloodlust was driving him mad and not even attacking and killing crocodiles brought him joy.

Neher needed to find somewhere else to hunt. There was nothing here for him any longer. He would travel north, far, far to the north.

~~~~~

Stay away from the sea-ice. That was what his parents always said, when he was a lad. Kallu was no fool. Many seasons had passed since he had laid them to rest, but he still honored his parents. He remembered the stories that told of the terrible creatures, the Qallupilluit, that haunted the waters. The Qallupilluit would lure children into the darkest sea-ice and drown them and eat them.

The sea-ice was too dangerous to go out on alone, so he would remain on the river ice. He walked on, spear gripped tight. It was late spring, which meant the bears would be nearby. Kallu feared the great bears, as did everyone else in his village. They were nearly as fearsome as the Qallupilluit, as tall as two men and stronger than five, with fur as white as snow.

His kayak was sturdy, made from the hides of caribou, stretched over whalebones and driftwood. Kallu placed a hand against the side of his kayak. He would be quick in his hunt and then he would return to his village. The last week had been cold. If luck was with him, he would find a fine seal, which would have enough meat to provide for the village for several nights. In a few more weeks, the caribou herds would start their migration and there would be more chances to hunt and gather for the village.

Kallu inhaled through his nose as he pressed through the river. The ice had not yet completely melted and there were many floes of ice that were solid enough to press against. This was a good thing and a bad thing. It was good as it meant the current was not particularly strong and he could paddle against it, but it was bad in that the ice could tear his kayak.

Through the gaps in the ice, the water was as clear as Kallu could remember, almost as if it wasn't there at all. Below the water, he could see dozens of small fish, but he didn't have the room to cast a net and gather any. The fish were quite small, no bigger than his hand. But the salmon would be returning to the rivers soon and there would be food aplenty. Kallu's stomach grumbled in anticipation.

The fish were all swimming in the same direction, along the current. Were they returning to the sea or were they swimming away from something? Kallu squinted against the sun. He didn't see any bears or wolves or even otters. He raised his paddle slowly. If there was nothing on land that frightened the fish, perhaps there was something in the water. Salmon could get as long as his arm, or longer, but they were not the largest fish in these waters. There were sharks in the sea and there were pike in the rivers. Kallu directed his kayak toward a stretch of land that didn't have much ice stretching out from it at all. He could dock there. He was more than capable of fighting off a pike, but he didn't want to risk losing his spear in the water.

He was nearly to the shore when something pressed hard against his kayak. Kallu was confused. There were no large rocks or logs that might have pressed against it. He turned to look over his shoulder and his blood ran colder than the river's ice floes. Something gripped the back of his kayak. It was as big as a man, but had neither fur nor scales. Its face curled into a snarl, and it hissed at him.

This wasn't a Qallupilluit. Those horrid creatures had green skin and dark hair and wore parkas themselves. This creature wore no clothing, and its hands were almost like an owl's talons. Kallu leapt from his kayak, splashing into the water. It wasn't deep, not even up to his knees, and his boots, lined with fur, kept his feet warm and dry. He raised the spear and held his ground.

The creature launched itself out of the water, landing in front of Kallu. It raised its talons and slashed at him, but Kallu stepped to the side. He stabbed at the creature with his spear. He had no idea what this creature was, but he would kill it. His first thrust missed, the creature leaping back into the water. Kallu frowned but didn't stop moving. Was it that the creature couldn't leave the river? That might make fighting it more difficult. Kallu's fingers curled around a stone and he threw it at the creature. The stone missed, but it still distracted the creature long enough for Kallu to dart forward. His boots pressed down hard against the pebbly shoreline, and he pushed as much weight as he could into the thrust. The spear pierced the creature's shoulder and Kallu wrenched his knife from his belt.

The creature was bleeding freely, but he'd have to get a lot closer to try to finish it off with his knife. Kallu swallowed hard and thought of turning to run, but he doubted he'd be able to outrun the creature. Kallu ran and slashed at the creature's chest, but it slammed its arm against him, knocking him to the ground. The knife twisted in the air, end over end, before splashing into the river. The creature roared at him and, just as a man would, pulled the spear away. It snapped the shaft into splinters and before the spearhead hit the ground, the creature knocked it back toward Kallu. He held his arm up to defend himself just in time, but the blade tore through his parka, cutting into his elbow. Kallu fell to his knees, screaming.

His knife and spear were gone. His arm was bleeding freely, soaking the fur of his coat. The creature snarled at him, going down on all fours. Kallu had to get away. He lunged back toward the water, toward his kayak. He would let the current take him away. Anything would be better than trying to face that horrible creature. He threw himself into his kayak and pushed the paddle against the silty bottom of the river. His grip slipped, but the current took him.

He could still hear the creature's screeches.

~~~~~

Neher snarled and thrashed as he dove back into the icy waters. He had haunted these waters for many years but never had his prey escaped him. There were far fewer humans here, but still more than enough to fill his bloodlust. There were no crocodiles or river horses here, nor were there lions or hyenas. There were wolves and bears on the shoreline, and in the waters there were sharks. There were whales, some of the largest and most powerful creatures that Neher had ever seen, but even they gave him a wide berth.

For seventy times seven years, he had lived under these waters. In that time he had killed warriors and hunters, fishermen and whalers, small children and the infirm alike. There were rumors of him — the natives of these lands feared and respected the ocean just as the Egyptians had feared and respected the Nile. But until today, none had ever escaped him.

Humans had fought him on occasion before, in desperate attempts to free themselves, to preserve their own lives. But he was mightier than any, so it had mattered little. Stone and staff and sword had been raised against him, but never before had his blood been spilled.

How dare they defy him! He was Neher, scion of Asbeel! Humans were supposed to be under his foot, not the other way around! Neher was the first of his line following the Flood—none of his sire's seed had survived the Flood, nor had any of the others sired by the Fallen. Neher had never met any of the others who had been born after the Flood. Neher was greater than any mere human. Already, his flesh was burning and the laceration was closing in on itself. He would not be killed today. He would not be killed on any day. He would seek vengeance and he would kill every last human in that village.

~~~~~

The rains came, the rains went. Ten thousand nights under the ice were not enough to freeze him, nor were ten thousand days under the scorching sun enough to parch him. Neher was still mightier than any mortal man. But something deep inside of him had shifted. It wasn't that he was necessarily getting older and slower. He was not an animal, bound to the same mortal failings as mankind. But things had changed, there was no denying it. He wasn't sure how, he wasn't sure what exactly, but something crucial had changed. It was as if the entire world had shifted…a vision of a torn veil kept flashing through his eyes. Was this something to do with the Creator?

Neher continued to travel the waterways. He had left the frozen waters of the north many years ago, but there was no shortage of rivers to haunt. One river was not as long as the Nile, but actually fiercer in its torrents. He spent many seasons there. The waters were rapid enough that it barely took any effort to drown the humans. Neher didn't even need to snuff out the lives of his victims. The water was volatile enough to do it for him.

Blood ran through the river and the people whispered of him, but they did not know of him the way the Egyptians had. They did not confront him the way the northern tribes had. That suited Neher fine. It was maddening, though—the peoples near these waters did not know the Creator, but Neher could still feel the Creator's favor toward them. Despite every effort, despite how many he slew himself, they continued to prosper.

Years passed and more humans came to the shores where Neher resided. Humans, true to their pathetic nature, took little time before they started fighting amongst themselves, not that they really needed an excuse. The petty wars that erupted between the humans mattered less than nothing to him.

Blood spilled, through sword and knife and bow. The victors consigned some of the conquered to the flames, dead and alive, and all others were pushed into the waters. Neher fed again and again. Not every human pushed into the water was dead when they went into the water, but none escaped him this time.

The locals told tales of him. They knew to fear Neher. They were not so foolish as the others from before. They knew of his prowess. In time, a few rose against him, local and invader alike. Neher was mightier than any defense they were capable of. Even setting their petty difference aside, the humans were no match for him.

His sire was condemned to fire and darkness, but Neher was cleverer than Asbeel had ever been. He moved along the currents, through ocean and river alike. Years passed and Neher fed and killed, but the world of humans continued to change. Ships were getting larger and more powerful, and mankind had mastered using fire and metal in tandem. Neher was still the mightiest and he eventually settled in the rivers in the mightiest of forests. The trees grew taller than any other, obscuring the sky, withstanding even the hottest fires.

~~~~~

Humanity had multiplied in recent decades, to levels that Neher had never imagined. Every river on the Earth had cities astride them — far grander than the tiny villages that had relied on the rivers to survive, the cities were prospering. Or they had been prospering. War had broken out again, with weapons that Neher had never imagined. Man had found a way to take to the skies, in tiny ships made of metal. They flew faster than eagles, wielding fire and lightning. Where there was war, there was death, and many humans in these strange metal ships had fallen into the sea.

Neher had been there, because even with their mighty weapons, humans were no match for him. Most humans had been killed in the battles before their ships fell into the ocean, but a fair few had been alive long enough to realize what Neher was. Of these, only a tiny handful had managed to keep their wits about them. Some drew their weapons and tried to fire at him. Neher had been there when humans had first tried to weaponize explosive powder, and while the destructive force had improved tremendously over the centuries, it still wasn't enough to stop him.

Larger ships, proper ships for the ocean, were destroyed in the war too. There, Neher feasted on humans — occasionally accompanied by sharks. Eventually, the war came to an end and Neher traveled the ocean again. It would not be long before humans turned against each other once more. It was in their nature. The first son of the first human had been the first murderer. And where humans killed each other, so Neher was able to kill those who remained.

Humans were expanding further and further, testing their limits. This infuriated Neher. He was stronger than any human, stronger than any human creation. Even beneath these tropical waters where he now prowled, there was nothing that could challenge Neher.

The humans were planning something — they had actually taken steps to take all of the creatures off of a nearby island. What this meant, Neher did not care. Humans were beneath his notice. What mattered was making sure that humans knew his power. At the next opportunity, he would kill enough humans to turn the ocean into blood.

The water was not particularly deep here, approximately thirty fathoms. Halfway to the surface, humans were experimenting with *something*. Whatever it was, Neher would ensure its destruction. He would bide his time — he was nothing if not patient, if the millennia of his survival were anything to go by — and then he would strike. There were no humans in the small metal tank, though it was large enough to house several, and there were several larger ships very close by. Neher swam closer to investigate. Humans may have mastered metal, but Neher was greater than that.

And then something shifted. The strange metal was a weapon, and it was hotter than anything Neher had ever felt. It was something unnatural. Something unclean. It burst out in all directions, obliterating everything in its path and as Neher's body was wrenched into vapor, he realized just how mighty were the ones who had been made in the image of the Creator.

~~~~~

The humans who detonated the atomic bomb *Baker* in the Bikini Atoll never realized what they banished back to Hell.

The End

BESSIE'S REVENGE
Sequel to the novella, **Bessie**
soon to be re-published by Ye Olde Dragon Books
Deborah Cullins Smith

Ned Barker cackled as he shuffled past the two young deputies. He hacked and spat toward the wastebasket next to Deputy Jim Walker but missed. Jim jumped back and the sputum barely missed his boots. He fumed as Ned chuckled and shrugged.

"Sorry 'bout that, Deputy. M' aim ain't what it used to be."

Then the old man shoved open the door and limped down Main Street. The two deputies in the office saw through the window he was carrying on a conversation with himself that he obviously found highly amusing. His raggedy clothes flapped in the mid-summer breeze, and his shaggy gray beard moved as he cackled to himself.

"We're letting him go? Just letting him walk on out of here?" Jim fumed as he pounded the counter with his fist.

"That ol' coot is laughin' at us," Henry Medford growled, his jaw muscles bunching in angry knots.

"What do you want me to hold him on?" The voice made both men jump guiltily. Sheriff Datweiler stood in the door to the interview room. "Do you really think that gimpy old man got the jump on two of this town's brightest jocks? Even if he caught them off guard—or with their pants down—Aiden Johnson and Larry Carrington were in prime physical condition. Top athletes in every sport and being scouted by colleges since their sophomore year of high school. You really think Old Ned could have murdered them both and created that mess at the campsite all by himself, as well as taking out Sophie Williams and Cindy Nagle? Even the girls could have taken Barker down and scratched out his eyes. They would have at least put up a fight. He doesn't have a scratch on him. There's no evidence against him, gentlemen, other than the fact that you don't like him. And that won't hold up in a court of law."

"So we're supposed to believe some monster in the lake got those kids, Sheriff?" Henry asked, his chin jutting out defiantly.

Sheriff Datweiler's hands went to his hips, his stance ramrod straight, and his gray eyes steely. Henry's gaze dropped to his boots. "No, we do not. We get out there and interview the friends of these kids to see who else might have had a beef with them. And we wait for Connie's report and hope she finds us something probative."

"Nasty old coot," Jim muttered, looking down with distaste at the mess by the wastebasket. Then he frowned. "Hey, Sheriff... look at this. There's some blood where ol' Ned hocked up that spit."

Sheriff Datweiler frowned. He started to say 'just clean it up,' but something stopped him. "Grab an evidence bag and collect that for Connie," he said. "Something tells me we might want to hang on to that."

"Collect it for evidence?" Jim muttered. "Sorry I mentioned it."

~~~~~

Connie Webber was the sole criminalist-slash-investigator for a five-county area, and she'd been on-site since the wee hours of the morning. Sophie's brother, Matt, had gone out to the lake when she hadn't come home all night. He had stumbled into the station after careening into town, jumping a curb, and crashing into the mailbox on the corner. He'd torn up the undercarriage of his Mustang, totaling the little convertible. That alone would have had his father in a homicidal rage if the Sheriff hadn't gone out to the lake immediately and witnessed the carnage where four teenagers had disappeared, leaving behind enough blood to drown any hope of finding survivors. The family was devastated — too distraught to care about the beautiful little car Joey Langley had towed to his junk yard, dollar signs glowing in his eyes.

They'd called Connie Webber for dual purposes. First, because she was the only trained forensic criminalist in the area, and second, because her full-time occupation lay in dog training. Connie had the best trackers in the state. While she worked the scene, her husband, Jerry, took their two best hounds out, carefully keeping them outside the perimeter of the campsite. But when the hounds had scented near the lake, they whimpered, and pulled their human back to the truck. Their tails tucked between their legs, they cried and whimpered, and they scratched at the door of the van, begging to be let in.

Jerry finally gave up trying to tug them back out toward the lake after the fifth attempt. They would not budge. They wrapped around his legs, tripping him with their leads. Finally, he opened their kennels and both dogs eagerly hopped in and burrowed their noses into the blankets that padded the floor of their cages.

Jerry scratched his head. "I've never seen 'em act like this. Never. They're always eager to get out and chase someone down. It's like a big game to them."

"Something sure has them spooked," Sheriff Datweiler said, staring at the lake with a frown creasing his forehead. "But what scares scent dogs?"

"Dunno, Sheriff," Jerry said, slamming the back doors of the van. "But Connie is not gonna be happy. I'll be wearin' this one. You wait an' see. She thinks I go too soft on the dogs and don't make 'em work hard enough. This'll all be my fault." He sighed.

Sheriff Datweiler chuckled and clapped him on the shoulder. "I'll vouch for you, Jerry. You pushed 'em as hard as anyone could have. They just wouldn't go near the water."

Jerry attempted a smile. "Thanks, Sheriff, but I'm still gonna catch it for this one. I just know it. Tell Connie I'll see her later."

"Sure thing, Jerry." The Sheriff watched Jerry slip the van into gear and pull out of the park. Then his frown returned to the placid water of the lake.

~~~~~

The Sheriff returned to town and waited for about an hour before approaching the site again. He found Connie stripping plaster-covered gloves from her hands as she stood and eased the kinks from her back and neck. He held out a super-sized Dr. Pepper and a Burger King bag.

Connie's eyes lit up. "My hero." She drank about a third of the cup in one long swallow, sighed, and belched.

"'Scuse me," she said with a wry grin. She eyed the bag, then the crime scene. Her stomach rumbled. "Traitor…" she mumbled toward her mid-section. She took another swig of Dr. Pepper. "I appreciate the thought, Adam, and normally, I'd be diggin' in like crazy…"

"I understand, Connie," Datweiler said, placing a sympathetic hand on her shoulder. "Which is why I got you the fish sandwich today instead of your usual Whopper."

Relief flooded her face. "Oh, bless you, Adam. You really are my hero." She took some hand sanitizer from her fanny pack and dowsed her hands liberally. Leaning against the squad car, she reached in and grabbed the box of fries.

"So how'd my babies do?"

As he reported on the dogs' behavior, she ate more slowly, her frown deepening. He even stumbled through a litany of praise for Jerry's attempts to keep them going. Still, she said nothing.

By the time she'd finished her fish sandwich, wrapped her trash, and sucked up the last of the Dr. Pepper in silence, Sheriff Datweiler was wondering if he should consider putting Jerry in protective custody.

"You need to see something," she said softly. "Come on. The plaster should be set by now."

He tossed the trash in his squad car for disposal in town and followed her back to the waterline. They ducked under crime scene tape, and she gently lifted the large plaster casts she had been making. There were seven of them. As she lifted them and flipped them over for him to see, his blood felt like ice in his veins. He had to help with some of the largest ones. Some showed huge webbed feet, about four feet across and two feet long, and they dug deep into the soft ground around the beach area. Others showed long claws, curled and sharp, and scaled padded paws.

"What am I looking at?" Datweiler stammered. "Are there two animals? Or one? Some sort of chimera? A fake?"

"I don't know," Connie said softly. "But if it's in that lake, it might explain why my dogs want nothing to do with it." She swallowed hard as she gazed out across the water. "I think these webbed feet might be the back legs, and these..." she pointed to the talons, "... might be the forefeet. But that's only a guess. I don't know what this is. But you'd better get someone out here who does, and fast."

"Connie." She paused and turned to face him. "I don't think we'd better tell anyone about this. Not just yet. We'll have every trigger-happy redneck within four states over there tryin' to shoot up the lake and the bodies will really pile up."

Datweiler noticed how difficult it was for her to meet his gaze. "Yeah," she whispered. She looked around. "I don't want to do this again."

He nodded, then he helped her load the plaster molds into her van. "You got someone you can call? Old buddy or professor from the university maybe?"

She thought for a minute, then nodded. "Yeah, biology major, but she loved paleontology."

"Call her."

"Adam." Her voice stopped him before he hopped back in his squad car.

"Better close the lake to swimmers and campers, and seal this area off," she advised. "I meant it when I said I don't want to do this again."

"Yeah," he said, adjusting his Ray-Bans. "Me neither."

~~~~~

Old Ned stumbled into the cave. Moonlight filtered through the trees and glinted off the scales of the beast that waited for him.

"How are ya', old gal? You been layin' low today?" He eased himself onto a rock and stretched his legs. He rubbed his knees. "That was a right smart walk through the woods, but I didnae want them coppers gettin' too close to our little hideaway here. We gotta be careful for a while, Bessie."

The beast lifted her long, scaly neck and grunted.

"Yeah, I know," Ned said with a groan. "We shouldn'ta' taken out all four of those young punks all at once. But I hate disrespectful young pups. And those 'uns were two o' the worst. Just got under m' skin. O' course, you didnae help matters much, comin' up on the beach and' spookin' those silly girls like ya' did." Ned chuckled. "But I admit I enjoyed it a mite." He coughed, rasping sharply, then spat into the sand. "They must have tasted pretty good too, if you've stayed put all day long without going fishin'."

Bessie grunted and pushed her shout toward the sputum in the sand. She let out a low moan and shook her massive head from side to side. Ned frowned at her. Bessie had never behaved quite this way before. Did those pesky teenagers upset her stomach? Give her indigestion? He took a step toward her, but she backed away from him, grunting and groaning with each move of her taloned feet.

"Wha's the matter with you, girl?" He stood uncertainly in the moonlight. Then he looked down at the sand. The glob glistened by the light of the moon. But it was black. Was it a trick of the light? With trembling fingers, Ned found his flashlight and aimed it on the ground.

The glob was dark red.

And the water in the lake was glowing dull green.

"What in the seven hells is going on?" Ned whispered. "Bessie, we need to get away from here! Sommit's wrong with this lake, girl! We need to git out." He limped toward the beast, his arm outstretched. "I'll find us another place to hide."

Bessie backed against the cave wall, still shaking her head from side to side. She had nowhere left to go. She was enormous, and the cavern gave her no room to maneuver. She rammed her bulk against the rock and wailed, what was left of her jagged teeth raised to the ceiling. Most of her foul-smelling mouth was now scaly gums, with a few rotting and broken teeth remaining to chew whatever Ned could scavenge to feed her.

If he cut it up.

Like he'd chopped up the teenagers from the beach.

But suddenly, she swung her head around and clamped those remaining teeth down on his outstretched arm. Ned dropped, slamming his aching knees against the rocks. He spun onto his back and kicked at the iron jaws with his feet. His work boots slammed into her jaws. Bessie howled and released his arm. Ned scrabbled backwards, cradling his bloody arm against his body. Bessie's head came down again and caught his right ankle. Ned screamed, and then his world faded to black.

~~~~~

Sheriff Adam Datweiler finished with his preliminary report and sent it off to Connie so she could include it with her findings for her friend at the university. They were hoping to hire Dr. Edith Armbruster without drawing a barrage of media attention, but the sheriff wasn't sure how long he could hold the news at bay once they learned that four teens had disappeared on the lake. That was the kind of thing that sold a lot of tabloids.

His phone rang.

"Sheriff's office."

"Adam, it's Connie."

"Hey, I just sent you my report so you could add it to your own for your friend..."

"Yeah, well, you can hand her a copy yourself," Connie cut in before he could finish. "Edith will be here at seven in the morning, and she's going to want you and me to escort her out to the lake. Said she's not going out there without someone packing some serious heat, so I hope you have something more than your sidearm."

"You can't be serious," Sheriff Datweiler scoffed.

"Oh, Edith was very serious," Connie said. "And she wanted to know if we had taken samples of the lake water recently. I think she's bringing along another professor with a more chemical-slash-nuclear background. She said this could be really nasty stuff, and a vitally important discovery."

"You've got to be kidding me," the sheriff muttered. "Connie, please tell me you aren't saddling us with some kind of three ring circus."

"I have no idea, but whatever we've got, it's hitting town in the morning. Lock and load, Sheriff."

And then he was listening to a dial tone.

~~~~~

When Ned awakened, the sun shone through the trees. He thought the light must be playing tricks on his eyes because the water was a peculiar shade of green in the morning mist. It had never looked green before!

Ned tried to sit up and pain shot through his body. Memory returned and he looked down to find his arm crusty with blood – and something green.

What is that? He swiveled his head and his gaze fell on the body of the great scaled beast, lying on its side only a few feet away. Her breathing was labored and he could tell she was only moments away from death. The rattle – the death rattle, his father had called it – was unmistakable, and the stench that rose from her mouth had the smell of decay already. But why now? What was killing her? Was it those rotten kids? They'd looked healthy enough. Had one of them been sick? Ned felt tears welling up in his eyes.

"You was sick, old gal. Is that it? That what made you turn on me?" he whispered. He inched his way painstakingly to her side. He spoke soothing words to her, but she shuddered at his approach, so he hesitated. It wouldn't do to provoke another attack. He probably wouldn't survive if she bit into him again. In fact, he wasn't so sure he would make it this time. Well, that was okay too. Maybe they'd just die together in this old cave. She raised her head and howled, the loudest, most mournful and horrifying howl he'd ever heard. Ned wanted to scold her, to tell her to be quiet – that someone might hear her.

But her head fell to the floor of the cave, her eyes rolled up and glazed over, and, after one more shuddering intake, her breathing stopped. Ned reached out with his good hand to pat her head, to caress those scales and tell her one more time how much he loved her. What it had meant to have her protecting him for so many years.

But his vision wasn't working right. He saw green scales on his hand, and webbing growing between his fingers. The hand began to shake. His world returned to black.

~~~~~

Edith Armbruster surprised Adam Datweiler. He had expected a mousey little lab rat, afraid of her own shadow, since she insisted on hard-core fire power for their expedition to the lake. She was a large-boned woman in her early forties with a firm handshake and a no-nonsense demeanor. She brought along her own high-powered rifle and produced the appropriate permit for it when asked.

So... not a wimp, he thought. *Just... cautious? But was it justified?*

She looked over the reports, the photographs of the scene, and examined the plaster casts Connie had made before they left the sheriff's office. By eight o'clock, they had loaded Connie's van, filled thermos bottles with coffee, and headed to the lake. Much to his surprise, they were met along the highway by a camper trailer towing a large motorboat.

"You're going out *on* the lake?" he asked Edith.

"We only have about a 50/50 chance of seeing this thing on land," she said. "So, yes, I do plan on scouting the lake a bit. And chances are about 80 to 90 percent that the beast has a cave or a lair somewhere secluded that won't be accessible by any of your roads. So if we want to find it, we're going to have to search the coastline around the outlying area. The camper is equipped like a remote lab, so we can do quite a bit of our processing without running back and forth to town. That means we can keep the town gossip to a minimum. Connie said that was important to you. So just keep the locals away from the lake, and we'll be fine. News crews and cameras too. I don't like them anyway. They waste too much of my time."

Sheriff Datweiler chuckled. "I agree with you there."

"So far, we've kept the media in the dark," Connie said from the back seat. "But this is a small community, and these folks are pretty shaken up. It's not going to take long for the word to get out. One upset parent will bring down the whole circus."

"Well, I tried to impress on them that we needed to keep this under wraps until we knew for sure whether the kids were alive or dead." The Sheriff shook his head. "They won't buy that for long. Sooner or later, someone will quote some crime show and insist that the media can help them find their kids. Or that it's a serial killer and we really need the FBI. Yeah, just what we need out here." He grunted derisively.

"Then let's get out there and find your beastie before they blow the whistle," Edith said, her mouth set in a grim line.

~~~~~

Henry popped out of his car, shotgun at the ready, when they pulled up to the campsite, which was still marked off with crime scene tape. Datweiler frowned. Henry Medford was an eager beaver, and wound pretty tight, but he wasn't usually the nervous, fidgety type.

"How'd it go last night, Henry?" he asked as he pulled up close to the deputy's car.

"Okay... I guess." Henry's finger was way too close to the trigger for Datweiler's liking.

"Then what's got you so fidgety this morning? I brought coffee, but I'm half afraid to give you any." He smiled to take the bite out of his words, but Henry didn't seem to notice. His gaze kept darting back toward the lake, scanning the woods around its perimeter.

"Somethin's out there, Sheriff."

"Yeah?" The camper and boat pulled past the Sheriff and

maneuvered to back the boat to the water's edge. While Edith, Connie and the young driver slid the boat into the water and unhitched it from the trailer, Datweiler waited for Henry to tell him what had him so spooked. Maybe he shouldn't have sent him out here alone, but this was a small department, and they were going to be spread pretty thin. Especially if this site had to be guarded twenty-four hours a day. "Talk to me, Henry."

Henry gulped. He finally leaned his rifle against his squad car, removed his cap, and ran shaky fingers through his short blond hair. "I didn't see anything, Sheriff. Nothing moved out here. But … well… long about four this morning, I heard the most terrible … I dunno… roar? Wail? Cry? It was awful. Inhuman. I never heard anything like it in my life, and I hope I never do again. I'll be hearin' that noise in my nightmares though."

Connie joined them in time to hear that last comment. "Henry, you heard a creature roar last night? Did it sound angry? In pain? Could you tell if there was an emotion or feeling behind the noise?"

Henry stared at her for a beat. Datweiler could see it in his expression. *He hadn't expected to be believed.* But as Henry looked from Connie's face to the sheriff's, he seemed to gain confidence in his ability to answer. Datweiler's pride in the young man soared, as Henry managed to stiffen his spine and restore his balance.

"I guess…" he thought for a moment, "…I'd have to say there was pain, but something like fear too." He frowned. "Sent a chill all the way up and down my spine, I can tell you."

"Could you tell which direction it came from?" Connie asked. She was hanging on his every word. By this time, Edith had joined them and was listening intently.

"Henry Medford, this is Dr. Edith Armbruster. She's going to be helping us to locate whatever is out here. So any information you give us will be a great help," the Sheriff said gently.

Henry nodded in her direction. "Ma'am."

"The direction, Henry?" Connie prodded him.

Henry took a deep breath, then pointed out to the right, past a dense growth of pines. "Out that way, around the bend, as near as I could tell. It echoed, like it was coming from a tunnel or a cave. I know there's a bunch of 'em out that way. It's gonna be hard to reach 'em though. 'Specially in something that big." He nodded toward the motorboat bobbing at the edge of the water.

"She's a 44-foot Express Cruiser," Edith said proudly. "Except I had a lot of the usual amenities stripped out of her. These things come with mini-bars and fancy grills, all the stuff for entertaining. We don't entertain on this boat. We hunt."

Henry eyed the name on her rear panel. "The *Mina*?"

Edith laughed. "Named her for the fictional character who hunted down and killed Dracula, Mina Harker. I hunt monsters too, Deputy Medford. Though I usually try to catch them, not kill them. With four teenagers dead, though, I think this time, I might be making an exception. Gotta find it first though. Let's go, Connie. We've got work to do."

"Go on back to town and check with Jim to make sure everything's okay at the office, then go grab some shut-eye," Datweiler said, clapping Henry on the shoulder. "We'll need you up and ready to go again later tonight."

"Out here?" Henry swallowed hard.

"Not alone," the sheriff promised.

Henry nodded in relief and headed to his squad car.

"No one's staying out here alone again," the sheriff whispered to himself. "Ever."

Sheriff Datweiler spent his morning watching Edith and Connie collect samples from the lake and run their tests in the makeshift lab, which was up and running in record time. Edith's assistant, Corey Tanner, had the process down to a science. A generator provided power to the equipment and computers, and he had a portable antenna set up within half an hour while they were still down at the lake. By the time the women were ready to use the lab, Corey had it ready for them.

"Why is the water so green?" Datweiler asked, frowning at the unusual glowing samples.

"Sometimes that indicates radioactivity, but not always," Corey said. "Sometimes it's an indication of certain pollutants. It can even be some types of pollen. Anyway, that's why I'm here." He flashed an impish grin. "Let's hit the lab, ladies."

"Radioactivity from what?" The sheriff followed them, his questions trailing in their wake. "You've got to be kidding me! How could we end up with a radioactive lake?"

"It's more likely to be pollution of some sort. And if you do have a beast out here, well… maybe it died in the last day or so and that polluted the waters. That might explain why you hadn't noticed the water changing colors before now. We won't know until we locate your monster."

Datweiler's radio crackled. He stepped outside the trailer and fiddled with the button to fine-tune the reception. "Say again, base."

"Sheriff, we've got a problem."

"What's going on, Jim?"

"The media just showed up. KLOW-TV and about six different tabloids. Seems that Cindy Nagle's mother called 'em and said she wanted someone to help find her daughter. She's down here too, and three sheets to the wind at that. Cryin' and screamin' that we ain't doin' nothin' to find her poor little baby girl. She's got 'em all wound up. Henry's out there trying to settle 'em down, but it ain't working very well. I think they might be headed your way soon."

Datweiler sighed and keyed his radio. "Okay, Jim. Call Tom Jackson over at County and ask him to send us some back-up. Tell him I need to seal the scene out here at the lake to keep the media out. And explain to him that I've got scientists and our criminalist out here working. I don't need a mob out here contaminating the evidence."

"Roger that," Jim responded.

"Well, you might want to press on, folks. Your job just got a little harder," he said, stepping back to the door of the lab. "The media is on the way, and they are fired up."

"Who blew the whistle?" Connie asked with a weary sigh.

"Agnes Nagle. Got liquored up and called KLOW, for starters. Tabloids picked it up from there. The circus is coming to town, and it's not a happy one."

"Can't you do anything to stop 'em, Sheriff?" Edith huffed.

"Well, ma'am, I'm sure going to try," Sheriff Datweiler drawled. "I've called in back-up from the County boys, but I'm just warning you that it's going to get a little more interesting than we'd hoped."

"Corey, get the damn boat ready to go," she snapped. "We need to make our first circuit before theses yahoos get out here."

"Dr. Armbruster, I can't leave the site until someone else gets here to secure the area. Right now, I'm all that's standing between the mob and this crime scene. If I take off to chase monsters, they could stomp all through here. Shoot, they could even vandalize your trailer. We've got to have police on the scene before we leave the area."

"Crap!" Edith muttered. "That's true. I didn't think that through very well, did I?"

"Well, I understand. But just do what you need to do here. We can launch as soon as my back-up arrives." He paused for a moment before asking, "Did you find anything?"

"Yes, it isn't radioactive." Edith pushed a lock of hair away from her eyes. "It's some sort of pollutant, but I don't know what type. I've never seen anything like this before. I'm really not sure what it means. But the size of those prints still alarms me. And I wasn't kidding when I said I wanted some heavy fire power out here. Whatever this is, it has the potential to be quite dangerous. Since four healthy young adults are already missing, presumed dead, I would say it's very dangerous. And that danger goes up if it feels cornered."

Sirens screamed from the entrance of the park, and within seconds, the flashing lights of three squad cars careened into the clearing. Sheriff Datweiler strode toward them to explain their needs and the dangers involved to his colleagues, while Corey proceeded to power up the boat.

~~~~~~

Ned opened his eyes and tried to focus, but his vision was blurry. And he couldn't seem to catch his breath. His chest ached and when he took a breath, his neck throbbed. The pain was wicked, like knives slicing his skin and flames setting it on fire. He groaned, and his voice sounded strange to his ears. He raised his hand to feel his forehead. Maybe he was running a fever. But his skin felt … different. Scaly, rough, pebbly. This was all wrong! And he wasn't hot—he was cold! He held his hands out and saw green and gold scales shimmering in the late afternoon sunlight. Why were there scales on his hands? The place where Bessie had bitten him had healed over with a row of red scales, thick and hard, like a protective callus.

What have you done to me, Bessie? His voice shrieked in his own head, but his words came out in a guttural roar. He stumbled over to the water's edge and looked down at his reflection. He stared in horror and disbelief. Gills fluttered along his neck, gulping at the air convulsively. His neck looked longer than it should be, and scales replaced his skin in most places. His clothes still hung on his frame, but they tore when they caught against the scales as he moved, shredding the fabric. He grimaced and saw his teeth had begun to sharpen and elongate in his gums. Ned threw his head back and roared one more time before falling forward into the water. As he struggled through the murky waters at the cavern's entrance, the gills in his neck began to work. He relaxed and his body floated, adapting to the environment. He kicked his feet. Swiveling around, he noted that even the place where Bessie had bitten his leg had healed over. It burned in the greenish-tinted water, but he could use it. He kicked again and propelled himself through the dim world beneath the water's surface.

Those kids! This was their fault. He wasn't sure how, but they did something to Bessie, and then she did something to him when she bit him. The townspeople had always been against him. But he'd show them. The lake used to be Bessie's. Now it was his.

And he would make them pay. He'd make them all pay.

~~~~~

At the campsite, everyone froze. The roar echoed over the water.

The county deputies looked less than thrilled as they muttered a few choice, and profane, words about not expecting to have to watch out for monsters.

"That wasn't pain," Connie whispered. "That's anger, raw fury. Something's got a whole lot of mad in its system."

"But it almost sounded ... human," Edith added, frowning. "Not quite human, but almost. Do you think we've got another victim out there? Could someone have slipped past your deputy last night to do a little hunting?"

"Could be, but I doubt it," Sheriff Datweiler said, listening carefully as the sounds faded away. "Henry was spot on about the direction though. Let's head out that way and see." He grabbed two high-powered rifles from the trunk of the squad car, pocketed three boxes of ammunition in his jacket, and slammed the door closed. "Let's rock 'n' roll."

Once aboard, he secured the ammunition and the rifles in the forward cabin. It was a handsome set-up, and Edith proved to be adept at piloting the *Mina* out into the lake. While the sheriff's inclination was to gun the engine and head toward those terrible sounds, Edith chose to slide smoothly around the bend, leaving little in the way of a wake. They eased through the water, glistening a dull green in the late morning sunlight. Clouds rolled lazily across the sun, and thunder rumbled off in the distance. Periodically, Connie went out and lowered a jar on a rope to catch another water sample, which she promptly capped and labeled with the approximate location and the time it was taken.

"Still green," Datweiler observed.

"And getting a little greener," she said grimly. "I think we might be getting closer to whatever the contamination is. This lake may be off limits for a very long time, Adam. That's going to upset a lot of locals. The kids all love to hang out here. It's been a summertime tradition for as long as I can remember."

"I know," he sighed. "One thing at a time, Connie."

Edith cut the engine. "I see what your deputy was talking about, Sheriff," she said, heaving herself out of the pilot's chair. "This cove is covered in vegetation. I can't remember when I last saw so many water lilies and bulrushes in one place. *Mina* can't wade through all this without gumming up her engines.."

177

"You don't expect us to swim, do you?" Datweiler eyed her dubiously.

"Of course not!" Edith's smile was grim. "Corey, break out the rubber raft."

~~~~~

Edith, Corey, and Connie had donned wet suits, just in case. Datweiler declined. His own clothes were sufficient, thank you very much, and he had no intention of leaving the boat unless there was firm ground to stand on. He was still relatively fit for a man of fifty, but that little roll around his midsection made him very self-conscious, and he wasn't about to squeeze himself into a skin-tight rubber suit that showed every body flaw. He'd rather risk getting a little bit wet and keep what was left of his dignity.

They rowed slowly into the cove, taking water samples, plant samples, insect samples and watching for signs of fish. There didn't seem to be any life in the water at all.

"Listen," Connie said, cocking her head.

"I don't hear anything," Datweiler said. "What is it?"

"That's just it. There's nothing." Edith's voice was grim. "No birdsong, no animal life. Just silence. It's not right."

Datweiler tightened his grip on his rifle. Ice water ran down his spine. They were right! Nothing moved in this area of the woods. But why?

"Look!" Corey pointed to the alcove in the far corner of the cove. He paddled the raft more rapidly toward the dim shadows he had spotted.

"Slow down, Corey," Edith commanded. "We don't want to startle anything living in this cove. Nice and easy."

He obeyed and slowed the raft to a leisurely crawl again, but they all felt the tension as they drew nearer to the recess in the rock wall around the end of the cove.

"What is that stench?" Corey asked, coughing.

Datweiler's eyes began to water. He and Connie exchanged glances. "Decomp." They said it simultaneously.

"But it's not a human one," Edith added. "This one smells... reptilian or amphibian — or both. Children, I think we may have found our creature already."

"Yeah, well... if we found the monster, I want to know what monster killed the monster," Datweiler said, his voice hard.

"Hey, someone may have done us a favor," Connie pointed out. "You want to arrest him or throw him a parade?"

"He violated a crime scene, and may have destroyed evidence,"

Datweiler said. "That's no favor."

"After what I cleaned up yesterday, I may just give him a big old-fashioned hug before you haul him away," Connie muttered.

They pulled up to the rocky outcropping around the entrance to a shallow cavern. Still, they heard no sounds at all, from inside or from the area surrounding the cave. Carefully, they inched forward. Connie and Corey held high-power flashlights, while Edith and Datweiler kept their rifles aimed, safeties off.

The stench became more overpowering as they approached the huge mound of scales toward the back wall. Its golden eyes were open and glazed, and flies buzzed around the open jaws, where jagged and broken teeth were faintly visible in blackened, rotting gums.

"Watch out!" Datweiler yanked Corey to the side, and the young man yelped in surprise.

"What was that for?" he asked indignantly.

"You almost stepped in that," Datweiler said, pointing to a bloody wet smear on the rock just to the right of Corey's feet. "Connie, can you collect that?"

"You want me to collect spit when we've got a monster on the floor in front of us?" she asked incredulously. "Adam, you amaze me sometimes."

"I think I might have something at the office for you to compare it to," he added, staring at the bloody sputum, as the dots began to connect in his mind.

Connie did as she was asked, then turned her attention to the beast. It was enormous, probably thirty-foot long if they could actually stretch it all the way out. The neck was long and scaly, and the head was wide. Once those teeth would have been ominous, but this was an old creature, far past her prime. Her teeth had been rotting long before death claimed her.

"What is that thing?" Datweiler whispered.

"I have no idea," Edith murmured. "But she's amazing."

"She?" Datweiler's voice rose a little. "It's a girl?"

Edith paused to give him a bemused glance. "Yes, Sheriff, it's a girl. Girls can be ferocious monsters too, you know."

"Yeah, guess you've met my ex-wife," he muttered, taking a careful step away from the creature.

Connie smothered a giggle and continued collecting samples from the pads of the paws.

Edith took samples of her scales, popping them into sample jars and bags. She added saline solution to them and carefully placed them in her backpack. Then she popped out one of the huge golden eyes. She carefully detached it, leaving dangling filaments of nerves and muscle to float in the jar.

"Amazing," she murmured over and over. "Simply amazing."

Connie examined the hind legs and the forefeet carefully. "These definitely made the impressions on the beach, Adam. Look at this." She pointed out the claws on the forefeet. Sharp and jagged as daggers, and fully capable of slicing skin. Connie discovered this when she got a finger too close to the business side of one claw and came away bloody. Corey quickly pulled out a first aid kit.

"We're dealing with a corpse. You don't want to get any of his bacteria in an open wound." He rinsed her hand thoroughly, disinfected it, and slathered it in antibiotic ointment before wrapping her finger securely and taping it with waterproof tape. Connie berated herself for not handling the claw more carefully.

"You'll be taking an oral antibiotic too," Edith said severely. "Connie, I'm surprised at you. You used to be more cautious around animal corpses."

Connie looked thoroughly chagrined. "I expected a sharp claw, but not like that. Can you excise that claw too?"

Edith grimaced but did as she asked, being much more cautious as she handled it. She still nicked her thumb, and had to undergo the same treatment from Corey, which made Connie feel slightly better.

"Bloody thing is sharper than any animal claw I've ever seen in nature before," Edith grumbled. "Even Kodiak bear claws aren't that nasty."

Datweiler winked at Connie when Edith wasn't looking.

By the time they had finished taking samples from the corpse and shooting photos from every angle, the sun was beginning to sink behind the trees. None of them had eaten since morning, although the stench in the cave was enough to quell their appetites for the moment.

"The university is going to want to send in a team to retrieve these remains," Edith said. "But we're going to need something to haul it out on. We can't get it on the *Mina*, but if we could hook a sled of some sort onto a hitch, *Mina* could tow it out. I'll contact the team as soon as we get back to the lab."

"In the meantime, I'll talk to the County Sheriff and get him on board for the long haul. Looks like we're going to be out here for a while," Datweiler said with a sigh.

As the *Mina* headed back to their base camp, Corey pulled some cold bottles of ginger ale from the refrigerator in the lower deck kitchen and passed them around.

"Better than just drinking water when you've seen and smelled what we just had to put up with," he said with a grimace.

"Think I'd prefer the water, if you don't mind," Datweiler said. "I can get it if you just point me in the right direction."

"There's water in the cooler right there beside you," Edith said, motioning to the side table between the leather passenger chairs mid-deck. Datweiler leaned down and found a miniature refrigerator cunningly tucked under the wooden table.

"Handy," he said, retrieving an ice-cold bottle of spring water.

"Every little space counts on a boat like this," she said with a laugh. "I even have a washer and dryer on board."

"A washer and dryer?" Connie laughed. "You're kidding, right?"

"Nope, they tucked it under the stairs. That staircase swings up, and voila! Washer and dryer. I don't use them often, but I have had occasion to need them, much to my surprise. We've had to wade through some pretty nasty swamps a time or two, and we didn't use our wetsuits." She looked pointedly at the sheriff when she said that. "We would have been pretty miserable and the whole boat would have smelled horrid for years to come without some terrycloth robes and that handy set of appliances. Always keep it supplied well now. Just in case."

Datweiler chuckled. "Good to know."

"What are you going to tell the press?" Connie asked. "You know you're going to have to give them something if we're bringing in a bigger team and hauling out a ginormous monster. Not to mention, round-the-clock police on site. You're going to have a media feeding frenzy if you don't give them something to keep them in line."

"The more you tell them, the more they're going to hound us for more details, Sheriff," Edith groused. "I'm all for a media blackout until we're finished with our work here."

Datweiler sighed, then cast an apologetic look in Connie's direction. "I can't call in an expert, then ignore her advice. Okay, Doc. If it's a blackout you want, I'll give it to you, but only for another twenty-four hours. Then we're going to have to come up with something we can tell these folks. If we don't, they'll start manufacturing their own stories, and believe me, that's a bigger and nastier kettle of fish than you're gonna want to deal with."

Edith grumbled but nodded in agreement.

Datweiler stared across the water. He blinked and sat up a little straighter to peer out the window.

"What is it, Adam?" Connie asked.

"I thought..." He blinked again. The sun was setting behind the trees and the shadows across the lake grew longer. It was gone. He shook his head. "Trick of the light," he said with a wry chuckle. "That and a long, stressful couple of days."

"Are you sure?" Connie asked. "What do you think you saw?"

"No, it was nothing." He shook his head. "Imagination and shadows. Forget it."

He settled back in his seat, but his gaze wandered over the surface of the lake. Watching for a ripple. Waiting for a scaly head to break the surface, golden eyes reflecting against the water. For a spiny fin to slip beneath the green-tinted lake.

"Adam." Connie's voice broke into his thoughts. "I just had a terrible thought."

"What's that?"

"The monster we examined in the cave," she spoke slowly. "I'd say it had been dead for at least eight to ten hours. Wouldn't you, Edith?"

"Yeah, I'd guess that." Edith's voice was soft as well.

Connie nodded. "Then what made the sound we all heard right before we hit the water? It couldn't have been that monster."

Adam felt his left eye twitch and a headache ramped up behind his eyes. He groaned. "You could have gone all evening without bringing that up, you know."

"The thought had crossed my mind," Edith said grimly. "I was going to suggest that you arm your cop friends appropriately tonight, Sheriff. We probably aren't out of the proverbial woods yet."

"Yeah, I suppose so," he said. "I just hope we don't attract any nocturnal visitors. Does this floating fantasy island happen to have any aspirin on board?"

"Set him up, Corey," Edith directed. "But not aspirin. I think what you really want is a good stiff drink, Sheriff. Will bourbon do?"

"I'd love one, but I think I'd better stick with the aspirin. You need me awake and alert tonight."

No one found that amusing.

~~~~~~

They found the County Sheriff waiting for them at the campsite. A tall man of Indian ancestry, Tom Jackson had the chiseled features of his forefathers and a long dark braid running down his back. He was built like a college linebacker, even in his forties, and his black eyes revealed both a curiosity and an intelligence that Datweiler found refreshing in law enforcement. Jackson was never one to jump to the obvious conclusion, but once his mind was made up, he was as immovable as Mount Everest. A good man to have on your side in any battle. Datweiler was especially glad to have him around for this one.

Jackson had a fire banked and some fish cooking over the flames. The scent of rosemary, dill and garlic rose from the foil packets, and their stomachs growled in unison.

"Please tell me you didn't pull those fish from this lake, Tom," Connie said, suddenly looking a bit pale as she eyed the flames.

Tom snorted derisively. "I wouldn't touch a fish from that lake. Water's been sick for several years now. You white men don't know anything about nature."

Connie heaved a sigh of relief.

"Bought 'em at the grocery store in town before I drove out. Label says they came from the Gulf, but I don't believe everything I read. I just know they didn't come from around here."

"So did you do a purification ceremony over them?" Datweiler asked with a twinkle in his eye and a poorly suppressed smile.

Tom looked up at him, deadpan serious. "No, but I purified the fire with sage, then I added a special blend of spices passed down from my grandfather's grandfather. That should do the trick." Then his lips twitched and he winked at Connie, who burst into laughter. He sniffed in their direction and frowned. "You might need to think about a purification of your own before you sit down to eat though."

They all looked at each other.

"You smell like death," he added.

The men took turns at the shower on the *Mina*, while the women stashed all the samples in the lab and made use of the shower in the trailer. After a couple applications of lemon-scented bath soap, they all agreed they felt — and smelled — much better.

~~~~~

"My boys said they heard something roar out here this afternoon. You find what you were looking for out there?" Tom asked as they opened foil packs and dug into the fragrant fish and vegetables inside.

"Well, yes and no," Connie said, swallowing her first bite and sighing with pleasure at the burst of flavor on her tongue. "This is perfect, Tom. Thank you so much. We found a beast out there in a cave. But it's been dead too long to have made the noise we heard this afternoon. It is, however, most likely the same creature that killed the kids on the beach two nights ago. The feet and claws look like they'll match the footprint impressions I took yesterday."

Tom frowned. "But you're saying there's another monster out there. We have a second predator to deal with now."

"Well, that beast has been dead too long to have been the scream we heard this afternoon, so yeah," Datweiler said. "I guess we have something else out there. We just don't know if it's the same type of creature or something else entirely."

"Well, what was it that you found?" he asked.

"We don't know." Edith answered this time.

Tom's eyebrows rose. "You don't know?"

"I've never seen anything like it before. It's either a totally new species, or a species so old, it's never been discovered before."

"And you didn't bring it back with you?"

"Too big." Edith was growing testy under Jackson's incredulous gaze. "I've already sent an email to my university, asking for help. We're going to have to have a team to recover this thing. You have no idea what we're up against. It was enormous. The four of us would never be able to move the carcass. And we can't load it onto the *Mina*. It would take her under."

Tom's gaze moved from Edith to the boat by the waterline and back to Edith again, disbelief creasing a frown into his sharp features. He looked to Datweiler.

The sheriff nodded. "She's absolutely right, Tom. You wouldn't believe the size of this thing. It's about the size of two squad cars. Scaly. These folks pulled samples off of it. They can show you after we eat if you think your stomach can take it. Frankly, mine can't. I've had all I can stand for one day. They took out an eye and put it in a jar. The thing is this big around." He held up both hands to indicate the circumference of the eyeball. "You see the bandages these ladies are sporting? They got those from one front claw on the beast. *One claw*. They barely touched the thing and got cut. What was it you said, Doc? Sharper than the claw of a Kodiak bear?"

Edith managed a wry smile. "I think you might as well drop the 'Doc' and call me Edith from now on."

Datweiler smiled and nodded. "Okay, Edith. Only if you'll call me Adam. Connie's about the only one around here who does. It'll be a nice change."

"Hey!"

"And Tom," Datweiler added quickly, dodging the open-handed

smack aimed at his shoulder. "But we just don't get to work together that often. You usually stay on the other side of the county."

"Yeah, well, you usually keep your side of the county working better, Chief," Tom muttered, forking up another mouthful of fish.

"That's true," Datweiler sighed. "We've had a few missing persons every year for about five years now, but this one is the worst."

"Yeah, that one five years ago. That was four kids too, wasn't it?" Tom said. "The Mason kid I remember, and that little blond cheerleader — what was her name? Jessica something?"

"Jessica Barnes," Datweiler said softly. "Danny Edwards, Karl Mason, and Diana Colches. All disappeared. No trace ever found. We questioned old Ned Barker back then too. But he just doesn't have the strength to take out good athletes like these kids. Same with the ones from two nights ago. Aiden Johnson and Larry Carrington were going into their senior year of high school with big prospects ahead of them for athletic scholarships. Sophie Williams and Cindy Nagle were both cheerleaders and active on the girls' volleyball and baseball teams. None of these kids were slouches when it came to physical prowess. They would not have gone down easy. We've lost a few people every year since those first four, mostly drifters or vacationers, sometimes a lone kid. Most of the time, it looks like suicide. You know, a troubled home, abusive home, or a runaway situation. Very little evidence to verify whether a crime even took place. But this time, it was all too obvious that we had a real live creature out here killing people. And we found a beast."

"But you're saying he wasn't alone. There's another one." Tom crumpled his empty foil into a ball and popped it into a trash bag. He held the bag open, and they all followed suit, crumpling their foil packs and tossing them in the trash. Tom nodded approvingly. No litterbugs here.

"Looks that way," Datweiler said.

"Adam, what *did* you see out there as we drove back in?" Connie asked.

"Hold that thought." Edith said, hopping up and scurrying back to the trailer. She returned with a bottle of Moscato and glasses. "We all need to unwind a little and we've earned this. And I don't like to drink alone. So no arguments please." She poured the wine and they each took a glass.

"Now, Adam, proceed," she ordered, sipping her wine and sighing with satisfaction.

Datweiler sighed. He took a sip of the sweet elixir and let it slide down his throat. It was the perfect end to a lovely meal, and it really did hit the spot. As long as he didn't allow himself more than one...

But Edith had already capped the bottle. Smart woman.

"I saw ... I think I saw a scaly head barely above the waterline. I saw golden eyes. The head wasn't as large as the one in the cave, so maybe this is only a juvenile. Then it seemed to duck under the surface, and a ... well, sort of a fin arched up and then disappeared into the lake. So this was more... fish-like than what we saw in the cave. But it can definitely breathe air too, because its head was above the waterline. If it wasn't all a figment of my imagination, or a trick of the light..." His voice trailed off and he took another sip of wine. He waited for comments, but none came. He glanced from face to face.

They were all taking him very seriously.

"I think I want to take a look at those things in your trailer now," Tom said, his voice deep and gravelly.

Without a word, Connie and Edith took him to the trailer.

Tom emerged twenty minutes later, his face set in hard lines. He tilted his head toward Datweiler, who managed to heave himself to his feet. He trudged toward Tom, stumbling over a tree root once along the way.

"I think this day is getting to me," he said sheepishly. "Must be getting old."

"Nah, you just need some sleep," Tom said, then he cast his gaze sideways and grinned. "Then again, you are pretty old. You white men age faster. You need to get back to nature."

"I've had about all of nature I can stand today," Datweiler said with a grin. They headed away from the campsite, to where the media waited out of sight, blocked by Tom's men.

"Not this kind of nature, my friend." Tom laughed. "We get this all behind us, I'll take you camping with me. Teach you how to really get back to nature the right way."

"So what do you think?" He motioned back toward the trailer. "About what you saw in there?"

"Bad medicine in there," he said, holding up a bandaged hand.

Datweiler snorted and shook his head. "Just had to touch it, didn't you? Didn't believe the women when they told you how sharp it was, so you had to see for yourself. And you think white men are gullible."

"Yeah, yeah, and you didn't touch that thing?" Tom asked. "Not even once."

"I didn't touch that thing with a ten-foot pole," Datweiler said. "I didn't even want to be in the vicinity, but I'm the hired gun. I stood at the ready with the rifle in case that critter twitched. One little muscle spasm, and that corpse would have some new craters in it. I had no desire to touch it." He held up both hands to show bandage-free digits.

"Gather 'round." Tom's voice boomed out as his deputies gathered from their various posts around the gate and the other areas surrounding the campsite. He walked over to the news media people. "I see even one of you cross this tape, and I will haul every last one of you in. You'll spend the next three days in lock-up where I will conveniently forget to post your paperwork. I might even forget to send food and water down to the hole for you. And that includes the ladies of the press as well as the gentlemen, so consider yourselves warned."

He walked away amid the clamor for comments. One young man started to follow, but a veteran reporter yanked him back by the collar. "That's Sheriff Tom Jackson, son. He means what he says, and I don't feel inclined to spend the next three days in his jail. So you best stay on this side of the tape or the rest of us will take you down and beat the snot out of you."

The sheriff grinned as he returned to his men. "Sometimes it helps when others do your job for you. Remember that." They all chuckled.

After stressing the importance of not leaking any information to the press, their families or friends, or posting pictures on social media, the sheriff briefed his men on their situation with full disclosure. Datweiler corroborated everything, adding any details that might be pertinent, and Tom sent them back out by twos. No one was to go anywhere alone. Two by the gate, two by the trailer, two between the campsite and the surrounding woods, and two by the boat and waterline.

"I'll be back out in the morning," Tom said. "But call me if things get interesting out here. I'll come back if I need to. In the meantime, you get some sleep, Adam. My men can handle this. Most of them are former military, and they're all tough as nails. You, my friend, have had a rough day."

"Thank you," Datweiler said with a sigh. "I planned on staying up, but I didn't realize how tired I was until I tried to stand up back there. I'm whipped."

"Rest. We tackle it again tomorrow." Tom clasped Datweiler's forearm, in an Indian-style greeting, which Adam returned. "Together."

~~~~~

The women opted for the beds on the *Mina*. Corey and Datweiler took the bunks in the trailer. Datweiler kept his shotgun close at hand, even though there were deputies patrolling outside. The memory of that head popping above the surface of the water haunted his dreams.

A shriek ripped the night and brought Datweiler straight up out of bed. He grabbed his gun and bolted from the trailer, grateful that he'd slept with his pants on. Another scream ended in a bubbly gurgle from the woods to the right of the trailer, and he ran toward the sound. Where were the deputies?

Then he saw their flashlights bobbing up ahead. He looked behind him and saw more men coming from the boat.

"No! Don't leave the boat and the trailer unguarded!" He waved them back, and they reluctantly returned to guard the women, who had responded to the screams as well. "Keep them back until we secure the scene!"

"You surely don't mean me!" Connie yelled.

"You're not armed, and you're not law enforcement. Stay put until we secure the scene." He pointed his finger in her direction and saw her slump in defeat. Then he turned and ran in the direction of the flashlights.

He skidded to a halt when he saw the blood, then the sprawled body of Corey Tanner. His face was a mask of terror through all the blood. His throat was one huge red gash with blood pumping out on the ground too fast to stop, and his neck was bent at an unnatural angle. Another rip across his abdomen had spilled his organs into a messy pile beside him. Both deputies stood stone-faced as Datweiler approached.

"What was he doing out here alone?" he asked.

The first deputy, a thirty-ish man, with a dark crew cut and a dark brown eyes swallowed hard before replying. "He said you'd had trouble getting to sleep and he didn't want to risk waking you if he used the john in the trailer. He was just going to walk a little ways out and use a tree."

The second deputy, a younger man with red hair and a smattering of freckles, picked up the narrative. "We heard a scuffle and tried to help him, but something was dragging him deeper into the trees. By the time we found him, it was too late."

That was the moment that Datweiler realized that this young man had removed his shirt and tried to staunch the bleeding before realizing that a broken neck wasn't fixable. His hands were stained red with blood, as was his white t-shirt. The uniform shirt on the ground would never be wearable again.

"Did you see it?"

They looked at each other. Neither wanted to speak.

"Just say it, no matter how crazy you think it sounds. You heard what we told you earlier. It can't be any worse than that," Datweiler said.

"We saw... well... it walked upright like a man, but it wasn't a man."

This from the older man. He clearly didn't think he'd be believed. But Datweiler did believe. He just didn't know what it meant.

Then they heard the women scream, and the sound of breaking glass. They all broke into a dead run.

"But the body..." the younger cop protested as they raced back to the trailer.

"He's dead," Datweiler shouted. "They're alive for now, and they need help if they're going to stay that way."

As they arrived, they saw one of the deputies raise his service pistol and take aim at a green scaly figure headed for the water. It walked with an off-balance gait, clutching something in its claw. As the deputy had said, it walked upright, but it wasn't a man. And yet it wore the tattered remains of human clothing. It lurched as bullets slammed into it from behind. Lifting its head, it roared. A shiver slid down Datweiler's spine. It was the roar from the previous afternoon! He was sure of it. It slid into the water and vanished beneath the surface, leaving a bubbly red trace in the water.

Connie was kneeling beside Edith near the steps to the trailer. The door hung by one hinge and water seeped down the steps in a trickle. Datweiler knelt to assess the damage to the women. Connie had a bruise beginning to blossom on her left cheek, but other than that, she assured him she was fine. Edith had a gash across her face that would require stitches, and one down her chest. That one would have been fatal if it had been any deeper. She had been lucky.

"The screams..." Edith stammered.

"Corey is dead," Datweiler said gently. "I'm so sorry. The creature caught him out in the woods. The deputies said he went out there to use a tree instead of using the inside latrine. Didn't want to wake me up. I wish he'd risked waking me."

"How bad is it?" Connie asked.

Datweiler hesitated before answering.

"Answer the question, Adam," Edith demanded. "How bad? Don't spare my feelings. Tell the truth."

"It's bad," he admitted. "His neck is broken, his throat was slashed..." The women both groaned, and Edith began to weep. "...and he was eviscerated."

The older deputy laid a hand on Datweiler's shoulder. "Sir? We're going to go back out and secure the body now. That thing seems to be gone for the moment. Lenny there put enough lead in him to make him think twice about coming ashore again. Maybe he'll just swim out and die before morning. Either way, we don't want other critters making a meal out of your friend. We'll take care of him until you can deal with the scene."

"Thank you," Datweiler choked. "Where's the other deputy? There were two of them on the boat."

A muscle tightened in the deputy's jaw. "Mark is dead. Lenny said that thing grappled with him when he came out of the trailer. It made a beeline for Dr. Armbruster, and Mark intercepted it. Fought with it and almost had it down until... it sliced his jugular with its claws. Mark bled out by the waterline."

"I'm sorry for your loss, deputy. He did his best." Datweiler felt a lump forming in his throat. There were just never the right words when a brother in blue fell in the line of duty. "Better call your boss. He wanted to know if things got interesting out here. I think this qualifies."

"Yes, sir, already done it. I just hope he doesn't lock us all in the looney bin, after the stories we tell tonight."

"Where's your first aid supplies, Edith?" Datweiler asked gently.

She gave directions to the bin in the trailer, and he returned quickly with enough supplies for Connie to triage her wounds temporarily. Then he headed for his squad car. Keying the mic on the car radio, he called the office.

Henry answered promptly. "Hey, Boss. Thanks for not giving me lake duty tonight. Guess last night just sort of freaked me—"

"Listen to me, Henry," Datweiler cut him off abruptly. "We've got trouble out here. And a lot of it. I need an ambulance on the double. Then I need you to go get Connie's kit and her van and bring it out here. She's got two crime scenes to deal with. We'll need the coroner too, so wake him up. Grab us some decent coffee. And make it quick. Better roll Jim out of bed so he can mind the shop too."

"Holy crap, Sheriff..." Henry's voice cracked. "Yessir. I'm on my way. Ambulance, coroner, Connie's kit, coffee."

"And don't forget to call Jim."

"He's sleeping in one of the cells. Said he had a bad feeling about tonight, so he slept here just in case we needed him. All I have to do is wake him up."

"Good man. Tell him I said thank you."

"Yessir."

~~~~~

Edith refused to be hauled to the hospital. She allowed the EMTs to stitch her up, using local anesthesia, bandage her wounds, then she proceeded to tape waterproof bandaging over the top of their handiwork from her own stash. They shrugged and shook their heads. She thanked them, signed all their forms, and sent them packing.

"You know you really ought to be resting in a hospital bed," Datweiler said.

"Pish tosh," she scoffed. "You'll need to hit the lake and search for that thing, won't you?"

"Yeah."

"You'll want my boat, won't you?"

"It would help, since it's already here."

"Well, I'm the only one who drives the *Mina*," she declared. "You need me here. Not lounging in some cushy bed somewhere."

"Never heard a hospital bed called 'cushy' before, but I take your point." He grinned at her.

"How's Connie doing on the recovery?" Her voice became soft.

"She's almost done," he said with equal softness. "She's taking a lot of samples from the wound tracks. This one left us a lot more to work with than the other beastie. Something green and sort of foamy. Might be the source of the contamination in the lake. We'll see. She's going to want to make use of your lab instead of running that media gauntlet up there."

"Two bodies. That poor girl is going to be exhausted." Edith shook her head.

"Yeah," Datweiler sighed. "Protocol demanded that she had to work the scene around the deputy first. That was no disrespect to Corey, Edith. It's just always done that way. You clear the cop's body first. But she's almost done with Corey now. They'll be taking him out soon."

"I'd like to see him…" Edith said.

"I wouldn't advise it," Datweiler said quickly. "Edith, let the funeral home work on him first. You don't want to see him that way. Please trust me on this. He was your friend. I don't think he'd want you to have to live with that memory. If it was me, I wouldn't want that for you."

Tears welled up in her eyes, but she nodded.

"I take it the blackout is over." Edith sighed.

"Yeah, I think so." Datweiler sighed too. "I'm sorry, Edith, but we can't hide two bodies going out of here in the coroner's van, especially when one is a cop. And if they start asking questions in town, they'll start getting more and more of the story. All the years of disappearances around this lake, and they'll blow it into some spectacular cover up that'll rock the entire state. We could all wind up under investigation. Better to just give them something to chew on. There was a beast on the lake. We found it. Now we know there's a second one. We wounded it last night. We're going out to find it today. Period."

"You think that's going to be enough?" she asked.

"We never had proof before this week." He shrugged. "As soon as we knew there was something out here, we did something about it. That's all anyone can do. Work the evidence. And we've never had sightings before. Now we've seen the big monster, and the creature from last night. Whatever it is."

"I found something you should see," she said, leading him to the waterline. They walked slowly, and Edith held on to the crook of Datweiler's arm. She leaned heavily against him a time or two, and he realized she was much weaker than she wanted anyone to know.

They reached the point where the creature had returned to the water. She pointed to the ground. There were dark blackish-red splotches with traces of green foam.

"What is this?" Datweiler asked with a frown.

"I think it might be the creature's blood," she said. "He was shot right here."

Datweiler stared at the blood on the ground. He remembered the lop-sided gait of the creature as it ambled back to the waterline. He remembered the bloody sputum in the cave. And he remembered the spit on the floor of his office. And the clothes hanging from the creature's body last night.

"You need to rest now, Edith," he said gently. "I'll get Connie to collect this as soon as she gets back. In fact, I've got evidence bags in my car. I'll collect it myself as soon as I get you settled back on the boat. We'll let you know when we're ready to go out."

"I don't want anyone else driving my *Mina*," she protested.

"If you're on the boat resting, we won't be able to leave without you. Okay?" He finally coaxed her back to her bunk and eased her down. She was asleep before her head hit the pillow.

He hurried to his squad car for an evidence bag and some rubber gloves. No way did he want that stuff touching his skin. He collected the sample, marked it, then scanned the shoreline for any further evidence of the creature. He found a few footprints that looked eerily like the larger back paws of the monster in the cave. But these were much smaller. What on earth did it mean? Was this the monster's offspring? Or did old Ned really have more to do with all this than they could have ever believed? *But how?* It just wasn't possible!

When Connie returned, her eyes were red-rimmed, and he hated to lay more on her shoulders, but he filled her in on Edith's findings, then on his own. She prepared more plaster molds of the new prints to add to her collection, while Datweiler stood watch with his rifle in both hands and ready to fire.

"What did you find this time?" The voice coming out of the darkness was familiar. The scent was not.

"That's not coffee," Datweiler observed.

"Nope. Herbal tea. Heap big Injun medicine." Tom offered one cup to Datweiler and another to Connie. "Figured you needed it after the night you had."

"I'm sorry about your man, Tom," Datweiler said, taking the cup.

"Thank you." His voice was stoic, but Datweiler knew it came from a place of great pain.

Connie sipped tentatively then laughed. "Heap big Injun medicine, my foot! This is cinnamon peppermint tea, Tom Jackson!"

"Who says that isn't Injun medicine? We've been drinking it for centuries." His face reddened under her gaze.

"You are so full of it!" she crowed.

"I think I'll take my tea back," he said, reaching for her cup. She pulled it away from him and swatted at his hand.

"Don't touch my tea!"

"Tell me about the footprints," he said, his voice losing some of the levity.

She sighed. "This creature appears to bear some similarities to the larger monster we found in the cave yesterday. And though he is much smaller, we found out last night that he is certainly no less lethal."

"So after he killed Corey, why didn't he just make good his escape?" Tom asked. "He could have gotten away pretty clean. Why trash the trailer? Why kill Mark and attack Edith? Those actions just got him shot."

Datweiler blew out a long breath. "I can answer that one. Edith went in and took a quick look around after the EMTs finished with her. We knew he took something, but we weren't sure what. Edith figured it out pretty quick."

He saw the dread on Connie's face. "What did he take, Adam?"

"He took the monster's eyeball back. This is looking more and more like revenge."

~~~~~

They gathered at the boat after a lunch of pizza from the local bowling alley. It was the best pizza around, and everyone ate heartily. They had even ordered an artichoke/spinach/ranch at Connie's request, since she wasn't sure she could face the meat and red sauce after another crime scene morning. It was just as well. The young red-haired deputy shared it with her.

Tom brought over the older deputy from the night before and introduced him to Datweiler. "This is Andy Lincoln," he said, as the two men formally shook hands.

"Thanks for all your assistance last night," Datweiler said. "I didn't get a chance to say it sooner, but you were invaluable."

"Happy to help. Just wish it had ended better for your friend."

"And for your partner."

"Andy was a Navy SEAL," Tom explained. "He's still got a lot of friends from his service days. I've asked him to call in some favors and we've got three guys coming in this afternoon. If we're going to hit this lake, I want the right kind of muscle going in after this thing. Andy feels his guys can get the job done."

"If it has to be done in the water, believe me, you want SEALs doing the job," Andy said. There was no bravado in his statement, just simple truth.

"Andy, I appreciate that, but there's a question of liability here," Datweiler began.

"Say no more." Andy cut him off. "We don't do this for money or glory. We do it to protect and serve, just like cops do. As far as SEALs are concerned, this is an attack on American citizens on American soil. We're in. All of us. We took the risk in the military, and we take the risk now when we feel the call to do it. That's all there is to it."

Datweiler traded glances with Tom. Both men shrugged. "Okay. You're in. You and your guys have your own gear?"

"Roger that."

"Let me know when you're ready."

~~~~~

At one o'clock, Datweiler and Jackson made a joint press conference and explained the bare bones of the case. They promised more updates to come, but stressed the importance of staying back, and the fact that remaining as far from the lake as possible could very well save their lives. So far, the press were behaving themselves. Then one of the reporters showed them a leaked picture of the original crime scene. It was both gruesome and bloody. Both cops blew an angry fuse and threatened to fire the man who leaked the picture to the press. Tom reiterated his threat to jail every last one of them if even one dared to violate the boundaries his men had set, and they stormed off in a snit.

194

"So 'fess up," Tom whispered so they stalked away from the reporters. "Was it you who sent out that picture?"

"Hey, I thought it was a genius idea," Datweiler whispered back. "Should have them scared to death, especially at night. Don't you think?"

"Yep, genius, my brother, genius."

They returned to the campsite chuckling quietly, out of earshot of the reporters.

~~~~~

At two o'clock, a gray van pulled up to the checkpoint. The newsmen swarmed the vehicle, but were rebuffed, and the van was quickly passed through the barrier and the gates closed behind them.

Andy Lincoln greeted the three men who exited the van and stretched their legs. Then he introduced them as Sylvester Gates, Donny Kemper, and Charlie Harmon. All three were built like Sherman tanks. They retrieved their gear from the back of the van, as well as gear for Andy, and began to load it aboard the *Mina*.

Datweiler headed to the trailer to tell Connie it was time to wake up Edith and head out. She was finishing up with the samples. He had even had Henry make a second trip out with the sample from the office.

"Well? Was I right? Please tell me it was a crazy idea." Datweiler wanted to be wrong this time.

"You were right, Adam. All three samples have a base DNA in common," she said slowly. He banged his head against the door frame. "But... there are significant changes to the DNA in the second two samples, and they are each significantly different from each other as well." His head shot back up.

"I don't understand."

"Well, quite honestly, neither do I. But it looks like Ned Barker's DNA is continually changing at this point. His body is morphing into something entirely new. He began as a human, but now he shares several traits in common with the monster in the cave. They aren't exactly the same, but they have some of the same strands of DNA. I've never seen anything like this. I've never known a man or beast who could jump species like this."

Datweiler sat down in the nearest chair, his head suddenly swimming. It was too much to take in. Ned Barker was the monster they'd seen last night? Impossible!

"There's something else."

He heard the catch in her voice, and he looked up.

"I don't know what it means, but I ran some of the blood through a few other tests as well, especially the first sample. Ned has a very aggressive form of lung cancer. I don't know if that affected his ability to assimilate the foreign DNA, or if his cancer affected the monster in the cave in some way. I haven't finished with the tests on the monster's blood yet. But the cancer does explain the blood in his sputum. I'm just not seeing the same level of T-cells in his blood in the more recent samples."

"You mean the monster's DNA is healing his cancer somehow?" Datweiler asked.

"No, not healing it exactly. Just changing it. It could be metastasizing it faster. But I'll have no idea how fast or where until..." She broke off.

"Until you do an autopsy."

"Well, on an animal, it's called a necropsy. I'm not sure this creature will qualify for a human autopsy anymore." Her face turned a little green at the prospect.

Datweiler could understand the feeling all too well.

They headed for the boat, and Connie took the stairs to awaken Edith. By the time Datweiler had helped the men load the last of the electronic equipment, Edith and Connie waded their way to the upper deck.

"Good grief! It looks like Cape Canaveral up here. Are you guys hitching a ride or planning on launching my boat into space?" She stepped gingerly over wires and cables to get to her chair and heaved a sigh of relief.

"Just want to see what we're walkin' into down there, ma'am," Sylvester said, with his most charming southern drawl.

"You planning on taking a stroll, young man?" She leveled a steely stare in his direction.

"You can talk me out of it, if you want to stroll around the deck with me," he said with a wink. "I can let the rest of these ugly lugs do the heavy lifting, and you and me can count the stars."

Edith's laughter was tinged with disdain, but she grabbed the bandage on her chest and grimaced. "Oh, don't make me laugh, young man. That hurts too much. Besides, I'm not in a funny mood today."

Charlie Harmon frowned and leaned toward Datweiler. "Shouldn't she be in a hospital, Sheriff?" he whispered. Sunlight glistened through the sunroof on his chocolate brown head, totally shorn of all hair. He reminded Datweiler of LL Cool J on that NCIS television show.

"I heard that, and no, I should *not* be in a hospital," Edith called out from the front seat.

Datweiler shrugged. "You heard the lady."

As they pulled away from the beach and out into the lake, the men began to pull on their wetsuits. Andy lowered a big round disc over the side of the boat and allowed it to float gently until it was floating several feet below the boat. Then he tied it to the boat railing and they checked the images coming back on their monitors. The world below the surface was a murky, misty landscape. Fronds of plant life waved at them as they passed, but they saw no fish at all for the first twenty minutes.

"How can this lake be completely empty of fish?" Tom asked. "It used to be the best stocked lake in the lower half of the state."

Datweiler shook his head. "Do you think the monster in the cave ate them all? I mean, something that big would have a huge appetite. It would take more than a few humans to fill up a gut like that."

"You guys really found a monster out here?" Donny Kemper asked. "This isn't some enormous practical joke, is it? Are we going to find some big movie prop from an old Loch Ness film out here?"

"I don't joke about six people dead in two days when I've had to sponge up the blood and guts, buddy," Connie replied sharply.

Donny turned as red as his closely cropped hair. "Sorry, ma'am. It's … just a little … well…"

"We realize it's pretty unbelievable, and we know it's like a bad horror script to everyone just coming into the picture." Datweiler tried to choose his words carefully. "But we've been living with this nightmare now for more than forty-eight hours on very little sleep, so please excuse us for not being in a joking mood, Mr. Kemper. We're all worn a little bit thin."

Andy stepped up. "Domino."

The three SEALs immediately sobered and stared at him in alarm.

"What's that mean?" Connie asked.

Andy eyed each of his buddies for another minute before turning to answer her. "When you're as close as we are, you tend to have some practical jokesters in the bunch. We have a safe word for those moments when the situation is so serious, we have to get down to business and stop screwing around. Use of the safe word assures us that it's no joke."

From that moment on, the mood aboard the *Mina* sobered. The men asked questions about the predator they were chasing. Connie and Datweiler filled in as much detail as they could about the monster in the cave, then Andy joined in with details about the creature they had fought the night before.

"So is this thing a man? Or a beast?" Sylvester Gates asked, running his hand through blond curls. He appeared to be the only one who had let his hair grow out after his military days.

"At this point, we aren't sure what it is. Maybe Ned has been sheltering the creature all these years. The old man has wandered around in these woods for decades, and he was known for telling tales about a monster in the lake he called 'Bessie.' Even his description of her more or less matches what we found, if the local teenagers are telling us the truth. But we had never seen any sign of a large predator out here until this week. We'd have the occasional missing person, but no solid evidence to show that it was a real monster. This week was a game-changer." Connie fell silent.

"Hey!" Charlie shouted. "What the hell was that!" He pointed at the monitor. He'd listened intently to every word they'd been saying, but his eyes had been trained on the monitors. The men clustered around the monitors.

"What did you see?" they clamored.

"Slow it down, Dr. Armbruster!" Andy's voice rose above the others.

Donny Kemper manned the joystick on the camera and maneuvered it to swivel slowly, panning the area.

"There!"

A flicker of fabric flashed past the camera, obscuring the lens briefly. When it floated away, they all saw the man-shaped creature swimming toward the dense overgrowth of bulrushes to the right. He flipped around and stared directly into the camera, baring his sharp teeth at them in a feral snarl before darting between the thick fronds and disappearing.

Charlie uttered a prayer under his breath. Sylvester's and Donny's words were far more profane. Andy's jaw clenched.

"Yeah. That's him. That's what we saw last night. He killed a cop and one of the scientists with this group. He's dangerous, so don't get careless."

"Cops don't have our training, Andy," Sylvester protested.

Andy leveled a stern look at him. "Mark Stevenson was a battle-trained Marine. Served two tours in Iraq, one in Afghanistan, then did a year as a drill sergeant. That thing took him out with one swipe of his claw. Opened his neck. Caught him just right. All it takes is a split second."

The men exchanged stunned looks.

"Don't lose focus. Watch each other's backs."

"Roger that." They each murmured the response.

Datweiler and Jackson watched silently as the Seals loaded up with stunners, knives in all shapes and sizes, spears, and finally harpoons. They had small utility knives in their belts and in straps at their ankles. Then they had larger blades, almost the size of Bowie knives, as well. Spears went into canisters strapped to their backs, the tips razor sharp and spiked. Whatever went in would not come out easily. The harpoons were the latest technology in gas propulsion. They would zoom through the water to strike their target without slowing down in the current.

"Following him into his den may not be the best idea," Datweiler objected. "You'll have terrible visibility, not only on the target, but with each other."

"We can't just wait for him to come out, Sheriff," Andy said. "He could just hole up in there indefinitely.

"What if we gave him a reason to come out?"

"What do you have in mind?" Tom Jackson asked.

The sound of a motorboat drew their attention.

"Now who in blue blazes is this?" Edith demanded, stomping from her chair to the back of the boat to get a look at the newcomers. "If this is a news media stunt... I swear..."

"If it's newsmen, I may scuttle their launch and arrest whoever I don't drown," Tom said grimly. "I told them not to..."

"Ah!" Edith cried in delight. "Reinforcements! Just in time! Adam, you wanted a reason for him to come out? I think I just may have one for you. This is my second crew from the university. They've come out to collect the body from the cave. That should bring your beastie out."

The second cruiser was almost as big as the Mina, but much dingier and older. Behind her, she towed a barge about twenty feet long.

"Jonathan, I told you to bring the big sled!" she frowned at the thin, bespectacled man who smiled from the side rail.

"Good afternoon to ... good grief, Edith! What have you done to yourself?" he gasped.

"Never mind that. Why didn't you bring the big one? I'm not sure she'll fit on the smaller sled."

"Some bigwig showed up and 'needed' Big Bertha for a hush-hush operation on the east coast. Offered big money. You know Jason is a pushover for donations to the university. Our own needs are secondary, especially when it comes to the science." He shrugged. "What do you want me to say? I did what I could." Jonathan eyed the heavily armed SEAL team. "What exactly is going on here, Edith?"

"Gentlemen, I think the party plan just took a radical turn," Datweiler said with a grin.

~~~~~

The second team came aboard and they anchored the two boats closely together while they hatched their plans. Among the new teammates was a familiar face. Chelsea Bailey had been involved with Karl Mason during the time of the first attack five years ago. Datweiler remembered interviewing her. She had been a sweet kid, and Karl had had a reputation as an opportunistic Romeo. She went to the lake with him but got upset and went home early. That one action had saved her life. Now she was studying biology at the university and had somehow ended up on this little field trip. She shivered as she looked around the lake.

"Does it feel a little surreal to be back at your old stomping grounds?" Datweiler asked her quietly when they had a moment alone.

She swallowed hard and nodded. "Did you really find... Bessie?"

He paused. "Yeah, I think we might have. The monster we found sure matches the description Ned's been talking about all these years. Speaking of Ned, Chelsea, do you remember anything particularly odd about him? About his manner or his behavior?"

"Other than his crazy stories about a monster in the lake?" She laughed. "Or the fact that he seemed to live out in the forest by himself?" She shook her head. "I don't know, Sheriff. He seemed to really believe in this Bessie story. Which I suppose makes sense, since it appears to be true after all."

"Did you ever run into him after that?" Datweiler asked.

She frowned. "You know, he did follow me that day. I ran away from Karl, from the lake. I was going to walk home." She smiled. "Stupid of me, I know. Ned Barker found me on the road. He said he had never lied to me, that the stories had all been true. Then he warned me not to change my mind and come back to the lake that night. He said I was better than Karl Mason. I deserved better than that. Then he disappeared." She shook her head and heaved a sigh. "I haven't thought of that in years. There was no sound in the forest after he left. No birds, no animals. Nothing. It was absolute silence. Eerie. Then Karl came screaming around the corner in that little convertible of his and insisted on driving me home. Of course, he was on his way to pick up Diana Colches, and I knew it. But it got me out of the woods and back to my house safely. I never came out to the lake again after that. It spoiled this place for me."

"Chelsea, we're ready to go," Jonathan called.

"I have to get ready," she said as she slipped away from Datweiler. He nodded and watched her make her way through the maze of wires then skip over the gangplank between ships to her own crew. She slid a wetsuit over her swimsuit and tucked her hair up in a bandanna. Then she jumped onto the sled in one graceful bound.

"There's no motor or undercarriage to get tangled in the vegetation, so they'll be able to glide over to the cave," Edith said, suddenly appearing at his left elbow.

"You aren't going with them?" he asked.

"They feel I'm too injured," she said, and her voice was bitter. Her chin motioned toward the sled. "Connie's going. She'll keep 'em headed in the right direction."

He saw the rubber raft going down next, and the SEALs caught up in quick order to the sled. They'd be safe. He looked to his right. Tom Jackson gripped the railing so tight, Datweiler thought he might bend the metal. The sled disappeared around the bend, but they heard loud exclamations coming from the cave, and knew the team had spotted the creature. They waited.

The sound of chains and pulleys, then calls to each other to pull, and pull harder. Then cries to stop. Catch that rope. More confusion. Silence for a few moments, then the activity began again. Suddenly there were cries of alarm, and gunshots rang out.

"Who took firearms?" Edith demanded.

"I gave one to Connie," Datweiler admitted, his throat tightening.

"Andy had his in the raft," Tom said, his eyes glued to the bend in the cove.

Screams and shouts, then splashes. Big ones. They heard Charlie Harmon's deep voice, saying, "Andy, stay here and guard the civilians. We got this." Then another splash.

Andy's voice echoed in the cavern. "Hurry up, people! Load that damn thing and let's get you out of here! Get the boy on the sled too. No, honey, don't worry, we're not leaving him behind."

"Oh, God..." Edith moaned. "Not another casualty. I still haven't called Corey's family."

"I can take care of that, Edith," Datweiler said, gripping her shoulder with one hand, his eyes still fixed on the cove. "Family notification is my job anyway. We've just been a little busy out here. But I can get the information from you or even from the school when things settle down here."

"No, he was my responsibility, Adam. I need to call them myself." They waited. Water churned beneath the water lilies and bulrushes. Something thrashed wildly out there in a fight for survival. Tom and Datweiler grabbed their rifles and shouldered them, ready in case the creature was the one to surface.

Then the sled came around the bend. The thrashing ceased abruptly, and crimson ribbons trailed out toward the boats. Andy manned one pole, Jonathan another, and a young student had a third. They poled in sync as best they could with Andy's strokes, as he was at the head of the sled, and they glided swiftly through the water toward their hitch. The carcass of the creature known as Bessie had drawn more insect activity, and the eye they'd removed had been rammed back into its socket. It sank into her skull, giving her a lopsided appearance that was grotesque. Beside the beast's body lay a young man, gasping and pale. Chelsea knelt next to him, pressing a towel to his chest and speaking softly to him as her hands grew more and more stained with the boy's blood. Datweiler felt a lump grow in his throat for the little girl who was once again facing the loss of a friend to a monster in this same lake.

Even if the first friend was a jerk like Karl Mason, he added to himself bitterly.

Then the water bubbled around the side of their boat. Datweiler and Tom raised their rifles again and took aim. Two wetsuits popped up, a third propped between them. They spit their air hoses out and shouted, "Give us a hand!" Both men charged down to the lower deck and reached over to pull the wounded man up onto the boat. It was Sylvester Gates. His blond hair was soaked in blood, and it poured down his face.

"He isn't breathing," Tom said, ripping off the air tanks and turning him on his back. "I'm starting CPR compressions. Get those men out of the water, Adam."

Datweiler reached over the railing again, his hand out to Donny Kemper when he heard Charlie scream, "Look out!" and a streak of green launched at him. Datweiler was knocked sideways and fell head over heels into the lake. Dazed, he struggled to discern up from down and fight his way back to the surface. Charlie held a spear in his hand and aimed at the scaled figure that swam directly for the sled. Donny floated motionless beside the *Mina*. Datweiler swam straight for Donny and shouted to Tom for help. A strong red arm grasped Donny and pulled him over the railing, then reached down again, and helped Datweiler back into the boat. Tom leaned down to check Donny, just as the man sat up and spewed water all over the deck.

New screams sent them both running to the other side of the boat, just in time to see it all end. The creature reared up on the end of the sled and roared. Its friend had been taken and it was angry. The students huddled around Jonathan, all except Chelsea Bailey. She sat beside her friend and stared into the eyes of the creature, her mouth open. Then she cocked her head to one side and stared harder. The beast cocked its head too, and there was a form of recognition in its stance. It paused.

In that moment of hesitation, a shot rang out and the creature's brain matter exploded on the sled. The body crumpled like a puppet with cut strings. Tom and Datweiler stared at Edith Armbruster, who held the smoking rifle, still aimed toward the creature on the sled. Datweiler stepped forward and gently took the gun from her hands.

"Nice shot, Edith," he murmured.

"That was for Corey," she said softly, her voice cracking.

She hobbled back to the SEALs on her lower deck. Donny sat beside Sylvester's body.

"He was a goner before we got him back to the boat, but we never leave a man behind," he said softly. "That thing got him in the spine."

"Guess I should have taken him up on that star gazing walk around the deck, huh?" Edith murmured sadly. She sighed and limped up to the upper deck and sat in her chair alone.

"Too much loss, too much pain," Tom said, watching her go. "She needs time to heal."

"She needs a few days in a hospital bed, but I doubt we'll get her there." Datweiler stared at Edith's retreating form.

Connie joined them from the sled team. "Adam, you're wet."

"You noticed."

"I'm a professional."

"You think you could direct me to those terrycloth robes and the shower? And maybe Edith will let me use that handy-dandy washer and dryer she talked about the other night."

Connie chuckled. "I think I can arrange that for you. I've already learned those ropes myself."

His eyebrows rose. "You have?"

"I've been working very messy crime scenes out here, Adam. And I didn't pack an overnight bag. Remember?"

She went up to have a word with Edith. While they conversed, Datweiler watched the team scurry to bag the remains of the second creature for processing, no doubt trying to prevent further cross-contamination between the two bodies.

But he wondered if they would ever be able to figure out how their DNA had merged in the first place. Was it a fluke or were they in danger of seeing another such freak of nature in their lake? And how long would the contamination last?

~~~~~

The teams dispersed. The media left. They had their story. Bodies went to the morgue; Connie went home to her husband and her dogs.

"The birds are back," Tom Jackson had noted before climbing into his squad car. Birds filled the trees, chirping and twittering from branch to branch. Edith had hugged him, but noticed a slight frown creasing his forehead when he pulled away from her. "You take care of yourself. You hear?"

"Sure thing." She had smiled. Was he sniffing her hair? The air around her? Maybe it was an Indian thing.

"Call me if you need anything," Datweiler said. "I'll be back out to check on you every couple of days. But if you need me sooner, just call. I mean it. Anything at all. Even if it's just someone to talk to."

"Got it. Thanks, Adam. I'll be fine now that we've got all the critters accounted for." She smiled wearily.

"You sure you'll be okay out here alone? I can stay in the trailer…"

"You've got family notifications to do. And I've got a lot of testing to work on. I'll be fine, Adam. Really. Right now, I just need some rest." She nodded reassuringly. "And thank you for offering to call Corey's folks. I should be the one, but…"

"I'll take care of it," he said, pulling her in for a one-armed hug. "You get some rest."

For the next two weeks, Edith would take water samples and monitor the contamination levels, and she needed time to recover before the long drive home. Jonathan said he would send a team back in two weeks to bring her pickup truck for towing the boat. They would keep the lab on-site as the team continued to test the water. It might take months before they could determine exactly what had occurred out here.

Edith scratched at the bandage on her chest. *Must be healing. It itches.*

Connie was going to return in the morning with some groceries. Datweiler's deputies had supplied sandwiches from Subway tonight. She still had a couple of extras in the refrigerator on the *Mina* for later, if she got hungry. Right now, she was just bone tired. She locked up the lab and stared up at the stars. Clouds moved lazily into the area.

Looks like it might rain tonight. Better make sure the moon roof is shut tight. Don't want the upper cabin flooded.

She boarded the *Mina* and set about securing the upper deck. Her shoulders felt tight, and sore. A shower would help. And her scalp itched too. Probably too much sweat from all the stress and anxiety this afternoon. She descended to the lower deck and pulled out a fresh terrycloth robe. It still smelled like fresh linen from her laundry soap. She had to remember to pick up more of that brand the next time she got to town. Maybe Adam would run her in to shop later this week. He was a nice guy.

She lathered up and rinsed twice, then she eased the bandage off her chest and soaped around the edges of the incision. Keeping the water on her back, she sponged around the area without soaking the stitches themselves. Then she carefully dried off and slipped into the robe. With it still hanging open, she stood before the mirror to assess the damage and try to rebandage the wound on her own.

Edith blinked.

Red and green scales were forming around the stitches, overlapping them, covering them, forming a protective shell over the wound.

"What in heaven's name is this?" She picked at the edge of one and it sliced her fingertip open. A bead of bright red blood appeared on the tip of her finger… followed by a stream of green foam that trickled down to her knuckle. Her eyes widened in horror. She looked into the mirror and noticed golden flecks accenting her warm brown eyes. She yanked the bandage off her face and saw more scales forming on her face. She shrank away from the mirror, tears filling her eyes.

"Noooooooooooooooooooooooo……!"

At her shriek, a flock of birds rose from the treetops and scattered into the night sky.

THE END

MEET THE AUTHORS

Darlene N. Bocek is an award winning author of YA Sci-fi. She is a pastor's wife living on a farm in Izmir, Turkey. She and her husband have a plethora of pets named after pop culture heroes, a son named after a sci-fi hero, two daughters practicing science-fact (dentistry), and a daughter studying to be an author. Her well-acclaimed first book, YA historical *Trunk of Scrolls*, will be re-released in 2024. See her books, join her club, find out about her Kickstarters, and download a free ebook at darlenenbocek.com.

Years ago, Mike Bogue suffered a sledgehammer blow to the cranium and survived, a testament—his friends say—to his hard head. A recently retired college educator living in Ozark, Arkansas, Mike has written for *G-FAN*, *Movie Milestones*, *The Lost Films Fanzine*, *Wonder*, *Castle of Frankenstein*, and *Mad Scientist*, as well as penning a regular column called "Kaiju Korner" for *Scary Monsters Magazine*. A graduate of Jerry Jenkins' "Your Novel Blueprint" course, Mike wrote the well-reviewed nonfiction book *Apocalypse Then: American and Japanese Atomic Cinema: 1951-1967* (McFarland, 2017), which received an NPR endorsement. As for Mike's head, it remains relatively impervious to cranial damage, a good thing since he needs it to finish his current writing projects, which include a post-apocalyptic novel.

Jordan Campbell grew up on the Central Coast of California and moved to Maine at the age of eleven. Long fascinated by stories, Jordan read at a post-college level when he was in the seventh grade. A graduate of the Honors College at the University of Maine, Jordan wrote a novel for his thesis. After years of writing mostly for his own pleasure, Jordan started submitting stories for publication. He has had two short stories published by *Raconteur Press*, in the anthologies *Space Marines* and *Space Marines 2*. He has plans for many, many more stories.

Rosemarie DiCristo got the idea for this story when she read about a real fish farm whose fish were being devoured by evil sea lions... who were not deterred by Frank Sinatra music. Despite her fondness for mistreated creatures and monsters, she meant the story to be told from the humans' point of view, but somehow Brady took over. When Rosemarie's not re-writing fairy/monster tales, she's writing flash fiction for kids and teens. Rosemarie has had several stories published in *Havok*, including one in their **Vice and Virtue** anthology. *A Fish Story* is her second story published in a *Ye Olde Dragon* anthology, and she is delighted to be a part of such a fine writing group.

Rachel Dib is a stay-at-home mom of three small children. After marrying a soldier, she left her home state of South Carolina to live in random places across the United States. Her short fiction appears in anthologies published by *Havok Publishing, Ye Olde Dragon Books, Iron Faerie Publishing,* and *Brigids Gate Press.*

Jim Doran is a genre writer who enjoys transporting his readers into worlds of wonder, mystery, and danger. Whether it's the fairytale hijinks in the five novels of his *Kingdom Fantasy series* or his multi-genre short stories, Jim has been published in *Havok, Every Day Fiction, Ye Olde Dragon's* **Moonlight and Claws** and **Who's the Monster?**, and *Havok's* **Casting Call** anthologies. When he's not writing, he's usually enjoying the seasons in Michigan or playing a board game.

Pam Halter is a children's book author and editor. Her picture book series, *Willoughby and Friends (Fruitbearer Publishing,)* have won Purple Dragonfly awards and a Realm Award. Her YA fantasy, **Fairyeater** (*Love2ReadLove2Write Publishing*), also won a Purple Dragonfly. Her short stories appear in several anthologies, including the *Whitstead books* and *Realmscapes,* as well as *Ye Olde Dragon Books.* Pam's family grew up in South Jersey. Her grandpa was in the Coast Guard and her dad was a SCUBA diver and fisherman. So, they went to the boat in Wildwood, NJ, like other families went to the campground. By the time Pam was ten years old, she could scale fish, clean lobsters, wash the boat, and check the crab traps. Seafood is still her favorite food, aside from pizza, of course. Learn more about Pam at *www.pamhalter.com*

On the road to publication, **Michelle Levigne** fell into fandom in college and has stories in various SF and fantasy universes' fanzines. She has a bunch of useless degrees in theater, English, film/communication, and writing. Even worse, she has dozens of books and novellas with multiple small presses, in science fiction and fantasy, YA, suspense, women's fiction, and sub-genres of romance. Her training includes the Institute for

Children's Literature; proofreading at an advertising agency; and working at a community newspaper. She is a tea snob and freelance edits for a living, but only enough to give her time to write. Her newest crime against the literary world is the storytelling podcast, Ye Olde Dragon's Library. Be afraid... be very afraid. Despite that, please visit her websites: *Mlevigne.com* and *YeOldeDragonBooks.com*.

Stoney M. Setzer lives south of Atlanta, GA. He has a beautiful wife, three wonderful children, and one crazy dog, and he is also a diehard Atlanta Braves fan. He has written a trilogy of novels about small-town amateur sleuth Wesley Winter (*Dead of Winter*, *Valley of the Shadow*, and *Day of Reckoning*). He has also written a short story anthology *Zero Hour*, featuring Twilight Zone-like stories with Christian themes. He has also had some of his short stories featured in such publications as *Residential Aliens* and *Havok*. Mr. Setzer is currently completing a novel featuring the fictional community of Sardis County, Tennessee, which is also the setting for his story in this anthology and has also figured into his previous contributions to the *Ye Olde Dragons* anthology. He hopes to have this novel completed and released later in the near future. Learn more at *www.tinniepress.blogspot.com* or on Facebook@ *stoneymsetzerofficial*.

Deborah Cullins Smith has been writing stories ever since she could hold a pencil, but she came to her actual career in writing rather late in life. In 2019, she published the trilogy, *The Last of the Long-Haired Hippies*, in a rapid-release timed for the 50th anniversary of Woodstock, which she covered in great detail in the second volume. *CWG Press* released *Shroud of Darkness*, *The Birth of the Storm*, and *Victoria's War* over a four-month period, a culmination of almost twenty years in development. Ms. Cullins Smith's first Mina Harker adventure, *Mina: Warrior in the Shadows* won the 2022 Realm Award for Horror Novel. Her next novel will continue the saga of Billy the Kid, which she began in the anthology *Moonlight and Claws* with the story *Habitations of Violence*, and continued in *Who's the Monster?* with the story *Phillippe*. Her love of historical research makes these books challenging, as she is devoted to maintaining as much historical accuracy as possible while sliding things sideways to suggest that a few characters might be more than we gave them credit for! (No disrespect intended.)

C.S. Wachter lives in rural Lancaster County, Pennsylvania with her husband Joe, two dogs, and two cats. They have been married for more than forty years and have three sons, one grandson, and one granddaughter. In 2018, she published the four books of *The Seven Words* epic fantasy series, followed in 2019 by a short story and a sequel continuing *The Seven Words* story. In 2020, she published *The Stone Sovereigns* YA Fantasy duology. In 2021, two of her short stories were included in the *Ye Olde Dragon* anthologies, **When Your Beauty IS the Beast** and *Moonlight and Claws*. She has also written various flash fiction pieces for *Havok*. She can be found at *https://cswachter.com/*

Angela R Watts is the bestselling and award-nominated author of *The Infidel Books* and the *Remnant Trilogy*. She's been writing stories since she was little, and has over thirty works in print, ranging from gritty adult novels to clean children's fiction. Some of her other titles include *A Solstice of Fire and Light*, *Winter of the Bees*, and *Where Giants Fall* (a fantasy anthology). Angela is a Christian, freelance editor, article writer for magazines and publishers, founder of Speculative Fiction Society, and artist. She lives in Tennessee with her family and many pets. You can get in touch with Angela on social media (@angelarwattsauthor) or subscribe to her newsletter at *angelarwatts.com*

A childhood spent obsessing over fantasy and role-play while haunting the landscape of Central Europe resulted in **Etta-Tamara Wilson** having a deep fascination with rarely told fairy tales. She's now preoccupied with reminding a whole host of fairy tale characters to mind their manners and be patient, while she helps the newly formed Fairy Temp Agency dream up future employment opportunities. When not writing, she's usually off learning new skills or dreaming of travel in lands near, far, or fictional. She has additional stories in the *Tales from the Tower* and *Who's the Monster?* anthologies.

So what's next at Ye Olde Dragon Books?

Well, we're going to be looking for submissions for our spring
Fairytale Anthology, of course!

TALES FROM THE FOREST
Spring, 2024

So, what fairytale are we going to shred this time around?

How about *Little Red Riding Hood*?

Maybe the fairytale we all grew up on wasn't telling the whole
story …

Think about it:
What if Red was bait in a trap?
*What if the wolf was an innocent bystander, but he got framed for
someone else's crime?*
*What if Granny was an unethical real estate developer and needed to get
the wolf out of the way so she and the Woodsman could chop down the
forest and start building cookie cutter cottages by the dozens?*

Okay, maybe the last is a bit of a stretch … but let your
imaginations run wild! (We know you will. We have faith in you!)

Check out the Anthology Submissions page on our website for
deadlines and specifications. And start brainstorming!

www.YeOldeDragonBooks.com

Printed in the USA
CPSIA information can be obtained
at www.ICGtesting.com
JSHW030055071023
49448JS00007B/27